THE
SEVENTH
STONE

NANCY FREEDMAN

THE
SEVENTH
STONE

A DUTTON BOOK

DUTTON
Published by the Penguin Group
Penguin Books USA Inc., 375 Hudson Street, New York, New York 10014, U.S.A.
Penguin Books Ltd, 27 Wrights Lane, London W8 5TZ, England
Penguin Books Australia Ltd, Ringwood, Victoria, Australia
Penguin Books Canada Ltd, 10 Alcorn Avenue, Toronto, Ontario, Canada M4V 3B2
Penguin Books (N.Z.) Ltd, 182–190 Wairau Road, Auckland 10, New Zealand

Penguin Books Ltd, Registered Offices:
Harmondsworth, Middlesex, England

First published by Dutton, an imprint of New American Library,
a division of Penguin Books USA Inc.
Distributed in Canada by McClelland & Stewart Inc.

First Printing, April, 1992
1   3   5   7   9   10   8   6   4   2

Copyright © Nancy Freedman, 1992
All rights reserved

 REGISTERED TRADEMARK—MARCA REGISTRADA

LIBRARY OF CONGRESS CATALOGING IN PUBLICATION DATA:

Freedman, Nancy Mars.
    The seventh stone / Nancy Freedman.
    p.   cm.
    ISBN 0-525-93424-3
    I. Title.
PS3511.R418S47   1992
813'.54—dc20   91–33672
                                                                         CIP

PRINTED IN THE UNITED STATES OF AMERICA
Set in Goudy

Designed by Steven N. Stathakis

PUBLISHER'S NOTE
This is a work of fiction. Names, characters, places, and incidents either are the products of
the author's imagination or are used fictitiously, and any resemblance to actual persons, living
or dead, events, or locales is entirely coincidental.

In memory of that other Momoko who,
twenty years ago, urged me to write this book.

I wish to express my thanks and appreciation to:

Masako Ohnuki
Kenneth R. Jackson
C. Scott Littleton
Ikuo ("York") & Hiroko Mukasa
Motoko Ezaki
Shauna Lin

Each in their own way deepened my understanding of the culture in which my story is embedded.

Special thanks is also due my editor, Laurie Bernstein, for her unfailing sense of literary truth. And to my representative, Suzanne Gluck, whose deep insights brought about the milieu in which my work flourished. While as always, there was my friend, Benedict.

If you meet Buddha on the way—kill him.

—*Zen saying*

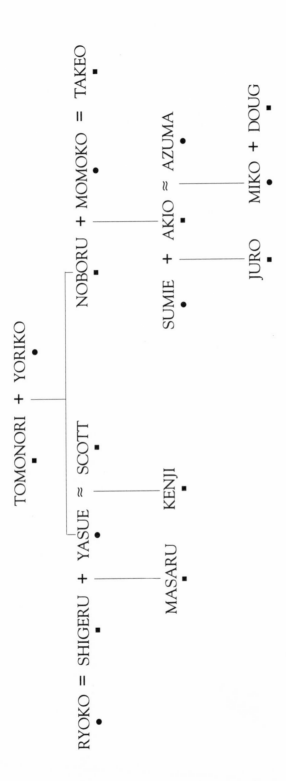

THE SANOGAWA FAMILY

TOMONORI + YORIKO

RYOKO = SHIGERU + YASUE ≈ SCOTT   NOBORU + MOMOKO = TAKEO

MASARU   KENJI   SUMIE + AKIO ≈ AZUMA

JURO   MIKO + DOUG

■ MALE   ● FEMALE   + MARRIAGE   = SECOND MARRIAGE   ≈ LIAISON

BooK
ONE

1989

A FRAIL, ELDERLY JAPANESE WOMAN IN TRADITIONAL KIMONO looked up from papers she was sorting. She had come across an old, mildewed copy of the *National Geographic*. A corner was turned down at a photograph of an Oka bomb that hung in the British Museum. Torpedo-shaped, it nestled innocently in the womb of the mother plane. She stared intently at the cramped cockpit with its clear canopy. It was this space that housed the Special Attacker as he homed in on target.

Yes, that was the beginning. It was the Special Attacker who by his certain death in the final months of the war set the family apart.

Kamikaze, the Americans said, suicide pilot. He was a member of the Shimpu, known as the Divine Wind. By his death in a cause already lost, he returned honor to a defeated country. And each member of the family made of the sacrifice what was needed for his own life, an excuse for love and revenge, for madness and suicide. While she, although she loved him, had not known how to love him until it was too late.

A tear fell upon the bomb attached to the Mitsubishi G4M.2e. She was surprised. She didn't know she had a tear left.

1945

THE LIEUTENANT OF THE 201ST SPECIAL ATTACK FORCE SAID SUD-
denly, "I do not hate Americans. John Wayne, Betty Grable. I love
them."

Captain Yokota, the pilot, did not feel worthy to respond to one
who held life lightly as a feather.

The Oka fighter seemed not to notice. "Japan will be defeated.
At Okinawa we were finished. Everyone knows this but they don't say
it."

Yokota stole a glance at the man beside him, who was no longer
of this world. How could he say what he was saying? He felt a rush of
pity. "Proud acts of the honored Oka fighter remind our people of the
warrior's way."

The Oka fighter's lips tightened into a grin, or perhaps it was a
grimace. "Lose to win."

Yokota thought that was what he said, but couldn't be sure, as
the words were lost in the noise of the engine; he felt as though he
were the one who would descend into the green bomb, a coffin twenty
feet long, which would carry the Kamikaze to his glorious moment.

"I do not hate Americans," his passenger said again, as though this puzzled him. "I used to see all the movies. *Stagecoach*, *Strike Me Pink*, that was with Eddie Cantor. *It Happened One Night*, do you remember that one?"

Yokota shuddered in pity. "May your death be as sudden and clean as the shattering of crystal." The Mitsubishi bomber climbed steeply to twenty-seven thousand feet. He scanned the sea, searching for the target. "There!" Yokota exclaimed, pointing.

Noboru Sanogawa stared at the distant dot, and his gut clamped together like a fist. He was disappointed at this involuntary reaction to death. He saluted Yokota briskly. "May the Emperor live ten thousand years!" were the words he chose as he lowered himself through the bomb bay and squeezed into the hatch of the small craft that depended from the mother plane. He reminded himself that he had crawled into the cramped cockpit at least two dozen times during training. But this was totally removed from training procedures just as he was removed from the idiot who had left a diary on a smoothed cot eulogizing a beautiful death. How could a beautiful death be achieved by hanging from the belly of a G4M.2e bomber?

An eerie cold wrapped his organs. He was cut off from humankind, entombed. *Mother, there is a note for you on my cot, my cot made up without a wrinkle. I asked you to forgive my undisciplined nature. I thanked you for my twenty-two years and asked pardon for preceding you. I promised to fall in purity like a blossom.*

It had been a John Wayne film. Elder Sister would have called it a three-handkerchief picture because although everyone seemed to realize it, John Wayne failed to sense that the woman he loved loved another. It was a marvelous film, with cloudscapes rolling over American prairies. Horses tossed sleek heads, nostrils working in and out, sides heaving, laved in sweat. These horses were not like the fierce white and gray of the samurai, just as the cowboy, while alike in demanding freedom and righting wrongs, was different.

Since the Americans did not have the tradition of the samurai, they made up their own version—cowpoke, cowhand, rodeo rider. The swinging barroom door, the brawls and fights over honor fit a niche carved into the psyche of every Japanese boy of twelve. John Wayne understood this. You knew, in spite of his round eyes, that he was a man who understood the heart, who made trips to view the cherry blossoms, and pilgrimages to enjoy the full moon over Mikasayama.

He was very honorable, one could tell by the way he dispatched evildo-ers and saved the woman who did not love him.

By now the film was almost over, and John Wayne finally admitted to himself that she loved his friend. This made his saving of her all the more heroic. He wasn't saving her for himself but for his buddy, to whom he owed his life. This was beautiful *ninjo*. Elder Sister, if she were here, would at this point have brought out another handkerchief.

The second obtrusion of Elder Sister into the plot of the film was disturbing. It reminded him he was not here with her and his mother, but had come without permission. He'd tried to obtain permission. But Mother was not home, she had gone out and taken Elder Sister with her. He was quite sure that had she been home, she would have allowed him to come. Reasoned this way, why should he not come simply because she was not there?

It was special as always to think of Mother. The Sun Goddess, the fierce and beautiful, must have looked like Mother. Although it wasn't by her face he knew her best; it was by scent and feel, from all the nights since he was born of burrowing into her flesh. He could almost remember the swaddled years when he rode her back, an exten-sion of her. All his life she let him know by fondling, by charming looks and smiles, that she belonged to him, that he was the one she loved beyond life. When he was angry she encouraged him to hit and punch and kick her. In childish rages he pummeled her breasts and stomach. *"Itai!"* she would cry, submitting to the childish blows. He was her little warrior, her only male child, her small stalwart samurai.

At night he slept curled into her. Over and over he explored her body, poking, punching, patting, smoothing. And her fingers showed him himself and why he was not a girl. Because of these protuberances he would inherit from his father, because of these he was a man-child and privileged. Spoiled by everyone, mother, sister, a tolerant father, doting grandparents, servants, he ruled like a divine despot. The ser-vants plied him with sweets, the grandparents gave him toys, and his mother bought him whatever he pointed at. He got first pick of candies and presents. Elder Sister had to take what was left. He was given presents when his sister was not. Also he bathed next after his father in the big tub. Elder Sister had her limbs pulled straight when she slept. He, on the other hand, was allowed to sprawl in the shape of a *dai*. He was catered to and adored for his maleness. Sometimes Mother would gather his genitals in her hand and bend her lovely neck over them. When she saw that she had stirred him, she withdrew her hand and laughed.

His father, large and clumsy, was his rival. But he was secure in the knowledge that his mother loved him best. Although sometimes in the night she stole in to Father. He knew this because he would wake and she would not be there. In the morning he would storm at her and beat her and she would say, "But, dear boy, I would rather be with you." She would tell him again how it had been when she first beheld a son, perfect, pure as a blossom, and had cried out, "What a wonderful child!" A son to carry on a proud name, to whom his father would pass on the sword of the samurai. He was called Noboru-chama and was the pride of the house.

When he was seven, a day was set for the *shichi-go-san* ceremony. Although it was unexpectedly cold and rainy, his father wouldn't hear of changing their plans, and the entire family trudged to the neighborhood shrine. His mother insisted on carrying an oiled-paper parasol whose sprightly decorations mocked the somber black umbrellas the rest carried. Noboru stood patiently in his fine clothes while his parents prayed for his future and explained the responsibility of being heir to the family tradition.

Until now he had been free to roam, to sail kites, play ball, tussle with the gang of *donen*, children who collected on the temple steps each morning. He was indulged at all levels. In those days the damage he did to rice-paper screens was a source of laughter. At meals he was allowed to drift around the room and stick his fingers in other people's portions. They only pretended to slap his hands as they exclaimed what a dreadful son they had. Even before he could count, he knew his mother gave him more candies than she gave Yasue. If he quarreled with his sister, she was chastised. She did not resent this because he was the only son. Frequently she too would cup his small testicles, paying homage to the maleness that resided there and ruled her life.

But from the day of the *shichi-go-san* things changed. It was explained to him that because everything would belong to him, the home, the land, the fortune, and the toy factory from which the rest derived, he owed more *on* than he could ever pay—to his family, his Emperor, and his country.

"Cold austerity" was a further circle that he learned naked on a predawn winter in an unheated house with pitchers of ice water cascading down his body. It was 4:00 A.M. "This is the hour when the gods bathe," his father told him.

The child looked at him admiringly. Oto-san was a remote presence whose authority was unquestioned. He was a fierce traditionalist who saw the Sanogawa family as upholders of their samurai past.

"You will be going to school now, and in order to study for good grades, you must harden yourself mentally and physically. In the days of our ancestors, the men of our family sat at dawn under the cold stream of a waterfall to practice self-discipline."

Noboru thought he would not have minded a waterfall as much as this dippered stream of ice-cold water over his head. But he did not flinch. He was striving for honor, learning that he must be strong for Emperor and family. Those claims came before the desire of the individual. Submission was strength. Submission to family was the highest loyalty.

"It is a virtue," he intoned after his father, "to repay insults as well as favors. The world tilts," he recited as a catechism, "while an insult or a defeat goes unpunished." Bowing with the palms of his hands flat against the floor, he repeated, "A good man returns the good that is done him many times over. A good man returns the evil also, many times."

And his father told him *The Tale of the Forty-seven Ronin*, explaining *chu* to one's lord:

A country baron attempted to assassinate Lord Kira, a nobleman senior to him in rank, who had disgraced him by advising him to wear garments unsuitable to the occasion. The baron was humiliated past enduring, for breach of etiquette was a crime that ranked with murder. To regain honor the baron waylaid the lord, but failed to prevail in the encounter. For daring to draw his sword on one of higher rank, the baron was ordered by the shogun to commit seppuku, which left his forty-seven retainers *ronin*, masterless men. Thereafter the only thing left in life for them was revenge. Lord Kira had them watched, but the *ronin* played a subtle game. They pretended to accept their master's death, gambled away their gold, denounced their fathers. And as final proof that they were scoundrels with no thought of revenge, they let their swords rust. This at last convinced Lord Kira and he was put off guard. The Forty-seven then put on their best armor and slaughtered the lord, completing the deed their master had left undone, upon which they in turn committed seppuku.

This righteous act of loyalty, his father told him, became part of the national tradition enshrined in the hearts of the people. To make sure the lesson sank in, Noboru was taken on New Year's Day to see the puppet-play version of the story, and later he saw it again in Kabuki. Then recently, his father capped these experiences by taking him on a pilgrimage to Sengakuji to visit the actual graves, planted with forty-seven cherry trees. Thousands of pilgrims came each year to pay homage, and bought, as they did, a ritual tear—a drop of water purchased on the spot. When his father bowed low, hands flat before him on the ground, Noboru imitated him, wondering if he would ever do anything so worthy that people might purchase a tear at his grave. John Wayne was worthy of cherry trees and tears. Like the Forty-seven, it was his nature to perform noble acts. Noboru wondered if he too might be made of such stern stuff. That would explain why he wasn't worried about his mother. She would certainly be angry and was sure to find some way to make him feel bad. She might even insist that he remove his futon from beside hers. She had threatened this in the past.

He was annoyed with himself for sowing a worry seed in the middle of a gunfight. The mirror behind the bar had shattered, whiskey bottles were breaking and guns speaking from the hip, while the bad guy, who pretended to be dead, inched toward a fully loaded six-shooter. John Wayne was in trouble, he had taken the last bullet from his gunbelt. Noboru wanted to push back his thoughts. He knew Mother would ask why, why had he gone off without permission and without anyone knowing? In some part of him he realized that with this rather minor infraction he was saying to his mother, "Unbind me, let me breathe, let me strike out in some small measure on my own." But this was what she could not permit. He was hers. That's whose son he was, her son.

John Wayne fell wounded. He would surely have to sleep alone and cold tonight. He wondered if he could lay his futon beside his sister's. But she might laugh if he did that. He couldn't take that chance.

Walking home from the movie, Noboru persuaded himself that he could handle his mother. But he was not prepared for the smooth face

Yoriko turned to him. It was as though a mask were stretched over her lovely features. She would not speak to him, but spoke instead to Elder Sister: "Tell him, Yasue, that it doesn't matter where he was or with whom. He is a son who did not respect his parents. He has forgotten what he owes them. Such a one is no longer son and brother. He is nothing. It is time he learned that a man does not exist alone. If he is not part of the fabric of the household, he has no place in its pattern. Tell that pitiful man-child who sets himself in opposition to his family that his family has taken the decision to cut him off from all honorable members. He is to leave this house at once, taking nothing with him."

To this point Elder Sister had a sly pleasure in relating his mischief and his fate to him. But now she faltered. Could her mother really mean this? But there was no wavering in the cool, imperious gaze.

Noboru was stunned. He had imagined her angry, punishing, but he had not thought that a John Wayne movie, an American cowboy film, could cause him to lose his place in life. Staring into her face, he looked for reprieve. He could not believe the love that had been there for him all his life was extinguished. Things were out of proportion. He did not deserve to be treated like this. He thought of appealing to his father. But he recognized this as futile. His father buried himself in the splendor of the Sanogawa past and removed himself from the household accounts and the disciplining of children.

Anger against his mother's injustice flared in him. He turned and marched toward the door, but he was prepared, if she called him back, to forgive her. Listening for her voice, expecting to be stopped, he put on his sandals. Her silence pounded in his ears. He slowed his motions, giving her an opportunity to speak.

He found himself outdoors. How was it possible? She loved him to distraction, he was her dearest, her boy, her son, her special favorite. Her breasts were his until he was four, for food or comfort. She told him often that was the time of her chief joy. She had looped an obi under his arms and coaxed him to walk, given him rice water when he was ill, cuddled and crooned to him, taught him while he was still strapped to her back, pushing his head down in obeisance to his father and grandfather. It was she who guided his small hands around the *hashi* until he could eat by himself, she who taught him the sitting position, legs folded back, instep to the floor, retrieving him each time he tumbled, replacing his legs correctly, not letting him fidget or shift.

But when it was over she allowed him to vent his frustrations by beating her with his child's fists and tearing at her hair.

How was it possible that this mother-creature who was submissively his could turn on him? Could drive him out? He knew it was mixed together with *ko*. *Ko*, that like the moon has its bright side and its dark, had turned its dark side to him. He had failed in *ko*. *Ko*, his father kept telling him, does not lessen with time, but accumulates interest.

The night wind cut into his shoulders and he hunched them together. The baseball game that took place daily near the temple steps had broken up and his *donen* had gone home to their suppers. At this hour, when light faded into dusk, men shared the world with spirits. He could see them darting fitfully, taking the shape of fireflies. For protection he sought the outer wall of the temple, but tonight it seemed a phantom place with himself standing at the edge of the world. At home, Ushiwaka-maru, his armored beetle, a sturdy little samurai with horns, would be hopping from one side of his cage to the other because he had not come with an offering of sugar water.

By now his father had been told of his lack of respect. He would continue to peruse the evening paper, not revealing his disappointment that cold austerity, periodic lectures on obligation, and even a pilgrimage had failed to develop his son's character. The servants would be whispering together behind their hands. And Mother? She had closed her heart. Her face had not been angry or in any way disarrayed. It had been closed.

The family would be eating now, clear soup with greens and bean curd. There would be a stew of white radishes, onions, perhaps a portion of fish. He was angry at himself for these thoughts. He must harden himself. Victory over the flesh was necessary if one was to respect oneself.

He was standing in darkness; not only was it past the hour of his dinner, but by now he would have drawn his futon to his mother's. He gave up believing that a servant would be sent to fetch him, and crouched by the inner wall. It seemed as good a place as any to sleep. He slid down further. Just beyond was a path into the temple garden, austere, the gravel carefully raked, the steppingstones washed each morning. There were smooth white rocks in this garden and yet no spot from which all could be seen, one always remained hidden.

He was part of the miniature landscape where even the stream was a sand stream, and the trees had been tortured into the gardener's design. Nothing was allowed to grow naturally. This week at school he had been taught to brush the word *ukiyo*—"sad world." But written in a different character it meant "floating cheerfulness." Everything had a front and a back, an *omote* and a *ura*, and you could not see all the stones.

Since he could not sleep he pondered his punishment. Seeing a foreign film was not bad in itself. He knew his transgression lay in the fact that he had acted on his own. He had failed to consult his mother, putting himself and his wishes ahead of hers. It wasn't as though he were an *ainoko*, a mongrel. He should have expected something severe would happen. Though he understood obligation, he had put it lightly aside, flouting every principle that had been instilled in him. He had gone against the *ko* he owed his parents.

His gentle, pliant mother was now another. Everything shifted and changed if she did. He had not seen the strength in her softness, he had not known the depth of her anger. He had thought himself loved, but it was the thought of him she loved, the concept of a son, the dignity she derived from having a son, the status an obedient son gave her. It was the relationship in which he stood to her that she loved. His heart broke at the discovery, and inside him tears flooded.

He thought of the agony he felt when he woke in the night to find her gone. He would not move, but lay listening to the rattle of the shoji screens as the rice paper fluttered with the lovemaking of his father.

He hated his father for possessing her in a man's way, while he only had of her what was given to a child. She was amused when she discovered he was aroused to an erection simply by pressing against her, and told him to take care of it himself.

In the morning she laughed with his father. He heard his name and knew what they were laughing at and was overcome with shame. He remembered running away to hide himself.

He no longer ran away. Mainly because it didn't do any good, but also because a boy who respected himself couldn't. Finally he closed his eyes, but the turbulence inside continued. He was talking to Elder Sister. He was angry and confused because in his heart he knew Yasue was not sorry that Mother had turned on him. She had been the single child six years before he was born. She had been petted and spoiled, then forced to stand aside and watch a baby brother supplant her, watch her mother caress him from toes to fingertips. If he wanted anything, he must have it and every life stopped until he was gratified. It must have been bitter. In his dream his sister listened politely while he accused her of deserting him, and politely watched the tears on his cheek. She had grown up and was quite removed from him these days, taking lessons in foreign cooking, music, and flower arrangement in preparation for the time she would marry. Her hair had been swept up with pink cloth in the elaborate "splitting-peach" fashion. She wore more silk and less cotton, and hiding in the shadows he had heard her tell her hopes of a husband to the moon. He could remember when Yasue wore her hair down her back, tied with a red ribbon, but even then she practiced with a pillow under her obi for the time when she would carry a son.

The sound of the temple bell passed through his body. He woke but did not move or open his eyes. This was a day of difficulties, and he gathered his mind so it would be steady to face whatever came. He recalled a story his grandmother used to tell of the samurai who hid from his enemies behind a screen. When they came to his hiding place they thrust a sword through it to make certain he wasn't there. The sword came out shiny and clean, without blood, so they went away. Once they were gone the stricken man staggered out holding his gaping wound together. As the sword was withdrawn from his body he had wiped it with the sleeve of his kimono.

Holding his gaping wound together, Noboru got to his feet. He took a few staggering samurai steps before becoming himself. He could see the monks moving about, one sweeping the steps, another at the well with a jug of water. He wanted water too, hand water for his fingers and to rinse his mouth as he did at home. But he was afraid someone would ask what he was doing at the ceremonial water trough. He didn't want to admit that he had slept all night in the temple grounds like a beggar. Better to go home, wait in front of the house, bowing to the ground, and see what happened. Perhaps Mother would no longer be angry, perhaps he would be told to enter and have his breakfast of miso soup and egg. Perhaps there would be a tangerine to finish it off.

But suppose she sent the servants to chase him away? Their house had a Western-style veranda encircling it on three sides. Inside it was Japanese, with shoji screens and tatami mats, except for the living room, which was used exclusively to entertain. The living room had a Knabe piano, oil paintings, a large overstuffed sofa in flowered chintz, a matching armchair, and a Queen Anne dining set. They even had a telephone, and its number was posted in large letters on the front gate. The telephone, his mother often said, cost as much as five servants. But he understood it was more prestigious, befitting one who, though of samurai blood, had flouted tradition to become the owner of a factory. Tomonori Sanogawa taught his children their line of descent through four hundred years. Only peasants and foreigners did not know their lineage.

They possessed other luxuries as well, a hot water system, a Chrysler car, and a sewing machine that none of the maids would go near. But Mother taught Elder Sister, who whirled away at it quite happily, making bride things for herself and her future home.

Elder Sister had a special look on her face when she sewed, and he knew she was thinking about that future home, and that those thoughts made her happy. He found this hard to understand. Home is where you are born and grow up . . . unless, of course, you cease to pay *ko* to your parents. Then you are cast out, nameless, belonging nowhere and to no one. How could he have been so un-Japanese as to put himself in such a position? He was a well-brought-up boy who called his teachers by the streets where they lived and did not presume to speak their names, as some children from modern homes did. And the diploma he had just earned at primary school with special mention in mathematics had its day of honor on the god shelf, which held a picture of the Emperor, a sprig of sakaki, the purity mirror, talismans of white paper prayers from the great Ise shrine, and small memorial tablets for his grandparents.

If Grandmother were alive his mother would not have treated him as she had. He could always go to Grandmother, and right or wrong she would side with him against his sister, his mother, even his father, whose mother she was. There were always candies in her apron pockets, and presents. It didn't have to be Boys' Day or New Year's or any holiday at all. It might be a very ordinary day, but she would say, "I think it may be time for a present hunt." That meant he was sure to find a gift, made by her, bought by her, or cajoled from his father's stock of toys. One morning she didn't get up. She, who was always the first to set the maids warming the house and laying breakfast.

The coffin was filled with ice and reposed in the living room. All his life he would hear the sound of the melting water dripping into the pan below—and see the faint insubstantial smoke misting her features. Every trace of thought and desire had vanished, leaving her face calm, chiseled. White death smoothed all lines. For three days relatives came, chatted, wept, and ate. They left funeral envelopes of money, fruit from California, tins of cocoa, coffee and tea. He recalled a string of salted salmon strung together by gaping jaws. He wished he could force all the gifts back, and death with them. Grandmother never scolded, she *expected* in a calm, serene way, so that everyone saw to it that what she expected happened. It was Grandmother who recounted the ancient legends. It was Grandmother who told him the roots of the mountains were in the sea, and that lions feared butterflies.

Even Mother slipped to the inferior status of daughter-in-law in her presence. From this recollection he built again the mother who indulged and catered to him, who loved him more than life.

By the time he reached home Noboru had persuaded himself that once he indicated his repentance his mother would rush out to him, throw her arms around him, and beg his forgiveness for the harsh and unjust punishment she had made him undergo.

But standing before the *genkan* of his house, he was attacked by doubts. He saw Fusa, sleeves tucked up, folding the bedding and stowing it away in the closet. They were all up, then.

Was his mother peering from a second-story window? Was she watching from behind half-drawn shutters as he prostrated himself?

He waited, his shame exposed to the world. Still, he would forgive her. If only she would come out he would forgive her.

No one came out.

By his right hand a stream of ants worked joylessly, foraging in long lines. He watched them. Moving a morsel of dirt with his finger, he cut off one of the ants from its fellows. It raced around first in one direction, then another. It was hopelessly alone on its side of the clod.

"Oka-san!" he called, but not loudly. His mother stayed inside the house.

After a while he stood up stiffly and wandered off. He felt aimless, a nonperson, someone outside the scheme of things. It didn't matter where he went or what he did. He walked about, bought some rice cakes and made his way to the railway station which was lined with vending machines and pinball games. He put money into their brightly colored slots and pulled their silver arms, following the progress of a ball that fell into one bracket and then another. He tried to tilt the machine to rack up a bigger score, but it was bolted down.

His friends were all in school. He could have gone to school also, but school did not seem consonant with being an outcast. Besides, he did not have his uniform, his book bag, or his hat.

When he had spent all his money he leaned against a post and watched the people go by. He tried to guess their occupations, an old man in kimono on his way to a mah-jongg parlor, a group of business-men wearing smiles and Western suits, going to lunch together at a good restaurant. A young boy hurried past holding a paper narcissus. Had he been given it, was it a love token, or had he picked it up in the street? Where were all these lives hurrying? Had they each a desti-nation? Was it only he who was shut out? He felt invisible, not part of the world he watched. Yesterday he was the only son of an important man, brought up to know his ancestors and his place. But none of that matters without *ko*.

Without *ko* one is nothing.

Once again he walked toward his home. When he reached it he knelt as before and, placing his hands in front of him, put his face in the dirt.

He was afraid to hope; there were no more bullets in his gunbelt. His father would be home from work, but it was doubtful he would inquire into the situation. All that was left to the wife. She no doubt had good reason for keeping their son on his knees before the house.

Gradually the day declined and no one came out to him. He studied a blade of grass. Its edges seemed sharp like steel, the steel edge of a blade of grass cut more deeply than a sword. But when his finger moved over its surface it was soft. The shadow of a tree length-ened into the space his shadow occupied, obliterating it. He got up and went away.

He had no destination, but returned by a circuitous route to the temple. For the second night he huddled against the inner wall of the courtyard. His dreaming was a struggle up Mount Miwa, where the *kami* live. If he could gain the summit they might be persuaded to help him, but he kept sliding back. The trouble was, someone was standing on his shadow. Even to escape his dream he didn't want to wake up. To wake would be to confirm that he had been sent in shame to *murahachibu*, the eighth part of the village.

He was too cold and uncomfortable to stay asleep. He blew on his hands to warm them. But afterward they were colder than before. Hunger was biting the inside of his belly. Why had he played pinball games with his money? Why hadn't he bought the vinegared raw fish with string beans cut like fine threads lying in tasty strips across it? Or the hot noodles with fried shrimp that were on sale? The last meal he could remember was small rice cakes he had bought yesterday at the station.

The sun was up, so he got up. He relieved himself against the wall but took no pleasure in it. Once more he walked to the station. This time there was no money for the pinball machine. He watched others play.

A vendor was hawking dried squid. There was ice cream, there was candy, but not for him. He picked up a torn comic book that someone had read and discarded. Perhaps it had something to convey to him, a message of some kind. It flashed into his mind that maybe things would take an upswing. Maybe he would see someone he knew who would suggest they have an ice cream together. But it was a world of hurrying strangers, everyone continuing the pattern of his life.

It was a three-handkerchief comic book about a wife whose whole existence was to please and benefit her husband. The wife stays in the background, hardworking, uncomplaining, while the husband rises in the world of business. The wife begins to realize that the drudgery of her life has made her old. She recognizes that her husband needs a young, attractive partner to be an asset in his career. So she goes away, entering a life of degradation, leaving him free to marry. On the wedding day of her onetime husband and a desirable geisha, the old wife is in the crowd of beggars watching the happy couple. Her husband, not recognizing her, throws her a few coins. It was the kind of story Elder Sister would have found beautiful.

He threw the book away, angry that he was asked to believe in a steadfast love. The love he knew was conditional. "I'll love you if . . ." wasn't worth having.

He watched himself from some other plane, knew he was hungry, yet food was unappetizing. Knew he was dirty. He had missed his bath for the second time. Not a day passed since he was born that he did not soak in the *ofuro*, going in after his father and sitting up to his chin in the hottest of hot water. Even cleanliness was no longer allowed him. But he was indifferent to his condition.

The Goddess Amaterasu Omikami climbed the sky. Where he had awakened cold and stiff, now he felt hot and somehow light-headed. He moved in the space between things and made not the slightest dent in the world. Some human beings did. The heroes.

He would like to be a hero. He would like to be John Wayne. But how? How did a boy impress himself upon history? It was not possible. Only heroes left a trace, the rest vanished, and teeming others took their place to vanish in their turn.

Except heroes. Heroes left a name.

John Wayne.

Noboru trudged toward his house past hunger, past hope, past despair. Into his mind came a phrase his grandmother had used often. Peering at him through the windows of her spectacles she would tell him, "Noboru, you must learn a life lesson. You must lose to win."

Lose to win, he pondered the words. Certainly he had accomplished the first part, he had lost . . . his mother's love, his home, his place in the family. There was no question that he had lost. How that could be turned into winning he didn't know.

Giddy with heat and hunger, he came to his home and threw himself on his knees, laying the palms of his hands flat on the ground and resting his head between them. One could not get lower, he was as prostrate as it was possible for a human being to be. He stayed this way through the first hour and through the second hour. The sun reached the meridian, light burned, an expanding radius bored into his brain, and in that flash of time the universe stood still. Noboru toppled over.

The servant Fusa turned him into her lap, felt his forehead and lifted the corner of his eyelids. She picked up his hand and squeezed it. "Obocchama, you are not dead, you are not even sick. Get up now and come into the house with me."

He continued to lie without movement.

"Obocchama, come. The mistress wishes it."

He opened his eyes at that and got up shakily, leaning on Fusa. They made their way to the house. "What a sight," Fusa scolded. "No one must see you so dirty, you are a disgrace. We will pop you into the tub, but first you must be scrubbed, there is dirt even under your fingernails." She took him into the washing room, undressed him, and scrubbed his body with a sponge. As a half-grown boy, this task was normally left to him. But Fusa felt the circumstances called for her ministrations and she did not go about it gently. Finally she allowed him to slip into the hot water. It laved him, and his body wanted to float away. If he could stay there forever! He didn't want a confrontation with his mother. He was afraid he would cry. No matter what happened, no matter what she said, he must not do that.

A yukata had been laid out for him. He put it on and followed Fusa to the kitchen, where she prepared him food. He hardly knew what he ate except that it was steaming like the *ofuro* and revived him further.

Afterward he followed Fusa into the six-mat room where his futon and bedding had been unrolled. He lay down gratefully. His mother came into the room and lay down beside him. She opened her arms and he crept into them. She stroked his hair. Noboru couldn't stop crying.

⛩

. . . The Oka fighter brushed at his cheeks but they were dry. He seemed a thousand times removed from that boy. A terrible cold seized and wrapped his organs. But he was not yet cut off from humankind, there was the voice tube to give or receive a last word, perhaps a correction of the approach angle. The dot in the sea was now identifiable as a cruiser. He judged the distance to be about twenty miles. He was already with those who had gone before, Adachi of the White Heron attack unit, Shimada of the Seven Lives unit, Matsuo of the True Spirit. Each had left a haiku behind on his cot, along with his letters and his wills. He had brushed his haiku last night:

> My companion in the skies of death
> —a falling
> plum blossom.

A ridiculous thought occurred to him: there was no shielding between him and the ton of explosives. Not the thinnest wall of protection had been provided. The chill he'd felt before crept over his entire body. Another memory, that of Takeo laughing, saying, "You notice they teach us how to sight, fire our rockets to gain altitude and steer. They don't bother showing us how to land." It seemed a shame that he would never land his craft, that when it crashed he and it would both explode.

Clouds piled against each other, drifting softly. The Americans believed the war started with Pearl Harbor. That was because they were unsophisticated and didn't know history. Five years ago his father had retooled the toy factory. The division of mechanical dolls and animals became the hub of a new operation; dolls and cuddly animals gave place to instrumentation paneling for Navy planes. Noboru had been set to studying this enterprise, for his father shared the sense of urgency that pervaded the nation. War was talked of openly.

It was recognized that the greatest benefit to come from their heavy industry in China was that it put the economy in high gear. In school, bets were laid as to when and where they would strike the Western Powers. In the street it was said the attack would be on a harbor in the Hawaiian chain, Pearl. His father thought this unlikely because it had been given such currency, but he did not doubt that war with the West was inevitable.

War had been extremely fortuitous for Japan in 1918. Although she was not an active participant, merely being on the winning side resulted in her picking up the German colonies in the East: the Marianas, the Caroline and Marshall Islands, as well as Tsingtao on the Chinese coast and the Shantung province. Japan was also given economic rights in Manchuria and Fukien, according to the terms of the Versailles Treaty.

All through Noboru's childhood there had been an uneasy relationship with the West. In 1938 Japan announced a New Order in Asia, the Greater East Asia Co-Prosperity Sphere, which included an unwilling China. Shinto priests began ancient chants, telling the people that Japan must cover the eight corners of the world and bring them under one roof. For too long their great country had lain at the end of the earth. It was time to become central, to assume a preeminent place among the nations, to swallow no more insults.

The Exclusion Act passed by the U.S. Congress was fiercely resented, for it was felt the honor of Nippon, its people, and the Emperor himself had been impugned.

In America equality was extended to everyone, even black people, but not to Japanese. In California they were not allowed to own land. The world tipped while the white race, large and clumsy, with hirsute bodies like apes, claimed genetic superiority when in fact they were incapable of speaking Japanese, and many people believed they had to lift a leg like a dog does, to urinate.

When Noboru was ten years old, Japan withdrew from the League of Nations over the occupation of Manchukuo. The reaction in the West had been a fresh storm of protest. But Japan imperiously held to its course of unifying East Asia.

The personal virtues of the fighting man were extolled in daily editorials; endurance in adversity, unswerving loyalty, dogged perseverance, unquestioning courage, *Yamato damashii*. These were heady times for a teenager who thought he wanted to be a soldier. The Imperial Rescript to Soldiers and Sailors was repeated at every gathering. A document part official, part holy writ, it embodied the elements that must be striven for if one was to acquit oneself of *chu*. Written in 1882 and given by the Meiji Emperor to his armed forces, it began, "We are the head and you are the body!" And continued, "Whether we shall be able to protect our country and repay the *on* of our ancestors depends on your ability to fulfill your obligation." It pointed out the chasm between *chu* owed the Emperor and private obligations.

There were five main precepts:

1. Attain virtue.
2. Observe appearances.
3. Cultivate valor.
4. Abandon honor.
5. Be frugal.

These five precepts were known as the Grand Way of Heaven and Earth and the Universal Law of Humanity.

"If the heart be sincere," it stated, "anything can be accomplished." And again, "Righteousness is the fulfillment of *gimu*."

Noboru wrestled with the fourth precept and finally took the puzzle to his father.

"Of course," his father explained, "we must abandon all, including such things as keeping faith and personal honor, when it conflicts with *chu* to country."

Three years later the Anti-Comintern Pact with Germany was signed, followed in 1940 by the Tripartite Pact pledging mutual assistance with the Axis Powers.

At this time Germany had been on the move for almost two years.

First Austria and then Poland were overrun. Noboru longed for a part in the coming war. His father had a series of conferences with cabinet members in pinstripe suits. The result was that he and a number of other small factory owners incorporated. They followed secret naval guidelines that came to them in code. His father told him to cut back on classes at the university and familiarize himself with every phase of the work going on at the plant.

He, Noboru, not yet eighteen years old, would be initiated into the code and learn his country's secrets. He would have a high-level clearance and wear a badge.

Belief in a uniquely Japanese spirit swept the land. Meetings at the Ministry ignited a new fervor in his father. "Our four small islands," he declared, "can no longer contain our spirit."

The West, people said, put its faith in material things. The Japanese drew their power from the spiritual. Eventually purity of purpose would be matched against the corrupt society of Hollywood America. A degenerate, luxury-loving population must bow down in defeat against the immaculate might of the chrysanthemum.

The West took fright at the fall of France.

But the Konoe government was inspired to cut Nationalist China's supply lines, occupy Indochina, and sign a joint German document guaranteeing the Vichy government in Paris.

The United States, in a state of fresh alarm, responded by freezing Japanese assets in America and declared a total oil embargo.

Noboru's father brought his fist down so hard on the lacquered tray that the sake cups jumped. "They have driven us to the moment of choice. Either we withdraw from China, bringing our industries to a halt for lack of oil, or we make a win-all, lose-all move."

"War?" Noboru asked.

His father's reply was to suck air through his teeth. "If we move now, we will hold Southeast Asia and the islands of northern Australia by summer. Then the nations of the world will each be assigned their proper stations. The British will be driven from Singapore, and all whites kept on their side of the ocean." He unrolled a map by which one could plainly see that the home islands of the Japanese archipelago were not as large as California. Even so, Noboru knew that in this land of soaring mountain peaks and impenetrable wooded valleys with bears and monkeys, people were able to live only along the edges.

"Besides not having room for our population, we have a paucity of resources. War for us is a necessity."

Xenophobia was rampant. The ceremony of *Oharai*, Honorable Purification, was carried out at the Grand Ise Shrine, while all through the land Shinto priests in pale *hakama* sprinkled salt and shook the sacred *sakaki* branch.

Purity of spirit was put into effect December 7, 1941. According to Japanese time it was December 8 when Admiral Isoroku Yamamoto proceeded against the Hawaiian Islands with a complement of six aircraft carriers, two battleships, three destroyers, and eleven cruisers. After hours of radio silence the news of total victory filled the air-waves; eight American battleships hit, five sunk, one heavily damaged. The count went on, two destroyers and nine other ships sunk or crippled. A hundred forty aircraft were destroyed on the ground, and eighty more damaged, with an estimated four thousand enemy killed and wounded.

Noboru was caught up in the general euphoria. That same day, Formosa-based bombers struck Clark and Iba air fields in the Philippines, destroying fully fifty percent of the U.S. Army's Far East aircraft. Two days later, Japanese forces landed on Luzon in an assault aimed at Manila. Manila was seen as a blazing jewel in the chain of golden battles, stretching back to Taira and Minamoto times, back to the first Emperor Jimmu, whose great-grandfather was the grandson of the Sun Goddess and whose mother, Tamayorihime, was the daughter of a sea god, down through two thousand years to the present Emperor, the *Tenno heika*, "heavenly king," whose reign is Showa.

The newspapers ran banner headlines; the Emperor was pleased. People thronged to temples and shrines. Gates flew white streamers, and fresh offerings were made to the *kami*. The supremacy of the white man in Asia was done, finished, along with the myth of racial superiority. Bigger was not necessarily better. The Americans who mated with any and all races and stank from a carnivore diet had caved in like a paper tiger. One huff, one puff, and it was over. The empire nation was drunk with a sense of destiny.

Tomonori Sanogawa did not join in these paeans of self-congratulation. It seemed to him it had been too easy. "They set a trap. Pearl Harbor was a trap and we walked into it."

"How could it be a trap?" Noboru was appalled at his father's pessimism. "They lost half their fleet."

"Exactly. The sacrifice was necessary. They maneuvered us into attacking. Only so could their President Roosevelt enter the war."

Noboru was not convinced. "Surely the price was too high."

The old man sucked air. "Battleships were sunk and disabled, yes. But the aircraft carriers were not sunk, and in sea engagements, which are the more important?"

However, the tide of public opinion could not be curbed. News arrived that Thailand and Burma had been invaded, and the British dreadnoughts *Prince of Wales* and *Repulse*, rushing to the rescue of Malaya, were pounded by Japanese aircraft and went down with all hands.

Noboru, standing with his father's factory workers, bowed in reverence, listening in hushed silence while the Imperial Rescript to Soldiers and Sailors was read, as it was before each posting of fresh military conquests. Shouts of *"Banzai!"* united their spirits.

It was in these frenetically joyous times when the country rode the victory wave that Noboru turned eighteen and personal joy entered his life.

Several things had been decided for him in family council, when uncles and great-uncles came to confer and explore with his father what was most fitting an only son's future.

Noboru was now subject to the draft and a commission in the navy could certainly be obtained. However, since his father's factory was subcontracting a vital guidance system for Internal Operations, and Noboru had been put to good use learning the technology, the question was:

Where did *chu* lie? Where the highest obligation?

No one thought to ask Noboru what he wanted. He was hoping to join up. Other boys at university with him had already enlisted. He masked his eagerness as well as he could, and waited with the appearance of disinterest for the matter to be resolved.

When at last he was summoned to the council, he entered with thumping heart and bowed deeply. His father's voice, in ceremonial cadence, informed him where *chu* lay, and the circle of males sucked on their cheeks and hissed approval. The gist of what was said was both expected and unexpected. *Chu* for him lay in the furtherance of the new guidance system for the Imperial Navy.

In his heart he had been afraid that was where *chu* lay. No splendid uniform with braid and ribbons, no toasts with fellow officers to Emperor and country.

But the council had not done with him.

"It is the wish of the family, Noboru-kun, that you marry as soon as possible. This is the duty of every male of suitable age at the home front. Do you understand? It is your obligation to start a family so that the strength of the nation is kept high."

This news astonished him and, when he had time to think about it, filled him with pleasurable excitement. Elder Sister had married and now hoped for a baby to dress in red like a little prince.

The decision itself unlocked tremendous energy around him. He was the eye, if not of a typhoon, at least of winds of change that blew through the house. His parents, after some hesitation, appealed to the same go-between who had arranged his sister's piano lessons and later her marriage. They discussed in detail the qualities that must be looked for in a girl of good family. His mother, while orchestrating the search, worried that he was still too young. But the family was committed and the marriage would proceed in the finest tradition. For an only son no expense would be spared.

A period of wartime austerity was about to be entered. This affair would be one of the last big social events, and his mother saw that things proceeded expeditiously.

The go-between did well; a factory owner's son met a factory owner's daughter. Of course, where such large enterprises were at stake, both sides employed representation. Noboru's family received reports on the prospective in-laws, which included full financial disclosure and a genealogy stretching back to the Tokugawa era. They sprang from a family who had early adopted things Western. The males learned Dutch and watchmaking, which in the next generation became guns and armaments. The wealthy *zaibatsu* clan were currently intent on buying a samurai son-in-law.

At the university the young men laughed at arranged matches. They were modern in outlook and swore to marry on their terms. But this was difficult to do, there were not many opportunities to meet young women. And every well brought up boy was shy with girls. If he were not shy it was assumed that he was a libertine. As an only son, great care had been taken with Noboru and he was particularly shy. He had not the least idea what one said to a girl.

His mother had been present at the council, but had not spoken. She sought him out now. "Remember, son, the marriage is not for your personal pleasure."

"I understand."

"It should not matter to you if the girl is pleasing to look at."

Noboru understood that he would be repaying more *on* if she were not. It occurred to him that his mother would be pleased if his wife was unattractive. In that case, he thought, I will not marry her, no matter how much *on*. But he did not say this aloud. It seemed to him there were two Noborus—one polite, sincere as an elder son must be, while the other, inward self speculated on how things would be if they were other than they were. For instance, sometimes he played tennis with Shigeru, Elder Sister's husband. Once as they arrived on the courts, a beautiful girl was leaving, laughing and swinging her racket. She was tall for a Japanese, almost his height, and there was inbred elegance in her most casual movement. For a moment their eyes met, and it was he who turned his glance away. But in that brief encounter he read approval.

Suppose the go-between brought him such a girl, with eyes like twin almonds, and hair cut and permed after the latest fashion? But in love there were strictures that said, Amuse yourself, enjoy . . . then turn to serious pursuits. Still, it was exciting that a girl was being thought of in connection with oneself.

Of the twelve holidays, the three days of New Year's were preeminent. It was the gift-giving season, with its beautifully wrapped packages, bright and fluttering ribbons, which began with gifts sent to Noboru's professor at Tokyo University, to the family doctor, to the go-between, to business associates of his father, as well as employees. And of course all relatives were remembered.

This year a special gift of a dozen bare-root cherry trees went to the family designate at the instigation of the go-between. The return gift arrived promptly, and Noboru was called to view a costly shoji screen with polished shells set into the burl of the wood. His heart caught like a stitch in his side until the gift won approval. When it did, he felt both proud and fearful.

On the eve of the celebration the women tied towels around their heads and cleaned the house from top to bottom, after which they feasted on wheat noodles that the old year might slip away more easily. The midnight bell tolled from the temple a hundred and eight times to purge everyone of the hundred and eight sins. Then a toast was drunk to expectations. There was, of course, a somber side that, if one listened for it, could be heard in the cadence of the bell, for a debtor is obliged to clear his name by this date, as is any person with *jisonshin*, self-respect. But in this year of victories, the usual rash of suicides was down. After an initial repulse, Guam was securely in Japanese hands, as were Makin and Tarawa in the Gilberts. So much glory washed the island kingdom on New Year's Day that all enterprises begun at this halcyon season were said to be certain of favorable outcomes.

From the first water used in the household, called "young water," the day was special. It was the day the families were to meet, the day he would see his future wife. On the god shelf the rice cakes were garlanded with the traditional white bean, kelp, and branches of sea grapes. Breakfast was served on lacquered trays that remained out of sight the rest of the year. Special New Year's sake was brought out, an imposing lobster was bedded on mounds of rice cake, and other festive foods were served with flowers.

The entranceway to their home was barred to evil spirits with the traditional rope of twisted straw and paper, and over the door hung a wreath of pine, plum, and bamboo boughs, symbolizing prosperity, longevity, loyalty, and purity. The whole house was decorated with blooms and sprigs of green. Mother and Elder Sister, in ceremonial kimono of costly silk, resembled flowers too. His mother owned eight sets of kimono for happy wear and two for sad occasions.

Not only was it the beginning of his country's world conquest, for him too it was a beginning. That morning he took out the bit of mirror that lay under his robes and looked into it long and hard. The mirror was a holy symbol of purity, for in it men, if their hearts were innocent, could look into their souls. In ancient times it was placed outside the cave where Amaterasu Omikami hid, taking the light of day with her. The mirror lured her out and caught her spirit, which men honor and worship to this day. The original sacred mirror into which Amaterasu Omikami looked was kept in the Grand Ise Shrine, one of three artifacts handed down from the One Who Dwelt Among Clouds to the present Emperor of Showa.

The more deeply Noboru looked into the mirror, the more surface he saw. Black, opaque eyes stared back at him. The cheekbones were classic, the nose slightly arched. Like a young god, his mother said. In height he had passed his father and was five feet six inches tall.

But who was this Noboru who did not fight for his country and instead built electrical circuitry and attended school part-time?

Would his future wife despise him because he was not in uniform, not fighting for the Emperor? When she looked as he did now, into his face . . . what would she see?

A mask not touched by life's experiences? Someone who has not been tried or tested, whose strengths are not known, whose weaknesses have not surfaced. Nothing to interest anyone, was his summation.

He began to dread the meeting that had for weeks absorbed all his thoughts. It was to take place this afternoon at the Shinto shrine of the sacred rock. Many shrines were located at the site of a sacred object—tree, lava outcropping, hilltop view. The one closest his home was in honor of a large table rock with a willow tree that drooped graciously, letting its shade fall upon it.

Noboru brushed the hair from his eyes in an old nervous gesture as they approached the shrine, which was thronged, as all holy places were throughout the country, with people come to worship and give thanks for the great victories being won daily. Trays of plants and flowers were set out everywhere, arranged by the local flower society. Strings of paper lanterns swayed from the eaves. Girls wore colored ribbons in their hair, and flowered hairpins. Overhead, kites flew. Gorgeous dragons, tigers, birds, and stylized warriors chased one another in cloudless skies.

He and his father and brother-in-law were dressed in Western business suits; his own had just been delivered by the tailor. The women walked behind in their second-finest kimono. His sister's kimono was part of her trousseau and had cost fifty yen. He did not know about Mother's, but it was even more beautiful, a pastel batik.

The family strolled through a grove of Japanese cedar that gave way to red pines, opening into the main garden. They walked under the torii gate and approached the hundred-times stone. Noboru looked past the great pillar to where some girls were playing badminton with New Year racquets. A small group approached, wearing happy faces.

It is said that the Japanese have three hearts, one to show the world, one to show their family, and the other hidden. His hidden heart opened to the girl with averted eyes. Walking between her parents, she presented herself in the prescribed manner, delicate as a flower swayed by wind, like the girls playing at the shrine, like the willow tree. The image she evoked was as elegant as Noh theater, as full of mystery as the sacred rock of this garden. There was a tortoise-shell comb in her hair. He forgot himself and sank into human feeling, allowing his eyes to rest on her face longer than protocol permitted. There was about her the essence of the unattainable, a refined and rarefied beauty, a thing created, cultivated, bred through generations.

Her name was Momoko—Peach Child. He stood there attempting to appear shy, refraining from looking at her, while his parents spoke of the happy chance that had brought about this meeting. Both families praised their mutual presents, saying how unworthy their own had been by comparison. Her parents went on to remark that they had spent the morning at the Imperial Palace waiting for the Tenno to appear, which he did twice a year, on his birthday and on the occasion of the new year.

Noboru's father, not to be outdone, mentioned deprecatingly a vivid memory of the time when he too had been in the Divine Presence. It was at a sumo tournament. The Emperor was known to be a fan of *rikishi* wrestling.

Momoko's father had the best of it, however, for he had heard the Emperor speak, a few words only to commend the bravery of the Imperial Forces and to pray for their continued victory. The two men got on well, and, it turned out, knew each other slightly as they belonged to a federation of factory owners. Several times they had been at restaurants together.

The prospective father-in-law was impressed that a Sanogawa should have gone into trade and done so well. "Men of war and men of poetry, that is the usual samurai tradition."

"Yes," Tomonori concurred, "but I am a man who moves with the times. My father perceived that destitution was not necessarily honorable. He was very progressive and at the same time a man who believed in tradition. These are my goals as well, and those of my son."

The wives met here for the first time and chatted casually, including Yasue and her husband in the conversation.

Noboru and Momoko said nothing. It was not seemly that they should. He gave the impression of a very shy, very well brought up young man. His mother was quite pleased with him. She felt he had observed the proprieties.

But she had not taken to Momoko. She had discovered while probing the go-between that the girl liked Western songs and novels.

Noboru's mother declared her preference for someone of more conservative tastes.

And not so beautiful, Noboru thought.

His father was not deterred by Western novels, and pressed for the match. "It is a most fortunate alliance. The bride comes well endowed, her father is respected, and his holdings exceed my own. His credit rating with the banks is excellent, and I thought the young lady exceedingly attractive."

"Really? Attractive? Well, in a somewhat cold manner. Didn't you find that she put on airs just a bit, Noboru?"

Noboru was careful not to appear enthusiastic. "If the match would help the family, I would not object to it."

His mother gave him a penetrating glance, his father a gargled sound of approbation.

His mother made it a point that evening to discuss what a man owed his parents and what he owed his wife. "A wife is necessary for one reason, to give you a son. A man must have a son. Tell me, was the girl Momoko pleasing to you?"

"She was okay."

His mother tried to penetrate this answer. She disliked American slang, especially now; it struck her as unpatriotic. "Just remember, Noboru, you will find there is pollution in most females. They play on a man's dependence on them."

"I do not understand," Noboru said.

"That's because you don't want to understand. It's a fine thing to gratify the senses, but gratification is not important in the scheme of things. And you must not confuse a woman with serious goals."

"I would be very pleased if you were pleased, Mother."

But his mother was not pleased.

Noboru wished Momoko were less beautiful so that his mother would like her. In spite of his mother's attitude, propitious signs were everywhere. Brunei Bay and Jesselton, on the northern coast of Borneo, were captured by the Imperial Forces, followed by Rabaul, the strategic base in New Britain. Gathering impetus from these successful spearheads, Japanese troops went on to take the Celebes and Kendrai. Next to fall were Gasmata, in western New Britain, and Kavieng, in New Ireland. The culmination of this string of triumphs was the capitulation of Singapore, with the capture of its British, Australian, and Indian garrison, ninety thousand strong.

In this good-luck period a second meeting between the families was arranged. Noboru's heart entered the Lotus Land and wandered among splashing fountains of clearest crystal, for this meant that his family had met with approval from hers. It also meant that he himself had not been displeasing to Momoko. He had been shy, he had been reserved, and in the quick flash when their eyes met, he had lowered his.

Could it really happen? Could such a beautiful girl belong to him, wait on her futon at night for him? Open her arms to him, allow him to touch, tentatively, her beauty, and then, as the final measure of love, allow him into it?

Could life really hold this for him? Again he wondered what Momoko felt toward him. Did she feel anything at all, or was she simply a good and obedient daughter? He must know, he must find out. Instead of going directly to the factory next day, he took the streetcar to the once-elegant house of the go-between.

She was a widow struggling to maintain her position. When she saw him at her door she turned pale, fearing the match had developed problems.

Noboru bowed low. The go-between bowed lower and motioned him to enter. It was an eight-tatami room from which children instantly vanished.

For propriety's sake he could not immediately disclose the object of his visit. He accepted tea and rice cakes, unobtrusively placing a plain white envelope containing his wristwatch on the tray.

The woman pretended not to see it. Beside it he laid a folded letter brushed in his best style. *If you are happy to have family with me, wear a flower in your hair.*

Noboru lifted the teacup and drank. Under veiled lids he saw watch and letter disappear into the commodious sleeve of the go-between's kimono.

The next stage in the honorable looking-over meeting was more formal, and was to be held at a Kabuki theater in downtown Tokyo.

Noboru loved Kabuki. He loved the magic of butterflies and birds on long sticks. Butterflies in Kabuki tradition are supposed to enrage red lions. He was properly intrigued by actors carrying around hatboxes in which reposed severed heads. Best of all was the resplendent stage horse trapped out in velvet, with an elaborate saddle, who, with the help of two prop men, pawed the earth, tossed his mane, and reared and fretted at the bit, before breaking into a canter. Each movement had been meticulously studied and translated into exquisite mime. His mother told him that the actor who rode the horse must tip the prop men. This was known as "hay money." If he failed to do so, he was slated for an undignified fall in front of the audience.

Lesser beasts—dogs, foxes, boars, and monkeys—were played by small boys in skins. Sea monsters, dragons and serpents, taken from Chinese mythology, required three or four prop men to snake across the stage.

His parents knew the entire Kabuki repertoire by heart. It had started somewhat disreputably in the seventeenth century through the impetus of a celebrated temple dancer, Okuni. In the beginning, only certain families portrayed the female roles, but the great actors began to essay all roles. And today the female characters were depicted by male *onnagata*. The plays were stylized, and the audience was completely familiar with the positions an actor assumed, even his vocal intonations. They anticipated the more famous lines and clapped in appreciation as they were about to be delivered.

Certain bits of business were under copyright to various acting families. But in spite of the fact that every stance, every furrow of the brow was traditional and done in a prescribed way, the more-famous actors somehow infused the characters with their own being and nuance. They grew up on the parts, watching their grandfathers and their fathers perform them. It was not, however, necessary to be a member of a great acting family. In the theater, talent is thicker than blood, and the young artist is taken into a family, given a minor name and allowed the family crest and *yago*, which his fans shout when he appears on stage.

Tonight they were to see *Benten Kozo*, a *Sewamono* play from the nineteenth century. In general there are three classes of Kabuki: *Juhachiban*, dealing with exotic spectacles of gods and goddesses; *Jidai-mono*, classical plays from the seventeenth and eighteenth centuries concerned with knightly wars and valor; and *Sewamono*, about the loves and sorrows of ordinary people.

The brilliant colors, the intoned poetry, the mystique were merely backdrop; the entrance Noboru waited for was not the frail and lovely *onnagata* wavering on high-platformed *geta*, but that of Momoko. She wore a kimono as lightly colored as spring. In her hair was a flower.

A flower, the sign to him that the marriage was not displeasing. With gravity she bowed to him. With gravity he bowed to her, not allowing the smile in his heart to reach his eyes.

The seating was arranged so that the two young people sat on adjoining cushions. He was conscious of an essence that wrapped the space around her and stirred his senses. A silken sleeve was close to him.

His elders were speaking of Kabuki's borrowings from the more sophisticated puppet theater. It occurred to him that their respective families manipulated the strings that activated him and Momoko. But he was happy to be played.

He stole a look at her. She did not look happy, she did not look unhappy. What she looked was beautiful. Her skin was translucent. The line of delicate neck slipping into her kimono was exquisite. The kimono itself held the five auspicious colors in patterned blossoms. She was more lovely than the young lady around whom the drama revolved. The pure and beautiful Senju-hime, on hearing of the death of Shinoda Kotaro, her betrothed, has come to the temple with a valuable incense burner to pray for his soul. She is amazed when a young man loitering there tells her *he* is Shinoda Kotaro, whom she has never seen. It seems to her wonderful that he is alive after all, and that she has found him. The end of Act One sees the consummation of their love.

But she has given herself to an imposter and a thief, Benten Kozo, who leads the girl into the woods to rob her. When he reveals his true identity, Senju-hime, overcome with shame, throws herself from the cliffs.

A single tear rolled down Momoko's cheek. Noboru exulted. He felt they shared the action, the tension, the blood of plots gone wrong. A wild love flared in him as bandits in flamboyantly extravagant costumes of skulls and dragons unfolded fans that became, according to the gesture, a sword, a bow, an arrow, even chopsticks. Opened, an *ogi* represented water or wind or the waves of the sea. Or a love that had just come into being. Closed, it commanded troops and directed battles.

The affianced young couple had no opportunity to speak, but when the climax of the play came, Momoko leaned toward him almost imperceptibly, so that he felt the whisper touch of her silken sleeve.

There was a further exchange of gifts between the families, a beautiful koto and a statue of Kannon for the Sanogawa garden. On their side, jars of finest silks for new kimonos and an eighteenth-century wood-block print of a blind lute player.

But Noboru was not satisfied. What did he really know, he asked himself, of her feelings? He was acceptable. Was that it, then, acceptable? How could that satisfy him when waking or sleeping he thought of her? But for all his thinking he did not, in fact, know anything about her. She had fastened a flower in her hair. A chrysanthemum, symbol of the war. Was there a reproach to him in this? That he was not a fighting man, an officer taking island after island in the name of the Emperor? There was no way to know.

The viewing of the moon was the occasion of the final meeting. At this encounter, scheduled to take place at the Meiji Shrine, where they were to be married, they would be permitted to speak. He wrote haiku for her, more than a dozen, but tore them up.

He was aware that his mother, during this period, watched him closely. It was not enough to tear the haiku across, they must be burned as well.

His mother found him abstracted, forgetful, heedlessly happy, and unreasonably gloomy. "Talking to him is like teaching prayers to Buddha," she complained to her husband, to her daughter, to any who would listen. "I tell you, the earth is too small and the heavens not high enough for that boy."

She became cold toward him and withdrawn. In the old days this would have brought him to her. Now he seemed not to notice. Her heart hardened against the marriage, but she could find no reason for it not to take place. It was advantageous to the house and to business. The gifts had been both rich and tasteful. To cancel now would be a breach of protocol, an insult that could not be allowed to stand. It was unthinkable that she embroil the family in loss of face. On the other hand, it was unbearable to see her son under the spell of this girl. She fretted and made herself quite miserable. She would have preferred Noboru to be miserable, but he remained for the most part stubbornly and idiotically happy.

They strolled in the grounds of the Shrine of Divine Brightness, past stone statues of Korean dogs and seated figures portrayed in ancient court costumes. This time the young couple not only bowed to each other but proceeded along the path together. Noboru, who was supposed to have his eyes on the ground, looked at her sideways and said, "Hello."

She responded demurely.

In a rush he added, "Momoko, I am very happy that we are to be married."

Her eyes crinkled and she smiled.

But he wanted more. "You're not unhappy, are you? You wore a flower and I thank you for that."

"Look at the moon, Noboru-san."

"I would rather look at you. You are very beautiful."

"I am glad I please you," she said formally.

"Momoko, I would love you even if our families had not arranged our marriage. I would love you anyway."

She looked puzzled.

"Don't you understand? That's what love is. It doesn't ask permission. It doesn't come because it is bidden."

Momoko did not pursue this rather unsettling conversation but opened up another. "I have a friend at university. She saw you. She thinks you are very good-looking." She laughed at her boldness, and the moon draped itself in a trailing scarf cloud. Their parents behind them murmured appreciatively.

"Is it not lovely?" Momoko exclaimed.

"Yes," Noboru answered, but forgot to look up.

On the family god shelf were set small white pennants, tokens of Noboru's coming wedding. All things seemed auspicious and rode the wings of success. Thick silk packages of various intriguing sizes and shapes were piling up in the entry, to be delivered to the bride. Fans of red and white were laid on the wedding gifts for prosperity. Many of the silken wrappings concealed stiff white envelopes with gold and silver tassels, which, when pulled, would reveal money offerings. Money was always hidden from view. Even when exchanged hand to hand, it was done quickly. But properly concealed it was an extremely nice gift.

The bridal couple received presentation tickets from both sets of parents to purchase housekeeping items at the Mitsukoshi department store. Momoko's dowry arrived two days before the wedding in a pair of trucks painted gold and blue with lucky figures of turtles and cranes. An itemized list was presented to the Sanogawas, stating that there were five sets of drawers, three of ebony and two of paulownia wood, holding kimonos and obi.

Noboru's father brought his accountant home to record the wedding gifts received and to make out a list of commemorative gifts that would be owing. Each of the guests must receive two and a half feet of brocaded *furoshiki*, with the inscription "Long Life and Prosperity" written in Chinese characters and sent out by the department store.

The day arrived. Beggars had gotten wind of the affair and lined both sides of the large black studded gates of his home, approaching as near as they dared. Noboru could almost persuade himself that the world was created for him out of gaily flying ribbons and Shinto prayers. It had snowed freshly, and ice crystals hung like blessing banners in trees and shrubs.

In the Meiji Shrine, old ways were preserved by priests of ancient lineage domiciled on the grounds. Oblivious of wars or social change, everything was done as in ancient times. The food offered to the deities each morning was prepared in cooking fires to which no match was ever touched.

By the time the wedding party arrived, the grounds had been swept and purified with holy water. They passed under the torii gate and approached along the compound of the absolution pavilion to observe a ceremonial rinsing of mouth and fingers in the atmosphere of divine brightness. They dipped water from a simple stone basin with a wooden ladle. The priests purified them with sacred chants, and the party moved on to the offering hall, a place for the recitation of prayers. The chamber lay between the main sanctuary and the oratory. As the company bowed in prayer, a priest raised a blessing wand over them.

They continued to the main hall, where offerings of fruit, vegetables, cakes, and flowers were piled against the altar. There they met for the first time with the bride and her parents and guests. Each side bowed ritually to the other.

Noboru stared at Momoko. Was it she? Her face was painted in the traditional white, her hair piled high in an elaborate coiffure and crowned in a bride's knot. In her red silk wedding *uchikake* with the family *mon* embroidered on it amid swirls of treasure boats, fans, pink-crested cranes, pines, and bamboo foliage, symbols of longevity, constancy, and perseverance, under which were kimono in layers, she might have been the heroine of a Kabuki play or the doll his sister secretly took with her to her marriage. Standing before the shrine of the Sun Goddess and the eight hundred *kami*, her face hidden under a white hat covering the horns of jealousy, she belonged to three thousand years.

Noboru no longer moved by his own volition, but gave himself over to the ceremony. A counterpoint of banners symbolizing the presence of the *kami*, ornamented with sun, moon, and clouds, waved above them. Priests with *kanmuri* hats clapped their hands three times to summon the Sun Goddess and the deities that attend her. The bridal couple were offered holy rice wine in a sacred earthen bowl, from which they sipped three sips three times. The music reached a climax, branches of the sakaki tree were waved over them, and Noboru and Momoko were married.

The bridal party was whisked by limousine to the banquet hall of the Imperial Hotel. Momoko slipped away with the go-between to change. She reappeared in a kimono of figured silver lotus sparkling between clusters of spring blossoms and took her place beside her husband at the center of the first table. They had been joined together, but he did not dare look at her.

The men were in Western pinstripe trousers and cutaway swallowtails, with a sprinkling of military uniforms. The married women of the family wore black brocaded kimonos, while the girls were bright in flowered prints.

The announcer gave a toast, the go-between thanked the guests for attending, and the dignified married couple who acted as honorary go-betweens and superseded the original go-between, bowed and introduced the newlyweds to the assemblage, reading the history of each family back to Tokugawa ancestors. The accomplishments of the young people were set forth, their schooling and hobbies, ending with a call for those present to act as guides in the future life of the couple. Noboru had been staring at the high ceiling, hand-painted with a myriad of colorful butterflies. At this point the twelve-course banquet for two hundred was served, carried out Western style. The guests struggled with knives and forks, seldom speaking in spite of champagne and cocktails, as talking at table was considered poor manners.

Momoko again excused herself. This time also the original go-between escorted her to the suite, where she washed off the thick paint and removed the elaborate wig. Her own hair was combed and arranged, and Western makeup applied. She donned a less ceremonious kimono, gay with splashes of flowers and grasses.

Noboru was overcome at the sight of her. Once more she looked like Momoko. He had not been able to make himself believe that this felicitous gathering was here to do him and his bride honor. He could hardly keep track of the sumptuous dishes, and did no more than bring the food to his lips.

The more important guests offered their congratulations, and finally ice cream and coffee were brought, along with peppermints, claret, vermouth, soda water, cigars, and cigarettes. This signaled the end of the banquet.

For their departure, Momoko put a brocaded *haori* coat over her kimono and, standing by Noboru's side at the door, bowed with him and their parents to the departing guests. When the last wedding guest had left, they said good-bye to their families and together walked the skylighted hall and gardens of Frank Lloyd Wright's imagination to the street, where they were taken by waiting limousine to the station.

This, his mother had explained, began phase two of the evening, which commenced by catching the 9:25 Atami train.

They had not yet spoken a word to each other. It was difficult for Noboru to abandon his role of shy young man, especially since he was uncertain how to assume that of husband. There were no guidelines for this. His life had been so structured that sudden freedom to say anything he wished seemed perilous. Nevertheless, as the husband, he must make the first move.

"You looked so beautiful, like the Sun Goddess," he said, "except . . ."

"Yes?"

"With the white makeup, I couldn't be sure it was you."

"The bridal kimono is very old. It was worn by my mother and grandmother. Did you like it best? I think I did."

"Yes, but what you're wearing now is very attractive."

"This was made for me."

An approaching train clanged to a stop, puffing and snorting steam like a dragon. The porter put down yellow stairs, and Noboru helped Momoko board. It was the first time he had touched her, and the brief contact made him conscious of the intimacy this night held. Noboru was convinced the porter knew they were newlyweds, and he avoided the man's eyes when he received back the ticket stubs. He found the compartment crammed with flowers, but hesitated. Should he sit beside her or opposite her? He sat beside her, it was closer.

After an experimental jerk, the train got under way. The city quickly slipped by and they were soon in the country. A gibbous moon hung in the sky, showing a muted, monochromatic world.

They passed expanses of rice paddies and the remnants of an old shogun castle, a *joka-machi*. One wall still partially stood, its ocher clumps of stone and mortar so much rubble at its base. It seemed to him the past was ushering in the future that he and Momoko were riding into.

Because he did not know her, he was uncertain whether the silence between them was of the kind that indicated harmony. And it struck him that he would very much like to see her laugh. "My father," he said tentatively, "told me that when this line was first built, the passengers removed their shoes before entering the train, leaving them on the platform. When they arrived at their destination they were shocked to discover—no shoes." Daringly he reached down, caught the hem of her kimono between his fingers, and raised the skirt an inch or two. He nodded. "Yes, I see you have your shoes."

Momoko hid her face delicately behind her fingers. Her laughter he took to be a good sign, she had not resented his forwardness. Human feeling was strong in him. He wanted to touch her. But he was afraid to do anything that would make him appear ridiculous in her eyes. "The go-between told my family that you were also a student at the university."

"Yes. I audited classes. But I felt strange. I didn't like wearing the student skirt they make girls wear over kimono."

"I still attend classes. And I think the student skirt works quite well. It is so unattractive that one seldom looks at the young ladies. And of course that is the idea, to keep your mind on your studies."

"What do you study?"

Noboru laughed. "I study world literature. To me the West is a puzzle. *Hamlet*, any Japanese can understand. But *Faust*? All that searching when knowledge is in living . . ." He hoped his young wife would take this to mean he himself was experienced in the art of living.

Momoko's contribution to things Western was an American who once came to their home. "He was a business acquaintance of my father's. He was very large and had a large nose. Do you believe they think with a different side of their brain than we do?"

"Biologically, I'd say it is not too probable."

"I like talking to you, Noboru-san. But I must be careful or I shall fall in love with you."

"Would that be so terrible?"

"It would be unseemly," she replied demurely.

"I don't see why."

She lowered her face so he could not read her thoughts. If he were a woman, he would know that a wife's place is more elevated than a human feeling relationship. As a woman she would have his children and keep his house. Condensing all this, she said simply, "I wish to be a good wife."

"I am sure you will be, Momoko. But that does not mean we cannot have special feelings about each other."

"Some things are unwomanly," she insisted.

He wanted to pierce her defenses, knock them down until, like the *joka-machi* castle, they were so much rubble. "It can't be wrong for you to love," he persisted.

"My mother told me love is for the geisha," she said primly.

He tasted this and, not liking it, tried another approach. "Do you read novels?"

"Of course. I love stories, especially sad ones."

"*I*–novels are filled with stories of love and lovers. . . ."

". . . who must commit *shinju* by jumping into a volcano together. I do not want to end my life for love, Noboru-san."

Recognizing that she saw her role very differently, he said nothing further on the subject. He himself would welcome the hottest lava if it demonstrated his love.

Momoko too was anxious to know her husband, to discover those likes and dislikes that made up Noboru. A moment later she was asking, "Do you admire the way foreign women look when they are beautiful?"

"Yes, but Japanese women are more elegant. You, for example. There is a delicacy about you that no foreign woman possesses."

Momoko wondered if other young men spoke like this when they were alone with girls. She couldn't imagine her brother doing it. She thought perhaps it was just Noboru.

They arrived at the station, which was filled with hawkers selling amulets, candy animals on sticks, and postcards. Leaving the compartment, she followed him off the train. Food vendors offered everything from small bottles of shoyu sauce to cuttlefish. Stolid country folk hurried into the night on straw clogs, bent under bulging bags and baskets. One basket walked away on chicken feet. Momoko watched it all, but Noboru watched her to see what amused her, what pleased her, what made her laugh and what made her sad. She did not allow any of these emotions to show on her face, which was at all times serene. But the *honne* that passed beneath, the reality behind the seeming, that was what he meant to know. His mother had cautioned him, "Even a great elephant can be fastened securely by the plaited strands of a woman's hair." Noboru chose to ignore her words.

They took a taxi past the gray-tiled roofs of the town to the hotel overlooking the sea. He had stayed here once, on a family pilgrimage when he was seven, and it looked hauntingly familiar. In the foyer they exchanged their shoes for slippers and were taken to their room, passing ornamental alcoves holding ancient scrolls, incense burners, and flower vases with red and white sazanka blooms and jade-like greenery. Outside the door were two pairs of exquisitely embroidered slippers to replace those that had taken them through the lobby. The attendant unlocked the door and, bowing low, placed their luggage against the wall.

Fresh-cut winter camellias from the hotel's private greenhouse had been picked for their welcome, and yukata laid out for them.

Noboru opened the wooden lattice that framed the window, and Momoko came up, standing slightly behind him. The air smelled of pine mingled with the sea. He put his arm about her. He had not thought about it first, it was an impulse. She didn't move.

He took heart from this and drew her against him, tasting her breath and her mouth, feeling her warmth, the smooth texture of her skin. He put her at arm's length to see if she shared his excitement, but her lovely face revealed nothing. "Momoko," he said, "what are you thinking?"

Now that they were alone, without crowds or distractions, she was apprehensive, and the kiss panicked her. But she made an effort to hide this. "Home thoughts have come upon me," she replied.

"Don't be sad, you will see your parents whenever you wish."

"But we will live in the home of *your* parents."

"They will want you to be happy," he told her. "And I want you to be happy." He searched for a way to reassure her. "Let us begin our first time together by following the Way of Tea."

His words produced the desired effect; she had learned the Way

of Tea in school, and the thought of a familiar ritual comforted her.
The four elements—harmony, reverence, purity, and tranquillity—
would be present in their marriage, and in their spirits. The prospect
of a *cha-no-yu* party with Noboru as principal guest was very pleasing.
"But we do not have a teahouse."

Noboru glanced at the hearth in the corner of the room. A deep
square of the tatami had been removed to make a place for it. It had
been lighted earlier in the day so that now soft coals glowed from it.
"A teahouse need only be small and separate. We will make our own."

"Make a teahouse?"

"Watch!" He began piling their luggage in the corner of the room
that held the hearth. "We will make it three tatami square." He outlined the space by placing upended suitcases as a boundary. "These
walls are a bit lower than other walls, but we will imagine them
higher."

Momoko fell in with the game. "We will not have to use the
bowl and utensils the hotel provides. My mother packed tea things
that have been in our family many generations."

Noboru stepped over the suitcases and surveyed his improvised
tearoom with satisfaction. Momoko came and stood beside him. "It is
a beautiful tearoom. Now you must go into the garden, Noboru-san,
and I will summon you when the tea is ready."

They bowed to each other gravely, and he slid back the door and
stepped outside. The cool night air passed over him in currents. Time
was suspended, deferred. He was a general waiting, poised for final
victory. He was a dying warrior, with release just beyond. He looked
around the *roji* in an effort to prepare his mind, discerning traces of
snow in the crevices of the rocks, and admired a stand of bamboo
beside a small pond. Stooping, he dipped his hands in the icy water.

The serenity he sought in the purity of water and plants shattered
when Momoko appeared. She bowed without speaking, but this silent
moment was a call, indicating that everything was prepared. Then,
like an apparition, she was gone.

Noboru followed and opened the window slightly, for the entrance
to a *cha-shitsu* is traditionally so small that the guests must creep in,
signifying that they have entered a different world in which one strives
to find the inner core of being.

Wriggling in, Noboru slid to the floor. On the wall opposite,
Momoko had unpacked and hung a Chinese scroll of the Sung Dynasty,

which depicted great mountaintops looming through clouds. The figures of human beings were small in the overpowering scale of the scene, but they had a place within it. He stayed quietly before the work, trying to capture the philosophy of its brushstrokes.

But the general was still poised, the warrior still counted his breaths, and Noboru joined his wife for the ceremony, sitting *seiza* fashion, his weight against his legs. Momoko was across from him, facing the utensils she had unpacked. In her right hand she held the tea caddy, in her left the bowl. The kettle was at the boil, and his hostess carefully ladled one-third of the water over the thick powdered tea, stirring the mixture vigorously with a bamboo whisk until it frothed.

Momoko was all concentration as she meticulously revolved the tea bowl a hundred eighty degrees before handing it to Noboru. Wayward thoughts broke her concentration; such intimate things were about to happen with this stranger. For in spite of his role as *shokyaku*, and in spite of receiving the bowl, turning it and taking it correctly in the palm of his left hand, he was a stranger. She watched him without seeming to do so as he protected the bowl with his right hand and sipped three times thoughtfully, before once more turning and replacing it on the low table. He then, as was proper, commented on the color, consistency, and taste of the tea.

It was all going as it should. He asked permission to examine the bowl, and to avoid lifting it and the possibility of damage, he leaned on his elbow, which rested on the floor, and was able from that angle to more properly observe the bowl. "By the glaze I can see this is from the Tokugawa period. The tea master Masakazu Kobori, lord of Enshu, whose school was Enshu Ryu, undoubtedly supervised the making of this bowl. It must be a family treasure. And on closer scrutiny, I see it is even earlier than I thought, from the Momoyama. Extraordinary."

Momoko inclined her head; the stories associated with Tea were a principal part of the ceremony. As hostess she began, "Many famous tea men were generals. But even a renowned general must ask permission of the great *kanpaku* to give a *cha-no-yu* entertainment. It happened that this bowl once belonged to General Yasuda, who had just returned from great conquests and was anxious to relax with the Tea.

"His guests entered, bowing so low that their faces did not show, but when they raised their heads, the principal guest had been replaced by the *kanpaku* himself, Toyotomi Hideyoshi, who, in great anger at not being consulted on the matter of the Tea, drew his sword and cut off the general's head. 'This is what happens when any become too important in their own eyes to heed custom,' he shouted. Just then a servant, very out of breath, appeared to say he had been unable to find the *kanpaku* and therefore had been unable to deliver the message. He had been charged with a humble request to hold a *cha-no-yu* party."

Noboru once more studied the general's bowl and asked to examine the other works of art, the spoon, the caddy, and the incense burner. For each of these there were also stories. But there came a moment when Noboru returned the bowl to his hostess, indicating the Tea was at an end.

"The first tea of our marriage," he said, and his smile thanked her. He watched her rinse and clean the implements, then, standing, stepped over the wall he had erected. "Now come."

She came hesitatingly, leaving the protection of the imaginary room regretfully, and asked if it was time to send down for a meal. He shook his head. She asked next if he would like the sake that had been ordered for them as a surprise and was set beside the bed.

"Yes, if you will have some with me."

"Is it permitted?"

"It's our wedding night. Try it."

She warmed it a moment at the hearth, poured and handed him a cup. Then, pouring some for herself, she raised her cup and, looking over the rim at him, drank.

"Do you like it?"

"Not its taste, but it is warm inside me."

After a second cup he said, "Momoko, let us visit the baths. You will bring the relaxing kimonos. I will put yours on you, and you will put mine on me."

The hot cleansing spa was a purification for the life they were about to embark on. When he stepped out, she bowed and held his kimono for him as he had directed.

He said, smiling, "Refresh yourself, Momoko. We will meet back in our room and prepare each other there." Ignoring the kimono, he slipped into trousers and a shirt for the return down the hall. She joined him minutes later, and once more brought the yukata to him.

"I cannot put it on over my clothes."

She looked at him uncertainly.

"Yes," he said.

Obediently she knelt before him. "Before I do as you wish, No-boru-san, I should tell you that my parents gave me a bride's book. It tells, well . . . how to do it. There are pictures."

Noboru considered this. "You will fetch the bride's book afterward. And afterward we will look at the pictures." With one hand he drew her into an embrace, with the other he plucked at her obi. "I think we are doing okay. Besides, I would rather make mistakes with you than get advice from a book just now."

He could hardly believe he had her naked in his lap. A confusion of sensual moments crowded his mind: his nurse's breasts against him as she bathed him . . . his mother on the night futon, her private underarm open to him . . . his sister, with the wind outlining her body.

The fine tracery of the window vine lay against Momoko's cheek. Shadows played over her flesh. Shadows sculpted the roundness of her belly and extended downward to the dark triangle.

The general charged, the warrior was released. It was a process that swept him along, like dying, like war, like birth.

She hid her face as he turned her, caressed her, explored her gentle folds and mounds. She saw desire rise in him, understood his body was a sword of love. The quick, unexpected pain and her own anxiety to do it all correctly gave way to a flash of feeling that carried her to a summit, a plateau. She opened and their love was wet.

He felt the contractions deep within her, and the world slid out of focus.

When the girl beneath him brought her legs together and the world was once more with them in the room, he lay back, having learned with his body, with all the subtle nuances of love, to know Momoko.

He opened his eyes to morning and spoke to her with elaborate casualness, remembering her in the context of the night, remembering the texture of their lovemaking, the throbbing, the opening, the warm moisture.

Momoko did not meet his glance, but when he started down the hall to the bathing room, she followed behind him, this time as a dutiful, submissive wife.

He was enjoying this married game, and asked her, as he had heard his father ask his mother, "Will you scrub my back?" Momoko picked up a sea sponge and complied. They were playing at being married, but it occurred to him to wonder where these games ended. He entered the *ofuro* asking himself if she had played at love last night, too. He became uneasy, wondering if he had learned to desire what he could not have.

Momoko bathed next, put on an unlined kimono, and, returning to their room, sat before the Western-style dressing table where she had laid her hair clips. This morning she put aside the jade ornaments and instead slipped a simple band over her hair. Breakfast was brought in. Noboru leaned across the low table. "If you will say that you love me a little bit, I'll take you for a walk."

She laughed behind her hand. "I love you a little bit, then."

He nodded at her response. "And I love you enough for both of us. Come, get dressed."

The light sprinkling of snow had vanished in the night. A warm sun shone, and the distance was lavender with campanulas. "Where are we going, to the beach?"

"Too many people. Let's go into the fields, past that wax tree toward the hills, and into the susuki grass." They passed a group of boys catching beetles.

"For pets?" she asked.

"No. They roast them on spits. They are good eating with sugar and bean curd."

"Buy one from them," she suggested, "and we will set it free."

He gratified her whim, and found that it brought him a good deal of pleasure.

He led her deeper into the woods. Momoko wondered what he thought when he remembered last night. She worried because she had given in to human feeling. The bride book didn't tell of feelings such as she had experienced. She must learn control so that Noboru would respect her.

They stopped before a stone shrine. It was a representation of a fox with pointed ears, and the inside of its mouth was painted red. Rice cakes had been left before it.

"A fox shrine. They say the fox gods loved men once. Then, many years ago, a man borrowed ten lacquered bowls from them and returned only nine. Since that time, so the story goes, they have stopped loving mankind."

Momoko looked pensive. "Why do men continue to bring them gifts, then?"

"They continue to hope." And he bowed to the shrine, his hands clasped before his body.

Because of an accelerated schedule at the factory, the honeymoon lasted just three days. The girl he played with at night and attempted to know during the day moved from his primary sphere of influence to that of his mother's. She was the daughter-in-law first, and only secondly a wife. His mother made this plain the first evening by pointedly sitting between them.

In the morning Momoko was not beside him, but had risen in the dark. Her mother-in-law explained to her that she must be up ahead of the servants and work harder than they, to set a good example. It was, after all, a disgrace for a young woman to sleep in daylight hours. Yoriko explained that she was expected to get a fire going in the brazier, heat the morning water, fill a metal washbasin and place it on a tray together with salt for cleaning teeth, and leave it on a bamboo mat outside the door to Tomonori's room. She was never to actually enter the room, but, from behind the sliding partition, kneel and inquire if the esteemed head of the house was awake. Upon hearing that he was, she was to pay her respects, open the sliding door, and, on her knees, slide in the tray. Momoko was amazed. This family, like her own, had a Western bathroom, but apparently they preferred a traditional morning ablution.

She was being instructed in the preparation and serving of breakfast when Noboru came downstairs. Momoko waited on him nervously under his mother's stern eye. As he brought the good warm rice to his lips he asked, "Have you eaten, Momoko?"

"She will eat when her husband has been fed," his mother answered.

He knew his mother believed in the burnt edges of rice for servants. He didn't realize she believed in it for daughters-in-law as well. Momoko disappeared into the kitchen. He himself had not been in the dark, spacious scullery since he was a child. Then he was especially interested in the storeroom that opened off it. It was a sort of pharmacy where green gentian hung from the lintel in readiness for stomach distress. Cranesbill was ground to a powder, to be dispensed for diarrhea. His mother was assured it had been culled on the Day of the Ox toward the end of summer. Lizard's tail was kept in a jar for swellings and boils, while pickled plums were ready for use against headaches.

What Noboru remembered fondly became a prison for Momoko.

The big brick oven was no longer used; small braziers were currently set out to prepare family meals. An old woman and her cross-eyed daughter gathered firewood, tended the stove, and cleaned the stone floor with rags, moving slowly along it like great, industrious beetles. Fusa, the mother, was in charge of preparing the evening meal. But a third drudge had been added, who now prepared the morning bean soup and tea under their supervision.

Their chief delight was when Momoko made a mistake and was scolded by her mother-in-law.

The most terrible confrontation came when a young ewe, which had been a triumphant purchase in these new days of wartime austerity, was brought home by Fusa and tethered in the courtyard. Momoko had never seen a sheep before and was intrigued by the pretty creature. Not realizing the significance of its presence or understanding the drastic cutback in food for the civilian population, she sneaked it small treats and bowls of milk.

And then Tomonori won a large government contract and a celebration was in order. An *eta* was sent for, one of the unclean class who, in the days before the Meiji Restoration, lived in villages unmarked on any map. Since that time they were euphemistically referred to as *burakumin*, "villagers," but they were still butchers and slaughterers. They prepared the dead, guarded prisoners, cleaned filth from shrines and temples, disposed of the carcasses of animals, and engaged in leather-working. When the *eta* arrived, following ten paces behind Fusa, the servant sought out her mistress and without a word made the vulgar sign, four fingers pointing down, meaning, "One who is no better than an animal that walks on four legs is here."

Yoriko nodded, indicating to Momoko that she was to come with her into the courtyard where the ewe was tethered. She sent Fusa back to the house, and nodded to the *burakumin*. The rough-looking fellow took a knife from his rags, and Momoko cried out. She had not until that moment realized the fate of the creature. "Oh, no," she pleaded.

Yoriko held up her hand to stop the *burakumin*, and turned eyes of cold fire on her daughter-in-law. "What did you say?"

"I—please don't kill it. It's such a sweet animal. We've become friends."

"I see," Yoriko said in a hoarse voice, "that you have been raised under a painted parasol, too dainty, too delicate to face the reality of war and scarcity. It does not matter to you that Mr. Sanogawa, my honorable husband and master of this house, has not tasted a strip of meat in his soup or on his plate since the day you became a wife. And now, when the Emperor himself has honored him, you cry out 'No!' " After a moment's pause she continued in the same inflexible voice, "I see I must toughen your spirit so that you are able to face the realities of life and the deprivation war has brought to us all. Take the knife," she snapped.

Momoko looked at her, totally uncomprehending.

"Give her the knife," Yoriko commanded the *burakumin*.

The fellow did as he was told, placing it in Momoko's numb fingers. She lost her grip, and the knife fell clattering against the paving.

"What is the matter with you?" Yoriko's exasperation spilled over. Although only the daughter of a merchant family, Momoko had been raised in luxury, like a princess, while she, Yoriko, of true samurai blood, had been reared on a farm to the north and had grown up impoverished, doing the hardest labor as a child. She looked at Momoko's soft, delicate hands with contempt and smoldering rage.

Tears came into Momoko's eyes, and she went down on the stones in a bow of self-abasement and apology, although she didn't exactly know for what.

"Pick up the knife, girl. . . . Well?" Yoriko exclaimed, losing patience.

Momoko shook her head in bewilderment. "You want me to . . . ? No, I can't. I don't know how."

"There's no mystery to it. On a farm one sees frequent slaughterings. A resolute jab to the throat and then a pull to the side, it's all over in a second."

Momoko kept her eyes on Yoriko, unable to believe she would force her to go through with this. It was unthinkable that she be asked to do such a thing. But there was no wavering in the glance her mother-in-law fixed on her. Momoko reset her fingers on the haft of the knife and hesitatingly approached the ewe. It looked at her, expecting a treat. With a great sob she turned and knelt at Yoriko's feet. "I don't know how," she said again.

"No more nonsense."

Momoko stayed on her knees. She didn't dare move or look up. A full minute went by.

"Very well," Yoriko relented, and she nodded to the *burakumin*, who reclaimed the knife.

Momoko remained still as a statue while the butcher stepped forward and with one hand pulled back the ewe's head and with the other expertly slit its throat. The animal's eyes glazed over and its front legs gave way. Slowly the body settled as the blood drained out of it into a pan held by the *burakumin*.

"Now then," Yoriko said briskly, "I will teach you the preparation of a great delicacy. It is extremely rare, as lamb is hard to come by. Portuguese priests introduced the dish centuries ago, and it is succulent beyond anything you've tasted. Here." She handed Momoko the bloodied knife. "You will finish up by making a lateral slit in the belly, running from one end of the stomach to the other. The animal is dead, you cannot still be squeamish."

Momoko accepted the bloody knife along with the humiliation, and pressed the point into flesh, which separated, layer after layer. Then she cut longitudinally, and the entire innards were exposed. To her horror she saw a transparent sac of a mucuslike substance holding three young, curled like toys.

"Lift them out," Yoriko directed.

Trancelike, Momoko plunged her hands into the warm belly; blood and viscous material enveloped them. She gave a tentative tug at the placenta.

"It needs more cutting," Yoriko said.

Momoko cut along the edge, causing hemorrhaging and a loosening. Then with a massive effort she pulled and the sac with the fetuses came away in her hands. One of the small things moved, and Momoko fell over in a dead faint.

She met the unborn lambs at table, prepared with peppers, rice, and pineapple. Since she ate at the end of the meal, after the men and finally Yoriko had eaten, no one observed that she did not taste a mouthful except Fusa's cross-eyed daughter. Eventually the girl brought the tale to her mistress.

Momoko bowed lower than ever, but instead of pacifying Yoriko, this subservience irritated her further. She thought she detected in the young woman a desire to outdo her in propriety. Each bow, each lowering of the eyes, seemed to her insincere. It was as though she were saying constantly, "I know my proper station and am correct in all I say and do. Therefore, I pass judgment on you." No woman of spirit would put up with such a superior attitude.

She complained to her son, being careful not to mention that she had insisted on Momoko taking part in a slaughtering. For she realized she had gone too far. Fortunately, Momoko herself would never speak of this defiling of her person to her husband. So, though unspoken, the two women arrived at an agreement of silence; both knew the matter would never be raised. "Your wife turns up her chin at me and everyone in the house. She thinks she has been raised in a better family than ours. Anyone would think it was she and not I who is a daughter of samurai."

"No, Mother, no. She just wants to please you. She is trying, believe me. Everything here is strange to her. It will take a little time."

"Of course you know better than I. I am the one who trains her, but you know better."

Noboru fell silent, remembering what his grandmother had once told him, that the sword wins which is not drawn from its scabbard.

His mother disliked allowing servants into the main house even to clean, and now there was no need. She supplied Momoko with a damp towel and set her to polishing the wood floor. It was necessary for her to crawl from room to room on her knees.

By April the peonies were coming into bloom and it was warm enough for the washing to be done outside, in the rear courtyard. This year there was a daughter-in-law to undertake the work. The washing was done with rice water, and the clothes hung to dry on bamboo poles. The sheets needed to be taken down, starched, and ironed. On top of this, as part of the war austerity, Yoriko decreed remaking the older bed quilts. The job required that they be pulled apart, washed, sewed and rewadded. Yoriko didn't bother instructing Momoko on the sewing machine, so it was backbreaking work.

At night, when Noboru reached for his bride, he found to his distress that she was drinking tears. With the back of her hand she attempted to rub them into her cheek.

"Momoko?"

"It is nothing. Home thoughts, that is all. I ask pardon for disrupting our harmony."

He understood that she was showing him feelings suitable for display rather than her soul feeling. "You are like a pearl, shut up tight within a shell. Open your mind to me," he begged.

"I don't please your mother."

He had known this long before the marriage. He had hoped it would change and that Momoko would win his mother over. Instead the fears he pushed down and ignored were confirmed, but there was nothing he could do about it. Parents were central in the pattern of *ko*, a wife's place tangential. He could only hold and stroke her and whisper encouragement. "Bend like the bamboo," he urged her, "that never breaks."

The time Momoko and he had together was under the night comforter. It was there she confided her worry to him that she was still without child. "Perhaps that is your mother's real anger at me."

"It is too soon to be distressed. In good time it will happen." Knowing Momoko was not happy, he considered speaking to his mother. But he suspected any interference from him would make things worse. He was unable to do what was right because of obligation.

When he thought of his marriage, it was to intertwine it emotionally with the uncontested advance of the chrysanthemum troops in the Pacific during the early months of the war. The first shock to public confidence occurred on the eighteenth of April, when American bombers appeared over Tokyo. This strike at the homeland had not been thought possible.

One of the randomly discharged incendiary bombs fell directly on the factory belonging to Momoko's father. Rushing to put out the fire, he was crushed by a falling beam and killed.

Momoko was devastated. Beyond the loss, it meant the breakup of her childhood home and the withdrawal of protection. Her mother, from being a lady of means, had to go with her remaining daughter as a cold-rice relative, to live in a cousin's home.

Momoko's position in the house worsened. There were no longer restraints, for there was no one to criticize. Momoko might have complained to Noboru, but she said nothing, telling herself she was not the first young wife to be ruled by a mother-in-law.

Before she had recovered from the blow of her father's death, she received notification that her brother had died somewhere in the Pacific.

Noboru attempted to console her, but although she listened gravely, he knew she was closed to his words. The double loss seemed too much for her to contend with. She put it by, refusing to talk about it. It was as though death were not in her vocabulary. Noboru was distressed for her, but he did not fully perceive how her losses, especially that of her father, affected her position in the household.

The news from the Pacific Theater was no longer solely of glorious victories and great advances. The Imperial Forces had landed on Lae and Salamaua in New Guinea, and captured Buka and Bougainville in the Solomons, but when they attempted to consolidate their position by occupying Port Moresby, a four-day battle in the Coral Sea ensued. The enemy they considered soft and decadent, who had caved in at Pearl Harbor, outfought them. It was rumored the light carrier *Shoho-maru* and a cruiser were sunk.

Noboru began keeping score, X's versus O's. The *Lexington* was destroyed, the *Yorktown* damaged; but the large carrier *Shokaku-maru*, though there had been no mention of it in the papers, limped into port crippled. He began another list, the toll of Imperial Navy planes shot down. This too was based on hearsay. There were no official accounts. But one thing was certain, the landing at Port Moresby was abandoned.

In an effort to achieve a decisive victory on another front, the Empire gathered its strength, four heavy and three light carriers, eleven battleships, fifteen cruisers, forty-four destroyers, fifteen submarines, and miscellaneous small vessels. The prize was a coral atoll called Midway.

Five hundred miles from target, the mighty fleet was intercepted by U.S. bombers. Noboru, with his X's and O's, deduced that in the course of the battle all four heavy carriers and at least one cruiser must have been destroyed, because the Navy began its first serious retreat. This clearly meant their first-line carrier advantage was lost. If that was true, most of their pilots had been downed as well. The papers made much of the fact that the *Yorktown* had finally been sunk. But it seemed to Noboru that the cost was terrible. With a heavy heart he guessed they were now at par with the Allied Forces, and that the initiative gained at Pearl Harbor was wiped out.

The cherry blossoms so radiant in the spring had fallen. The character of the fighting underwent profound changes; it was no longer a valiant adventuring with victories and honors to be won. The turning point was August 7, when the U.S. First Marine Division poured ashore and secured the airfield on Guadalcanal. The Japanese strengthened their garrison with six thousand fresh troops and attacked the beachhead, but the United States was successful in mounting an engagement off Cape Esperance and the Santa Cruz Islands and was able to land reinforcements.

Nothing was substantiated, but it was said that the final evacuation of Guadalcanal in January 1943 was a debacle, leaving behind twenty-four thousand dead on the ground, to say nothing of a significant loss of shipping. The brave drive to the south was ended. The Imperial Forces were reduced to fighting a defensive war.

The battles became a grim hanging-on in the face of vastly superior troops and weaponry. Increasing casualties struck almost every family, and the mood in the home islands was one of spreading misery.

By 1944 Japan had given up any thought of invading New Caledonia, Fiji, or Samoa. It concentrated what energy it could muster to defend the key position on Rabaul against Allied encirclement.

Noboru felt the same sadness when he unrolled the scroll map of the Pacific as when he thought of Momoko. It had all gone wrong together, or so it seemed to him.

Though the seeds of disaster had been planted at the beginning, the fact that Momoko was still barren gave her mother-in-law leverage. She had failed in the one area where wives must not fail. Noboru attempted to excuse her, saying they were all in wretched physical condition. It was a blessing, he said, that there was no child.

His mother's response came during a meal Momoko was serving. Yoriko uttered the word *divorce*.

"Divorce," his mother said. "It's the only way."

Momoko did not indicate she had heard, but continued handling each bowl as prescribed. Appearances must not be affected by reality. The image of perfect family harmony must be preserved, though it cracked and broke into pieces. But the sharp edges cut into Noboru's soul.

"Forgive me, Mother," he broke out. "I cannot hear this."

"There! You see how my son speaks to me. Because of this woman he has lost all sense of *haji*. He no longer respects himself. Parents, country, Emperor, what are they? Nothing, compared to the calculated smiles of this woman. When you speak, Noboru, you are like a pomegranate that gapes open, showing all its heart. You constantly expose your feelings, blurt out your so-called love. I feel *haji* for you. Do you feel none for yourself?"

Noboru bowed his head. "I feel it. It is hard to bear. I am tangled in obligation."

"Three years of marriage and there is no child. She eats our rice, of which there is little enough these days, and what does she give back? Nothing. I say divorce."

"When I was small and you bathed me, Mother, did you wash my neck clean only for the sword?"

"So! At least you acknowledge the years a mother gives a child. You slept on my breast, and yes, I bathed and tended you. And this is my reward, that you default in your obligation."

Noboru bowed before her. "Thank you," he said, meaning, I am sorry I must take on all this indebtedness. Getting up, he indicated to Momoko that she was to follow, and mounted the stairs to their room. Once the door was closed he said through his teeth, "Never. Do you understand, Momoko? I'll never divorce you."

For the first time she wept. When he put his arm around her she fought free. "How can you do this to me? I know *haji*. I accept your mother's decision. Why can't you?"

"Momoko, if I love you too much, it is not out of disrespect. From the first moment there was love. My mother guesses, and you know, that I love you more than I should. Come away with me now, tonight, we will hide in the countryside and be our own family."

"I cannot believe what you are saying. You would leave the house of your birth, your parents? Then you would be no one!"

The pause between them was unbridgeable. Those were her feelings, one could not argue with feelings. He withdrew to study the course of the war.

Although his maps portrayed a bleak picture as island after island capitulated, it was the battle raging within himself that occupied him. The death of a thousand men meant less to him than one tear shed by his young wife. To calm this seething chaos in himself, Noboru called on Zen. He slowed his breathing, cleared his mind. But when the exercise was over, once again it was Momoko who filled his thoughts. He prayed for something, anything that would postpone the edict and prevent his mother from carrying out the threat against his wife.

He didn't know he prayed for fresh disaster. Tomonori suffered a heart attack. He didn't die, but sat at home looking frail and disconsolate. This was not the end he had envisioned for his country, and it was not the end he had imagined for himself. He and his country had suffered grievous body blows, and it was doubtful either would survive. For Yamato the end approached as surely as it did for him. It was winding down in squalor, hunger, mismanagement, and a hollow bravado that refused to acknowledge its own death throes. It was not a death for a son of samurai, it was a dog's death.

Yoriko accepted the heavy responsibility thrust on her. The once head of house sat lost in a lassitude from which he could not be roused. Noboru worked at a feverish pace and was never there. It was necessary to set the problem of her daughter-in-law temporarily aside. The girl was a daytime lamp, of no use to anyone. There were immediate problems to solve. The shortage of food grew acute. Yoriko ordered that barley be mixed with their rice, and even so there was not enough to go around. Next she was forced to strip herself of family treasures. Each possession, each heirloom, each trinket sold out of the house was like parting with some bit of herself. She moaned continually that they were reduced to nothing. "We are paupers," she wailed over and over.

Noboru tried to encourage her. "To lose face is to lose everything. But to lose everything is not necessarily to lose face."

His mother stared at him blankly. This piece of wisdom, supposedly from the brush of the Emperor, held no meaning for her and certainly no comfort. How could words, no matter how lofty, replace her best kimono with the jasmine pattern?

By constructing air bases on every island they occupied, the Allies blocked all westward movement. In an attempt to halt this island-grabbing, three hundred more planes of the Imperial Navy were deployed. Most did not return to base. Even more serious was the loss of the Emirau Islands, which isolated Rabaul and Kavieng, immobilizing a hundred thousand troops.

There were further Allied landings on Hollandia, which was converted into the major command post for the entire Southwest Pacific area. The large Japanese contingent entrenched at Wewak held out, but the way things were going, people said the war would last a hundred years.

The withdrawal from Tarawa in the Gilberts and from Wake could only mean they had incurred desperate losses. They rallied to make a new stand in the Marshalls, since it was obvious the Americans were taking aim at the Philippines. Admiral Nimitz, however, gave them no time to regroup, but bombarded the Kwajalein atoll incessantly until the U.S. infantry could swarm ashore. Again the Japanese were routed.

The Marianas were next. The Allies threw five hundred ships and 125,000 troops at it.

The Imperial Forces responded with Operation A, deploying their remaining land-based aircraft in the Marianas, the Carolines, and western New Guinea. As nearly as Noboru could figure, the present strength of the Imperial Command included nine carriers with 450 aircraft.

Word trickled back to Tokyo that in spite of fierce resistance, much of Saipan was in the hands of the enemy and its two commanders had committed seppuku.

People were stunned. Until now losses had been concealed. Noboru had a more realistic picture since he was engaged in refitting crippled shipping as it limped into port. But the population was unprepared for such news, and on July 18 General Hideki Tojo's cabinet fell. General Kuniaki Koiso took his place.

Grim details of the fighting on Saipan continued to leak out. When the Americans secured the island they found a thousand civilians hiding in caves against the constant pulverizing bombardments. Rather than surrender, they threw themselves into the sea. Women holding infants and tugging the reluctant hands of children, old people, a sprinkling of young disoriented soldiers, all struggled to the top of cliffs and followed each other like lemmings in mutual destruction.

Of the original 32,000 soldiers stationed there, only three thousand remained, and they were in a pitiable condition, with no food or ammunition. As the U.S. Marines moved inland through the jungle they flushed out men who attacked them with bamboo sticks and bayonets. The corpses piled so high the Americans were forced to move their positions to see over them. Even those Japanese being treated in hospital poured out to join their comrades, limping and in bandages, holding each other up. They were a macabre sight as they marched into the machine-gun fire.

Rows of soldiers knelt before their officers, waiting to be honorably beheaded. Others, to avoid capture, chewed their tongues in an effort to strangle on blood, still others tied grenades around their waists.

Prime Minister Koiso emphasized that Operation A was challenging the U.S. Fifth Fleet in the Philippine Sea, and that there was still resistance on Saipan.

These sporadic efforts were broken and the Japanese forces retreated to Okinawa. Noboru crossed off two more carriers and, at a
guess, another three hundred planes. Admiral Jisaburo Ozawa committed the combined fleet to the Battle of the Philippine Sea.

In the Burmese jungle, troops fought Wingate's Chinese battalions
and the Indian contingent under General Slim that Stilwell put together as his NCAC force. Caught in this pincer movement, it was
whispered, 30,500 men died in combat, at least eight thousand were
lost to disease, and upwards of thirty thousand wounded.

Koiso's cabinet sought to calm reaction at home, but by the end
of October 1944 the Allied forces landed four divisions on Leyte and
were poised to retake the Philippines.

Vice-Admiral Jisaburo Ozawa replied with *Sho-Go*, Operation Victory. Several refitted ships joined the pulverized Imperial Navy, which
massed four carriers and 106 planes that were still operational and
sailed south in an effort to lure the U.S. carriers away from Leyte Gulf.
Vice-Admiral Takeo Kurita, sailing from Singapore, split his fleet into
two commands to converge on what he hoped would be a Leyte Gulf
undefended by sea power. The two Japanese fleets planned to rendez-
vous at Leyte from the north and northwest. However, Kurita's main
group was sighted off Palawan, and the *Musashi*, Japan's mightiest battleship, was sunk from the air. Nevertheless, Kurita managed to get
through the San Bernardino Strait and inflict heavy damage on three
groups of U.S. escort carriers.

Bad news awaited him at Leyte Gulf. The supporting group, under
Vice-Admiral Nishimura, had been detected in Surigao Strait and virtually annihilated by the U.S. Seventh Fleet. Kurita turned back, and
the way was open for an American reconquest of the Philippines.

Japan, like a terminal patient, convulsed in a further effort. When
defeats were reported in the papers, statements also appeared to the
effect that those in charge had anticipated that particular outcome.
The airwaves carried the same message, the war was going as expected.
No single defeat had any effect on the ultimate victory that unquestionably would be theirs.

The people, hearing this on their radios, hardly understood. Dazed
from hundreds of hours of war work, and nights spent in air-raid shel-
ters, suffering hunger, seeing more and more devastation around them,
they responded with silence.

In February Manila fell, sending shock waves throughout Japan.

The first daylight raids over Tokyo occurred March 9, when incendiaries were dropped. The family fled with the servants to the nearest shelter, passing unreal scenes of chaos and destruction. Two electric wires fell onto the street in front of them. There had been one wire, but it broke apart and thrashed like a great snake, fire and hissing noises spurting from it. Clouds of white chalk, which were once walls, coved arches, and stairways, settled about them. A steel girder crashed down, exposing struts that a second before were plastered over. The sky could be seen through their massive ribs.

Sky sharks swam the sky, and the city erupted in shards of glass and fire. The Americans, like Wild West Indians, raided in daylight, and Tokyo canted at odd angles, seeming to slide out of view. Fire was everywhere, unchecked, eating at foundations already burned. A building exploded to the right of them, its contents projectiles rocketing hundreds of feet into the ignited air. A series of shock waves pounded the ground; sound was heard with echo-chamber distortion. Noboru wondered if his inner ear had blown through the side of his head.

Molten streams of debris, dismembered floor planks, sifting plaster and massive chunks of masonry settled and oozed like internal organs.

The Americans with their American know-how had done all this, exploding rail ties and cotton driving-belts into the air, creating meteors of brick and fire that fell everywhere in showers, twisting electro-technical machinery into superannuated shapes. The iron foundry and the chemical plant leaped at each other. Hot, violent breath of gas ignited with a rush, sucking away the air. Buildings symmetrical one minute assumed elongated shapes like burned punk before buckling and collapsing.

Overhead, the underbellies of the sharks flashed silver, their brains hooked into a control tower somewhere on Iwo Jima. The efficient predators wheeled in perfect formation, their bombing runs precise, discharging their loads without malice. The Americans killed as they produced, by assembly-line methods, annihilating everything. Suddenly, a rosette of living smoke where one of the metal sharks had been!

So, Noboru thought, they hadn't knocked out all the antiaircraft guns. The rosette trailed thin, disintegrating into the general cloud of smoke rising from the city. A strand of pleasure wove through his fear.

The city was devouring itself. There was fascination in seeing the

great geometric ruins of a modern city strewn surrealistically between
pedestals of smoke and a broken water main. Abandoned bicycles,
elevators of freight and grain, houses of wood and rice paper, shrines
with torii gates, all had a common purpose, to feed the conflagration.
The lining of his throat seemed to have caught fire. Is this how you
died, in your throat? Was it a separate death for each organ, did each
organ wage its own battle?

It was not Noboru, but the servant's cross-eyed daughter who died
a dog's death, her intestines bursting in a steaming mass from her body.
The smell was very bad. Noboru pulled Momoko away, then reached
for his mother. In a frenzy of anger she refused his help. He had
thought of his wife before her.

Noboru cursed himself, she would never forgive him. They had
reached the mouth of the shelter and he pushed his father and the
women ahead of him through the forbidding arch. It smelled foul and
was crammed with docile, vacant-eyed humanity. What had become
of the cleanliness ethos? The very walls stank.

A loudspeaker secured overhead blared a government-sponsored
message. In crisp tones the anonymous voice urged them to spend this
time in the shelter constructively. Calisthenics was suggested. Exercise
would keep them fit and healthy. Those who listened were too shocked
and weak to understand. Hardening oneself, the radio told them, was
the Way of the Samurai. The Japanese spirit was shiny as a naked
sword. And like the sword, the voice exhorted, their spirit was free of
rust and indomitable. Therefore they would prevail.

In the cramped space, people stared straight ahead, occasionally
scratching, or swatting vermin. The reverberation of the bombardment
shook them to their bones.

In the crush, Noboru and Momoko were separated from the others. She lay against him shuddering. His hand moved in a quieting
gesture over her, but his mind was preoccupied with death as he
doubted any of them would survive the next hour. As his hand moved
in the automatic arc it had established, it hesitated, then stopped to
retrace her body and particularly her abdomen.

She caught her breath and did not seem to let it out.

"Momoko?"

She answered with a sob, then haltingly, "Do not be angry, Noboru-san. I beg pardon for bringing more burden to you, another to
feed."

"Ahhh," the sound escaped him, but no words. Perhaps twenty minutes went by, then he said in an altered voice, "This should be a happy thing to learn. It should be a thing to rejoice the soul."

"Yes."

They had prayed for this. But now, when they were defeated and starving? In the dark, his face pressed against the child, he cried.

"Forgive me." She held him against her.

He thought of his life as writing held to a mirror. It made no sense at all, and held no meaning. He and Momoko had never seen the cherry trees in blossom, or visited the shrines or taken part in festival days. The war did not permit personal happiness. It did not permit the coming of a child.

After a while Noboru spoke again to ask, "Will it live, do you think?"

"Even though I bound myself, it is strong within me." She hesitated. "But there is a woman I could go to if you wish."

"No. If it can live, let it. Perhaps we have a son."

She looked into his face. The smile that was in his voice was not on his mouth. "Does my mother know?"

"No. I am afraid she will send me away."

"But she was angry with you for being childless."

"I know." She did not elaborate. She did not need to, they both knew his mother's anger was unreasoning. In spite of it being a misfortune, he kept his hand on the miracle of life he had caused inside her.

The all-clear sounded, and they listened to the sudden silence. Slowly limbs unfolded from frozen positions, people straightened and tentatively began to move toward the entrance. Noboru found his parents. They did not speak, but went toward the entrance together.

They came out from underground and stood staring at what had been a city. It was leveled to a smoking mass of powder. Occasionally a jagged, unsubstantial wall was backlit by fire. Smoke and flame gobbled the edges of unrecognizable shapes. The dead sprawled grotesquely, already part of the rubble, almost indistinguishable from it. The town of Edo cried its death agony, finding voice in the whimpers coming from those trapped beneath its debris. People called to each other that the grounds of the Imperial Residence alone remained green and untouched. The *kami* had protected it, how else could the miracle be explained? The family bowed toward the palace in awe before picking their way through the nightmare landscape. A hand beneath embers clutched repeatedly at the air.

As they moved farther from the main part of the city they saw that here and there homes stood, or partially stood, and as the radius increased, so did the homes that were unscathed. Hope rose in them, struggling against the fear. Was it possible they could escape the fate of sixty thousand whom these last hours had made homeless?

When they saw that their house had survived, they fell to the ground wordlessly. The *kami*, whom they had fed and worshiped at the home shrine all these years, had protected them. They entered the house, they bowed low to the *kamidana*.

In the night the storage shed was plundered and the sacks of grain and vegetables Noboru had traded for in the countryside were gone. The servant who had not wept at her daughter's death, set up a loud wailing and keening and threw her apron over her head.

Each family survived as best it could. Noboru went several times a week to the country to barter, stripping the house gradually of beautiful old comforters, costly kimonos, obi, the tea spoon. The trips were dangerous, there were roving bands of teenagers turned outlaw. Noboru armed himself and began traveling with neighbors. His father remained at home to guard what stores they had. There was no law, no police. The government was in tatters.

They were told not to despair. They were told there was salvation. Where? What could save them?

A thundering propaganda blitz responded with the Special Attack Force, the 201st.

The Shimpu unit was composed of young men who volunteered their lives to change the course of the war. This dedication of the Japanese spirit was known as Kamikaze, the Divine Wind. In 1281, when there seemed no way to repel Mongol invaders and things were at their blackest, a divine wind sprang up that sent the marauding ships to the bottom of the sea and proved the Japanese were a god-protected race.

Prayers were said in shrines and temples, and in homes incense was lighted for the Oka fighters. Like Hitler's V-2 rockets, these were their secret weapon, their cherry blossoms, the soul of the nation, *wakon*, against which *yosai*, the knowledge and steel of the West, would falter and break. The people hoped again and priests purified the land.

The father of the Oka fighters, the man in whom desperation mounted at a dwindling air force, a crippled navy, the chronic lack of supplies, was Vice-Admiral Takijiro Onishi. He conceived the notion of a special attack force following the high example of the sure-death missions of individual pilots who, in an effort to stop the bombing of Tokyo, attempted to use their own wings to shear off those of incoming planes. Onishi's idea was to institutionalize these individual acts of heroism, and the Shimpu squad, the 201st, was formed.

Onishi was in personal command of the land-based air operations at Mabalacat in the Philippines, and in a position to assess accurately the superior American forces. He had witnessed the massive Allied buildup of firepower, ships, and men. He believed the only possible way to overcome the absurdly pitiful odds was with a resolution that would sweep aside such considerations as superior numbers and unlimited oil, gas, and matériel. He called up a kind of mystic nationalism that caught the imagination of the people. After almost seven hundred years the Divine Wind would blow again.

But the first time he stood before the boys he had trained, to send them to certain death, he faltered. They were his sons. More, they were the spiritual sons of the nation.

On the spot he dedicated his own life, vowing to commit seppuku at the appropriate hour and join his young Oka fighters in a pure death.

Today in flower
Tomorrow scattered by the wind.
Such is our blossom life.
How can we think its fragrance lasts forever?

The first Shimpu attack began at dawn on March 21, 1945, against seven carriers sighted three hundred miles southwest of Kyushu. Vice-Admiral Ugaki, commander of the Fifth Naval Air Fleet, gave the signal, and the Divine Wind was unloosed. Eighteen twin-engine Mitsubishi bombers took off, all but two of which had Oka bombs in their bellies. The pilots who manned these devices were the Divine Wind boys. But who exactly were they? Where had they come from? As a group they were between nineteen and twenty-one years old, mostly university students and mostly liberal-arts majors. There were copies of Hemingway and Thomas Wolfe beside them on their mission, poems by Baudelaire and William Butler Yeats, as well as Lady Murasaki.

They called themselves "body-smashers" or "flesh bullets." The mission itself they referred to as "self-blasting." On takeoff they joked that they would meet at the Yasukuni Shrine, where war heroes were interred. They were not coerced or drugged as the Americans claimed. Many volunteers applied, few were accepted. Only the elite were allowed into the ranks of the Oka, only a few given the honor of paying ultimate *chu* to the Emperor-Priest, the Tenno.

A tradition quickly grew up among them. They assembled at an early hour for departure. A roll of drums and each man pledged the Emperor in imperial sake. Around his head in samurai fashion each tied a white *hachimaki* cloth, ancient symbol of heroism. Above them a white standard was raised with the inscription *Hi Ri Ho Ken Ten*, glorifying heaven and truth over wrong. It was here Vice-Admiral Onishi waited to speak to them. He had a set speech, but it always brought tears to his eyes. "The salvation of your country is now beyond the powers of the ministers of state, the chiefs of staff, and a lowly commander like myself. It can only come from you. Your hundred million countrymen ask this sacrifice, I ask this sacrifice. You are now *kami*, without earthly desire. Your efforts shall reach the throne. I ask you to do your best."

The prayers of the country focused on the 201st. They were perceived as the incarnation of the samurai tradition. The results of their strikes were greatly magnified and the difference they made to the war immensely exaggerated. But the public, reading of their splendid deaths and blazing glory, took heart.

Our flesh against American steel, the young pilots themselves said, and wrapped themselves in mystic belief.

The certain death facing the Oka fighters was almost easier to bear than the relentless high-altitude bombing of Tokyo. Initially the bombing was limited by the amount of fuel the bombers could carry, but once Iwo Jima was taken, the distance was cut in half and B-29s swooped the city mercilessly. If it were a question of flesh only, but it was nerves, shredded, raw ganglions of nerves inflamed by the pounding that daily took its toll. Spirits ebbed in bodies already dangerously malnourished. The attacking planes left fires everywhere, preventing produce and supplies from reaching the city. Food shortages were alarming, inflation spiraled out of control. Hordes fled the city, scavenging food along the way, plundering fields. Even roots were pulled up and devoured.

People prayed for the storms that a year before wreaked havoc on American shipping. But the seas remained calm. The storm was in the hearts of the people. There were rumors that Americans drove their tanks over Japanese prisoners. What had happened to John Wayne?

The Prime Minister issued a statement in which he acknowledged that "military developments in the Pacific Theater are in a state that does not admit of optimism." Then he added, so as not to seem defeatist, "The greatly extended supply lines of the enemy on all fronts are exposed to our attacks. In this is to be found an opportunity to grasp victory. Now is the time for us hundred million to give vent to our flaming ardor and, following the example of our valiant men of the Special Attack Corps, demonstrate our spirit of sure victory."

The country was apathetic, past caring. The *kami* did not seem to notice the gifts brought daily to shrines throughout the land—flowers, bright papers, prayer strips. The *kami* looked away and the darling children of the 201st Attack Force fell like blossoms into the sea.

The people of Tokyo were hungry.

Hungry.

Hungry.

When his mother discovered Momoko was pregnant she became very quiet. "You hid it from me," Yoriko said in soft tones. "You deceived me," spoken conventionally, gently. "Why would you do this if it were my son's child?" She used the polite idiom, and her voice was silken. "Instead of coming to me, as is proper, you procrastinate until the last moment. And when your condition can no longer be concealed, you confide in Noboru. You attempt to set my own son against me."

Momoko put her forehead against the floor. Her docile acceptance of this abuse provoked the woman further, but it was the arrival of Yasue and her husband and small son that caused her to lose control. Her daughter's family had been bombed out. They had saved nothing. They had nothing. They stood at the door.

Family feeling demanded they be taken in. But where would it end, and what were they to do? It was past enduring, and rather than vent her feelings against her daughter, Yoriko lashed out at Momoko. "You are mistaken if you expect us to keep you. You and your deceitful ways! And now some brat of a child who has no father. I said it before, but now it must be. My son will divorce you. It is too much," she cried to the walls. "For almost four years she did not conceive, the gods know by what means. But now when the family is in disarray and there is no food, now is the time she chooses."

Noboru listened to his mother rampage with stubborn resentment. The old fantasy returned: he and Momoko would go away together, deep into the forest, they would buy a little seed and tend a patch. He would defend it and her and the child when it was born.

When last he spoke like this to Momoko she had looked at him as though he were mad, saying, "If you left your family and this house, who would you be?"

"I would be Noboru."

"No one, that's who you would be, no one!"

He tried again, with the same result. "Momoko," he urged, "the war is over."

"No. Don't say that. It can't be."

"It is. Come away with me. We could make it through." Looking at her face he checked the wild thoughts tumbling through his mind, and accepted the reality of their position. He said simply, "If my mother drives you away, where will you go?"

"To my brother-in-law." For Hiroko had married two years before.

"Your mother now lives with him."

She acknowledged this was so. "There is nowhere else."

That night, as Momoko served the expanded family a pitiful morsel, her mother-in-law spoke her decree. "This is your last meal under our roof. I have discussed it with my honorable husband and he agrees you must leave." She paused, waiting for Noboru to object, but he said nothing. "Noboru, my son, you will divorce this woman for the sake of harmony."

Noboru bowed to his parents. He was enmeshed in *gimu*, there was no use struggling. The more one struggled, the tighter one drew the skein. Like an invisible spiderweb, but strong, heavy with the strength of obligation, he was trussed and thrown at the feet of his family. From this humble position he spoke.

His words, however, were not humble. There were few moves he could make consistent with personal honor, but one had occurred to him. The kernel of it had lain in his mind for weeks. "I hope my honorable parents will pardon my presumption at speaking. I know I have not served you as well as you wished, Mother, Father. And for you, Momoko, I have not done what I wanted. But I can still pay *chu*. I have decided to volunteer for the Special Attack Force under Admiral Takijiro Onishi. I believe I can die well, and I ask your blessing."

His mother was shocked. What his father felt he could not determine. He hoped Momoko would tell the child of this moment, when, on his knees, he claimed the right of the splendid death. His actions would win her a reprieve with his family. He was confident that now she could stay on.

Into the silence his father, who had scarcely spoken in months, said, "It is too late for our country. What is the point, my son? Nothing can save Yamato, not even those valiant warriors."

Noboru, with his head pressed against the floor, acknowledged what his father said as truth. Nevertheless he replied with the words of his grandmother, which he at last understood: "Lose to win."

There was nothing to add. He, the descendant of samurai, claimed a samurai's death. His parents were mute. Momoko lowered her head, crushed by secret feelings. Yasue began to cry, but at a word from her husband she pushed down the head of the small child on her back to teach him to honor such *bushido*.

Before being admitted into the fabled ranks of the 201st, Noboru underwent days of interrogation and examination. Why one should be in top psychological and physical condition to be considered for a death mission he didn't comprehend. Apparently Yamato rejected all but her most perfect sons. He had gone through the motions without estimating his chances, but one morning he was issued a uniform and received the sword of a lieutenant in the Shimpu unit.

The ceremony stirred him, and he was momentarily lifted from the somnolent state through which he had moved. The stern faces of his superiors were smiling, sake was handed around, and he was welcomed into the ranks of those to be honored. Ceremony had its place, it got one through another day.

Noboru was flown to Mabalacat on a transport plane. His first impression was of steam rolling along the earth, traveling up by the roots of jungle vines, causing the intense heat and light to appear as waves. Involuntarily his eyes narrowed against the slicing brilliance. This was the staging area for the death process. It seemed odd there was so much activity. The base, carefully camouflaged by palmetto and palm fronds, had been hacked out by machines and kept open by machetes.

He was saluted and returned salutes on his escorted tour of the facility. It was quite primitive. The large barracks had been hastily erected. There was a command center and a number of smaller storage huts at the perimeter, for weapons, tools, and parts for Zeros and Mitsubishi bombers.

Entering the bare, aseptic barracks, Noboru was assigned a cot in a long row of cots. His fellow pilots gathered around, smiling, introducing themselves, shaking hands. But in the back of his mind was the thought, Whose cot had this been, whose footlocker into which he poured his few toiletries and fewer possessions? He had a strong feeling it was recently vacated.

Noboru was invited to join a game of cards, but declined, looking around him at the young men who joked, laughed, talked, smoked. They did not seem as he had imagined Oka fighters. He probed underneath the schoolboy bravado for the steel that had to reside at the core of each. Yes, there it was in the shadowed figure whom no one approached and no one spoke to.

The young man sprawled on the cot next to his, following his eyes, leaned over. "He's been chosen for the morning show."

Noboru nodded. He could pick them out now. They were the quiet ones, those hunched over, reading letters, engaged in writing their wills. Around them men shot craps and played cards.

There was a bombing raid during the night. The Americans were looking for the base, scourging the jungle in the hope of a lucky strike. Noboru felt the explosions in his bones; they seemed to reverberate to the pounding, and he had the sensation that his teeth loosened.

An incoming mortar shell struck close, lighting the night in a stark, unnatural glow that gave everything a harsh edge.

Noboru got up. If this was it he wanted to be on his feet. He went to the window and looked out. A few crippled planes had been wheeled out of the jungle and hidden under coarse fiber nets. These carcasses were being worked on by a battery of gnomes who swarmed over them, oiling, greasing, soldering. Noboru watched in awe as the ground crew scavenged parts from disabled Zeros to repair those planes that still had the possibility of becoming airborne. Slowly the realization struck him that he had not seen a single operational aircraft.

In the morning Captain Nakajima ordered the refitted planes onto the runway, and a mission was scheduled. The men were called to assembly, standing at attention while their comrades tasted a token slice of bonito, a sip of imperial sake, and saluting, ran to their planes. The rest of the unit was dismissed.

"If you've ever wondered about the Japanese spirit, this is it." A young man with hands in his pockets was watching him. "Amazing, isn't it? It looks like a plane, but will it fly like a plane? That's the reason they dismiss us. They're not anxious for us to see that half of them don't get off the ground, and most of those that do turn back or fall into the sea."

"No," Noboru said, "that can't be."

But at that very moment an Oka pilot burst into tears when the engine of his plane failed to turn over.

The young man clapped Noboru on the back. "Well, don't worry about it. We will be the lucky ones, you and I. By the way, I am Takeo Kuroda. I saw your name on the roster. Will you play a game of go, Sanogawa?"

He led the way through the spartan barracks to a corner cot. Underneath it was a woven case with a lid containing several books, writing materials, and a go board. Takeo sat on the cot and waved him to do likewise, as though inviting him to sit on a richly embossed cushion. There was a quality of grace about him that Noboru found charming.

"You get no leave here," he told Noboru, "no chance to go to the nearest pub and get drunk like in World War One movies of the RAF. For us, once we've joined up, that's it. What made you do it, anyway? You know it's absurd."

Noboru had thought about this a good deal. "The Shimpu attack force will not win the war for Japan, if that's what you mean. But it will be a point of pride to build on."

"You mean toward a spiritual rebirth?"

"We have never been a defeated nation. The 201st will be a memory to hold on to."

Takeo arranged the stones. "You're right, of course. Personal sincerity and the purity of our decision, that's what we have to set against this insane and useless war." They played in silence through the opening moves.

"Who goes tomorrow?" Noboru asked. "Have they been selected?"

Takeo nodded, indicating a slender boy lying on a cot in the second row from them. He lay with his arms folded under his head, staring into space, puffing on a cigarette.

"Mukasa drinks the imperial sake in the morning. And Kawase, at the far end of the room, and Yamaguchi, who is out inspecting his plane. They are already wrapped in their death, testing the parameters of human will."

Noboru pondered this awhile. "Do they find tranquillity?"

"Sanogawa, you have forgotten to move."

Noboru told himself it was foolish to have made a friend when there was no time left. But it fell out that way. When they were called up for morning ceremonies they stood together. As the drum roll sounded, side by side they saluted their chosen comrades. Too often they heard the catch of a failed engine, or saw a tailspin crash and spurt of flame.

Vice-Admiral Takijiro Onishi, father of the Oka fighters, took personal charge of their training. He was a heavyset man of fifty-four and there was about him a sense of being driven. One felt that his round face was meant to wear a jolly expression; instead its habitual look was of determined doggedness. Takeo said under his breath, "He grew up Navy and has flown every aircraft made. It is well known he despises a parachute. He says it takes away a pilot's honor."

Noboru nodded. He had great respect for this man who would not compromise. Onishi set them to studying the profiles of American vessels. "I want to count on your instant recognition," he told them. "This is important, as you will position yourself for impact differently depending on the class of ship you intercept. For instance, in the case of a carrier it is best to come in on the flight-deck elevator. With a cruiser you must try for the funnels." He sketched the torpedo-like shape of the bomb on the blackboard, with its stubby wings and tail. "You will notice the cockpit is set well back, just in front of the tail. It is, however, the long nose section we will focus on, that contains the warhead—a ton of explosives." This information was met with heavy silence.

The course consisted in familiarizing themselves with the instrument panel, as well as guidance and crash procedures. Nothing was left to chance. Instruction was also given in the few moves necessary to lower oneself from the bomb bay of the mother plane into the strike vehicle. "Did you notice, there's no landing gear on our bombs?" Takeo laughed. "Sometimes I wake in the night and wonder what the shit I'm doing here. It's not that I'm afraid," he added hastily.

"I know. I argue with myself too. The war is already ended. The cause already lost. We must find harmony in our souls, Japan for living, you and I for dying. The priests tell us it is all the same." But he wondered about his friend. Takeo seemed to take an interest in everything. He had enthusiasm for the world, for art, for the theory of war, for politics. He launched into dissertations that consisted more of questions than answers. Realizing this, he would break off, smile, and say, "Well, I guess I'll never know. Or on the other hand, I may find out very soon."

It had rained heavily the day before, the planes were mired, and the runway was turned into a bog. They were sitting on Noboru's cot, talking as they often did. Takeo had a great love and admiration for his elder brother Kichiro, who had been killed in the defense of Iwo Jima against the U.S. Marines two months ago. It didn't take elaborate calculation to estimate that it was at that time Takeo left graduate school to enroll in the Special Attack Force. Perhaps he traded personal revenge for death, perhaps it was a family decision to have a son replace a son in fighting for the Emperor. In either case it no longer seemed strange to him that Takeo was here, and Noboru listened with compassion to the stories of his brother.

"When I was seven my family was vacationing at Lake Nojiri. Of course I had been told not to go into the water alone. But," Takeo shrugged, "it happened that Kichiro came out on the dock to fish and saw an inverted pair of feet sailing by, held up by water wings. The damn things had slipped to my ankles somehow and it was impossible to get my head up.

"These incidents always seemed to happen on vacation. I must have felt that everyday rules didn't apply, because the next time we were at a ski lodge in Hokkaido. There was a frozen lake behind our hotel. It was toward the end of the season and the ice was no longer considered reliable. I remember skipping stones at the edge and losing a particularly good lager, you know the kind, thin, smooth, and round, that fit in your hand perfectly. It lay a few yards from shore and I figured it would be no problem to retrieve it.

"I have never experienced anything as terrible as the sound of the cracking under my feet, the cracks split and sheared off, and I was tipped into a numbing cold that knocked the breath out of me. I remember raking the smooth surface ice for a purchase, but it was no use. I slipped under and the cold scalded me. I flailed out frantically, got my head above water . . . and there was Kichiro, on his belly, extending a ski pole.

"He made me run all the way back to the lodge, wouldn't let me stop to catch my breath. I remember how painful the *ofuro* was. But Kichiro chafed my arms and legs. He always knew what to do, and even more important to me than not drowning, he didn't tell our parents."

"He must have been in a position of great responsibility in the war," Noboru said.

"Yes, he was a natural leader. There were letters of commendation at his death. But our relationship was not based on any of the stuff I've been telling you. He opened the world to me, history, politics, finance . . . he had a mind that encompassed everything. I wish you could have known him, Noboru."

"Perhaps in knowing you, I know him a bit."

"I don't think so. I would like to think so but I don't. Still, perhaps there is something . . . you see, my mother and I were very close. Then when I was ten she was placed in a sanitarium for a lung condition. It was the worst thing that had ever happened, being separated. But Kichiro took over. The things Mother and I used to do, I found myself doing with him. We went to baseball games, to the movies, he even tried very seriously to see that I continued painting, which was one of the things I did with Mother . . . but he was no good at it, and we gave it up." Takeo paused and said, "You can't really be interested in my brother. . . ."

"You're wrong."

"We climbed Mount Asama once. As you know, it's volcanic. So when we got to the top we walked right to the edge of the crater and we each threw a soft-drink bottle in." He laughed and stretched, and the sudden gesture knocked a small black diary on Noboru's knee to the ground. They both bent to retrieve it, and in that flash Takeo saw the face of a girl pasted to the open page. The soft look of her pinioned him.

"My wife," Noboru said, putting the book in his pocket.

Takeo was astounded. "Here I've been spilling my guts. And you never even mentioned being married."

"We were married at the beginning of the war, when things were hopeful."

Takeo shot him a quick glance. "What is her name?"

"Momoko."

"Momoko. Peach Child . . . If I had a wife like that I would not be here."

Noboru turned the conversation, speaking of his parents, his schooling, the war work he had done, the toy factory that now built sophisticated guidance systems for the Navy. But of the girl in the picture he said nothing more.

Takeo longed for another glimpse of her face, but he never saw that small black book again.

Noboru somehow assumed that he and Takeo would be called up together, that they would share the last adventure. But he was chosen with others, and Takeo was left for another day.

Takeo was desolate. He kept shaking his head. "I don't understand it. I've been waiting longer, it should have been me."

Noboru did not go to Takeo's cot that last night, but took formal leave of his friend. He spent the next hours attempting to put his soul in order. Sometime during the night Takeo roused him with a hand on his shoulder.

"What is it?" Noboru asked, starting up.

"A favor, Noboru."

"What favor?" he whispered back.

Takeo placed a deck of cards between them. "Match me for the mission. It should have been mine, you know it. If I draw the high card, I go. If the *kami* meant this for you, then you will choose the high one." He went on arguing for his point until Noboru finally agreed.

Takeo fanned out the deck and laid it facedown on the cot. "Pick," he challenged.

Noboru's hand hovered a moment, then he drew.

He smiled at Takeo and put down a dark jack.

Takeo concentrated and drew in his turn. He laid a king on top of Noboru's jack.

Once fate had intervened Noboru could not bear to look at his friend.

Takeo put his arm around him as always, but he was merely repeating a gesture they had both become accustomed to. There was no reality to him. He laughed and told jokes in whispers, but it was false. Can a ghost laugh? Can a ghost tell jokes?

Takeo returned to his cot to attend to the final details of his life.

From time to time Noboru stole looks in his direction. He seemed busy, his head bent over his writing pad, as his had been. Was he also making a will, brushing a haiku?

When he looked next, Takeo's face was pressed against the single blanket issue. His friend's sudden terror was familiar, it was part of his own body. He got up in the dark and crossed the room. "Give me back the mission."

"No. I won it."

He knelt on the floor beside Takeo.

"I can't go with a lie between us." Takeo's face once more pressed the blanket. Noboru bent to hear him.

"It was a lie about my brother. Shall I tell you what happened?" He turned to Noboru. "He was shot in the back. Shot dead by his own men as he surrendered to the Americans. His men were incensed, ashamed that he was trying to save his own life. They shot him to prevent loss of honor to them all.

"That's the story, that's what happened. And now you know why I'm here. My parents were distraught. My mother's brother fought in China and distinguished himself. For four hundred years we have been a military family.

"All right." Takeo sat upright. "Kichiro was a coward. But that wasn't the only thing he was, he was generous and loyal. He was elder brother. And I tell you, this night has shown me that every man knows terror as he sees his life end. Kichiro's only shame was in acting on that moment. The shining death of an Oka fighter will win a place at the Yasukuni Shrine, and that wipes out the rest."

Noboru fumbled for his hand and seized it in a wordless grip. The handclasp was firm. Noboru knew he could return to his bed.

At some point Noboru opened his eyes, it was daylight. For a moment he thought he was going. Then he remembered. When the drums called he would be standing alone.

Takeo came up to him, thrusting out three envelopes. On the topmost was written, "Property of the Late Captain Kuroda." He had already elevated himself the full step in rank that he would obtain in death.

Noboru saluted him and pulled him into an embrace, whispering into his ear, "The cherry blossoms last only a week."

Takeo looked into his eyes, then strode out on the field with the others selected for the day's mission.

Noboru followed more slowly, noting subtle changes in Takeo's appearance. The family *mon* was pinned to his collar. Wound around his helmet was a *hachimaki* cloth decorated with a rising sun, ancient symbol of determination. A flowing white scarf lent a dashing, carefree touch.

Slim and straight, Takeo stood before Onishi in his flight uniform. Noboru thought Onishi might challenge him. But either he did not notice that they had switched places, or he let it pass. Takeo wore a *senninbari* around his waist. This was a belt with a thousand stitched blessings. The mother of the warrior went into the streets and asked a thousand virgins to contribute their pure prayers by adding one stitch to the belt, which was to go with him in his final hour.

Noboru watched as Takeo tasted the austere breakfast of rice and dried bonito strips laid out on the table with its white cloth.

He watched as his friend lifted the sake cup in a last communion. The drums rolled.

Takeo turned toward his plane and climbed into the cockpit. Noboru ran after him waving, calling . . . good luck!

Takeo laughed back at him and, pulling off his scarf, threw it to Noboru.

The motors caught, the planes were airborne . . . some were airborne, Takeo's plane was. The roll of drums ceased abruptly. Takeo's plane faded into the sky. The *kami* had chosen.

Noboru felt suddenly fatigued. He was bone-tired. It was impossible to think anymore, impossible to feel.

There were long days and more nights to get through. Other groups were chosen, always the night before, to give them time to put their souls in order. And to do such last-minute things that those with certain knowledge of their fate have always done, brush final letters, bring their diaries up to date, lie back with their thoughts and smoke from a package of cigarettes imprinted with a chrysanthemum—a gift, their officers told them, from the Emperor.

When they felt sufficiently composed, those who were already dead wrote a haiku. And, last act of all, a will was drawn that included a lock of hair and nail parings for burial, as that was all that would be left.

The evening came when he too was taken aside . . .

He took the voice tube in his hand. "May the Emperor live ten thousand years!" he shouted a final time. His voice sounded strong. He disconnected the line and with the same movement pulled the release handle.

His small wood-and-steel craft disengaged; the mother plane swooped low, saluted with a dipping of wings, and was gone. He allowed himself to glide through a gradual angle of descent, like a wild blossom shaken from the tree in purity.

Realization that it was ending had seeped into him last night when he set out the white flyer's scarf Takeo had tossed him. Now there was new realization. Not only was it ending, but ending on this sunny morning filled with fluffy cirrus clouds.

The green toy with its burden of destruction floated through the woolly clouds lighted from within, piled against each other, soft, radiant. Mother, Father, my letter to you is on my cot, my cot made up without a wrinkle.

It was harder to think of Momoko. What becomes of the feeling I carry in me for you and our child who is about to be born? Does it fade like a nameless star into nothing? Takeo could answer that, by now he knew.

Along with the tumult of thought was a cool, professional appraisal of the angle of descent and a mental review of the steps he must put his craft through. He was well-positioned above his objective and, reaching behind his head, he activated the three solid-fuel rocket engines.

The final phase, the dive, began. Almost instantly he accelerated, hurtling from twenty thousand feet at five hundred seventy miles per hour. Momoko, I lived through a dark night last night. I must die well, Momoko. I must not close my eyes.

The death process was rapid. He was tossed and spun on waves of a sonic bombardment. Antiaircraft fire pierced the air around him.

Preparing for the end, the Oka fighter increased the downward angle, plummeting toward the fast-approaching deck of the cruiser. He kept his eyes open as he had promised himself, and targeted the funnels on the forward deck as Onishi had taught him. His hands froze on the steering stick. In samurai treatises the characters for dying and those for madness are combined in one word, *death-frenzy*. He braced his body for the annihilation of his soul. The floor of the deck was coming at him. Oh, Momoko, reason can tell us nothing.

Two and a half tons of trinitroanisol hit.

The death throes of Japan and the body-smashing impact of a young warrior were one. He knew at the last . . . screaming sound, tearing flesh. A glory-blazing death, they called it.

The Americans called it an "idiot bomb." They crowded around the gaping hole. Splattered brain, shards of burned flesh, shriveled tissue. They began to hose down the deck.

"It was a fucking Betty. Those Japs just ain't human."

A Moebius strip, life and death one strand. Life catapulted from the birth canal, soggy with blood, screaming silently. Ejected from the womb, forcing its way toward light, the warrior's son exploded into life as he imploded into death.

Momoko gave herself up to the inevitable contractions, but even through the agony she was conscious that it was her mother-in-law herself who wiped the sweat from her forehead. This did not seem strange but was part of the new reality. The deepened sense of joy in travail allowed the possibility of other opposites such as compassion where there had been only scorn and jealousy. Momoko smiled up at Yoriko; she would accomplish this woman-thing without a tear.

But a tear splashed onto her face. It wasn't her own, it was Yoriko's. . . . She is crying for my pain, Momoko thought, and before the thought was erased in ultimate spasm, a son was laid in her arms.

Yoriko bent over the child. "He is perfect," she said, "perfect in all his limbs, a straight back, strong shoulders, and the face is Sano-gawa. Our little samurai is pure as a cherry blossom. You did well, Momoko."

Momoko looked up at her. "The tear was yours," she said.

Tomonori came to see the child, and then Yasue and Shigeru. They said the right things, but there was something lacking in their joy.

Momoko turned to Yoriko. Then she, who had not cried out in labor, screamed, for she read Noboru's death in the other's face.

Yoriko nodded. "Yes," she said. "Here it is, the notification. Noboru was made a captain. They will forward his officer's sword to us
with other personal effects."

Momoko buried her face in her child. This bit of humanity was
all that was left. . . . Noboru, Noboru, you'd no right. What use is it
to your Emperor or your country that you are dead? Didn't you know
my life would end too?

No, he didn't know that. How could he know what she'd never
told him?

Her name, Momoko, meant Peach Child. She was fair and pretty, like
a peach. As a little thing she ran about the courtyard of her father's
house, petted by all, given sweets, given toys, but always after her
brother. She accepted this stricture. She could have anything in her
turn. Boys came first, then came pretty little girls.

She thought she understood how things were regulated in her
world. But she didn't.

When Momoko reached the age of seven there was cataclysmic
change, an upheaval that took her from the carefree life she led and
hedged her about with restrictions. At night when she slept, Nurse
held her by the ankles and pulled her feet together into the modest
kinoji position. It was not seemly for a girl-child to sprawl. She must
be conscious, waking or sleeping, of each movement. Her body must
be composed, her gestures studied and full of grace. She was taught
the slightly pigeon-toed walk of the Japanese woman. She practiced
the respect bows, and learned to whom she owed them. She was told
to watch her mother, who bowed even when she spoke into the telephone. She must at all times present an image of harmony. Her voice
too was modulated. She could no longer chatter on about anything
that occurred to her. She was not to call out to her brother or friends.
Silence was valued. If she had opinions, they were to be kept to herself,
for of what use were the opinions of a girl-person to either the adults
or the males of the family?

She no longer ran about her father's courtyard and there were no
free areas for play. She was sent to school.

In the beginning she was taught to read and brush her characters with the boys. But after the first several years the girls were selected out of classes in mathematics and science, geography and civics. Instead she learned to sew. She took music classes and learned both the koto and the piano. She liked to feel music under her fingers, it was a surprisingly wonderful sensation. Her body wanted to sway and move, but of course this was not allowed, nor was singing. So she sang inside. That was the rule, only *ura* thoughts were permitted . . . those kept inside. *Omote*, all things externalized, were forbidden. You lived deeply in the interior of your being, never telling your feelings.

A girl of good family, a girl who would marry well, must start early to prepare for her life role. She was given a little red silk pillow to strap on her back in lieu of the child that would one day ride there. To be female meant that she was the vehicle, the vessel through which the continuation of the family was assured. For this she was bred and educated. For this, clothed and fed and allowed a place in the structure of the larger family, the *ie*.

There was a younger doll in the family, a sister who ran about and slept unheedingly and called out in excitement. As Momoko watched, sadness tugged at her heart. Hiroko did not yet understand that although everything was lavished on her, none of it was for her. It was for a moment in time when she would marry. It was as if a contract had been drawn at her birth that upon her wedding would be fulfilled.

Hiroko did not know how soon she was to be corraled, gathered in like a wild colt, and broken. Momoko tried to hint to her sister what was in store. She did this through stories, for Momoko had always spun herself tales. Hiroko loved the stories but didn't seem to understand that the girl who must sleep in the shape of the spirit of control would soon be herself.

Momoko often cast longing looks at her brother's geography book, which he left about. She knew that her country was a series of volcanic islands at the end of the earth. Korea was across the strait and Russia rose menacingly beyond the island of Hokkaido and past the Northern Territories. China was a huge land with an undisciplined population that needed to be shown its proper place. More hazy in her mind, but infinitely more interesting, was America, far away on the other side of the Pacific Ocean. That's where they made the films. Their women were exotically beautiful with light hair and eyes. Blondes. Many of the Japanese princesses in Momoko's stories looked like Ginger Rogers.

The men of the white race were overly large and coarse and seemed quite frightening. It didn't surprise her that after a while they were at war.

Her relationship with her parents was formal. She loved her nurse more, and her sister. Her brother, Toshiki, was a respect figure. It surprised her that one day she had the courage to take his geography book. She crept into the garden with it and pored over its colorful maps and charts. There were so many places in the world she didn't know about. Africa, the Dark Continent, and Europe, cut into many countries.

The book was struck from her hand. Her brother stood over her, his eyes bright with anger. He was breathing in and out very fast. "What are you doing with my book? You'll ruin your future if you fill your head with things that don't concern you. A woman's world is her family. No other exists for you. And you'd better understand that."

She bowed low to hide the shame and distress and, though she tried to repress it, the anger. "*Onii-sama*, I'm sorry."

"I speak for your own good, Momoko."

"I know that. Thank you." She watched him walk away with his book. It had been titled *Many Lands*, and was of green leather, bound in imitation of foreign editions. If a question can be described as a rebellion, then there was a small rebellion inside her. The question was . . . Why? She did not try to repress it but let it grow in her mind. Why couldn't a female know what the world that she was born into was like?

The garden was her favorite spot, not only for reading but for musing as well. It was laid out in a controlled design with many gardeners to tend it. She didn't know what the house that she would someday enter would be like, but she knew its garden would have a free area reserved for whim and whimsy. Here she would plant anything that appealed to her and in any order. Nor would she uproot a shrub simply because it was shocked by transplanting, but give it a chance to come back. She felt an affinity for anything that depended on her. If flowers drooped or their leaves yellowed, or aphid holes appeared, she was immediately busy with trowel and mulch to rectify things. Even in her practice of ikebana, she would prune out the dead stalks but preserve any leaf that still had life. When she was reprimanded for this unusual procedure, she bowed her head in seeming submission. But on the next occasion she again prolonged the existence of anything that showed signs of life.

When she heard that Toshiki's science class was going into the woods to collect specimens of insects to dip into his formaldehyde jar and pin, she went there first and hid as many insects as she could find, especially the caterpillars that would become butterflies.

Momoko was not filled with the same glee as the others of her household at the onset of war. But she recognized that the country had set a course from which there was no turning back. *Oharai*, the great purification, was performed, and the shrines were thronged as for a holiday. White blessing banners flew in the wind, and the Emperor himself sat upon a white horse.

The United States Army's Far East aircraft were destroyed at Pearl. Clark and Iba airbases in the Philippines were captured, and Luzon fell to the Imperial Forces early in January. The nation went wild, intoxicated by victories that followed one after the other.

Offerings of thanks were made to the *kami* who watched over the land. The Imperial Rescript to Soldiers and Sailors was read on all public occasions. With shouts of *"Banzai!"* the people learned that the *Prince of Wales* and the *Repulse*, two great British warships, had been sunk. And Momoko learned she was affianced.

It happened just after New Year's. She and Hiroko had been sent with a servant on their yearly excursion to the beach to gather strings of kelp and bunches of sea grapes. Once home their treasures were added to the groupings of flowers set about the house, and they were ready to welcome the coming twelve days.

At the sounding of the temple bell her father drank a toast to the continued success of the Imperial Forces, and gave thanks for the glorious victory at Guam, also Makin and Tarawa in the Gilberts, that had fallen to the might of the chrysanthemum.

The day after Young Water, a personal maid, was assigned to Momoko. Bowing to her young mistress, she rearranged her hair, with the chignon lower and divided. What had been a single bud now opened into two. Momoko, staring into the mirror, was considerably impressed. When her parents called her to their private quarters, she realized something special was taking place. For one thing, her father seemed to see her when he looked at her. Not only see her, he appeared to be appraising her. She lowered her head.

The silence in the room continued until the Father of the family was ready to make his pronouncement, which he did with a great clearing of his throat. "I see, daughter, that quite without my noticing it you have grown up. But if I have not noticed, others have. There has been an inquiry regarding you. The Sanogawa family, of ancient samurai stock, have honored us. The head of house is, I believe, a man of substance, indeed he is a member of my guild.

"In view of this I have agreed to an honorable looking-over. The son of the house seems to be of good character. But I will check this further. You have my word that you will not go to a man with any blemish on his reputation."

Momoko bowed deeply. Her heart was beating so she could hardly speak. "Thank you, Oto-sama," she murmured.

Her father's brows drew together. "Remember, Momoko, you hold the honor of this house in your hands. Acquit yourself well."

"I will do my best, Oto-sama."

Her father dismissed her, and her mother followed her out. "This would be a fortunate alliance, daughter. The boy Noboru is the heir brother. They have no other son, only a daughter. Which means your son will inherit."

Momoko asked, "His name is Noboru?"

"Yes, Noboru. He works at his father's factory, which is under contract, so I understand, to deliver an important guidance system to the Navy, and yet he manages classes at the university as well."

"Did they send a picture?"

Her mother gave her a disapproving glance. "He is not a hunchback, or lame. If he had any gross deformities the honorable go-between would have mentioned it. We can assume he is sound of body and mind, and that's all that should concern you."

"Yes, Mother."

Some memory of her own youth must have come to her, for she added, "Of course, that's not enough for you. You want to know if he is handsome and tall."

Momoko lowered her eyes, and the delicate peach of her skin deepened. She was ashamed of such frivolous thoughts and ashamed her mother had guessed them.

"Never mind, never mind," her mother said. "It is natural. But remember, this man is not to be your lover. That is for stories and romances. He is to be your husband and father your children. The geisha and the bar girl will play sex games with him. Those creatures have no dignity. Your role is a noble one. Keep harmony, see to his needs. I will instruct you further as the event draws near."

Not since her babyhood had Momoko been the center of so much attention. Beautiful old kimonos were taken from between layers of scented silk. A dressmaker was called in and bolts of material unwound on the tatami in streams of colors.

Momoko clung to the few scraps of information that had come her way. His name was Noboru. Her dream husband now had a name. And he was important in his own family. She was marrying the heir, a young man of birth and breeding, tracing his lineage to samurai who followed the way of the sword and the horse. There were seeds here for the stories she told in her head, but she dutifully snipped the wandering threads of these tales, not allowing them to degenerate into romantic love. She worked hard at keeping them proper, proper vehicles for a soon-to-be proper wife.

When it arrived, the day of the first honorable looking-over was brushed in joy. There was no cloud in the sky, not one. They went as a family, even Hiroko was included. Looking at the girl, Momoko thought, That was myself yesterday.

They rode to the shrine in their Lincoln. She tried to still her racing pulse, but it was difficult, knowing she was about to meet the family under whose roof she would live for the rest of her life with a boy called Noboru. A few moments more and she passed through the torii-gated entrance. As they proceeded along the gravel path, she listened to the crunch of their feet, father, mother, brother, sister.

There was a group approaching; she heard their voices, saw the shadows they cast. One of them was Noboru, who was neither hunchbacked nor lame and had no gross deformities . . . who was, she saw as she looked into his face, handsome.

Quickly she glanced away. The parents on both sides pretended they had met by chance. The men recognized each other from their guild meetings and introduced their families. By a subtle rearrangement the two young people found themselves walking together in front of the others. They did not speak. They did not even look at each other, but at the pine needles fallen on the path.

Momoko felt a heightened sense of awareness; she was changing, emerging from the amorphous state of preparation she had lived in all her life. This new Momoko walked behind and to the left of a slim young man. And her heart soared with the kites.

The following day a New Year's gift arrived from the Sanogawa *ke*. The dozen bare-root cherry trees were a sign that they were ready to proceed.

Hiroko could not contain herself; she told Momoko over and over how good-looking Noboru was. "I love him myself. I wish he had a brother exactly like him for me."

Momoko smiled from the distance of her new persona. What a charming, silly little puffin of a girl her sister was. And to think she had been just like her, a laughing, chattering girl who made up stories in her head.

She joined with the other grown-ups in the family, giving thanks at the shrine for the forward movement of their undefeated forces who had taken Rabaul on New Britain and Kavieng in New Ireland. Gasmata also fell before the troops of Yamato. They were unstoppable, a fresh string of victories stretched from Kuching to Brunei Bay, from Jesselton on the north coast of Borneo to Balikpapan on the east. From there they struck Celebes and Kendrai. The British, Australian, and Indian garrison on Singapore surrendered.

She saw how foolish she had been to fear the war. The *kami* granted glory, and daily the power of her country grew. The crane of good fortune spread its wings over the land and all enterprises were blessed. Even the small affairs of her house floated in the general felicitous mood toward a happy resolution.

Then something unexpected happened, and the unexpected, Momoko had been taught, is never a good thing. She was allowed more free time these days and was in the garden reading when on the street side of the large wooden gate there came a small sound. She put down her book to listen.

It was a sound not as bold as knocking. It came again. She identified it as scratching. Someone was scratching at the garden door.

She went to it and unbolted it. The gate swung open to reveal a servant, not of her house, a strange servant. The man bowed and delivered a note.

It seemed to her that not only was her breathing suspended, but life itself, until she opened it. The characters were brushed with flair. She read, "If you are happy to have family with me, wear a flower in your hair." Where before she could not breathe at all, now her breath came too fast and seemed out of control.

In a flash her mind made a picture. Noboru had taken the samurai sword of his father, struck off her father's head, and, placing her on the saddle of his horse, galloped off with her. . . . Why had he done this rash thing?

Why had he left his role of shy young man, pushed her parents aside, and taken matters into his own hands? This was an outlaw thing to do. As outlaw as the mad picture that had come unbidden into her mind.

She felt panic. The dream-husband she had made up would never act so impulsively, would never have written such a note, indeed any note. Her panic increased as she realized she was marrying someone she did not know.

She felt he made it very difficult to know him by being so unexpected as to write her in secret and send a servant in secret.

She had never heard of anyone who had ever done such a thing. And though she was troubled, she honored his wish and at the next honorable looking-over, which was at a Kabuki play, pinned a flower in her hair.

When his eyes went to it she flushed and looked away. Still, she was more conscious of him than of the dashing Benten Kozo, the hero-villain of the piece.

Noboru refused to keep his eyes on the play unfolding before them, alive with bright, symbolic creatures. It was a breach of protocol and quite unsettling that he looked at her so often. This confirmed her suspicion that he did not altogether fit her idea of a husband, and it unsettled her even more.

When the forbidden love of Senju-hime for Benten Kozo was consummated at the end of the first act, for some reason she identified Noboru with the brigand. She felt it would be as dangerous to love this young man as to love Benten Kozo. She suspected it might be easy to allow love, but recognized that their lives would not be anchored in the rules and traditions she had grown up with. She told herself she must be on guard. She told herself she must be careful. For who knew where Noboru's unexpected nature would lead?

The play once more commanded her attention. Momoko did not think Benten Kozo would behave so badly. He betrayed Senju-hime who loved him, and in shame she threw herself over a precipice.

Momoko felt the sting of a hot tear hanging in her lashes; she tried to blink it back, but it rolled down her cheek.

With the arrival and acceptance of an eighteenth-century wood-block print, the intentions of the two families were sealed. The wedding would take place.

There was a final honorable looking-over, but only some great and grievous matter could change the course of events at this juncture. Short of a shameful or criminal act being uncovered, both sides were committed.

The final encounter came about at the viewing of the moon. On this occasion the families joined each other and strolled in the courtyard of the Meiji Shrine, where the marriage ceremony would be performed. Once again Momoko walked ahead with Noboru.

They spoke together for the first time. Things were proceeding in a reassuring manner with appropriate comments when all of a sudden Noboru stepped out of the ritual and said impetuously, "I would love you even if our families had not arranged our marriage. I would love you anyway."

She didn't know how to respond to such a wild remark.

"Love doesn't ask permission," he went on in the same outlaw way.

A surge of excitement swept over her. She thought of Senju-hime, who had loved and died. She had to be careful or the same thing would happen to her. She had been taught that if you did not follow the respect rules, you were lost with no guide for your life.

Even after their marriage Noboru remained unexpected and unpredictable in his ways, and did not resemble her idea of a proper husband. He was more the brigand who stole kisses in the dark. When she was with him her heart beat fast and it was easy to lose her resolve to make things conform more to her image of what her marriage should be. This was made difficult by the enmity of her mother-in-law. To escape the constant harassment, she stole time from her chores to plant the private garden she had promised herself. She chose a faraway corner, outside her mother-in-law's daily tour of inspection, and partly hidden. Some flowers she transplanted, others she raised from seeds in small cups kept in a sunny spot. Nothing grew in straight rows. She tamped in seeds haphazardly, as though the wind itself had carried them. And when they bloomed, she gave her flowers the utmost freedom, permitting arrays of colors never seen next to each other, allowing them to grow in crowds of wild, spectacular shades.

Momoko rejoiced in this beautiful nook. It reflected what she could not have in her life, the freedom to let love and passion find their places. Under their quilt at night, Noboru was gentle. He would look into her face, touch her hair. Then slowly his body awakened hers, and he would whisper, "Shhh." The rice-paper partition between them and his parents was thin and they did not dare make a sound. Her eyes would close and his too. Then together, silently, they experienced the breath-stopping feeling.

Those private times were like her garden, secret. Only she and Noboru knew what they were and what they meant.

But of the garden, only she knew. Until the day it was discovered. Fusa's cross-eyed daughter found it and went to her mistress.

When Momoko came to water the hidden patch, there were only trampled, broken stems and petals lying in the dirt. She knelt down, searching for a root that might be replanted. But it was destroyed past any help. Her garden was gone.

Yoriko didn't say anything about it, but Momoko sensed her mother-in-law's satisfaction. It had to be her, the servants wouldn't dare. But why? Why couldn't she be permitted this one pleasure? Momoko went through the day stoically and did not cry until she was alone in her room.

Noboru came in, and when he saw her huddled miserably in a corner of the futon, sat quietly beside her. After a while he took her hand and put it against his own chest. This gesture of allegiance broke her reserve, and the story of her garden poured out.

"It was very small, it hardly took anything away from the large garden."

She was surprised to see that Noboru was crying.

"Why?" she asked, placing a finger on his cheek. "It wasn't your garden."

"It was."

That night she did not retreat in any part of her, but clung to him as fiercely as he did to her.

In the morning she was severe with herself, reminding herself that she had been undisciplined. The role of a wife is formal.

That evening Noboru brought a small box filled with good loamy earth to their room, and several iris bulbs. Once more Momoko's resolve faltered.

"Bring them to the window for a couple of hours of sun," he told her. "The rest of the time you'll hide them in the cupboard."

When the planes came over and the whole house shook from the bombing, they brought out the iris and sat with their arms around each other, looking at them. They brought them out at other times too, to celebrate their ultimate moments.

During the day she went about the heavy tasks laid on her and endured Yoriko's complaints, thinking, She guesses what happens at night under the quilt and is punishing me. This is what I deserve for not adhering to my role of a proper wife. I have gone against my training, my mother would be displeased, my father dishonored.

The year dragged on, shocked into focus by death. She kept shaking her head, refusing to believe her father had been killed. But the reality of it seeped into her thoughts at every turn. And then, just days later, Toshiki. She couldn't take it in. Both? She couldn't react the second time. She felt numb; even as she burned incense she felt nothing. The future seemed to her dark and without hope. And when the future became the present, she saw that she had been right. It was the third year of the war, the country was sunk in quagmire, the people quiet, sullen, moving like ghosts.

When New Year's came around again, she wrote to her sister reminding her this was the third year they had not gone to the seaside to gather kelp and sea lace. She apologized again for not having attended her wedding. It was too far and there was no money for a trip to Moji. The true purpose of her letter was to ask Hiroko's advice on conceiving, for though she had been married only four months, Hiroko was already pregnant.

Momoko was desperate. She had prayed. She had left gifts for the priests. She drank concoctions of squid ink, but still must bow her head before Yoriko's wrath. She had failed in the one thing expected of women. She had failed to produce a child, and Yoriko threatened her with divorce. Noboru set himself firmly against this, which made Yoriko more determined.

And Noboru himself must be resisted. He wanted to run away with her and live in the mountains. It was her duty to help him overcome such mad schemes and foreign thoughts. His impulsiveness would bring about the disaster he dreaded. She knew it.

The future poised itself like a painted wave, about to crash, but not moving. Then in September of the third year of the war she found herself pregnant. Initial elation lifted her to an almost out-of-body joy. But it was quickly punctured by the reality they all faced, hunger.

There was not enough food. How could she bring a child into the world to starve? She hid her pregnancy. For even though Yoriko commented daily on her barrenness, once she learned the truth she might make her get rid of the child. Momoko's instinct told her to make no confidences. After four months she bound herself.

The moment she dreaded came as they huddled in the air-raid shelter. She was relieved, almost glad Noboru had found out her secret. The pregnancy said for her the things she didn't allow herself to say . . . it said, Our love blossoms in me.

He didn't order her to abort the child, of course not. He did what he had always done, showed her his love.

But what he felt and what she felt didn't matter. It counted for nothing. They had many whispered conferences on how best to relay their news to Yoriko. Momoko allowed herself to hope that her persecution was over. She even imagined Yoriko smiling at her.

When her mother-in-law knew and called her child bastard, Momoko was suddenly like the comatose war wounded, hardly capable of response.

It had been a year since Yoriko had first brought up the subject of divorce. Now she was adamant. Noboru was frantic. Once again when they were alone he pleaded with her. "The war is all but over, Momoko. We could make it through."

For a moment it even seemed possible. They would go into the mountains, which were steep and inaccessible. She saw herself following him. He would brush creepers and branches from their path. He would find a place for them; the shelter of a cave would be enough. She would pick the wild asparagus she had once seen growing, make a soup of dandelions, gather herbs . . . and he would keep them safe, protect her and the child until the war was over. Her heart leaped at the crazy prospect, just the two of them, outside the law, outside the world, outside the war. This reaction on her part totally demoralized her, for she saw plainly that it was a mirage, with no reality to it. She drew away from him, afraid and confused.

At the end he sacrificed his life for Emperor and country. She couldn't understand this when all through the war he had said, "I do not hate Americans."

Why did he say that? Why? Everyone hated the Americans. . . .

The last terrible minutes that they were alone were branded on her. Noboru asked for her blessing. As he stood before her, waiting, she struggled with feelings she couldn't express, a great paroxysm of questioning. For the first time she questioned everything. Had he the right to be a hero, to choose Emperor, country, and a glorious death?

What about the child, who would have no father? What about the turbulence that choked her, that she didn't know how to manage?

It was as though a spell had been laid on her. She was paralyzed, unable to move. Against her training, against the propriety instilled in her from the beginning, she had come to love him in the wild, free way he demanded.

She watched him go, imagining that she was running after him, calling him back, telling him the things he wanted to hear and she wanted to say. Begging him to stay, agreeing to anything.

It was too late. He was gone. And which part of it had been in her head she couldn't say.

Momoko had not left the house since the birth of her child, which was tangled in her mind with Noboru's death. It took the historic event of the Emperor's speech to bring her into the streets. Beside this torn-up girl knelt her mother-in-law and the master of the house, Tomonori Sanogawa. As Noboru had foreseen, it had not been honorable to banish the wife of a war hero, a warrior of the 201st. Momoko was grateful. The Sanogawa *ke* was the only link with Noboru, and she clung to it.

Besides, Yoriko was a mother to her. She sometimes had to remind herself of the years of hostility and persecution. Akio's birth changed that. Yoriko chose to forget that before his birth she had called him "Momoko's bastard." In her eyes he was a little Noboru. She doted on the infant, clearly preferring him to Yasue's boy. But there was more to it. She was able to share the dead with Momoko as she had not been able to share the living. It strengthened her to know they prayed the same prayers.

So though things were easier in the house, Momoko could not be easy in her mind. She looked back in pain at the stubborn girl who had been herself, and who refused to tell her young husband that he came first, ahead of duty. She had not known that she had bonded with him in the way he wanted. And now that she did know, it no longer mattered. He was dead and she wished that she were.

Of the family she cared least for Yasue's husband Shigeru. But it was apparent to her that there was no one else to run the business if things returned to normal after the war.

After the war, the phrase was on everyone's lips. This in spite of the fact that Russia had declared war and invaded Manchukuo. Why would they do this at this late date, except to be in on the kill when the spoils were divided? The only certain thing was that the country was sunk in a morass from which it could not extricate itself. A million men were under arms on far-flung islands, thousands of civilians were uprooted, forced to work in mines and munitions factories, countless others drifted homeless in search of food. Their armbands read, "Volunteer Worker." In the moribund city half-starved children picked over the sprawling ruins of its wood and concrete carcass. It was August 14. The papers printed the news that the Emperor was to speak. Loudspeakers had been set up and all over Japan crowds thronged into the streets.

No one dared speculate as to what it might mean. In April, when the U.S. Marines landed in Okinawa, the Koiso cabinet fell. In a desperate effort to stabilize the government, Admiral Kantaro Suzuki was named Prime Minister. What had he counseled the Emperor? The people wondered as they assembled, what could they be asked to give that they had not given?

They bowed, waiting to hear the voice they had never heard. The Ruler from Ages Eternal, the hundred twenty-fifth Emperor of Sun lineage, absolute monarch and Shinto deity, was about to address his people. It was a happening unprecedented. Nowhere was it recorded that the father or grandfather or any remote ancestor of those present had been so honored. But, and they asked themselves this nervously and in fear, what could it mean? What would be asked?

The Sanogawa family were among those who poured into the street. Momoko's three-month-old son, Akio, was strapped to her back, and she reached over her shoulder to push down his head in deference to the occasion.

Static spat from overhead speakers, alerting the people, who strained to hear the divine voice. The shock at the Emperor's first words was compounded by the refined cadence. The Tenno was speaking a strangely accented, arcane Japanese made all the more difficult to understand by the sputtering of the radio. Although his sincerity was obvious to all, after a few seconds the gist of what the Tenno was saying was borne in on them.

"The situation has developed not necessarily to our advantage." Throughout Japan people knelt.

"The enemy has begun to employ a new and most cruel bomb," the royal voice quavered, "the power of which to do damage is indeed incalculable, taking toll of many innocent lives."

There had been rumors all week. Four B-29s had flown reconnaissance over Hiroshima at seven-thirty the morning of the sixth. The all-clear sounded, people went into the streets and resumed their day. A day that ended in windstorm, fire, and death.

The Tokyo-Hiroshima train was stopped at Fukuyama. No one knew why, not even the railwaymen or the conductors. But in Mihara, seventy miles away, they saw the blue flash as flames spewed from the sky over Hiroshima, and the windows of the Etajima Military Academy were blown out. A black rain fell from a clear sky. Thirty hours passed; after forty hours there were reports of burned flesh separating from bone and falling off. Someone said the bank building calculated to be two hundred meters from the center of the blast had a human form seared into its steps. Was that what the Tenno meant? They heard that an instrument-bearing parachute had been dropped first, before the bomb itself, to lure the curious into the streets and increase the kill. But it wasn't enough; three days later they dropped a second bomb, on Nagasaki.

The Emperor continued reading the prepared text. The airwaves crackled. "How are we to save ourselves, to atone before the hallowed spirits of our imperial ancestors?" The question, they recognized, was not addressed to them. The voice seemed weakened, but it went on, "We have therefore ordered acceptance of the provisions of the Joint Declaration of the Powers. . . ."

All over Japan the population began to realize they were hearing a speech of surrender. The Emperor was inseparable from Japan.

Japan was saying, "We've no choice but to endure the unendurable and suffer the insufferable."

The voice ceased.

The radio was silent.

There was stunned comprehension and incomprehension.

Shimpu units of the 201st, farmers, merchants, the dispossessed . . . all tried to understand.

Three and a half million had died, cities were decimated, industry at a standstill. Still, their army was undefeated.

Later they were to say, "The Emperor spoke and the war ended."

But it was not quite like that. Many on the street did not get up but remained on their knees. Others cried openly. Some committed seppuku in front of the Imperial Palace. The great majority wandered dazed and demoralized. What had it been for, the dead, the wounded, the hunger, the fear?

Only their Emperor could have reconciled them to defeat. Until he spoke it was the duty of every man under arms to fight on and the duty of those at home to support them, no matter at what cost.

But he had spoken.

They had heard the divine wisdom. They were told to put before the eyes of their mind a new course, and that course was peace. The decision came from the one at the center of their lives, temporal and sacred. The crane fluttered from the hand of the Tenno over the land.

Momoko's father-in-law, after he bowed in reverence and submission, was never able to stand erect again. He walked and sat in a half-crouched position. It was he, however, who sought and found the spirit to instruct his family.

"Remember," he admonished them, "to draw one's sword within the castle of Edo is punishable by death. Our Emperor in his belly has always been an Emperor of peace. The politicians overruled him, that is what happened."

Yasue wept aloud. "Evil comes from the Americans. What will they do to us? Will we all die?"

Her father addressed a more important issue. "Japan will retain her identity no matter what is to follow."

When they reached home Momoko brought out the tea bowls to calm their spirits.

"I hope," Yasue whispered to her, "this day will not leave its mark on our sons." The two young women had become close, they were both mothers of sons.

The men sipped tea and the name of General Douglas MacArthur entered the house, along with a foreboding of what the Occupation would mean.

The house was kept shuttered up and the outer gate locked. Even Masaru, the two-year-old son of Yasue, was kept inside. He cried to be allowed to play in the garden, but his mother distracted him with a few morsels of sweetened rice. Yoriko insisted that the blinds also be drawn. And so the family walled in their fear.

Rumors reached them by way of the servants who, before dawn, were in the streets foraging and trading for food. Black rain had fallen in Hiroshima. And terrible winds blew out of nowhere, seeming to bring with them a strange light.

"Will that be here?" Yasue asked.

"No, no," Shigeru reassured her, "that was caused by the new bomb. That will not be here."

Not satisfied by her husband's explanation, she turned to her father. "What is your opinion, Oto-sama? Are we to be made slaves by the Americans?" she asked.

Raising his voice, the elder replied. "Are there no chores to be done in this house, that you congregate like cackling geese?"

There was a monstrous American warship in Tokyo Bay. A delegation was sent to the *Missouri* and asked the question, What is to be done about the Emperor? No final answer was given. Some thought he would be deposed, others that he would be tried as a war criminal. Tomonori maintained that if they spared Japan, they must spare the Emperor.

Word was out that the surrender was to be signed aboard the battleship. People said that the Americans insisted on unconditional surrender. Yasue, bowing, asked her father what this meant. He replied impatiently, "How can I know?" And quoted an ancient canon:

> *"I cannot control the*
> *waters of the Kamo River,*
> *the roll of dice,*
> *or the hearts of men."*

The son-in-law replied more practically. "We can only wait."

It seemed unlikely that the Americans who had dropped two atomic bombs would have any spark of humanity. Life continued as gray as the powder of their ruined city. It was lived at a subsistence level that was harder than wartime. No one was trying any longer to kill them, yet each day was a silent struggle to stay alive. The water the vegetables had been cooked in the day before was often their only food.

On August 29 the Americans made their first broadcast to the people of Japan. The State-War-Navy Directive enunciated the new policy: "The Supreme Commander will exercise authority through the Japanese government machinery and agencies, including the Emperor, to the extent that this satisfactorily furthers U.S. objectives. The Japanese government will be permitted, under his instructions, to exercise the normal powers of a government in matters of domestic administration."

The reaction throughout Japan was relief. The fear that revenge would be taken against the Emperor was without foundation.

The *Yomiuri-Hochi* editorialized, "This is the beginning. . . . It has taken national defeat for the Japanese people to lift their minds to the world to see things objectively. Every irrationality that has warped Japanese thinking must be eliminated by honest analysis. It takes courage to look defeat in the face, but we must put our faith in Nippon's tomorrow."

The people were told to give up feelings of lassitude and notions of shame. This was hard to do in a burned-out city of blackened bricks, with shards of glass still underfoot and three walls knocked down for every one standing. Even the water in Tokyo was polluted, and no longer flowed from pipes. It was necessary to remain at the faucet up to twenty minutes, catching rusty, clouded drops that then had to be boiled.

An optimistic attitude was hard to sustain while watching short coffins carried through the streets. Because of a scarcity of planks, caskets were made four or five inches too short and the body pushed and tugged, in some instances actually broken, in order to cram it in.

Things eased somewhat for the family when Shigeru, owing to his knowledge of English, found employment with a major newspaper chain as a translator. It was this money that both households managed on. In recognition of this, and because they no longer had a son, Yoriko insisted that her husband officially adopt Shigeru. It was done, and they all felt the merit of having regularized his position in the Sanogawa family by naming him heir.

In spite of gearing up for the inevitable when Americans would run the city, they were unprepared for the sudden pounding at the front door. They looked at one another and no one stirred.

The pounding came again.

"Open the door," Yoriko screamed at the servant, but the servant hung back. "Momoko, go to the door!"

Momoko crossed the room, certain she would be struck to the ground by a black American with a tommy gun. But a Japanese stood there, a young man in a captain's uniform. Momoko gasped and steadied herself with her hand against the wall. She had almost thought . . . Noboru, in the commemorative photograph sent home with a lock of hair and nail parings, wore that uniform.

With correct manners the young man introduced himself. "Forgive the intrusion. I am Takeo Kuroda—friend of the son of this house. We were in the Shimpu Attack Unit, the 201st, together."

The father of the household stepped forward. "Welcome, honored friend of our son."

Momoko on her knees laid out guest slippers. She still felt shaken. Yasue fetched cushions, placing them in preparation for tea. They could not entertain in the Western part of the house, there was no furniture left.

The men seated themselves and the women glided behind sliding doors to direct the servants and to listen.

"You were one of those waiting, not yet called up?" the head of the house asked.

"No. I was sent on an earlier mission, but we had engine trouble and the plane fell into the sea. The pilot was dead on impact. I managed to climb on top of a wing section and floated for three days. Okinawans in a fishing boat picked me up. I lived in their village until my family made payment and arranged for a boat."

"How long have you been in Tokyo?" the senior asked.

"Two weeks. I looked for Vice-Admiral Takijiro Onishi. He, as you know, commanded the 201st."

"He is in Tokyo? I did not know that."

"Sir, like the storytellers of ancient times who wandered the country, I have come to tell you a tale that puts in perspective the death of your son, my friend. Noboru knew Japan was defeated. But he believed his death was needed to restore *bushido* so our country would build an honorable peace.

"My story is how the peace came about. I have it from my distinguished uncle. For until the Emperor actually made the phonograph record of surrender, all was confusion, no one knew what ultimately would be decided. You can't imagine! There was a peace faction and a war faction, and the Emperor was caught between."

Takeo paused to taste his tea before continuing.

"As early as two months ago the Emperor called on the Supreme Council to find a way to end the war. They even made contact with Russia to ask her to mediate. Instead, as you know, the bastards declared war. Vice-Admiral Onishi couldn't accept defeat. He really believed that the spiritual strength of his Special Attack Force would turn the war around. Those last days I think he was completely insane. He got to everyone in the Diet, trying to persuade them to continue fighting. To surrender, he claimed, was to cease being Japanese.

"On the final day before the broadcast he even waylaid Prince Takamatsu and begged him, palms flat to the floor, his forehead pressed against stone, to send a representative from the Emperor to the Great Ise Shrine for correct guidance.

"But the crane had taken flight; no man could stop it, although they tried. There were officers, desperate men, I will not name them, that would be dangerous for them and for me. But I tell you this because it is well known, they raced through the palace looking for the Emperor's recording, which they had sworn to destroy."

Momoko moved on her knees to refresh the tea. The father of the house, referring to Takeo's account of events, said, "Of course they did not find it. I, with my whole family, heard the Emperor's voice telling us we must bear what is unbearable."

"That is correct, they did not find it." In a quiet tone Takeo related that on the day of the broadcast Onishi wept, and in the evening invited several staff officers to his official residence. He sent out for an elaborate meal and they drank sake and talked until midnight, when Onishi dismissed them. Then he called back the youngest man, Kodama, to ask for his short sword.

Kodama handed it to him reluctantly, saying, "This is not necessary, Admiral. You did all a man could do."

Onishi replied simply, "I am dedicated." His friends left and Onishi retired to his second-floor study, where he spent the next hours in preparation. He went to the toilet and emptied his bladder. Then he bathed, shaved himself carefully, and rouged his cheeks so his death face would be the color of cherry blossoms. Next he dressed in a fresh uniform, tying a white *hachimaki* around his forehead.

He sat cross-legged on the tatami, and wrote out a will; then, placing the sword before him, brought his mind to a state of one-pointedness, and brushed a farewell haiku.

Now all is done,
and I can rest
a thousand years.

The faces of the young men of the 201st passed before his mind, and he wrote: "I wish to express my deep appreciation to the spirits of the brave Special Attackers. They fought and died valiantly with faith in our ultimate victory. In death I wish to atone for my part in the failure to achieve that victory and to apologize to the dead fliers and their families.

"I wish the young people of Japan to find a moral in my death. . . . You must abide by the spirit of the Emperor's decision with the utmost perseverance. You are the treasure of the nation. With all the fervor of the Special Attackers, strive for the welfare of Japan and for peace throughout the world. But do not forget your pride in being Japanese."

He read back what he had written, wrote instructions for the disposition of his body and consolation to his wife, then undid the lower buttons of his uniform jacket, freeing his arms from the sleeves, which he tucked behind his knees to prevent falling backward, for the soul must fly from the abdomen in a forward fashion, and it is in that position all samurai must die. Next he pushed down his belt and trousers to the white loincloth, and with a calm spirit but a determined hand rammed Kodama's sword into the lower left side of his abdomen and, pulling the haft sideways and sharply up, slit himself open.

He immediately vomited blood and his gut vomited out his bowels. They kept streaming from the cavity in a raw, gleaming stench; slipping, they fell onto his thighs and genitals. Uncoiling, the viscera began to turn gray.

The borrowed sword had not been sharp enough, he did not die. The agony was acute. To end it he stabbed himself in the throat, but the military collar got in the way. Red froth issued through the opening, and the hissing sound of his breath continued.

Once more, this time with great difficulty, he raised the short-handled sword and jabbed it into his chest. But he had weakened and the wound was superficial. He still did not die, but continued in a limbo of pain.

He continued until six o'clock in the morning, when the servant appeared to make morning tea. Onishi had toppled over onto the blood-filled tatami. The man fled at the sight, returning with Kodama and two other naval officers who rushed to him.

"Do not," he gasped, "do anything to keep me alive."

The two other officers retreated a few steps, but Kodama would not leave his side.

"If your sword had been sharper," Onishi admonished him, "we would not be having this final talk."

Kodama was distraught and grabbed hold of the sword to use it on himself. But Onishi stopped him. "Don't be a fool. Young people must go on living and build Japan again." Blood stopped speech; it poured from his eyes, his nose, and his mouth. But his five senses helped the sixth, which is in the mind, and he was able to lift himself from earthly sordidness. His expression became tranquil, there was no observer-self left. He no longer felt suffering, he had attained *muga*.

Kodama, to get through the time until death, began reciting mantra with his eyes closed. Finally one of his brother officers touched him on the shoulder. Onishi was dead, his *chu* returned to the God-Emperor. He had joined the wonderful children of the 201st.

Takeo's story was finished, and they watched in silence as a large beetle accomplished its journey from one mat to another.

Momoko began clearing the tea things.

The head of the house sucked through his teeth. "Our son wrote of the honorable Vice-Admiral Takajiro Onishi. Noboru admired him. But now the reputation of Japan must be defended through the peaceful art of life."

The guest nodded. "It is called *do-mok-ra-sie*."

The elder gentleman tasted the word: "*Do-mok-ra-sie*."

Their guest, though most circumspect, had been observing Momoko. Since the birth of her son there was a fragile quality about her, delicate hands delicately handling the bowls, a whispered rustle of sleeve as she supplely removed the last trace of the tea.

Shigeru returned home, and when he heard that their guest was from the same Shimpu unit as Noboru, he bowed deeply.

To set a guest-meal strained the resources of the house. Still, receiving a call from a friend of their dead son was an honor that compelled them to improvise as best they could. Once there would have been an excellent fish well seasoned with powdered seaweed, salted sesame seeds on festive rice, and a bean sauce with sugar. However, the women plundered the larder and set out a boiled potato, finely sliced and served with diced pickles tastefully arranged in their remaining bowls. Momoko's slender neck bent as she served, as though the weight of her thickly piled hair was too much, and the kimono sleeve fell away from her wrists.

Takeo tasted the food thoughtfully. "Harsh times may lie ahead."

The father of the house nodded. "What conditions are most spoken of?"

"My uncle is in the Diet and I now work for him. One hears everything. But one thing is certain, there will be purges."

There was a silence of understanding as the three men ruminated the possible consequences.

"Who is to be purged?" Shigeru asked.

"Those designated as war criminals. Any who were prominent— generals, admirals, and the *zaibatsu* families who aided the war effort through munitions or the building of ships and planes. As it was phrased in the Potsdam Proclamation, 'There must be eliminated for all time the authority and influence of those who have deceived and ruled the people of Japan into embarking on world conquest.' "

"If they dismantle the *zaibatsu* families of Mitsubishi, Sumitomo, and Mitsui they destroy our way back," Tomonori interjected.

"Perhaps that is their true intention," Shigeru observed.

After a silence Shigeru said to Takeo, "It is being said that the Americans judge us by you Special Attack boys. They believe we will not submit to occupation."

Takeo smiled. "I have heard it more brutally stated. They consider Japan a nation of fanatics with no regard for human life. In the Diet they even say that Harry Truman's decision to drop the bomb was due to fear of the Japanese population if American troops were forced to invade. He thought on the one hand there might be wholesale terrorist attacks and a bath of American blood. On the other hand he thought the entire population might commit seppuku in a sort of mass frenzy. Are we responsible for such mad ideas even in part, we of the 201st?"

The elder man laid down his *hashi*. "It is hard when cherry blossoms are bespattered by irresponsible rain."

Takeo bowed before his words.

"In the streets," Shigeru said, "returning soldiers are spat on."

"In other wars," the elder replied, "homecoming soldiers were dressed in white and bowed to by strangers with respect."

"The Potsdam Proclamation assures the nation that Japan will retain her identity and her people will be left free to decide their future form of government," Takeo reminded them.

"Once we have been purged."

"Of course, yes."

"Will our shrines and temples, our priests be left in peace?" Tomonori wondered. "Have you heard anything said on this matter?"

"I have heard the word 'disestablishment' used."

"It has a bad sound," the old man commented.

"It is believed that no worship of Shinto will be allowed. But this may be rumor. It is best to hope for respect relations with the Americans."

The young warrior friend of Noboru's had stayed the requisite three hours and now, bowing his thanks, he prepared to take his departure, inviting the men of the house to join him in town for dinner later in the week.

Before he left, the father of the family asked a question that had been on his mind. "How far down do you imagine they will reach in their purge?"

Takeo shook his head; he could not answer.

⛩

The golden days of autumn slipped away and boys no longer banged on kerosene cans to chase the sparrows from the rice paddies. It had been inevitable that the two great forces guiding Japan would meet. Winter snow fell before the event occurred, and winter waves lapped grayly in Tokyo Bay. But when the meeting between General Douglas MacArthur and the Emperor of Japan took place the populace regarded it almost as a scene from Kabuki. It was not lost on them that it was the Emperor who presented himself at MacArthur's headquarters.

The whole world was to know what the two rulers discussed when on New Year's Day the Imperial Rescript announced, "The ties between us and our people have always stood upon mutual trust and affection. They do not depend upon mere myths and legends. They are not predicated on the false assumption that the Emperor is divine and that the Japanese people are superior to other races and fated to rule the world."

Japan was stunned. The Emperor had publicly renounced his claim to divinity. He had, as the Americans said, "de-godded himself."

MacArthur's reaction to the Emperor became known around the world: "In that instant I knew I faced the First Gentleman of Japan."

The photographs printed in all the papers were studied with grave care. How small their Emperor appeared beside the towering shogun general in his open-throat shirt. They had never seen their Emperor as diminutive, but he was. Should they measure the mighty war that had exhausted their resources, their spirits, and their bodies in the same scale? What kind of blind national madness had seized them, to suppose they could have pitted their puny strength against the industrial giant of the West?

People were getting used to American servicemen in the streets. The children smiled shyly at these tall, hairy *gaijin* and offered flowers. The newspapers excoriated the homeless for congregating at the railway depots to sleep, as the Americans would notice them. There was great politeness on both sides. The Japanese were scrupulously polite, and the Americans made a strenuous effort in that direction. But they had a hard time reconciling this low-key, deferential population with the maniacs who had attacked their fortified positions with bamboo spears and wild shouts of *"Banzai!"* The politeness on both sides masked deep distrust. The Americans felt a million slanted eyes watching every move they made, evaluating, speculating. The Japanese watched the well-dressed, well-fed Americans and were impressed by their efficiency, but bewildered at the haphazard way it seemed to be achieved. The informality of Americans was indeed puzzling. "Supreme Commander for the Allied Powers," that they understood. It had dignity. Its acronym, SCAP, hadn't.

Nevertheless it was SCAP they lived under. General Douglas MacArthur didn't need the dignity of an organization, he himself was the embodiment of dignity, which, together with his aloofness and bearing, won Japanese admiration. He seemed almost a messianic figure, and the population was in great awe of him. But more than figureheads were needed to restore the ruined country. Inflation soared; ex-soldiers wandered the streets as beggars, exposing disfiguring war wounds; people tried to grow food between the ties of the railroad.

Without the Americans they would have starved. Most food came from the United States, half a billion dollars' worth from one agency or another. It was strange and unappetizing. A good deal of it was corn: corn flakes, corn on the cob, creamed corn, corn niblets, corn muffins, and even corn syrup and something known as popcorn. Corn traditionally was fed only to cattle and swine. It was an insult. Especially as AID or RESCUE MATERIAL was stamped on every package.

Repugnant as it was, thousands were kept alive by these shipments. The family's own cupboards held corn and other unfamiliar goods. The rest they bought on the black market from the Koreans.

Momoko's instinct was to distrust anything *muko*, "from over there." The fact that *gaijin* help was needed to survive was unfortunate. The fact of *gaijin* in the streets of her world seemed a disaster on the same scale as typhoons, tidal waves, volcanoes, floods, and earthquakes.

Earthquakes were measured by intensity. At intensity five, windows broke and gravestones toppled. At intensity six, fissures appeared in houses and roads. The intensity of the Occupation was not yet known.

External and internal worlds had to be rebuilt. But where did one begin? Was total nihilism in order? Tear down what remained in order to build anew? Did this apply to their psyches as well as their city?

Could one look to the Americans? They spoke of a new constitution. MacArthur had rushed a draft to the newest Prime Minister. But even if it pointed out an honorable road for them to follow, how could a piece of paper feed, clothe, and provide them with jobs?

Takeo called. He had just returned from Okinawa, where his uncle had sent him as part of a delegation to advise where American construction teams should put their efforts. He brought neatly wrapped gifts, persimmons, a jar of green tea, dried seaweed, a cuttlefish, and a portion of rice. He showed his breeding by including among the gifts a clay pot for making *kama meshi* and flower bulbs, indicating that he did not bring them food from pity, but merely included it among the presents.

Takeo was given guest slippers, served sweets by Momoko from a black-lacquered tray, and brought tea, which he took with the men of the house. Courtesy demanded general conversation, so he spoke of the large military base being built on Okinawa. "It seems the Occupation is totally American, with a few Australians. The Soviets have refused to place troops under MacArthur's command, and Chiang Kai-shek cannot spare men, he is too busy fighting the Communists."

Tomonori nodded. "We are more used to Americans. We have had American missionaries and American teachers. The Emperor himself had an American tutor."

"Working with my uncle," Takeo said, "I see SCAP officials in action. I sense that they are becoming more accepting of us, that they are ready to believe in our ability to set a new course."

"Yes," Shigeru said somewhat bitterly, "we are cooperative."

At last Takeo could mention the reason for his visit. Although he had kept his eyes studiously from her, the reason was Momoko. He humbly asked permission of her honored father-in-law to take her walking.

If surprise was felt by the family, it was not shown and the request was solemnly granted. But Momoko found it difficult to orient herself. A friend of Noboru's, an officer in the 201st, was asking for her company. How could she be seen on the street in such a ragged kimono?

Takeo did not seem to notice her patched condition. He preceded her out the door and, turning, hands on thighs, bowed a leave-taking of the others. He hurried her past groups of Koreans who had been brought over as cheap labor during the war. Because they controlled the black market they walked aggressively through the streets. Momoko stayed close to Takeo's heels.

"I thought we might walk by the Fukiage Palace along the Abyss of a Thousand Birds," he suggested.

She murmured assent. She had always felt that the Emperor's presence added a special grace to the city.

"Do you remember before the war," Takeo said, "they used to string paper lanterns overhead along the moat, and there were vendors with carts heaped with flowers?"

"I remember the narcissus," Momoko said.

"Yes, there were narcissus."

Shacks and hovels had been erected from the rubble of the street, covering the city like scabs. Takeo turned from the spindly ginkgo trees that lined the road; they had been bombed into stark, grotesque shapes, jagged and broken. He followed a byway that led under camphors and ancient oaks, which, being near to the palace, remained untouched. "At the vernal equinox there were stalls set up everywhere. And acrobats, do you remember the acrobats?"

"And the puppet theater. One could buy sweets and so many good things to eat." She stopped self-consciously.

They had reached the beginning of the long, narrow parkway that bordered the moat surrounding the Imperial Palace with its groves of pines, and could see the Sakashita Gate. A ragged child approached them, selling fortunes. In pity, Momoko said, "May we?"

"Of course." And Takeo dug into his pocket for the price.

They selected from a wooden box. "Mine says . . ." she began, but her voice died in her throat.

"Well?" Takeo asked.

She looked down at printed Zen sayings: "Footprints recede. . . . The sound of clapping is done. . . . The bent twig snaps." The words struck desolation in her. His footprints had receded. His clapping was done. The twig of his life had snapped. It would not come again. She dissembled as well as she could, and laughed, saying, "Oh, the usual nonsense."

When he reached to read it for himself she crumpled it in her hand, telling herself as she did so that she was being ridiculous, *bakamitai.*

Takeo tossed his fortune away too. He looked into Momoko's face. "When I was in the village in Okinawa, I kept hoping that Noboru had been reassigned. But of course I knew that was impossible, that he had to be dead."

"He was made a captain," Momoko said. "They sent me his sword."

"We were close friends. It was strange, perhaps it was the circumstances. When you know you're to die, everything takes on a heightened quality. There was no time for friendship, neither of us sought it. It happened. It was as though we had found a brother. There was nothing we didn't speak of . . . except you."

Her hand went to her throat.

"And if I questioned him about you, he evaded lightly but emphatically. What was between the two of you he refused to share. From this I knew how deeply he cared for you, Momoko."

Momoko said falteringly, "I accept what you say as a gift. And because I know it to be true." Of the wild passion that a bird might feel when it flies too high, she could not speak. How could she when she had withheld it?

Takeo could no longer see her face because she was one step

behind, so he dropped back a pace. "There is something I must tell you. One night we were talking on Noboru's cot, when his diary was knocked to the ground. We both bent to pick it up. It was lying open and your picture was between the pages. Your face looked up at me, Momoko. And it stayed with me. Floating all those days on the water in and out of consciousness, I talked to you. You replied. Momoko, if you had not, I think I would have died out there. Then later, those weeks I lived in the village . . . the habit was formed. Whenever I saw any lovely thing, a drop of dew holding an entire rainbow, a sunset that lent its color to the water . . . I would say, 'Look, Momoko.' "

He caught her hand, and released it immediately.

It was an exceptional afternoon. A day set apart for her pleasure was something that had not happened in a very long time. She tried to tell Yasue about it, but Yasue made her look at it in a different way, a way she had not wanted to confront.

"So, what do you think of him?" she asked.

"Takeo is very nice. One could not help like him."

"You know what I mean."

"He is Noboru's friend," Momoko said defensively.

"And I suppose you talked of Noboru the whole time?"

". . . Part of the time."

They were in the garden, making figures of hollyhocks for Masaru. "He is courting you, Momoko, and you know it. What will you say if he asks you to marry him?"

"You are making me angry, Yasue. I love your brother."

"Noboru is dead. You are young and so pretty. You need a husband. Your child needs a father."

"I don't want to hear talk like that."

"Then why did you go out with him?"

"I told you, because of Noboru. We both needed to talk about him. I'll tell you right now, Yasue, I will never love another man."

"Hmmmm," was Yasue's comment. "Well, in case he asks you again, you can borrow my ivory kimono."

"I don't understand you, Yasue. Noboru was your brother."

"That's why, my little goose. I want what he would want for you."

Momoko shook her head. "It's you who are the goose."

When Takeo asked her to accompany him on an outing to a nearby park, she hesitated, but the prospect of another light-hearted, pleasurable day won out. She salved her conscience by refusing the loan of Yasue's ivory kimono.

Takeo bought a ferocious-looking kite in the shape of a scaly dragon and ran with it. She laughed, clapping her hands, to see it mount into the sky. Finally she ran also. She forgot she was a lady who had a child, as the wind whipped her hair and her blood raced. When he came to a stop she ran into him.

"I'm sorry." She was breathless, her hair across her face.

He reached out and smoothed one wayward strand into place. "Now I know what you were like when you were twelve years old."

"I had forgotten what it is to play, to be young."

"I know, I also had forgotten. You make me feel alive, Momoko." Having said that, he grew quiet and, though he walked at her side, was preoccupied. At last he broke out, "I never meant to tell you. I swore I wouldn't. But I've no choice, I have to. You have to know what happened.

"Momoko, we traded missions. It was my fault. He was assigned ahead of me, but I'd waited weeks longer. I persuaded him to cut cards. High card went. I drew it. I took his mission and lived. He took what should have been mine and died."

He stopped speaking and looked at her as though she held his life in her hands.

Momoko staring back at him saw Noboru. Saw him engulfed in flames. Her lips parted, but instead of his final cry, words poured out. "When I opened the door to you that first time, my heart stopped. I thought it was him." Her voice dropped to a whisper. "Why are you standing here in your captain's uniform, when he is dead? You tricked him. You stole his life. You should have been the one to smash and burn on the deck of an enemy ship.

"How can you live with it? Of course he died. Maybe his plane had trouble too, but he wouldn't give up, he wouldn't let the pilot. But you saw a way out . . . a way not to be blown up on a ship's deck, a way not to be burned and mutilated. Can't you see I hate you for being here! I hate you so much!"

Takeo was as one turned to stone. He watched her go.

門

Momoko confided a good deal of the dreadful scene to Yasue.

Noboru's sister was appalled, not at Takeo's revelation, but at Momoko's reaction. "You have to understand how it was. Takeo couldn't have known, neither could Noboru. The *kami* decided. It was meant. It wasn't Takeo's fault. How could you have behaved like that, Momoko?"

"I don't know," she said distractedly. "He was wearing his flight uniform. Just like the first time. When I opened the door and he was standing there in it, I almost fainted. Yasue, it's the same captain's uniform that Noboru is wearing in the picture forwarded from his unit, the one on the *kamidana*. And . . . I don't know why I said those things."

"Momoko, you must write him immediately. Try to explain, apologize."

"Yes, yes, that's what I must do."

Yasue regarded her cryptically. "But first you must sort out your feelings. If he gets such a letter from you he may come back. Is that what you want?"

"I don't know. You say 'sort it out.' That's the trouble, I can't. I think perhaps I lost a second chance to be what someone wants and needs. Why am I such a fool, Yasue?"

"Write the letter," her sister-in-law advised emphatically.

She didn't write it. She didn't write it because she couldn't imagine what she would do if he actually stood in front of her again. She thought she would probably die of shame.

"What should I do?" she asked her bright-eyed one-year-old. And for some reason she thought of her sister. Hiroko lived in Moji, a day's journey by train and ferry. They hadn't seen each other during the war, just letters on New Year's and when Hiroko's daughters were born. She had written one other letter, telling of Noboru's death and their son's birth.

Of course that was what she should do, she should go to her sister and her mother who now lived with her, show them this beautiful son whom they had never seen.

"I should have done it months ago," she said to Shigeru, when she laid her plan before him.

"I think," Yasue spoke up, although she hadn't been asked, "that it is an excellent idea. Things are better for us now, we can afford the fare. And certainly Momoko's family should see the child."

Under this wifely persuasion, Shigeru capitulated.

The trip was a major excursion for Momoko, who, except for her honeymoon in Atami, had not been anywhere. She dressed Akio in his red silk bunting, which by now was too small for him. She had made it while waiting for his arrival. With what care she had cut the pattern, stitched and lined it, adding padding for warmth. And here he was laughing up at her from its silk splendor. As the train rattled along she remembered with pride that she had delivered her child without crying out. From the time she was seven she had known she must do this woman-thing with the bravery of a warrior. There had been a secret fear that her body would betray her and she would find herself screaming, but she had controlled herself as the wives of samurai had done for a thousand years.

She remembered Yoriko bending over her, she remembered Yoriko's tear on her face. From that moment they shared a birth and they shared a death.

Akio returned her to the present. He had been lulled by the movement of the train, but now he woke, and she gave him the breast. To keep him entertained she recounted the ancient Kojiki myths of creation, and he gurgled his delight back to her. "Your father"—her stories always began with Noboru—"was a mighty Oka fighter. And your Emperor is divine back to Jimmu, whose father was the great-grandson of the Sun Goddess, whose mother was the daughter of a sea god. . . ." She remembered telling the same stories to her sister. She looked forward to establishing the old bond. Perhaps she and her mother would also find common ground. But though she told of shoguns in their walled castles, of blind lute players and of a one-footed umbrella, her mind kept reverting to another matter. . . . Even if she wrote, he probably would not forgive her. She had spoken in an unforgivable way. The kindest thing he could think of her was that she was mad. If only he hadn't worn his flight uniform. . . .

Akio rejected the breast and grew restless. She promised him that someday he would see many water birds, herons, storks, grebes, and cranes, and best of all, they would watch the cormorant, who is trained with a band around his neck to catch fish for men. "When you are bigger," she said. *When you are bigger* was a recurring theme with her. "When you are bigger, you will have a cicada in a bamboo cage. But you must catch him yourself. On a hot summer day we will go together into a pine forest and he will lead us to him by his drowsy song."

The travelers arrived weary and dusty at the gates of her brother-in-law's house. It was a substantial home, with servants who admitted them.

An *ofuro* and tea refreshed her. But the ladies of the house she hardly recognized. Her mother, who had grown old, inspected Akio, murmuring approval at his sturdy body, his few words, his attempt at walking. Momoko unwound her obi and, putting it around him, showed them he could do even better when she encouraged him. He experimented with more steps before finding himself sitting down. They all laughed at the surprised look on his face. Momoko was very proud.

Hiroko had two children, but they were girls. Perhaps that was why her sister did not show her secret heart, but did everything formally and correctly, from serving tea to serving conversation. It was hard to believe there had ever been confidences between them, or that she had told this self-possessed young lady ghost stories.

They spent the night, but she began the return journey as soon as possible, telling herself severely that she must face the fact that she was alone, that no one cared about her or Akio, with the exception of Yasue and perhaps Yoriko. It's my fault, she thought. I don't know how to be close to anyone anymore.

The rhythm of the train induced a half-sleep from which she suddenly startled up. A terrible thought had occurred to her. She realized that she had castigated Noboru for dying and Takeo for living.

"Poor baby," she said aloud to the child in the red silk bunting, "your mother is a madwoman."

Momoko had been home less than two days when Yasue came into her room with an excitement she attempted to repress. "Takeo is in the garden."

"He's here?"

"What garden do you think I mean? Of course he's here. He asked for you."

"Oh, Yasue . . ."

"Don't ask me, I don't know. I don't know how to advise you anymore. Besides, you don't listen to me anyway."

"Tell him I'm not here."

"I said you were."

"Tell him I'm sick."

"No."

Momoko took a long breath, but when she entered the garden it was with the composure of an *onnagata*. There were no signs of inner turmoil.

The first thing she noticed was that Takeo did not wear his uniform, but a Western suit. Knowing he felt the same constraint she did made it somewhat easier to begin. "Thank you for coming, Takeo-san. I wrote you a letter in my head. It was a letter of apology, a letter that asked, no begged you to forgive me."

He came toward her, but stopped a few feet away. Thoughts of Noboru lay between them. His guilt and her hysteria under the wind-swept trees were in both their minds.

"I loved him too." Takeo used the words as a lash. "I keep thinking about him. I miss him very much. They say when a man lives putting his whole being into it, keeping nothing back . . . such a man is a golden lion. Noboru was a golden lion."

Momoko nodded. "I hope someday you will tell Akio about his father."

"I didn't mean to live, Momoko. You must believe me." His straight black hair fell across his forehead, hot tears hung on his lashes.

Momoko put her hand out to him tentatively. "Takeo-san?"

He turned away.

"Takeo-san, I know you did not cry when you were shut in your bomb alone with the thought of your death. When you floated on the water all those days, you persevered. Do not cry now." Her hand touched his shoulder.

He would not turn around but shook his head stubbornly. "*Kataji-kenai*," he replied, using a double word, the common meaning was "thank you," the original meaning "I have lost."

"I know you loved him. It was an accident, you were his friend."

He turned then and looked at her. "You know that?"

"Yes."

"And you do not blame me? You don't blame me for not dying when he succeeded? You don't blame me for standing here?"

"Of course not. Please don't remember the awful things I said. I didn't mean them. I never blamed you for anything."

"Not for loving you?"

She hesitated. The ache of her useless love intensified. It spilled over and extended to his friend. Could she love the friend who loved him? It was the best she could do, the closest she could come. "I do not blame you."

With this chance at happiness, Takeo's face lightened.

Momoko gathered up her son, strapped him to her back, and ran most of the way to the Yasukuni, where war heroes were enshrined. She had to talk to Noboru. She needed his permission.

The attackers of the 201st had a special memorial tablet. She located his name and asked to see the relics, the lock of hair and the nail parings. She remembered something very clearly that she had forgotten, the way he had, in moments of stress or indecision, of brushing back the hair from his forehead. Takeo had adopted the habit.

Suddenly she was choking, that was what happened when you tried to swallow tears. She thought she was past tears. She composed herself enough to reach around and press down her baby's head. "Noboru, this is your son. Do you love him? He looks like you, the eyes, I think. And the line of cheekbone. He's a good baby. He never cries. Not like me. He's too young to understand yet, but think of his pride when he knows his father was a Shimpu fighter. When he is older I'll try to explain. I couldn't now. I'm still not reconciled to the uselessness of it. I still can't accept it.

"The war ended in August. August twelfth. So you see, you were right, we almost made it through together. I still ask why, Noboru. Why couldn't I show you my hidden heart? Would you have reported for duty if I'd asked you to stay? Would you be alive? I think because of honor you would have gone. But I'll never forgive myself.

"I hope you can forgive me, though. I know you can. I know you've even forgiven me my silence when you asked for my love and blessing to take with you. I was stupid, tied up, bound fast with ideas that were stifling me. I couldn't tell you how I felt. I wanted to, I tried to. But I couldn't." The silence of the great hall closed in on her.

"It's Takeo," she confided to him. "We both love you. He is a good man, as you know, and he loves me. And he would take care of our son." She hesitated, and then went on, "But all that means nothing if you are hurt by this. Give me a sign and I won't marry him. Or if you think I should, could you somehow let me know? . . . ." Her voice trailed off and she listened again to silence.

She left the Yasukuni Shrine, and outside on the steps, but to the side where she was not observed, she took Akio from her back and nursed him.

She had another stop to make. Since Disestablishment, many of the Shinto shrines had been turned into nursery schools, and she was taking Akio to inquire about registering him for the following year. When they arrived she was told by a severe-looking young lady in Western dress that Akio would be too young for the first semester, but if there were enough applicants they would open a midyear session. She signed him up for that.

On the way home she took a different route to keep Akio amused, turning up streets at random, peering into gardens. As she was passing the west gate of a Buddhist temple she heard a bell and a voice. Drawn by the sound, she entered the paradise of all-saving Buddha, and saw a monk sitting *seiza*-fashion, reciting prayers for the dead, periodically pulling on a long rope that tolled the bell. Along the rope were tied the pretty kimonos of children. These, she recognized, were the clothes of dead babies for whom the monk prayed. She dropped coppers into his bowl and fled.

She knew the healthy child on her back aroused the envy of those pitiful dead. If they could pluck his life from him, they would. Even in the street she ran, until there was no breath in her, until she stumbled against a wall where she leaned, panting.

Then it seemed a great light illumined everything. Of course, this was it. This was his answer. She had asked Noboru what she should do. And in the incident of the dead children he had answered her. . . . In these uncertain times their son needed a father.

It started when Prince Konoe was served with an arrest warrant and drank poison. General Hideki Tojo was seized as a war criminal, and others followed daily. Chaos reigned.

The Home Ministry was abolished, the National Police Force disbanded, the Education Ministry gave notice. A new constitution was being drawn. The old peerage was outlawed, women were to be given the vote. And the powerful industrial combines, the *zaibatsu* corporations, were in danger of being broken up in a rampage of trust-busting operations.

The world they knew was gone. The *gaijin* were making a new one. But this new one they did not know.

One day there were three American military men at the Sanogawa door. No guns were in evidence, one of the privates carried a clipboard and a fountain pen. The officer bowed and spoke in stilted Japanese to Yoriko, who had opened the door.

"We are sorry to disturb you. But it is necessary to arrange suitable billeting. May we go through the premises and decide how many men can be accommodated?"

Yoriko returned the bow with a sinking heart. The men brushed past her, tearing up the tatami with heavy shoes before the officer could stop them.

The Western section of the house was a find. They were delighted with the few pieces of furniture the family had begun to buy back, and particularly pleased by the indoor plumbing. "Great. Great," the officer exclaimed.

"Mark it for officers, sir?"

"Yes, officers."

"A garden too, with a pond. This is all right."

Tomonori Sanogawa, head of the house, came forward. "You require?" he asked in textbook English. His demeanor was stiffly correct, his bow correct but minimal.

"The United States Army is billeting two men here. Officers."

"May I see the order?"

Though the question was asked politely, the lieutenant was of-

fended. He slapped his pockets roughly. "I've got it here somewhere."
Where did these Japs get off, anyway? You'd think they'd won the war.
"Here it is." He handed the paper over. "As you see, everything's in
order."

The Jap bowed and handed it back. "As you say."

These little delicate men seemed effeminate to him, and the short
stocky ones comic, like strutting bantam roosters. The women, on the
other hand, looked like pretty dolls. And the thing about them that
was especially appealing was that they knew they were women, they
never forgot it. The small stature that repelled him in the male was
charming in the female. And his gaze traveled from the wizened gentleman before him to the patterned kimono disappearing from view in
the garden. He had glimpsed a pretty laughing face and a child. They
appeared to be chasing dragonflies. Scott Williams decided one of the
requisitions would be for himself.

Takeo was again in Tokyo on business for his uncle, and requested a
personal interview with Tomonori Sanogawa. From the tone of the
request it was understood the visit was of an official nature and to be
conducted according to tradition.

Momoko worried about this meeting. In the old days before the
war, it would have been unthinkable that she marry again. She would
have lived out her life a memorial to her dead husband. But tradition
was turned upside down by simple expediency, the scramble to exist.

Yasue was strongly in her corner and mentioned to Shigeru, who
was attempting to start up the factory, what the patronage of a young
man already of some influence and his powerful uncle could mean.
Through this contact the Americans could be approached, and any
undertaking fortunate enough to have the support of the Americans
was sure to prosper.

"My husband will be your ally," she assured Momoko. And then
she spoke her fear. "But will my parents allow you to remove their
grandson?"

Momoko had given some thought to this. "There would be no
possibility if they did not have your son. But they have a grandson to

honor them. And they know that Takeo will do well for Akio. Besides, it will be easier for the household if there are two less to be responsible for."

Yasue pressed Momoko's hands. "Leave everything to me," she said.

The conferences that followed were many. There was the conference between Yasue and Shigeru, between Yasue and her mother. Yoriko then spoke at some length to Tomonori, and finally Tomonori and Shigeru went out to a restaurant and returned very drunk and very late. At each stage Yasue reported to Momoko on the progress that had been made. The only real opposition was the natural reluctance of the old people to lose a grandson. But Tomonori replied to Takeo's note, setting the day and hour for his visit.

When the time came, Momoko was banished to the depths of the kitchen. Yasue reported to her when Takeo arrived, adding that he presented himself in Japanese robes. Yasue whispered that he looked very romantic. His gift to the head of the house left no doubt at all as to his purpose. He presented Tomonori with rolls of silk and a rare Imari water jar.

Her father-in-law acknowledged the richness of the gifts with words that meant both "thank you" and also "I am sorry I must take on this indebtedness." His stiff bow was from the waist.

They spoke, as protocol demanded, of things in no way connected with the proposal Takeo had come to make.

"We are glad to see you, Kuroda-san. Does your visit to us mean that you have completed your assignment in Okinawa Prefecture?"

"I wish that were the case. No, I am in Tokyo only for the afternoon. I am acting as my uncle's courier."

"Are you permanently assigned in Okinawa, then?"

"No, I hope to finish up within the next few months and be back for good. Even in the time I've been gone, Tokyo has changed, with building starts everywhere. On the way here I saw many more American soldiers on the street."

"We have two billeted on us. Officers. They keep to themselves, but their voices are not harmonious." They sipped tea in silence. "Ever since the surrender my stomach has given me trouble. At times I think it is my heart acting up again. But probably it is gas."

Takeo nodded. "I myself did not sleep for a week after it occurred."

"I was ill again when the Emperor was made to humble himself. He did it for the nation, but I was up all night. For me he is the Tenno."

"Still you must not distress yourself. Can a flood be stopped by a grain of sand?"

"True. We live in confusing times. Our police don't know if they have power or not. Our teachers don't know what they are to teach. Things are uncertain."

Takeo felt it was time to shift the conversation to the purpose of his visit. "In the midst of relocating I was unable to come by a suitable go-between. But I will find one to negotiate for me further. For I hope to create a small space of order in my own life by taking a wife."

Behind the screen, Yasue convulsed in silent giggles and signed Momoko to come closer.

Tomonori nodded and, with the look of a wise old turtle, replied, "A good decision. Commendable. It is difficult to rise to a position of power within the government if one is a bachelor."

"I have heard this," Takeo agreed suavely. "But my reason for wishing to marry stems from the human feelings which I have for your esteemed daughter-in-law."

The head of house sucked his lip in seeming surprise. His reply was ritual: "My daughter-in-law is a very unworthy young woman."

"Yet to me she seems gentle and in harmony with everything around her."

"I believe she is a good mother." Tomonori took out cigarettes and offered one to Takeo, who refused. He himself lit up and inhaled. "Have you thought that you would be marrying a woman with a child?"

"It is the child of my friend. It would be an honor to adopt Akio."

Tomonori Sanogawa smoked awhile in silence. At last he said, "The only son of an only son who is dead cannot be replaced." On the other side of the partition, Momoko drew in her breath sharply.

"How clumsy of me!" Takeo exclaimed. "I should have made plain to you from the beginning that Akio's primary obligation would be to the Sanogawa *ke*. He would say the prayers for his father and, in that distant future, for your honorable self."

"Then you would not insist on an official adoption?"

Takeo, seeing it was the only way, made up his mind with lightning rapidity. "As long as his home was with his mother and me, I would not insist. His first obligation would be to this family."

The head of house had discharged his duty. "My dear Takeo, we must celebrate. Yasue! Bring sake cups."

She had them in readiness and, kneeling, pushed aside the rice-paper screen.

The men got very drunk, Tomonori explaining that you never really knew a man until you drank with him. The head of house sang complete passages from Noh plays, while Takeo was intent on telling of glider pilots who, during the last days of the war, had taken up quarters on Mount Hiei in a Buddhist sanctuary. "They practiced jumping off the cliffs so that when the invasion came they would tie grenades to their bodies and explode on top of the enemy. It was sad for them that the enemy never came." He told other stories of pilots and airmen, and when it was time to leave, Yasue whispered to him where to find Momoko. He overtook her in the hall. "Momoko!" he called, coming abreast of her, "I thought I'd have to leave without seeing you. You heard everything?"

"Yes."

"Momoko, my family is old and honorable. My prospects are good for the times we live in. My honorable uncle is well placed in government. As you know, he works with the Forces of Occupation in the reconstruction of Okinawa, and because I learned the dialect he still has need of me. I must go back. But when I return I will be in a position to marry. . . . It will be good, I promise you. Noboru would understand. He would be glad. We will not live with my family in Osaka, but here in Tokyo. I will be a new man on the scene . . . old cup, new tea. We will be a modern couple and live in an apartment."

A tear splashed onto her hand. She attempted to smile. She didn't know if she could go through with it.

During the four months Takeo was gone, Momoko lived in and out of dreams. Very often she would take the cracked mirror from Noboru's chest and stare at her lovely face. It gave her reassurance, like a wealthy man examining his bank account. She ran her fingertips along the flowerlike countenance, with its delicately arched brows and wide velvet eyes. Her nose was slender and patrician, her mouth full and appealing. Her face had made her a petted and adored child. Her face had brought her Noboru, and now another man was drawn to it. A face without flaw, a complexion like ripened peaches, these were the best assets a woman could be endowed with. In spite of all the suffering in her life she felt like a girl again, and the cracked mirror assured her she looked virginal and young.

From the day Takeo formalized his intentions, Momoko's position in the household changed radically. With no word said, the servants handed her a rice bowl when Yoriko and Yasue were served.

Momoko greatly prized her new status, and believed the *kami* had, with Noboru's blessing, sent his friend to restore her son's place in the world. For when Tomonori adopted Shigeru, his son and not hers became the Sanogawa heir.

Why, when she and her son had a fresh chance, did she so often find herself crying? In the old days of bombing and hunger she never cried. Why now, when the bad times were gone and she was about to marry a man she liked and respected? Rummaging in her mind for an excuse, she could not find one.

She didn't want to think that it was fear. Did she fear because the world had opened up to her again and held out tantalizing possibilities? She tried to remember when this gnawing feeling had started. She thought it was when Yasue whispered to her that perhaps she would be the mother of a second son.

Those words caused a kind of numbness, setting up a series of contractions in her womb. After Akio's birth her woman's rhythm lost regularity. There were many months when she did not menstruate at all. Yasue told her this was not unusual and could be laid to the deprivations she had lived through. But now, with everything else returning to normal, her body still had not straightened itself out. Surely, she told herself, this was a temporary condition that with time would come right. And if it didn't? She couldn't contemplate this possibility. Takeo would expect children, especially since he wasn't allowed to adopt Akio. His parents would expect children.

The worry seed was deep within her, part of a generalized fear. This vague apprehension was a floating anxiety that people everywhere seemed to share. It was fueled by the presence of the soldiers of Occupation. In the streets she hurried past them with lowered eyes. But in this very house rough voices and boisterous laughs were sometimes heard. At night she would startle awake, knowing this was the hour the American MPs removed the newly dead from doorways where they huddled.

Then there were the stories that kept coming out of Hiroshima and Nagasaki. Yasue's husband's sister had gone to visit her aunt in Nagasaki and was there on August 9 when it happened. She aborted a five-month child. It was a son and she was inconsolable. She whispered to Yasue that no one from outside would marry anyone from Nagasaki. The women bleed constantly. The men are bent over with pain, yet can't tell you where it hurts. She cried in Yasue's arms, saying she was haunted by the terrible things she saw. Especially by a head swollen very large. She saw it drinking at a water fountain, it had no features, but seemed to be composed of huge clusters of soy beans.

Reality intruded in the form of American MPs at the door. Huge and towering, they presented the arrest order, insistent on explaining the charges. There was nothing any of them could do. When a document is embossed and has enough stamps and signatures, it does not matter if it is wrong and vicious. Tomonori Sanogawa was accused of war crimes. And though Yoriko burst into prayers for the dead, they took him as he stood, with no chance to pack anything.

Shigeru, as son-in-law and now nominal head of house, set a quiet investigation in motion. It was learned that the charge emanated from the fact that the *gaijin* had somehow learned of the guidance system perfected by the Sanogawa company. Tomonori was not personally charged, but he was in the category of those charged, which included former officers, administrators, teachers, top politicians in the former Konoe government, and those heads of businesses engaged in war work.

"How serious is it?" Momoko asked.

It was a poor time for that question. Hideki Tojo and former Prime Minister Hirota were in solitary confinement, a sign, people said, that death by hanging would be the ultimate verdict. Prince Konoe had only escaped the wrath of the Americans by suicide.

Shigeru procured the services of a well-known attorney. They tried to get a trial date set, but there were more important persons than Tomonori Sanogawa to occupy the attention of the Far East Tribunal.

In this the family found hope. So far they had been unable to see Tomonori, but through the lawyer he communicated to them that he was well, and asked for a change of clothing.

Shigeru began to make decisions for the family. Momoko wished he wouldn't; it would be better to let things drift until the head of house was back. To do otherwise seemed to her lacking in respect and to invite bad luck. But her opinion, which she whispered to Yasue, counted for nothing. Still, she fretted about it and even wrote Takeo. But what could he do from Okinawa Prefecture in the Ryukyu island chain?

She tried to keep busy and not think about things too much. By seven o'clock the futon was shaken and hanging out the window to air, the floor of her compound washed, the breakfast bowls put away and the baby bathed and dressed.

She and Yasue often took the children to the park. Subtle changes had come over Yasue. Momoko attributed these to the fact that with the war behind them, Yasue was able to find joy in the simplest things, a leaf that yesterday was curled up and today unfurled itself, a bird perched on a thread of grass blade that couldn't possibly hold it, but did. Yasue would stop at the sight of these small things and press her hands together. There were times, however, when she seemed lost in some reverie of her own, and conversation with her was either a beat ahead or a beat behind.

They had a daring talk, she and Yasue. It seemed the Americans were serious about giving women the vote. SCAP decreed it. SCAP believed women should hold an equal place with men. Such an idea made them giggle.

"Are American women equal with their men?" Yasue wondered. "It must be that they are."

"Could the vote mean the end of *danson johi*—honor man, despise woman?"

Again they put their fingers to their mouths to hide their reaction to such an improbability.

Momoko took Yasue's hand impulsively. "You are my sister, whether you are equal or not equal."

They planned another outing for the following afternoon. They were going to take the children to the sand drawer who did such unique compositions in the temple courtyard. But it was already well past the hour. Momoko had dressed Akio and he had fallen asleep. What could be delaying Yasue? She wondered if perhaps something had happened to Tomonori that they were keeping from her. Was it possible he had suffered another heart attack? Perhaps he had been executed. The Americans had the power to do as they liked.

Akio stirred. She snatched him up and held him over the bucket. Once he had accomplished that, to reward him and to pass the time until Yasue came, she told him a story of Izanagi-no-Mikoto's heavenly jeweled spear, which he used as an organ of procreation. "It is this spear from which the race of Japanese come, Akio."

Yasue arrived full of apologies, saying she thought Masaru might be coming down with a cold. Momoko, watching the energetic child, was certain it was not so, and wondered why Yasue would make up such an excuse. Yasue had completely forgotten about the sand drawer, and then tried to cover it up.

That was the first of many discordant things that occurred on subsequent afternoons. The irrepressible happiness of the past weeks had given way to a subdued mien. Often Yasue was inattentive, and her obi was not always in harmony with her kimono.

Momoko asked after Tomonori, but there was no further news of the head of house. So it wasn't that.

What, then? She wondered, as she often had, how well Yasue got on with Shigeru, whose exploits with women were well known. Yasue never complained of this, or mentioned her husband in any way. Was it possible that some fresh attachment of his had caused this change in her? More than once Yasue raised her voice at her three-year-old when Masaru was simply being his bubbling self.

Finally Momoko spoke her concern and Yasue chided her. "There is nothing wrong, Momoko, nothing. You go on and on so."

This was unfair, since she hadn't mentioned it before. But she said in a conciliatory fashion, "All right, I won't ask any more questions, I promise. But in turn you must promise that if there *is* anything I can do, you will let me."

"There, you're doing it again," Yasue cried at her. "Assuming there is something, not listening to me when I tell you there isn't. I'm leaving."

Momoko was stricken with remorse. "You can't. I haven't given you tea yet."

"I can't stay. I shouldn't have come."

"What have I done?" Momoko was bewildered.

"I'm sorry, I'm sorry," Yasue said distractedly, and, taking her child in her arms, ran from the room.

Momoko stared after her, a poisonous feeling spreading in her. She felt threatened, she didn't know by what.

The next day Yoriko had the seamstress in to line the winter kimonos, and she had to go over the work that was to be done.

Yoriko, looking worn and harried, said, "I'm very nervous. There's still no news, but according to the *Mainichi Shimbun* the Far East Tribunal has condemned sixteen so-called war criminals to life imprisonment. The most serious cases, where conviction carries the death penalty, are still before the court. I don't know what they will do to my poor husband. The law catches flies but lets hornets go free. He only did what was asked of him by his country. You know he is a good man. It is the world that has turned upside down, pretending he is an important oak when he is only a simple tree fern."

Momoko accepted tea from the kitchen maid who in the old days used to bully her. Another pleasant reminder that she was soon to be a married woman. And, like Yoriko, had borne a son. They were equals. She wondered how she could ever have feared this woman. Setting down her tea bowl she asked why Yasue had taken no part in deciding which kimonos were to be refurbished.

"Yasue is not well. I don't know what is the matter. She won't let me call a doctor."

"Perhaps it is flu."

"No. There are no symptoms that I can see. But she won't leave her room. She had no breakfast, and she didn't even ask about Masaru. Perhaps you can cheer her up."

Momoko nodded and went upstairs to the section of the house Yasue shared with her husband and son. Stopping on her side of a drawn screen, she called Yasue softly by name.

There was no answer. Momoko tapped discreetly. There was still no reply and she opened the screen a crack. Yasue was lying with her face to the wall. Momoko spoke her name again and, when she did not turn around, entered and knelt beside her.

"Elder Sister . . ." She plucked at the sleeve of her yukata. "Are you ill?"

"No. Yes. I am ill."

"You're not."

"No."

Momoko took one of her hands in hers and stroked it. It was slender, delicate, and cold. Yasue turned and looked at her—not exactly at her, but at the space she occupied. "The world is dark."

"Why, Yasue? Why is the world dark for you?"

Yasue stifled a sound in her throat. Had it been a laugh, a cry, what?

"You can tell me. We are sisters, you can tell me anything. Is it your husband?"

"It is not Shigeru. I care nothing for Shigeru."

"What, then?"

"Oh, Momoko, he's left. They transferred him. I'll never see him again."

The pause itself was a question mark that forced Momoko to ask, "What are we talking about?"

"About Scott. Do you despise me, Momoko? I can't help it if you do."

"Scotto?" Momoko's tongue had a hard time getting around the unfamiliar sound. "Is Scotto a person? Who is Scotto?"

"There are so many ways to answer that." Yasue took hold of her hands and her voice was eager. "Scott was one of the officers billeted here."

Momoko gasped.

"Yes, yes, it is as you think. We love each other. The reasons not to love are so many. You don't have to tell them to me. But, Momoko, have you ever seen a small wild plant growing out of cement with no nourishment? Scott and I were like that, cut off from any soil. But when it happens anyway, it is so strong, so tenacious that nothing can impede its growth."

"But how . . . ?"

"Mother sent me with towels and linen to the Western section of the house. Scott was studying Japanese. He had bought a small book that listed various customs and holidays, and he asked me about them. We started talking about Kabuki. I remember telling him that Kabuki actors never take curtain calls. It began that simply.

"Because his Japanese was very primitive, like a child's, everything came out directly. He asked me if I had visited Hiroshima and how I felt about it. I told him no, I could not bear to go. I told him the town used to be known for oysters. 'It won't be known that way again,' he said, and I agreed with him.

"The next time a change of linen was required, Mother asked you to do it. Do you remember? But I said I'd take care of it. I put back the coarse towels Mother had laid out and exchanged them for some with a soft, lovely weave. I don't know why I did that. I think I wanted him to have a good impression of Japanese people.

"He was very happy to see me, he told me that several times. No one had ever told me that. I was happy to see him too, and I said so. There didn't seem any harm in it.

"He found the Japanese language difficult and asked if I could help him a bit. He was studying a book of poetry and we sat down at the desk to read. The poem was a *renga* from the Muromachi period. And I explained that *renga* were made up of chains of verses contributed by more than one person.

" 'Really? That's fascinating.'

" 'You see, they're love poems.'

" 'Oh. So *he* makes up a line and *she* answers with a line?'

" 'Yes. There are thirty-one syllables. The seven-syllable lines occur twice. Then three lines of five-seven-five. *Renga* require a great deal of skill.'

" 'And a great deal of passion.' Until he said that I hadn't realized how close to him I was sitting. He reached over and we were kissing. Human feeling took over in a way I didn't know it could. I was trembling and he quieted me. His stroking was very gentle and he was whispering to me wonderful English words.

"The stroking become intimate and I guided his hands myself, afraid he might stop. The world didn't exist, only the two of us. And I wanted it to go on forever. When we finally let go of each other, we stayed as we were, enjoying each other's bodies. This *gaijin*, this stranger with the exotic blue-gray eyes, held me and I, him. He was of another race, American, large, strange, beautiful.

"He carried me to the bed and, taking our clothes off, we learned each other. Every way that was possible, we clung. He taught me to be at home with the foreign sound *Scott* . . . and said he must never lose me from his life.

"He called me by my plain name, no one had ever spoken my name exactly like that. Can you believe, Momoko, that I, a woman who had borne a child, had never felt before what a woman can feel? Only with him, this beautiful American."

There was silence in the room. Finally Momoko said, "Yasue, I

ask you as your friend, how could you have done this thing? You knew
he would have to go."

"But not so soon. Neither of us thought it would be so soon. Oh,
Momoko, it doesn't seem worthwhile even to start a day that does not
include him."

"The only thing to do," Momoko said, "is to pretend you dreamed
a dream about an American soldier. None of it happened, it is not
real."

"It is the most real part of my life. I'll never forget him. I don't
want to forget him, and you shouldn't ask me to. Momoko, you don't
understand how it was, we laughed together, and talked and wrote
renga. We loved each other."

Momoko didn't utter a word.

"I'm sorry, I'm sorry. You *do* know, you *do* understand. And finally
so do I."

Things should have gradually reversed themselves after this. Even
if they couldn't return to normal, the intensity should have lessened
and gone out of it. But that didn't happen.

Two weeks went by. Yasue crept around the house, going through
her tasks at one remove. She is fighting her pain, Momoko thought,
and she is not able to win out.

Then came the day when she realized Yasue was not in the house.
This realization did not come all at once. At first Momoko simply
went to her rooms to ask if they could take the children to the park.
Not finding her, she thought she was probably with Yoriko, sorting
linens.

She was surprised to find she wasn't there either, and asked her
mother-in-law if she'd seen her. Yoriko replied crossly that when there
was work to be done everyone seemed suddenly to have other things
to do.

Where is she? Momoko asked herself. For the first time the question came with urgency and she began a systematic search. As the
possibilities narrowed, a kind of panic descended. Was it possible that
Scotto had contacted her? Yasue told her he had been transferred, but
perhaps he had found a way. Perhaps Yasue had gone somewhere to
meet him. Or in the disturbed state she was in, she might even have
run off with him.

Momoko dismissed this notion. Masaru was in the kitchen playing with the cat, she would never go off without him. Momoko's searching became hurried, frantic, she was running from room to empty room.

The telephone that Shigeru had recently installed, that the entire *ie* looked on as indicating that the company had started up again with prospects of the old prewar prosperity, the telephone that reposed on its own table, rang.

Momoko ran toward it. It would be Yasue calling to explain, to say where she was. But when she picked up the receiver an American voice, a man's voice, spoke crisply. "This is Sergeant Whitcomb from Allied Headquarters. There's a woman here, a Yasue Sanogawa. She gave this as her home phone. Is that right? Does this person reside there?"

There was a pause while she attempted to assimilate this strangely inflected Japanese. The difficulty of the language was a bulwark against the *gaijin*, a line of defense; even when they thought they spoke it, it was a protective cloak.

Rallying herself, she answered him. "She does, yes. Is she all right? Has anything happened?"

"Well, let's say that plenty's going to happen if someone doesn't get down here. She's causing a disturbance."

"A disturbance?"

"That's what I said. She insists on talking to an officer who isn't here anymore. But you can't get through to her. Now if you don't get down here I'm going to have to file a report."

"I'll come get her."

She knew where the household money was kept, and took enough for a cab. She remained calm; it was as though she stood outside all activity as an observer.

The taxi pulled up in front of a massive building flying the American flag. There were soldiers on guard flanking the entrance. "Wait here," she said to the driver and walked up the steps as a dozen light round eyes watched her.

She went to the reception desk. "I had a telephone call. My sister is here."

"Sanogawa?"

"Yes."

"Second door to your right."

She followed directions, knocked, and was admitted. Yasue sat at a desk opposite an officer; her head was buried in her arms, which were stretched out on the desk's surface. Her body shook with inaudible crying.

Momoko rushed to her and knelt on the floor, trying to peer up into her face. "Yasue, it's all right. I'm here. We're going home."

Yasue shook her head. "I can't. I must find Scott."

"Yes." She spoke placatingly. "All right. But this isn't the way to do it."

Yasue raised a tear-stained face. "Ask them where he is. They won't tell me."

The sergeant behind the desk said, "Lieutenant Williams was transferred over a month ago. Look, if she doesn't leave quietly . . ."

"She will. She will leave quietly."

But Yasue shook her head. "Make him tell you, Momoko. Please. I must find Scott, I must."

"Yasue, come with me now. And then we will think what to do."

A convulsion ran through Yasue's body. "His fingerprints are on every part of me."

"It's all right," Momoko said again, pulling Yasue to her feet.

The sergeant leaned toward them across a desk full of disorder. "Now for her own good I'm telling you to keep her away from here. It's not part of my job to deal with hysterical females."

Momoko nodded that she understood and backed toward the door with her arm around Yasue. Yasue leaned heavily on her, and she guided her out of the building, down the stairs, and into the taxi. Yasue started talking almost immediately in a hurried breathless way.

"It's the *gaijin* who roomed with Scott. He came in on us once. He saw us together, he thinks I'm that kind of woman. After Scott left he said he'd take over for him. He laughed, but he meant it. He trapped me in the hall and wouldn't let me pass. He had done this before, laughing as though it was in fun and then letting me go. This time it was different; he did not intend to let me go. I knew it. I saw his eyes, like blue ice. He pushed me into his room, but laughing, as though it were a game. I dropped one of the towels I had come with. He thought that was funny. He motioned me to pick it up. When I bent down he threw my kimono over my head and tied it with something so that my upper body was in a sack of my own clothes. He lifted this sack-me onto the Western bed. He bent over me. A smell like rancid butter came from his body. He was sweating. I breathed as shallowly as I could.

"He began pressing into me. He pulled off my woman-cloth, and did things to me. His fingers were large and he had a jagged nail. Finally, when he had played enough, he shoved his organ in. It spread my bones like childbirth. I hoped the pain was enough to kill me. I don't know if he hated women, or hated Japanese. When it was over I was alive. He untied the kimono and it fell around my feet.

" 'Come tomorrow,' he said, 'just like you have been doing, with towels, whatever. I know you've got to make it look good, with your folks around. Now if you don't come I'll tell them, first about Scott, then about me. I wonder what they'd do? And you looking so innocent. How many have there been, Sue? That's your name, Sue, isn't it? Come tomorrow, Sue. I mean it. You come and we'll have some more fun. That was fun, wasn't it?' He wouldn't let me go until I said it was."

"Yasue, you didn't do what the American told you? You didn't go back?"

The taxi pulled up at the gate of their home. Momoko took her in through a rear entrance and up to her room without anyone seeing them. She spread the futon and Yasue collapsed on it. She began crying again. She who had given advice and been elder sister was now helpless.

Momoko asked quietly, "Do you still . . . go back?"

Yasue nodded.

"You will not go again." She left Yasue cowering on the futon and went down the hall. If she had been asked what she was going to do, she wouldn't have been able to reply. But some part of her knew exactly. Going straight to Tomonori's room, she knelt before the Sano-gawa swords. Choosing the *katana* with its sharkskin hilt, she inclined her head before it, then in a single movement took it from the display rack on top of the bureau and unsheathed it.

Momoko lifted the curved, single-edged blade in both hands over her head. Carrying the sword ready to strike, she returned to the hall and entered the Western section of the house, throwing open doors, looking into rooms. Then came one that opened on a man who was seated at a desk filling out some sort of forms. He was the *gaijin* with the long, lanky frame, cropped sandy hair, and watery blue eyes that blinked in disbelief at the apparition in the doorway. "Sue . . ." he began, in an uncertain tone. Then: "You're not Sue."

Momoko strode into the room, the sword held high. The door to the clothes closet was ajar. A dress uniform hung there pristine with braid and ribbons. This became her target. She sliced through it in one blow, cleaving the material, cutting from shoulder to inseam.

The man watched in disbelief. When she turned, he upset the chair in an effort to get behind the desk.

Momoko walked past him without seeing him, and proceeded along the corridor to Tomonori's room. She returned the sword to the display rack.

The next day the officer moved out.

"What did you say to him?" Yasue asked.

"I said nothing to him."

Yasue gave her a strange look and stayed quietly with her head in Momoko's lap. They had changed places. Momoko was now elder sister. She stroked Yasue's glossy hair and hoped that she would cry. It was good that the officer had acted on her warning. For he knew and she knew she would not stop there. This capacity for violence in herself was something she accepted as due to the war. No one could live through bombings, hunger, death, defeat, and remain the same. You died, as many did, or you found a reservoir of strength. It was this she had tapped into.

Not Yasue. She trembled if any hand touched her and started at every sound. She told Momoko she could not sleep at night and lay many hours in the dark by Shigeru's side with wide eyes, never moving. Then, her head still in Momoko's lap, she confided, "My husband wanted me last night. And when he held me I thought I was tied in the sack of my kimono. I fought to breathe, I didn't know I was fighting him. And Momoko, he liked it. He started laughing and pinned me down like the hairy *gaijin*. I thought it was the *gaijin*. My stomach flooded through my nose and my mouth. I threw up, Momoko. And he is furious."

"Not to worry," Momoko soothed, "not to worry."

Momoko chatted away for both of them. She had heard that American women only have a nine-month pregnancy whereas, as everyone knows, it takes ten months to create a Japanese. "I have heard while we count in terms of our cycle, twenty-eight days, they count by the calendar month. But I don't think that's it at all. It's just that they are not Japanese."

Yasue was not ready to be pulled from her misery. When she

raised her head she said, "I'll never forget what you did for me, Momoko. Never."

Momoko glanced at the pond where Akio selected leaves for Masaru to sail. Over his padded kimono Momoko had put a white smock, which he could get as dirty as he liked. Both boys had their sleeves pinned back, for it was February and too cold to allow them to get wet. She corralled the children and, setting them on her lap, began a story she intended for Yasue. "I will tell you about a prince of long ago whose ricefields were drying up because of drought. Instead of turning a bright yellow they were shriveled and dun-colored as far as the eye could see.

"Now this prince was clever. One day he appeared in the wilted fields with a large doll the size of a real child. The doll was dressed in red silk and it carried a bucket in its outstretched hands. People came from all around to look, because this doll had moving parts. When water was poured into its pail it would lift and pour the water over its face.

"Everyone was delighted by the beautiful doll with the unusual mechanism and brought water to work it. And as word of this spread far and wide, the prince's fields were saved."

With the story done she said to Yasue, "You don't owe me *on*. I was only the doll in red silk. So let us forget everything. The *gaijin* is gone and that's the end of it."

Yasue nodded, but she did not want to forget everything. Each day she looked for a letter. Momoko began another story.

But the previous story had not concluded. MPs came, a gang of five. In horribly accented Japanese they read a brief statement to the effect that the Sanogawa family had not surrendered all weapons as required by law. They had a report of a sword hidden on the premises.

Report? Who reported? Momoko asked, but she knew. She watched in silent rage as the Americans plunged rifle butts into ricepaper partitions and stamped over tatami mats, overturned a low lacquered table, and knocked the god-shelf to the ground. The picture of Noboru in his uniform fell underfoot, its glass shattered. The sprig of sakaki and the white paper ribbon were ground into powder.

Momoko followed behind the marauders, watching their systematic destruction. Most damage was done in the Western sitting room. The padded hammers were ripped out of the new piano, the stuffing of the replaced couch torn open and the insides pulled apart. They moved on again, down the corridor.

She could have told them where the swords were, any one of them could have, and stopped the pillage. But no one betrayed the swords.

They were not hidden, but displayed on the rack in Tomonori's room. With triumphant cries the Americans seized them and, taking them by their sharkskin hilts, tested them on the *zabuton*. The swords flashed and sliced cleanly.

Why not? Their thousand layers of iron and steel crystals had forged a matchless edge of utmost strength. In Muromachi times, toward the close of the fourteenth century, the master swordmaker daily commenced his work with prayer and purification. This ensured weapons of loyalty and honor, which in the hands of a samurai would cut through armor and decapitate heads.

The soldiers clowned around. One of them brandished the short, sturdy *wakizashi*, and in mock fury made as though to run Momoko through. Her eyes closed involuntarily but she stood her ground. Little Akio stood beside her and did not blink.

"What do you know, a little samurai!"

Akio stared at them from opaque eyes.

The soldiers laughed and ruffled his hair. "We'll be fighting you one of these days!"

The sergeant examined the elegant *katana* further. "It's a real beauty. Both of them, really, they're a pair. Collector's items, I'd guess." He handed them around, and the souls of the swords glinted with humiliation. They had not been forged for the hands of enemies. The family was cited and fined.

The women purified the home shrine with salt and prayers and holy water purchased from the priests. Momoko smoothed Noboru's photograph and purchased another frame. Yoriko arranged a fresh bunch of sakaki and set out new paper blessings.

Momoko confessed before the shrine. "It is I who am responsible, no one else." But admitting her guilt did not ease her, and she wrote Takeo.

"Takeo-san, I am at fault in the matter of the Sanogawa swords. They were confiscated because of me." She gave no details; she couldn't on account of Yasue.

Takeo wrote back, "Perhaps I can locate the honorable Sanogawa swords. Perhaps they can be bought. I will try. However, samurai swords are a source of barter among the occupiers and hard to come by." And so the matter rested.

Momoko understood Yasue was not healed. She continued to divert her with stories, and gradually Yasue began to listen. The soul behind her eyes inhabited its place again. Momoko told of the time at the end of memory when Japan had been a matriarchy and the Empress Himiko ruled. When she died, a hundred men and women were buried with her. "I wonder," she paused to ask Yasue, "what she would think of women having the vote."

The boys didn't care about the Empress, they would rather hear that Japan rested on the back of a giant, basking catfish. Whenever it twitched, calamity followed.

Was that what happened? Did the giant catfish shiver and move ever so slightly?

If so, she didn't notice. There were so many things to look forward to and to teach Akio. "It is *hari-kuyo*," she told him, "a wonderful day when we say prayers for all the sewing needles that were broken during the year. See, I saved the needle I broke mending your yellow sweater. Here it is, poor thing, in two pieces. But look—a bit of tofu. Watch me, Akio, I place the needle on it to rest. The needle is happy because the tofu is soft."

She bundled Akio into his jacket and set out with him for Sensoji in the Asakusa ward of the city, where the god of medicine would receive her needle along with a gift of fruits and a sweet cake. She chatted to Akio as they went, reminding him how fast her fingers flew when she sewed. "That is because of the kind spirit of the needles. It is also a very good festival for all little boys, because if broken needles are brought to the temple, they will not find their way into tatami mats and stick someone's little feet."

She laughed and Akio laughed. They went on many such small excursions.

The next afternoon was rainy, and they were at their favorite occupation when Shigeru joined them, contributing a story of his own.

He told about a certain Air Force captain, a man of great responsibility and honor. After a battle it was his duty to enter in his official report the names of all those safely returned from the sortie.

"This particular day he was seen to walk somewhat stiffly to his headquarters, as though," Shigeru said, "he had two samurai swords buckled on. However, he carried out his duty, recording the names of his men. Then he dropped dead.

"But the curious thing is that he was already cold, for he had been dead from a bullet in the heart for some time. The force of his will enabled him to carry out his commitments before giving in to his own death."

Momoko shivered. She did not like his story. "The war is over now, Shigeru-san."

"Certainly. The new Mac constitution says that now we are to pursue happiness."

" 'Pursue happiness'? What does that mean?"

"Well, *pursue* means to run after. And *happiness* is happiness."

"A running-after-happiness. What a strange idea." Was the new constitution telling her to take her life in her hands and fashion it, make it something wonderful? Could she and Takeo, with her little son, all three together run after happiness?

She discussed it further with Yasue after Shigeru left. Yasue was momentarily intrigued. But very few things seemed to interest her. What she pursued was not happiness, but her own melancholy thoughts. Momoko, however, kept returning to the idea. She remembered the garden of her parents' home, and her resolve to have quite a different one of her own, which led to the small patch she had tended secretly, and its destruction. I must take a step or two, she told herself, before I run, even after happiness. The first step, once she was married, would be to plant a garden. A garden of her own had become a symbol to her of all she wanted. But events occurred that pushed thoughts of personal happiness away.

Denial carries a sound that bursts from the human throat and ascends to the *kami* on Mount Miwa. The reaction in any who hear it is to still the hands and stop the blood. That sound pierced the young women who sat together in Momoko's rooms. Yasue looked wildly about. It came again. Galvanized, they were on their feet, running.

Shigeru had returned home to ring the bell on the *butsudan*. Yoriko stopped screaming as suddenly as she began and watched him with an almost vacant expression.

"Mother!" Yasue went up to her as though to embrace her, but stopped to ask Shigeru, "It's my father?"

"A heart attack. This time it was fatal." He was right to state it starkly; that made it real.

"They killed my brother and they killed my father." Yasue began to rock back and forth to a cadence only she heard.

Shigeru had reopened the family toy factory, adding a sophisticated electronics section that depended on American orders. He said nervously, "Your respected father was not mistreated."

"He was not mistreated, but he is dead," Yasue replied.

Momoko sided with Yasue. "You do not put an ill man, a man who has suffered a heart attack, in prison and expect that all will be well."

Shigeru did not speak again in defense of the Americans.

The body was brought an hour later.

"Did you know," Yoriko addressed no one in particular, "that up until the war my husband employed only those of samurai blood in his plant? He took them off their poor, impoverished farms and brought them to the city. He gave them hope, showing them that in the modern world it is not dishonorable to work. My husband was a very progressive man. He was also a man of strictest principle who held with tradition."

By a piling-up of silences the others affirmed that this was indeed so.

The three women kept the deathwatch, sitting with the corpse all night and replenishing the incense. Momoko slept fitfully, dreaming she saw two *hashi* standing upright in a bowl of rice, the way it is offered to the dead. Toward morning, Yasue too dozed off and woke in the middle of a scream.

"They killed my brother and they killed my father," she said again in exactly the same way as before.

Employees came, supervisors and engineers from the plant, neighbors, friends, distant relatives, all congregated in the house. It was not like the old days. The fruit and vegetables that were served had to be arranged to make the platters appear full. But there was enough, not what befitted the head of house, but enough. Considering the times, the family made a respectable showing. Face was maintained, and the many white envelopes contained enough money to bury Tomonori Sanogawa.

"Your good husband has escaped the floating world," Yoriko was told many times. She was composed, and agreed with everyone. Looking at her, Momoko wondered if she had loved him. The thought seemed almost irrelevant. They had gone through it all in tandem, even a war, and they had become old together.

To Momoko her father-in-law had been a remote figure, but the hole left by his death was large. Even when he was cremated Yoriko remained calm, receiving visitors, listening to formal expressions of consolation, all without comment. Since her initial outburst she had become resigned.

But it seemed to Momoko that Yasue was as much plunged in grief as ever. Momoko worried about her, remembering when she had lost her own father, early in the war. A father was a respect figure, a figure of massive authority. When he is dead you are vulnerable in a way you never were before. For if this can happen to the one under whose protection you stood, then you are without help in the world, and alone.

Yasue would not accept comfort, not even from Momoko, but shut her out with politeness. Momoko understood that this grief came too close upon the other, and understood her need to be alone. She had to find her own path. And to give her time, Momoko did Yasue's chores as well as her own, helping her mother-in-law as in the old days.

Yasue did not come for breakfast, and the servants looked after Masaru in the kitchen. Momoko waited awhile, occupying herself with mending. Finally she cut the thread, tucking her pearl-handled sewing knife in her obi to return to her room later. Akio was fussy, and she gave him the breast before settling him for his nap. Yasue still had not come, so she set about finding her.

Convinced finally that she was not in the house, Momoko glanced toward the garden. It was March, hardly spring, but the narcissus were already blooming. Of course, that's where she'd be, and she followed the twisting path to the stone bench hidden by bushes. Out of the corner of her eye she saw color—surprising, this time of year, for a water lily to bloom.

She turned toward the edge of the pond. It was not a water lily, it was a kimono, Yasue's best kimono of ivory and lavender. Long strands of hair floated with tuber stems to the surface.

The pond was not deep. She must have deliberately forced her head down, kept herself from breathing. The surface meant life, and she had fought against it.

Who could do that when eyes bulged and tissues expanded past enduring in their demand for air? Staring at the drenched beauty of the kimono, Momoko felt that last struggle against life inches above her, knew the sharp, intense pain as water rushed in and drowned her lungs.

Momoko reached into the water, grasping the folds of the sub-merged garment. It was unexpectedly heavy. She dragged at it with all her strength, dislodging a stone at the side of the pond and sliding partway in.

The shock of cold water went through her, but she continued to tug at the body until she dragged it onto the shore. She knew Yasue was dead. Clammy, cold, and dead. So the sudden movement brought a strangled cry. The movement had not been made by Yasue, it came from her belly.

As she looked down at the body, so many things tangled in her mind. Why had she kept it secret? Why hadn't she told her, instead of binding herself so tight? Momoko knelt and, to make sure, placed her fingers against her abdomen and traced the outline. There could be no doubt.

She placed her fingers on the flesh of her throat anyway. There was no pulse, no breath, no life. "Forgive me, Yasue." Setting her teeth and gathering all the strength of will she possessed, she asked the *kami* for more. She took the sewing knife from her obi and inserted the blade into the folds of material, making a cut, and with both hands tore the garment away from the body. There was a stomach band compressing the child. She sliced this away.

Yasue was watching her. She had to stop to close her eyes. Her breath came in short gasps as she began to slit open the belly. Layer after layer of flesh parted under the blade as she reached the placenta.

She saw the infant in the fetal position behind curtains of blood, and, reaching into the abdominal cavity, attempted to pull it out. It was still attached. In a sudden kaleidoscopic rending of thought, she was a bride in this house, with her mother-in-law standing over her, forcing her to take embryonic lambs from a warm womb. She cut again. The melding continued in her mind as she wiped away strings of mucus in order to see. Clearing her head once more, she bent over the fetus, reaching in for it. She had it. She pulled it free and it was in her arms. She began mopping at the red froth. Then froze in horror. How could a child with ice-blue eyes be born?

Momoko had always loved stories, she loved to hear them and to tell them. But there was one that frightened her. It was about the gods. It seemed that gods were easily bored by eternity. The floating world below them was their theater. And they watched the myriad lives that played out their roles before them. Man's laughter became their pageants, their circuses, their comedies. But tears, tears were the heart of drama, and the gods could never have enough.

The baby that she took from Yasue lived. He was called Kenji. Shigeru was more upset by his appearance than by his wife's death, and Yoriko gave him to the servants to raise. Having done that, she considered her obligation to the dead was met. She shook her head often and said repeatedly to Momoko, "I never knew my daughter."

Momoko stole in every now and again to hold the baby. After all, he was an infant and no one else went near him unless absolutely necessary.

There was a dichotomy of feeling in Momoko too. The child was Yasue's, but whether by her lover or her rapist, who could tell? In another culture the baby might be considered beautiful. But the light-sky eyes with their odd round shape struck her with repugnance. They did not fit a Japanese face. When she looked at the child she thought of Yasue's desperation. She thought of her death. But she continued finding time for Kenji because there was no one else.

Three-year-old Masaru took to wetting himself. He had frequent nightmares, and she let him sleep on one side of her while Akio slept on the other. Often she was up for hours crooning to little Masaru. She recited a haiku by Basho.

The old pond,
The splash of a frog
Jumping in.

Mother, she told Masaru, had attempted to pick the purple iris reflected in the water and had fallen in.

"Like the frog," he said.

"Mother loved you very much," she assured him and, catching him up in her arms, said that now she, his auntie, would love him and take care of him, that her heart was big enough for both Masaru and Akio.

Akio flew into a rage at this and stamped like the unruly wind god Susanoo-no-Mikoto, beating her with his baby fists. Momoko held his fury in one hand and wiped Masaru's tears with the other.

The country was drifting, exhausted and unsettled. People repressed their rage, papered it over with daily tasks, daily conversation, daily living, daily dying. But it burst out inappropriately. Neighbors who had gone through the war together quarreled over such things as fences or a plum tree. The papers printed an account of a woman who murdered her sleeping husband and four children with an ax. The wind behaved oddly, blowing from unaccustomed directions. Sea creatures too were traumatized, no longer by depth bombs, but by spreading oil slicks and polluted waters that killed the birds, which later washed up on the shore, their feathers sticky and useless. From many coastal communities came disturbing rumors that whales were beaching themselves.

Then, on the thirteenth of March, there was a newspaper account of the death of a young poet, student of the famed Tamiki Hara.

Momoko only nodded, the gods were insatiable.

It was said Jun Fukui committed seppuku because of a dear friend who had fled to Hiroshima during the bombing of Osaka. When the terrible light came, she held up her arm to shield her face. And now, all these months later, the arm suppurated and hurt so much that she tried to tear it off.

But it wasn't that, or the sight of the man who had part of his stomach skin grafted onto his back. It wasn't even the stories of the hands, the hands of those dying beside the road that reached up and clutched at the living as they hurried by.

No. Jun Fukui committed seppuku because of the slugs.

It began to rain in February and continued into March, and the slugs began coming up from the ground. They were of an unusual size, fat and gray, and no one had ever seen so many. People caught them by the hundreds and drowned them in tin cans filled with salt water.

Jun Fukui could not bear to think what the slugs fed on that made them so fat. He committed seppuku, and the gods recognized that as first-class entertainment.

People reading of the suicide were puzzled. They felt his timing had not been propitious. March 13 was not a significant day. It was not the day the war ended, or the day the surrender was signed, or even the day the Emperor had de-godded himself. And if he wanted to make a statement about Hiroshima, why had Jun Fukui waited until seven months after the event?

The Americans didn't know what to make of the suicide. It struck them as very Japanese. *Stars and Stripes* summed it up in a single paragraph commenting on the waste of an idealistic young man and promising poet. There was no mention of slugs.

1947

WITH ONE EAR SHE LISTENED FOR THE WELCOMING GREETING. IT WAS almost five months since she had seen Takeo. She was excited, anticipating, yet fearful.

Then she heard her brother-in-law's *"Irasshai."*

He was here. O-Bon could begin, the festival that lights the visiting spirits of the dead on their homeward journey.

Momoko kept her movements calm and leisurely as she entered the room. She bowed deeply, a tinge of a smile on her face. Takeo had brought a most gracious present, dark tea from the district of Uji, which grows the finest grade. Takeo Kuroda understood protocol.

Nevertheless, he wasted no time in getting the two of them quickly out of the house, explaining that he had train tickets for Kamakura. "My mother's people come from there. And to do honor to my mother's brother, the uncle who has so generously sponsored me, I wish to spend O-Bon there, and to take your daughter-in-law."

They joined the throngs of holidaymakers. He was full of high spirits and completely at ease with her. This was the first festival since the war that people had thrown themselves into. Last year it had fallen in the dire days of surrender. Now the country was attempting to emerge from the cloud of defeat and ravagement. The crowds were light-hearted, perhaps determinedly so, anxious for things to get back to the way they had been. The station was jammed, as was the Kamakura train. No one minded. If someone bumped into you, you only laughed. They did not even allow the "Allied car," kept for the sole use of the Americans and today totally empty, to dampen their spirits.

It was an hour's ride. With Takeo beside her, it seemed possible that she could at last let go of Yasue's death. She was sure it would not have happened had Takeo been there. His presence would have restrained the *gaijin*. They would have recognized an officer of the 201st. Even her father-in-law might not have died.

"Your eyes are bright, Momoko. What are you thinking?"

With sudden shyness she glanced away.

They arrived at Kamakura, visited the great Buddha, then walked along covered, sun-protected streets toward the beach, carried by merry-makers on a tide of laughter and fun. Square-sided lanterns were strung on overhead wires. They were magic things, each housing its own hearth, which would be lit at sundown.

The regular beat of drums against the lyric cadence of flutes and the rhythmic shouts of bystanders filled their ears. The dancing got under way with posturing and gestures but little motion of the feet. Girls in white and blue kimonos dipped and swayed in arched lines. Their long hair was combed straight, tied with ribbons, and allowed to flow down their backs.

A puppet theater had been set up, and they stopped before it to watch a battle scene. Lifelike warrior puppets were dressed in armor made of overlapping plates of rawhide, lacquered gold for one army, black for the opposing force. The costumes were accurate to the last detail; miniature fierce generals carried iron military fans replete with ribbons for signaling their troops. The master puppeteer stood prominently before his diminutive theater so that the audience could follow his skilled and dextrous movements. It was an old story from the seventeenth century.

Vendors passed among the audience with soft drinks, Peach Wow and Kirin's Jive. Dried squid and candied rice balls were hawked. Takeo bought flavored ices and they walked past some boys who had taken off their wooden clogs and were chasing and hitting one another with them, dodging in and out among elderly gate ball players.

They passed a stall of brilliantly colored origami, stiff folded paper animals, flowers, boats, hats, and pinwheels. The next cart held clay dolls and red balloons with whistles attached to the end of their strings. A boy sold cicadas in small cages, and there were fortunes for sale. This time Momoko didn't want one. She knew her fortune, it was with the man at her side.

Young men played baseball on the sand and young women hurried from the water to the shade of their umbrellas, not risking their complexions. Rowboats and sails bobbed gaily on the water.

Walking along the shore in the sand, it was difficult for her to keep always to the left and slightly behind. They fell to walking side by side.

"Tell me about Okinawa."

"I dislike it. It reminds me of when I was forcibly in their village. It's hot, humid, and, worse, it's an exile from you and from starting our life. I can't figure out why the Americans decided to put their main naval base there."

"Don't tell me about Okinawa, then. Tell me about your home."

"It's in Osaka, near the Tennoji Temple. I used to go there often with my mother on painting expeditions."

"I didn't know you painted."

"I'm afraid I hadn't much aptitude. My mother is a fine painter, however, and she chose the exercise of painting as a way of showing me the world. Sitting by a turtle pond in the outer court we discussed wars, history, inventions. All the time she would be sketching the pious people who fed the turtles hollow 'balloon rice' before going to the red hall, which is part of the temple and has a large wooden image. Cures were said to occur when one rubbed the part of the image that corresponded to the hurt in their own bodies. Peasants came from all over, and the monks sold them medicine made of dead turtles."

"Were they cured?"

"I don't know. I tried it once when I had an earache, but it didn't work—I suppose because I didn't expect it to. . . . When I think of my home, I think of the fields and the bluffs and the woods, all these places I learned through my mother's eyes.

"We used to set out together with brushes, ink, and scrolls all packed into the bamboo case that held our lunch. We'd walk and climb and ramble 'over the world,' she'd say. And it seemed to me that indeed the world lay under our feet and we could claim any part of it by painting it.

"We'd keep going until one of us would stop and exclaim, 'Look at that!' And that would be the sight we'd paint, whether it was a whole valley or one stunted pine. If it was a picture, we somehow both knew it.

"She would paint it as though from a great distance, with perspective built into it. I, on the other hand, would grub my way into it, making it appear to be right on top of me, whether it was a mountain peak or an ocean. Then we would compare our two views and laugh that the same scene could appear so different." He paused and regarded her solemnly. "My mother needs more family since my brother died."

"Your brother?"

"He was killed at Okinawa."

"My brother died at sea early in the war."

"I know. Noboru told me."

"Takeo-san, I can't marry you without telling you that I don't love you in the way you want."

"I know. I've always known that you love Noboru. It's all right, Momoko. I love him too. It's a strange way to start a marriage, with the three of us, but I don't want to lose him either."

Silence looped its net over them as they thought of him and of their other dead who must be lighted on their way this evening.

"And does your mother still paint?"

"She's very frail. It's a combination of the war and my brother's death. She hasn't the physical strength for it any longer."

"But she is important in your life. I hope to be important in my son's life."

Takeo nodded in agreement. "Without her I never would have understood space."

"Space?"

"She said one should look at the way figures cut into space, be concerned with what the space looked like, and the solid forms would take care of themselves."

They walked perhaps an hour more when she settled herself in the sand, positioning her parasol against the low rays of the sun.

Takeo watched. "It seems to me, Momoko, that you are in harmony with the world."

She smiled up at him, and he hunted through the cooling sand for a shell. He handed it to her. It was small and closed. She opened it.

"I'm not the same anymore, Takeo. Since Yasue died, I'm . . . tempered, like the stolen Sanogawa swords."

He sifted sand through his fingers. "If you're speaking of the child you saved, it was a warrior's deed, but was it right to bring a child into the world without its mother?"

"I had to do it. When I saw there was movement, when I saw there was life, there was no other choice. It was terrible. I still tremble when I think about it. When Kenji wakes me in the night, I look into his round eyes and wonder if I did the right thing. He is Yasue's shame. Her shame lives and she is dead."

"Don't think about it that way. Besides, who could be sure the child was not Shigeru's?"

"Why are things so difficult? It was the war, wasn't it, that made it this way?"

Absently he had drawn the outline of an Oka bomb. When he noticed this he quickly threw sand over it.

But Momoko had seen it. "And what about you, Takeo-san? One can't dedicate one's life, be an Oka fighter, and then continue living as though it never happened."

"I am twenty-three," Takeo said, "and the only one in my squadron to survive. When I see myself unexpectedly in a mirror or a window, I am surprised that I am still young."

There was silence between them. Takeo spoke again. "Momoko, there is something else, one other thing I didn't tell you. I loved Noboru . . . but I hated him too. Don't pull away, let me explain. I felt a crazy kind of jealousy because he'd experienced everything with you that I wanted to. My feeling for him isn't one seamless surface, it's made up of many feelings, a sense of loss, a sense of love, feelings of remorse, shame, guilt.

"I see him running beside my plane, calling to me, waving the scarf I threw him. He was crying, I was laughing. Or maybe it was the other way around. . . ."

After a while she said, "This is O-Bon. I think it's time for the dead to leave us."

"Noboru?" He shook his head. "No, I don't think so. I think he is real and we are the ghosts."

"Hold me, Takeo-san. I need to be held. No one has held me for so long."

Takeo took her in his arms, pressing her to him. Her eyes were closed, human feeling strong. . . . The name she murmured was Noboru.

1952

MOMOKO STOOD IN THE KITCHEN OF THE TINY APARTMENT, POKING her fingers into the soil of the window box. Because they had the full afternoon sun, the azaleas required more water. This was not the garden she had dreamed of. But she had selected every plant and it was a beginning. Like her life, she thought.

The apartment itself was typical of what a young man with SCAP connections could expect. Her pride was the black-faced telephone. Her telephone-calling was limited to the old house. But it was not far away and she preferred to take Akio and visit. Somehow it was still her home.

The bulky Kelvinator refrigerator that took up most of the floor-space in the kitchen was a tangible symbol of their prosperity. They were acquiring things very fast. "Too fast?" she asked Takeo when a gleaming white washing machine was installed. It came with complete directions. So far she had only admired it. Secretly she still rinsed things out in the sink and hung them to dry in the three-mat porch.

Akio, seven now, was at school. Takeo gave a good deal of thought as to how to educate the boy, exploring various possibilities with Momoko. "Ideally, the schools should explain fully everything a child uses in the course of a day. For instance, he should not turn on a light switch before understanding electricity."

Momoko burst out laughing. "Then we should all have to live in the dark."

Takeo gave up his theory reluctantly. "But you see, if he were cast away on a desert island, he could start up civilization again by the time he was twelve."

"Providing the island had supplies of oil and coal and . . ."

Takeo laughed, "I see the pupil is cleverer than the teacher."

Momoko smiled at the recollection. She had already tidied the apartment, and peeled shrimp were chilling in the Kelvinator. With the afternoon stretching in front of her, Momoko decided on a walk. She was almost out the door when the telephone rang. Picking it up, she bowed to its black face.

It was Takeo. An afternoon appointment had been canceled and he'd been able to shift another, so he declared a vacation for the rest of the day. "I'll pick up Akio and be home in half an hour. We'll go to the Kameido Tenjin Shrine and view the wisteria blossoms."

She smiled at the telephone. These wonderful trellised wisteria had hung in luxurious clusters over the pond in the days of her girl-hood. Destroyed by air raids during the war, they had been brought back and once more grew beside the arching bridge. How good it was of Takeo to remember her fondness for the spot. Like everyone else he put in the ten to twelve hours required at work, and many times it was more, stretching into an evening with his colleagues. But he managed surprises for her as well, taking a perfectly ordinary day like this and turning it into a special occasion.

Takeo had been patient with her. Even after they were married he waited for her to come to him. She understood why Noboru loved him. After a while she loved him too. He was never the enigma to her that Noboru had been. Or perhaps it was simply that she had grown up. Takeo was an eminently civilized man. He had a large capacity for enjoyment and made beautiful harmony of their lives, fulfilling her in every way. Though in almost five years there had been no pregnancy. She brushed this shadow-thought away and hummed an American jazz number as she prepared a spur-of-the-moment picnic.

Her men, large and small, appeared, the small one riding the shoulders of the large.

They found a shady spot under an elderly oak and sat close, drinking in the fragrance of the thick lavender wisteria clumps on their twisted branches, watching Akio follow an ant trail.

"I wish," Momoko said, "that my world could be encapsulated in this moment, never moving on in time, just being this forever."

His fingers interlaced with hers.

Akio finished his pursuit, and Takeo felt in his pocket and brought out a red balloon. "Now this is not a regular balloon. It's an exploring balloon."

Akio looked skeptical. Takeo went on, "First we blow it up," which he proceeded to do. "Then we tie it with a string, but we haven't finished. Mother will hold the balloon while we write out a message."

"A message? What kind of message?"

Momoko watched the child's eager response to his stepfather and knew Takeo was a blessing banner in their lives.

"Well," he smiled. "That's for you to say. We're going to tie your message to the tail of the balloon and let it sail away, over the city, over woods and plains. Who knows where it will land or who will read it? But we will put on your address and ask whoever finds it to tell us where it came down, and on what date and at what hour. That way we will have a good idea of its journey."

Akio was enthralled with the plan, and wrote his name laboriously. "I want them to know it's mine, and that I sent it."

Akio released the balloon, and all three clapped as it rose into the sky. For a while it bobbed overhead, but after twenty minutes or so a gentle zephyr sent it soaring, and it became a mere speck sailing out of view.

Akio shared another pleasure with his stepfather. Very often Takeo got out the go board. It was Akio's delight to set up his nine black handicap stones on the marked points. Momoko smiled at their two heads bent over the game, for Takeo allowed the boy to try moves in order to discover the consequences. Akio's face held a look of rapt attention as Takeo showed how the enemy ranks might be separated, cut off, and rendered helpless.

Commenting on this later, Takeo said, "It will be difficult for Akio, son of an Oka fighter. Without a war it is difficult to be a hero."

Momoko nodded; the intensity of her son's nature was a worry to her.

It was during this period that the uncle who was Takeo's mentor died suddenly, and a large estate came to him. The change in their fortunes was radical. "I'll buy you a garden," Takeo told her.

"I never heard of anyone buying a garden."

"Of course it will have a house on it."

"A house? A house of our own?"

They set about looking at properties. Before the seven grasses of autumn appeared, Takeo was elected to the Diet and Momoko found the garden she wanted to tend. It occupied three-tenths of an acre in the heart of Tokyo.

Momoko was not to move in. She often wondered if her instinct that day at the Kameido Tenjin to encapsulate the moment had been prescience.

She and Takeo never discussed being childless, it was too painful. The first several years she hoped. Then it was like the war, a thing you didn't think about, that you refused to allow to surface, that you put behind you.

A letter from Takeo's mother made that impossible. The letter informed them that she and her husband would make a visit.

A second letter came from his father. From that moment Takeo withdrew from her. He had the look of a man torn by *ko*. What had his father written?

"It's leukemia," Takeo told her that evening. "The news of my uncle's death was too much, Mother's own condition has worsened. My father says she is dying. She is another casualty of the war."

He was silent on the subject from then on, moody and preoccupied. She knew he was thinking of the turtle pond at Osaka.

Momoko was certain that the reason behind his mother's coming visit was to beg her son not to let her die without a grandchild. Momoko had already lived through this agony with Noboru. She could not face it again.

She didn't blame Takeo's mother. How could she blame a dying woman who was thinking of her son? Shouldn't she also think of him? When he looked into Akio's face he did not see any lineament of himself or his family. Akio's eyes were not the eyes of his mother, or the nose of his father, nor did Akio's chin resemble his. It was natural that he want a son of his own, and right that he have one. He had not been able to adopt Akio, and a man must have a son. Especially a man in Takeo's position. He showed an instinct for management, and there were rumors he might be moved to the Ministry of Finance. Such a man should not be distracted. Such a man should not be worried.

After restless nights and the swallowing of many tears she knew what she should do. What she should *not* do was force Takeo to initiate things, force him to the cruel words he must say in order to obtain a divorce. She resolved not to drive him into this corner.

Still she hesitated. She had watched the affection that developed between Akio and his stepfather, seen Takeo foster it with the care and patience that were typical of him. He told her once that he culti-vated patience because he had brought about Noboru's death through impatience and so he strove to rectify this fault in his nature.

And now she was to be instrumental in depriving Takeo as well as Akio of this bond. She didn't want her boy to lose his father, not a second time. Then there was the practical matter of inheritance. Since Shigeru now headed the Sanogawa family, *his* son, not Akio, would inherit. And if she removed Akio from the Kuroda *ke*, he must forfeit what would surely be another fortune. But she could not allow such considerations to dissuade her. Honor demanded that she give Takeo his freedom, and though she looked at the alternatives long and hard, it remained a box that opened only one way.

That night Momoko served the tea herself, a special mark of her respect. Takeo looked at her in a way that was itself a caress. This would make it harder.

She was, however, determined in her resolve, and when Takeo set down the cup, said from the floor, "Takeo-san, forgive me." She saw that this formal mode of address surprised him. She looked away, repeating what she had rehearsed. "I have been happy. And Akio has been happy. But his prayers belong to another *ie*. There is no one to pray for you, Takeo-san, because I have failed you. The war still lives in my body and makes it impossible to conceive. Before your honorable parents arrive, I would like to be gone."

Takeo, to whom this outburst was utterly unexpected, put his hand to his forehead in a confused gesture. Distress showed in his face. "No, Momoko, no. Akio is my son. It is enough."

"Takeo-san, it is not enough for your mother. I cannot see you so torn. She is dying and your father is old, you owe them *ko*."

Takeo got up and walked to the window. Momoko had spoken the thoughts that he denied. He stood looking out, but the landscape he saw was interior, layered with obligations and duties against which he set his love. The conflict went on in him. Finally he turned to her. "Momoko, no."

She bowed her head. "Takeo-san, it must be yes."

They faced each other silently. As clouds contain a storm, the silence gathered. She watched his struggle, she had already passed through it. At last Takeo bowed from the waist.

⛩

Change, Yoriko knew from experience, was rarely for the better. Even when it had the appearance of good, it must be viewed with suspicion. They had gotten used to the Occupation and come to respect General MacArthur. The country straightened out under his leadership, and people had begun to feel a modicum of prosperity. A deep feeling of shock and foreboding ran through Japan when the general was recalled. The shogun MacArthur was recognized as a fair man, while nothing was known of Ridgway, the man sent to replace him. His job, as the Americans put it, was to wind things down.

The Americans had proved neither cruel nor vindictive masters. But they did not know this part of the world and had mistakenly gotten into a war with Japan's old enemies, the Koreans.

The negative aspect of this was that the replacement soldiers were not of the same caliber as the original fighting men. They were young draftees who got drunk at every opportunity, destroyed property, and were disrespectful. Their own MPs had trouble controlling them.

The positive aspect was that large orders began pouring into the factory. The war matériel the Americans banned before, they now wanted. This demand produced a radical change in all segments of the economy. In the Sanogawa factory the electronics section doubled. Everyone began to prosper. Shigeru in particular had a knack for making money. To be so successful struck Yoriko as somewhat tasteless, and revealed his merchant background. He had, she thought, the soul of a ricemonger. He had wasted no time marrying again, and every year a child had been added to the family. They were not of her blood, and she found them a squalling, unattractive lot. The new wife failed to satisfy him, and Shigeru was more profligate than before. The only sword he paid tribute to was the one between his legs. But he was the heir and Masaru, his heir. There was no question that he was firmly in control of the family.

The family, like the country, was dealing with change. For the country she feared inflation and a turn away from peace. For the family she perceived uncertainty and internal jockeying for position. The balance of power within the household these days rested with Ryoko. It was hard to see an outsider usurp her place simply because she was married to Shigeru, whom she herself had positioned. Before Momoko's marriage, she had planned to gradually place the running of the household in her hands. Since Momoko had been trained by her, the routine would have continued along the lines she had established, with designated times for washing, sewing and cleaning. Besides the traditional observation of festivals, there was the preparation of meals and baths to see to, the children and the servants to keep track of, the art of flowers to attend to, bills to pay, money to bank, and selecting the best schools for the boys.

But when she married, Momoko moved away. Shigeru married shortly afterward, and brought a wife into the family. Yoriko found herself deposed. Ryoko changed everything around; even market day was now on Wednesday. Yoriko bitterly resented this new wife who had taken her daughter's place. So, although she was upset when after five years Momoko returned, in many ways she was glad, hoping things would revert to normal. Momoko, however, took little interest in household chores and seemed content to follow Ryoko's instructions. For the first few months she did this quietly and with dignity.

Then a change occurred and she began to hum to herself as she went about the house and garden. Yoriko felt keenly that this cheerfulness was not appropriate, either for a bereaved widow or a discarded wife. After all, the circumstances of her return were lamentable. To be divorced was bad enough, but to be discarded as a barren woman brought shame not only on her, but on the entire Sanogawa family. If it had happened to her she would not be able to raise her head, but Momoko seemed to have no clear comprehension of her position. Perhaps it was just as well, since fallen flowers cannot return to their branches.

Yoriko reluctantly admitted that in spite of her ambiguous role, Momoko was a comfort to her. They shared the past, and she began to wonder if they shared the same dream of the future. For a plan was taking shape in Yoriko's mind. It was built around Akio.

However, it proved no easy task to get next to the boy or win his confidence. Akio wandered about, silent and morose, mourning his stepfather and the life he had known with him. His cousin Masaru made many overtures, all of which Akio ignored. He preferred to be by himself, and even to amuse himself.

Even in this he did not behave as a child, but as a miniature person. When the seven-year-old did childish things such as throw a ball against a building, he did not seem to do it for pleasure. It was as though he were fulfilling a duty, throwing the ball as a businessman might attend to some detail of office procedure, with a tired and weary expression. He appeared to be contemplating life, making up his mind whether he deigned to live it. Ryoko declared that he would grow up to be a monk. Yoriko did not think so.

Though they lived communally, the inner life of each was insu-lated from the others. Akio had become the center of Yoriko's interest. His principal pastime was to collect snails and beetles, tie them into parachutes that he designed from thread and silk, and send them bil-lowing from the roof onto the courtyard below. Though this led to improved design, insects with damaged shells soon littered the pavement.

Masaru was large and strapping, physically resembling his father. But he had a nature as sensitive as his mother's. He could not bear the sight of so many injured insects. He created a sickbay from a box, installing the creatures in rows. Broken shells were taped, and favorite grasses placed beside them for food. Masaru also tended animals; there was generally an injured rabbit, cat, or field mouse mending in a cage. Birds, too, took their turn in Masaru's hospital.

Watching all this, Yoriko was more than ever convinced that Masaru lacked the mettle needed to run the Sanogawa *ke*. Who ever heard of a tender warrior, or a laughing samurai who told jokes? It was easy to like Masaru. If you liked him, he liked you back. She was aware this was not true of Akio. You could like him if you wished, it was up to you. But your liking him put him under no obligation. This very independence of character convinced her the wrong grandson was the heir cousin.

The cousins were watched not only by Yoriko but by a third child. From the bowels of the house and from behind shoji screens, from dark and distant corners, light blue eyes followed them. Kenji's status was that of servant, but the other servants kept out of his way. Those light eyes rested attentively on everything, took in everything. No one ever knew what conclusions were reached, no one asked. But the cousins fascinated him. Fusa had told him Masaru was his brother. But this only embarrassed Kenji, who shied away from Masaru's kindness as he did from Akio's scorn. Nevertheless he continued to watch them from a distance, especially Akio's strange behavior.

Yoriko accepted that it was her fault Akio felt so strange and uneasy on being returned to his old *ie*. Was it not she who had urged adopting Shigeru as a means of ensuring his loyalty to the company? But that did not make it proper for a son's son to be pushed aside in favor of a daughter's son.

Yoriko had taken to communing nightly with the commemorative photograph of Noboru in his officer's flight uniform with a *hachimaki* bound around his forehead. He looked out from the *kamidana*, fearless and proud.

"Help me set things right," she asked her son, placing flowers before him, and felt she had struck a bargain. From that moment she stepped up her campaign.

She found sweets in the pocket of her apron for Akio and, pulling him into her lap, said, "Now that you have returned to your proper place, it is time you knew your heritage, Akio."

Until now he had not fully understood about his father. His mother had taken him to the Yasukuni Shrine and pointed out his father's name inscribed there. But he had not known in a visceral way. In the past he had pieced together certain things from the talk of grown-ups, like a family dog distinguishing intonations of grief and identifying grief words by the timbre of the voices. There had been *Father*. There had been *his father*. There had been *Oka fighter*.

And now his grandmother told him directly, "Never forget that your father volunteered to die, a human bomb. His blood and charred flesh were splattered on the deck of an American cruiser."

Momoko, overhearing her mother-in-law, was appalled. "I don't want the child's head filled with war stories. The war is over." At the first opportunity she took Akio into her room. "I want to talk to you about your father."

Akio felt he had new knowledge of him. But he nodded.

"He wasn't a bloodthirsty fighter, or a fanatic who fought on long after there was any possibility of hope. Actually he was a very moderate man. He liked Americans."

"I don't believe it," Akio said.

Momoko was unprepared for this defiance. "You must believe it, Akio. It's true."

"My father was a Special Attacker, a hero. He wanted to kill Americans and win the war."

"No, Akio, the war was already lost. He died as an act of courage, to give us courage, to show our spirit was undefeated."

"He was a warrior, an attacker, a fighter," Akio stormed at her.

"Akio-chan, please listen to me. It's important that you understand."

But he wouldn't listen. He ran off and hid from her the rest of the day. He mulled over everything he had been told. And when he had it all straight he emerged from his corner and folded a paper plane. He flew this plane with a solemn face. Watching it leave his hand, he clenched his teeth as it soared. His whole body tensed as the plane dipped, almost bowing to him. He watched without taking a breath as the wings leveled out, cutting through the air. Nothing could stop it now, the crash was predetermined by the sharp angle of descent. Nevertheless he jumped out at it, arms waving in an effort to intercept it, to halt the inevitable. It ended with the plane hitting the ground and him standing over it, looking down, seeing the deck of an American cruiser.

This new game by which he sought identification with his father seemed to him a betrayal of Takeo. He had heard Masaru speak of a pain that is measured in the laboratory in *dols*. His was of another kind, woven into the fabric of his being. He did not even recognize it when he first felt it.

No one did.

Except Masaru.

Masaru realized his cousin's sense of displacement. He watched the pantomime with the paper plane, guessing at his divided loyalties. He felt a special bond with the younger child. In their early years they had been brought up almost as brothers, and ever since he participated with Akio in the *shichi-go-san* ceremony that brought him officially into the family, the bond was strengthened. He recognized that Akio's withdrawn behavior was not directed against him but was an effort to fend off hurt he could not understand. When Akio's fresh distress exhibited itself in the form of a paper plane, he decided to intervene.

It seemed to him more important than mending shells or a kitten's paws.

"Akio," he said, touching him on the shoulder, "I have something to show you." He took him to the far end of the garden near the pond where he sometimes burned incense to his mother. Kneeling, he began to scrape earth away until a bit of cloth was revealed. Soon a good-sized packet emerged. He shook the dirt free and unwound the cloth. Inside was a magazine wrapped in oiled paper and sealed with adhesive tape— a *National Geographic*. The corner of one of its pages was turned down.

Masaru squatted beside Akio and laboriously deciphered the English: "In the Science Museum of London, suspended by three slender cables, an Oka bomb hovers inconspicuously at the back of the third floor. It is overshadowed by Hawk Hurricanes, Supermarine Spitfires, and Gloster Turbojets. The small, frail craft, known to the Japanese as a 'cherry blossom bomb' and to the Americans as an 'idiot bomb' or a 'Betty,' carried a single warrior to his fiery death."

Masaru looked up from the article. "This is what it meant to be an Oka fighter."

"I knew this. I've seen his hair and nail parings at the Yasukuni Shrine."

"There is something else, something you don't know."

"Tell me."

Masaru regarded him in silence and finally said, "It's about your two fathers. They met in the last months of the war. They were together at Mabalacat in the Philippines. They belonged to the same Shimpu unit, the 201st. Did your stepfather ever tell you anything about this?"

Akio shook his head.

"Don't you think that strange? After all, they were friends." Masaru broke off. "Before I tell you anything else, we must be friends, more than friends, more than cousins. We must be brothers."

"Brothers?"

"We will have a ceremony. You must steal sake and two sake cups from the kitchen."

"Now?"

At Masaru's emphatic nod, Akio left the garden.

"Why are some children always underfoot?" old Fusa complained. "Out with you."

"I'm thirsty."

"Well, then, get the water yourself. At your age, don't expect to
be waited on."

Akio watched her go into another part of the house. He took the
sake from a cabinet. Then, by climbing onto a shelf, he was able to
reach the sake cups. He hesitated over them, choosing two of the
oldest and most beautiful. Hiding them in his clothes, he started back.
Kenji emerged from behind a door and began following at a distance.
Akio threw stones at him. "Get back where you came from, Ainoko."
The child ran off, and Akio returned to Masaru.

Masaru was astounded at seeing the cups. "You didn't have to
take the best ones."

"Yes, I did."

"Okay, then, one cup we will fill at the pond, and when we have
found our *kami* in it, we will swear an oath and from the second cup
drink sake."

Akio followed the older boy's example, even to copying his grave
expression.

"Now," said Masaru, dippering up the water, "repeat after me:
We are brothers begot by sisters."

"We are brothers," Akio intoned, "begot by sisters."

"Arrows that are tied together never break, and our brotherhood
will last until the day these cups are smashed."

Akio again repeated his words, watching as Masaru stared into
the cup. When at last he caught a glimpse of the benevolent *kami*, he
set the cup down and drank sake from the second. Only then did he
give the divination cup to Akio.

Akio looked long and hard into the water. Filtered light moved
upon the surface, and when he had seen his *kami*, he too drank sake.

It seemed to Akio he drank fire.

Masaru observed him approvingly. "Our brotherhood is sealed."

"Then tell me about my two fathers."

"First we must put back the magazine, and bury the cups with it."
As he spoke he rolled them all into the cloth and, digging the cavity
deeper, buried them. Then, turning to Akio, he began.

"They were waiting to be called up. Takeo had waited longer,
several weeks longer. But it was your father, Noboru, who was scheduled for the morning. Takeo felt it was unfair, and pleaded with Noboru to trade missions with him. Noboru refused. Finally Takeo

suggested they draw for it, high card would go. Noboru gave in and Takeo won the mission. His plane had engine trouble, it fell into the sea, but he was rescued and lived."

"And my father, my *real* father, took his place and died?"

"Yes."

Akio's face became masklike. "I don't believe you. It's a lie."

"No. Your mother told my mother, and the servants overheard. I tell you the man you are feeling guilty about, the man you miss so much, is responsible for your father being dead."

The pupils of Akio's eyes rolled up out of sight, his body convulsed, and he lost consciousness. Masaru bent over him, then ran for help.

Momoko chafed his hands and Akio opened his eyes.

"What happened?" Momoko asked, but neither child would tell her.

That night Akio took his pallet from his mother's side and placed it beside his brother. Momoko felt a twinge of sadness; his futon had lain beside hers all his life. On the other hand she was pleased that the older boy had taken Akio under his guidance. Her son could benefit from Masaru's easygoing ways.

Yoriko was not pleased by this move. Akio's futon was a symbol of his allegiance.

This was not the only change to occur that particular night. Akio woke in a fit of screaming. From then on he seemed utterly lost in tantrums, as though he couldn't find his way out of them. He would burst out yelling like a madman over some small thing of no consequence to anyone but himself.

Neither his mother nor his grandmother knew exactly what called out these rages. Tantrums in young males were generally tolerated, as it was believed they engendered a warlike spirit necessary for manhood. But Akio's excessive rampages were unnerving. At such times he was unreachable. Strange glints danced in his eyes, and the tendons of his neck knotted. It seemed to his family that such a small child should not have the capacity for such prolonged bursts of temper.

Yoriko was fearful that he might be possessed by an *oni*, a grotesque with horns, who wears pants made of tiger skins and runs away with children. The *oni* wished to devour Akio's soul; perhaps he already had, as neither entreaties nor bribes nor anything influenced him to a calmer, more rational way.

She confided her fears to Momoko, saying that perhaps one of those restless spirits who wander the earth looking for a way to bring peace to their unfortunate souls had entered into Akio, that he was storming to expel it and the *oni* was storming back. How else could such maniacal behavior be explained? Surely no child was capable of it, let alone able to sustain it hour after hour.

Momoko had another explanation, but since it involved her own deep-seated guilt, she preferred Yoriko's version. Perhaps after all there were *oni*. It was easier to believe in them than accept that she was responsible for these frightening aberrations in her child.

Yoriko reached her own decision about the boy. Purification with *moxa* could no longer be avoided.

"No!" Momoko said, backing away. "I can't do it."

But the grandmother had no such compunction. She had not given birth to him, he was not her child. Besides, it was necessary to know if he possessed the steel of his samurai forebears. She lit the cone of gray powder and let it burn itself into his flesh.

The servants held him, but there was no need. Akio had braced himself for the ordeal and did not pull away from the smoldering herbs. He had prepared himself to meet it, and when it scorched his flesh he laughed, somewhat wildly, but it was a laugh.

Momoko shuddered. Yoriko had been right, it was an *oni*.

There was a rule that *moxa* could be applied only three times. At the third application Akio still laughed.

Momoko cried, but he continued to laugh.

Momoko laid soft cloths dipped in a healing unguent on his chest. He thrashed from side to side under her tenderness and finally allowed himself to cry. Momoko cried with him. This was her doing. She had not thought she would be banishing a happy child who laughed up into your face, in exchange for this out-of-control boy.

The tantrums continued. She began to believe in Yoriko's demon. If it was a demon, it had not been dislodged. There was no recourse any longer but to take the boy to the priest for purification. It was necessary to put a rope around his waist, since he would not listen to them or go willingly.

The two women pulled the child most of the way. He rushed at them, beating them, breathing in jagged sobs. When he saw the torii gate of the shrine he fell in the dirt, his body as rigid as a board, and refused to get up.

Momoko pulled him to his feet. He snarled at her, attempting to bite. Momoko backed away from her own child. His grandmother slipped another coil of rope around him, this time pinioning his arms.

The shrine was surrounded by a spacious cloister, but the women went around to the back. They found a priest sitting before a sacred tree. They waited respectfully for the Holy One to return to the small reality in which they stood in need of his attention. The old eyes, which had been clouded with other vistas, cleared as he took in the situation.

"What have we here?" he asked, getting arthritically to his feet and peering at the bound child.

"We do not know, Ancient One. Perhaps the boy is possessed."

The priest approached Akio, who kicked at him, screaming and rolling his eyes.

The priest took hold of the back of his neck and lifted him a little way off the ground. "My eyes see a small child who thinks he has a great woe. But I will show you woe." He removed the rope from him, and perhaps because he had freed him, Akio followed the priest into an alcove where a fresco covered the walls. He gazed at an extremely brutal depiction of samurai at the bastion of a shogun's castle. Retainers had fallen in defending it. Their bodies were being hacked and dismembered. The scene ran red with blood and viscera. In the foreground a boy about his own age was held by his ankles and swung against a stone wall.

Akio stared at the graphic depiction and forgot to scream.

"This, boy," the priest said, "represents trouble. This represents pain. This, my child, is the representation of it. You have felt your first pain and rebelled against it. But you will know more and greater." He reached out and pulled the straw rope attached to a bell. "There, do you hear? I have summoned the kami from the Divine Body Mountain. As they travel to us through the essence of things the kami behold the rich and the powerful and smile with compassion. To them the world is like a map of a foreign country. But they will come to free you of your pain." He turned to the grandmother. "Ghosts have visited him. They held him as you saw." The priest once more focused his attention on Akio. "What is your name, child?"

"Akio."

"Listen to me, Akio, this strength in you, this power which you have, you waste in futile noise and bad temper. The ability to feel is a gift not to be spilled out. Hoard it within yourself, and you can be a leader. But control is necessary. You must protect your anger, save it, hoard it as you save and hoard your semen." His voice trailed away.

He folded his hands together. He had left them.

Akio was quiet. There was no further need of the rope. On the way back he did not utter a sound.

"I do not think the priest was right about the pain," Yoriko said. "What could a child his age know of pain?"

"Still," Momoko replied, "the priest drove out the impurities, and he spoke well." She remembered Takeo saying that to be the son of an Oka fighter would be a burden for Akio to carry. But the boy returned to normal and there were no more outbursts.

Shortly after this, in accordance with her secret plan, Yoriko insisted that Akio undergo "cold austerity." Momoko opposed the idea, but Akio himself wanted it. He enjoyed the trial; the shock of cold water was something tangible to stand up to.

He proved his worth to himself and called Masaru to come test his spirit by this means.

Masaru laughed. "What is the purpose, except to catch cold?"

"He doesn't understand the warrior's way," his grandmother whispered to Akio. She had observed the absorption with which he listened to his mother's stories, and had started a story of her own. It was an ongoing narration about two brothers. Gradually the theme became apparent: the wrong brother, who was a fool and not capable of running the vast estates that would be entrusted to his care, would inherit. Then one day Yoriko reminded him that Masaru and not he was the official heir. "Even though you are the son of an Oka fighter."

Akio absorbed this. He had always acted as though he were the heir cousin, as though everything—home, land, factory—belonged to him. They didn't, they belonged to Masaru, who accepted his good fortune lightly. Finally he said, "Masaru is older."

"But he is only the son of a daughter. You are the son of Captain Sanogawa."

Akio was angry with his grandmother for forcing him to think about such things. But the poison of envy and discontent had been injected.

It did not end there, a second humiliation trailed the first. A boy transferred to his school from the neighborhood where his mother and he had lived with his stepfather before the divorce. He was asked, "Aren't you the son of Takeo Kuroda?"

There followed jeering, taunts, and name-calling. Hopeless battles ensued. Hopeless because even if he won, he lost. Where else could they find such a defenseless target as his mother? For a woman who is put aside is an object of scorn. Even an Old Miss was given more respect. Because of his mother he was often made to walk home with pebbles in his shoes. And once they forced him to wag his penis like a tail and jump about like a dog.

Masaru protected him from the *ijime*-bullying when he could. Once Akio had been grateful, now he resented it. What right had Masaru to put him in his debt and make him wear an *on*? Masaru was placing a hard burden on him. But since he loved him, he bore it and did not complain.

Nevertheless he hoped Masaru would see the position he put him in and restrain his outrush of human feeling. It never happened that way; the next time Masaru saw him pinned beneath a gang of boys taking a beating, he rushed in and saved him. It required a great deal of generosity on Akio's part to put up with so much from his cousin.

Momoko knew she had failed her son twice: once when she left Takeo's house, and again when she tried to impose her view of his father's sacrifice. She wished for the time when she wrapped him in his red silk bunting and carried him on her back.

1960

THE BOYS GREW UP IN A JAPAN THAT HAD PAID ITS REPARATIONS and, although still regarded in many quarters as an outlaw nation, had sought and gained admission to the UN.

At fifteen and seventeen, Akio and Masaru were already taller than the last generation. They were looked on as special children, the first to be unmarked by war. The two faced each other across a go board.

Akio regarded his opponent quizzically. "*Atari!*" he said, signaling he was preparing a kill.

Masaru saw that his cousin's white pieces were menacing him. In hopes of shifting the combat area, he tried *osaeru* to block Akio's line of stones and prevent encirclement.

Akio smiled at this evasion. Masaru was only putting off the inevitable.

Masaru charged in desperation, *kogeima kakari*, attempting to control a corner. Akio analyzed the threat without immediately responding to it. Even when he was absolutely still, as now, there was the feeling that he was poised inwardly so that the possibility of action and physical confrontation was always imminent. "I am thinking of applying to the National Go Academy of the first Hon-inbo," he said offhandedly.

Masaru looked up startled. "The Nippon Kiin? But it's a monastery, you have to take vows."

"That's right. The first six years of your novitiate you're kept incommunicado. I think in six years I might understand some of the principles of the game."

"What principles?"

"There must be some reason why go was forbidden to the common man for centuries, reserved only for noblemen."

"I suppose so."

"Why, for instance, should a go master of the ninth *dan* be called Sorcerer-Living-in-Mountains? It would be valuable to know that, don't you think?"

Even though Masaru knew Akio had no intention of joining that august institution, the Nippon Kiin, and that he was merely exploring the ramifications of such an act mentally, he was nevertheless disturbed. Akio's approach was always too intense, too personal. He became the thing he did.

With a flashing move, Akio launched *oi otoshi*, a totally unexpected onslaught. Masaru narrowed his field of concentration to meet it, and after some seconds managed to place a stone so as to at least keep his lines of communication open.

"Did you ever think"—Akio's voice dropped and his words were audible only by an effort of will—"that we might be stones placed in someone else's game?"

Masaru was uncomfortable with the thought. "Like whose?"

"I don't know, anyone's. Grandmother's. President Eisenhower's."

"You're crazy, you know that?"

Akio considered that possibility. "No, I don't think so."

"You wouldn't know. Crazy people never know they're crazy."

Akio's control of the center outweighed the stones Masaru had clumped in a corner position. Inexorably, White moved to surround them. "Not too crazy to beat you," Akio laughed.

Although he was two years younger, Akio generally found a *sente*, which forced Masaru to move in his favor. Winning was important to him, but he tried not to show this. His emotions were kept under strict control.

Recently he had discovered a remarkable outlet for his feelings.

The boys at school kept diaries, it was the fashion, and he had bought one himself but been too lazy to keep it up. One day he came across it and started to toss it out when a use for it occurred to him. He worked the better part of the day compiling a list of names.

A hit list.

Every name there was destined to be overtaken by great misfortune. Akio was uncertain whether drawing attention of the *kami* to the names would be sufficient, or whether he himself would have to engineer the punishments.

The first name he entered was his stepfather's, Takeo Kuroda. But Shigeru had a prominent place on the list as well. He had never been told directly, but over the years Akio had pieced together the tragedy of his aunt Yasue, his father's sister. He blamed Shigeru. What man would allow such a thing to happen to his wife? Akio felt he bore responsibility. His uncle was dimly aware of his censure. In his turn, Shigeru resented Akio's lordly attitude and that he always prevailed with his son. If truth be told, Shigeru was somewhat intimidated by him.

Akio entered the name of Shigeru's second wife, Ryoko, whom nobody liked, and the four brats born to her in this house. His mother didn't like Ryoko because she felt it would be disloyal to Yasue. As for the children, they were completely undisciplined and grew like wild seeds. Akio disdained them, and Masaru seemed embarrassed by his half-siblings.

Nor did Akio hesitate to place his grandmother on the list. She was there for marring his friendship with Masaru. Ever since she had been at pains to explain to him that Masaru would inherit, his own lowly position in the household irked him. And he had regarded his cousin with critical eyes.

Masaru was not on the list. Sometime in the distant future he would have to deal with him. But for eight years they had been two arrows bound together in the same quiver. Masaru was the one person Akio loved.

When he was little, Akio's idea of revenge was to have anyone who harmed him boiled in oil. Then his nurse had given him another idea when she forbade the towel-snapping that he and Masaru indulged in, aiming at each other's buttocks when they came out of the *ofuro*. His nurse said it made a sound like that of a head struck from its body.

As he grew older, less ferocious ways of dealing with people occurred to him. He committed some of these schemes to paper, enjoying concocting various plots of revenge, and waited for the day when he could close the circle.

It happened sooner than he expected. The *kami* chose Ryoko as their first victim. Actually, Ryoko was one of the least important people on his list, and his enmity did not run deep. He placed her there for insisting he include her oldest boy in a game. "It is only right," she said.

"Why? He's not my brother. None of your four have anything to do with me. We are not related. I would as soon play with Kenji."

"You should feel *haji*," she shrilled at him. "They are your uncle's children and have more right in this house than you do. Kenji indeed, your blue-eyed spy."

To avoid quarreling with a woman, Akio walked away from her, but she called after him, "You're not the heir cousin, you know."

That decided him. A woman who had no feeling for respect within a family deserved to be taught a lesson. That night her name was entered in the book.

It troubled him that she had guessed about Kenji. Kenji could fix anything and operate any kind of machine. "Yankee know-how," the family said scornfully. But Akio prized this ability and made use of it. His skates and bicycle had both been repaired countless times. And as he worked, Kenji told him things he thought might interest him, the intrigues of the servants, and the story of his own bizarre birth, which Fusa had taken a spiteful pleasure in relating to him.

Although Kenji didn't say it, Akio was able to figure out that the strange child, just a year younger than himself, was his cousin, related to him as closely as Masaru. From then on Akio was even more brusque with him, for he shared in the general feeling that Kenji was one who should not have been born. The boy was made to understand that there was no place in the world for a half-caste, and that blue eyes in a Japanese face were an abomination. But this was no news to Kenji.

Among the things he told Akio was that Shigeru kept a mistress.

About a week later Akio and Masaru were invited by Shigeru to the closing night of the Tokyo *basho*, which ended the fifteen days of the spring sumo tournaments. It came about partly as an effort on Shigeru's part to break Masaru's addiction to television. He found the boys lying on the floor, roaring with laughter at the antics of two pseudo-wrestlers. The slapstick match featured a plucky youthful contender pitted against a suspiciously American-looking foreigner.

There were shots of the audience booing and yelling and pounding the floor as the immense *gaijin* entered the ring, bumping his head on an arch that had been erected for that purpose, shaking his own hands, and yelling, *"Haro, haro."* ("Hello, hello.") He wore a white mask with bright blue eyes painted above his own and a huge false nose plastered on. The boos and hisses from the audience accelerated, to the delight of the boys.

The young contender also wore a mask, a World War II caricature of the Yellow Peril Jap, with buck teeth and thick Coke-bottle glasses. He resembled a gasping fish, and the boys collapsed on each other, holding their stomachs.

The giant foreigner began scratching his armpits and jumping around like a monkey. This brought renewed laughter and boos, at which he turned, glared at the audience, and spat.

The boos became vicious, and this set him off. The hulk turned and grabbed the poor Japanese, who tried valiantly to defend himself. But the monstrous *gaijin* constantly took unfair advantage of him, and only the end of the round saved the day.

The young Japanese staggered to his corner, where friends removed the Yellow Peril mask and revived him with "strength water" to his temples. He bowed his gratitude to them, and when he was in this vulnerable position and while it was still between rounds, the vicious American rushed him from behind. Somewhere he had picked up a steel chair, which he swung over his head. The crowd, with one voice, yelled, "Look out!"

The warning came almost too late; once more the *makoto* Japanese seemed defenseless against such brazen tactics. Passions were running high, hysteria mounted. It looked as though the young, true-spirited Japanese must be defeated if not killed. Someone in the audience threw a chair at the giant. Immediately there was a rain of items bombarding the ring. It did no good. Again, only time-out saved the younger athlete. But as he turned to walk to his corner the *gaijin* went for him. It was against all rules, all sense of sportsmanship and fair play, and the audience screamed and banged the walls and stamped the floor.

Then a wonderful transformation occurred. The innocent young man called on the glorious strength of spirit that is in every Japanese boy and stood up to the frothing foreigner, dispatching him with several rather standard ploys.

Shigeru snapped off the TV in disgust. "This is crap. Why do you waste your time on junk like this? I've got tickets for the real thing. How would you like to see some classic wrestling? I'm speaking of the Yokozuna."

The boys looked at each other; was he serious? The grand champions of sumo?

Shigeru was carried away by his own generosity. "I tell you what, we'll make a night of it. Dinner, the works. What do you say to that?"

In honor of the occasion the boys decided to dress. Akio was looking through his clothes chest for his tie with blue dots when he heard someone crying on the other side of the sliding door. His first thought was that it was his mother, and an oppressive feeling of hopelessness spread in him, for what could a son do for a mother who had been both widowed and divorced?

Having made his choice and married her, why couldn't Takeo have been loyal and overlooked the fact that she bore him no children? Not only was he responsible for his father's death, he was responsible for his mother's public humiliation. His mother always made excuses for him, claiming he had divorced her out of deference to his parents. Takeo's dying mother wanted to see grandchildren, and his sense of obligation to her kept him from anything he might owe a wife. Yes, he knew that story.

Even though he had behaved so badly, Takeo had been able to make peace with the Sanogawa family because of the swords. Shortly after the divorce he found and returned the swords that were confiscated during the Occupation, and for which he had never stopped searching. Everyone in the Sanogawa ke now honored him, except Akio, who hated the idea of owing on to this man whose son he had been. He had many memories of this time, and because they were happy he did not forgive Takeo.

Being discarded as a barren woman, his mother, and he along with her, would certainly have eaten cold rice except for the fact that his father was a war hero. This did not prevent his anger turning against Takeo, who should have protected them, who should have remained a father to him. It was for this failure that Takeo headed the list.

In the eight years since he had divorced Momoko, Takeo had prospered. He made a good second marriage and had both sons and a daughter. He was a man to reckon with in the LDP, the party in power, and was said to wield a great deal of influence in the Ministry of Finance. So far he had not suffered. Perhaps now that he was preeminent on Akio's list, things would be different.

Hearing his mother crying, fierce anger flared in him that Takeo had made her life so bitter.

Actually, Akio often felt she was not as bitter as she should have been. The movies he and Masaru went to were filled with the sufferings of mothers. It was a genre known as *hahamono*, or "mother-things," in which the mother invariably accepted meekly the blows fate heaped on her, and took on herself additional trouble to spare those she loved. But his mother, unlike the heroines of these films, hid her hurt too well and did not allow her suffering to show.

It was he who harbored resentment while she gave every appearance of content. By being happy, she denied him the opportunity to commiserate with her. If they could have shed tears together over her fate, he would have loved and reverenced her. But not only did she bear no resentment toward Ryoko, she appeared to harbor none for Takeo, whom he hated so deeply. She put a gulf between them by refusing to share his animosity. She seemed to feel that the return of the Sanogawa swords absolved him.

Of course she did not know of the harassment at school on her account. Nevertheless she owed him at least some measure of unhappiness and he listened to the tears on the far side of the sliding panel with more satisfaction than compassion. . . . until he realized it was not his mother. Because now there were words and it was not his mother's voice, but Ryoko's.

Noticing a splinter of sunlight on the mat he guessed that the panel was open a crack and quietly went to it and looked through.

Ryoko sat before a pile of unpaid bills and, one after another, crumpled them in her hands and threw them on the floor. "No, no," she said at one point, "it is too much. It isn't fair." And her tears made the ink run.

Akio stole away to ask his grandmother about it. She was drinking tea with Momoko, laughing and speaking in half-whispers. They broke off and looked at him.

"What's going on with Aunt Ryoko?" he asked. "She's back there crying."

The two women exchanged glances and Akio guessed that was

what they had been discussing. Yoriko began laughing again and his mother looked uncomfortable.

"Ryoko," his grandmother informed him, "has the task of keeping Shigeru's accounts. And among his accounts are bills for flowers that arrive daily at a certain apartment."

"The boy isn't old enough," Momoko protested.

"What? At fifteen? He's old enough to keep a mistress himself."

Both Momoko and Akio blushed.

"The thing is," Yoriko went on blithely, "last month there was a bill for a necklace. But that was nothing. This month it is the rent on the girl's apartment." And she laughed aloud at the thought of Ryoko having to pay for her husband's philandering.

Akio nodded. For the first time his own bookkeeping balanced. Though she herself was insignificant, the fact that justice had been done, and payment extracted, renewed his faith that in time the rest would be appropriately taken care of.

"Hurry," his mother said, "your uncle is waiting for you."

The women looked after him as he left. Yoriko voiced the thought always uppermost in her mind. "That young man was born to head the Sanogawa."

The evening began with a Hawaiian dinner in a private *zashiki* of a restaurant in the Ryogoku. What made it particularly interesting was that a girl about their own age was waiting for them, an exceptionally pretty girl made up skillfully to appear as though she used no makeup. She got to her feet when she saw Shigeru, and bowed deeply. He responded with a swat on her behind. "Azuma, this is my son and my ward. I hope you don't like younger men."

They both laughed at this sally, and the boys refrained from looking at each other. Akio felt Masaru's embarrassment, not over his father's sexual conquest, but that he had brought them to witness it.

They helped themselves from a large wooden tray with a hibachi in the center on which were warmed great *poo-poo*, consisting of chicken pieces wrapped in tinfoil and spears of pork, pineapple, and lichee nuts garlanded with small orchids. Shigeru ordered Chinese *lao-chu* wine to which he added crystals of white sugar. Azuma did the same, and the boys followed suit.

Shigeru pretended he had added so much sugar he could not stir it, and grabbed the spoon as though he were wielding an oar. Azuma went into peals of laughter at his antics.

Akio smiled at his plate. So this little girl was the great rival over whom Ryoko wept. Perhaps she was good at the oral skills he had seen alluded to in the less reputable newspapers. Or did she dance naked on his uncle's body, bringing him pain and orgasm?

Shigeru and the girl drank steadily. Shigeru's face became flushed and he began feeling her up under the table.

Akio, who was seated on the other side of Azuma, dropped the hand closest to her under the table onto her naked thigh. He didn't dare go higher for fear of encountering Shigeru's hand, so he grabbed hold of a firm buttock instead. Azuma reached forward on the pretext of helping herself from the round platter, and he felt further. He started fooling around, and she kept jumping forward to twirl the platter. She laughed most of the time, and Akio wondered what Shigeru was up to from his vantage point.

"Your boys are so cute, Shigeru-san. Really handsome. If you aren't careful I will run off with one of them."

Much laughter from Shigeru, who was by this time quite drunk and wanted to take her breasts out of her dress.

She slapped his hands playfully. "What will your boys think?"

"They'll be jealous, what else? Besides, they have to grow up sometime."

Masaru had become morose. He pushed his food around on his plate without tasting it. How much he knew of what was going on, Akio couldn't tell. For the first time in his life he was glad he didn't have a father to make a fool of himself.

More dishes were brought, and by the time they were cleared away another round of *lao-chu* wine appeared. Shigeru pounded on the table. "Dance, Azuma. I want you to dance." And he boosted her onto the table.

As she stood there somewhat waveringly, he produced her underpants and waved them under his son's nose. "I just happen to have . . . but I wonder where they came from?" He got up and, leaning forward, peered up between her legs. She spread them obligingly. "Come, boys," Shigeru urged hospitably, "have a look. Just a look, mind you. That's all. Masaru?"

Masaru's mouth was clamped into a hard line and he shook his head.

"He's shy," Azuma cried in delight. "I think that's sweet."

"Well, I know one that isn't shy. What do you say, Akio?"

"Why not?" Akio bent forward and had a long look. It was shadowy under the short skirt, but he saw the long red gash bulging with moisture, and his own response was automatic.

"That will do," Shigeru said, "a look is all you get. The rest is man's work. You haven't got it in you yet, you just think you have." As he set Azuma down on the floor he asked, "You don't have a little sister, do you, who would show a couple of virgins where to put it?" He doubled over with laughter, but Azuma winked at Akio over his shoulder.

Once out in the air, Shigeru sobered considerably. He had chosen this particular restaurant for its proximity to the Kokugikan. Outside the stadium were colorful *banzuke* advertising the event. Entering the auditorium with its press of bodies was a visceral experience. There was the usual smell of soap, and an American smell as well, the smell of sweat. They were caught in the crowd, and the sumo song was already blaring over loudspeakers.

"They don't recognize it," Shigeru told Azuma. "It's *Kimigayo*, the national anthem, but they don't know it. Kids today have no patriotism," forgetting that applied to her as well. He gave her his arm like a foreign gentleman, and she took it as though she were a Hollywood star. She'd had no time to put her underpants on, they were stuffed in her purse.

Akio was amazed to see that Shigeru had purchased good seats down front. Again he made sure to sit on the other side of Azuma, although without a table there was no opportunity to do anything.

Masaru slumped on the far side of him. He hadn't said a word for hours. Suddenly he seemed to come to life; Akio felt a sharp jab in his ribs. He turned and looked at Masaru, who indicated with his head the direction he was to look.

Unbelievable! Beside Masaru sat a yakuza, a real, actual yakuza whose pinky finger had been amputated. Wow! Akio could hardly tear his glance away. The yakuza were the most feared fraternity in the country. They were the rough boys, the punks who did the persuading for the big-gun politicians. And just as in the comics, this one sat there in a pinstripe, three-piece suit that, at every move, gave glimpses of tattooing extending to his wrists. Even though it was an evening event, the yakuza's outfit was topped by sunglasses. The rings on the fingers he still had called attention to the missing pinky.

This was already a great night, and the wrestling hadn't begun yet. Sumo originated in conjunction with fertility rites performed at the Imperial Court in ancient times. The ring was a two-foot-high stage of pounded clay covered by a film of damp sand and outlined by a hemp rope. There were five judges seated by the side, recognizable by black *haori* over their kimonos.

They were about to see serious sumo. The *rikishi* from the east entered ringside in brilliantly colored *mawashi*, each accompanied by two attendants, a dew-sweeper, and a sword bearer for the parade ceremony of the Grand Masters. The announcer proclaimed each *rikishi* by name, giving his rank, home prefecture, and "stable" or team.

When the massive athletes were assembled they faced inward, performing a short series of foot-stamping gestures with sexual overtones, enhanced by the huge exposed buttocks. They filed out by way of the aisles, replaced by *rikishi* from the west, who performed the same ritual. The audience was spellbound until the last topknot disappeared.

The first *rikishi* reappeared, stripped to their loincloths. Throwing salt into the circle of the *dohyo*, they squatted facing each other in ready position. Eye contact was crucial. The *gyoji*, in his colorful kimono and hat, judged the finer points as the bouts were played.

Last came the Grand Masters of the Makuuchi. This moment, when the Yokozuna faced each other was what everyone waited for. The pillars of flesh braced. One grand champion lunged at his opponent's throat and, with an iron headlock, forced him off the mat. There was the final *yusho*. The audience exploded in applause; they had seen what they had come to see.

Afterward, Azuma begged to go back to the *shitaku beya*, which was not so much a dressing room as a place for fans, managers, and media to gather. There was a wait before the public was allowed back, and they filled the time at a noodle shop. Shigeru was amazed that the boys could eat again. Finally they observed a group of fans being ushered in by a rear door, and they joined them going back to the dressing rooms. Several newspapermen were there, laughing and joking with the Yokozuna, while around him a group of girls waited for a *tegata*.

The master obliged by inking his hand on an ink pad and bringing it down on spread-out cards in assembly-line fashion. Azuma marched up to him, took her panties from her pocket, and, smiling sweetly, said, "Put your handprints on these, please."

With a roar of laughter that shook his mound of belly, the Yokozuna placed his great hand on the red ink pad and brought it down on her underpants. Shigeru hurried her away.

Outside the stadium he gave the boys money for the subway. "I'll be staying in town," he said with a broad wink.

Masaru refused the money. "I think I will walk."

His father shrugged and left with Azuma.

"I'll walk too," Akio said.

Masaru turned on him angrily. "Why don't you take the subway?"

"I don't want to."

"You were disgusting with that girl. I saw what you were doing."

"Oh, that."

"When you're as old as my father, you'll be just like him."

"I'll never need to prove to my son that I'm a man."

"God, I hate him."

"He's no worse than any other grown-up. They're all buffoons."

"I hate him," Masaru said again.

"He may have done us a favor. We can go see Azuma whenever we want."

"I don't want to see her."

"Think about it."

"You think we could?"

"Why not?"

"We might get a disease."

"Your father must have checked her out."

"But we don't know where she lives. My father saw to that."

Akio laughed. "Ryoko knows. She must have a receipt for the rent."

They walked in silence a while. "Can you play go tomorrow?" Akio asked. "While we were watching the wrestling I devised a new move."

"I thought we were going to the Tachikawa air force base tomorrow and see if we can get close enough to throw stones at the F-101s."

"We'll do that next week."

"Okay."

Akio, moving for White, consolidated two groups of stones, threatening *naka oshi gachi*, an early victory by a large margin. As usual he identified with his army, making himself part of the play. He had gotten out his Juku school *hachimaki* victory band and tied it around his forehead to intimidate his opponent. When he saw this, Masaru only laughed.

Something had been happening recently that was disconcerting; Masaru was beginning to occasionally win a game. This was puzzling to Akio, because Masaru lacked insight into the game, and certainly possessed none of his ability. It was understandable that he beat him with regularity at the paper-scissors-stone game, because, played with hands and fingers, it required only quickness and luck. But abstract thought was something Masaru balked at. He had a different way of knowing, an intuitive way. And Akio guessed that on those occasions when his cousin triumphed over him, it was not by knowing go, but by knowing *him* and figuring out what he was most likely to do.

This was a disturbing thought. Masaru seemed to have an instinct that he himself lacked. His cousin repeatedly came down on the side of right, honor, compassion, good. From his mother's description of Yasue, he thought Masaru must have inherited her nature. He *was* honorable, he *was* compassionate and good. He probably understood Akio's father's death better than Akio did, and in the same situation would act as Noboru had.

About himself Akio wasn't sure. Did he lack that nobility of soul? There was always the moment at which common sense stepped in and said, "Whoa, wait a minute."

But for all his common sense, and in spite of his brilliance, Akio suspected his cousin held values he himself could never attain. And this although he was mediocre in school. It was sacrilege to think it, but perhaps you had to be a bit dumb to be a hero.

Kenji was hanging around. Akio yelled at him and the boy scurried off. Akio frowned. While appearing to be trapped and helpless, he was secretly gathering strength for a *tachiai* into the other's territory, and then a quick encircling *nodowa*.

At this critical juncture someone rattled the broken lock at the front gate and, calling, "Hello, is anyone there?" pushed it open.

A young woman stood there walking a bicycle. She wore the navy and white sailor suit of a schoolgirl, and her hair was bobbed. Neither boy recognized at first that it was Sumie, their playmate in that long-past free time when they were small children.

"Masaru-san," she called, as though they were still seven, "is that you? And Akio-san, I'd hardly know you. Has it been so long?" She approached, wheeling the bicycle up the path.

Was it really Sumie? How pretty she'd become, how tall, how graceful.

"The chain came off my bike. I was right outside your gate so I thought I could leave it here and telephone for someone to come get it."

"Kenji will fix it for you," Masaru said, raising his voice and calling him back.

Kenji squatted by the bike and studied it, spinning the wheels.

"We're playing go," Akio said pointedly to Sumie.

She came close to see. "Who's winning?"

Akio lost the thread of his attack. It was inappropriate for a girl to look over his shoulder and inappropriate that she was beautiful.

Masaru replied jokingly, "If you counted up all the games we've ever played, the odds favor Akio. It's more or less his game. Too much long-term plotting for my brain."

Sumie laughed, the sound like bells in a gentle wind. Her middy blouse and serge skirt only served to emphasize that she had outgrown such a childish costume, for it did not disguise the swell of her breasts or the curve of her hips. Even as he noticed these details, Akio chided himself. To beat his cousin he had been using what in Zen is known as "pillar-standing." Originally it was invented for the art of fencing. At first one practices in a courtyard, using all the space, but through concentration the orbit of play can be narrowed to the patch of ground beneath one's feet. Then, if the swordsman becomes truly proficient and secure in Zen, he is able to duel on top of a pillar without dizziness or fear of falling.

Sumie was embarked on a description of the tennis club near the Myoko-ji Temple in Yokohama. "My family has just joined. It's marvelous. My game has improved a hundred percent. On the weekends we usually stay for dinner. They have a band and it's a lot of fun."

"Look out," Masaru laughed, "or your family will have you married off."

"Oh, no, I'm too young. I'm only fifteen. But I have it all figured out. I will marry when I am twenty-five. My husband will be twenty-seven and our second child will be graduating university when he reaches retirement."

"Then I can't marry you," Akio said. "We are the same age."

"Fate is kind to me," Masaru laughed. "Guess what? When you're twenty-five I'll be twenty-seven."

Sumie dimpled and couldn't seem to find a spot in the garden to look at.

"Twenty-five is cutting it close," Akio said, falling into the old teasing way he had used when they were small. "If you don't watch out you'll be a Christmas cake."

A Christmas cake, like an old maid, was not good after the twenty-fifth. Sumie didn't care for his remark. "Really, Akio," she responded much as she had then, "are you still in the habit of saying such things now that you are grown?"

"What do you expect? You come in and interrupt a go game, for which it is possible to study one's entire life. And you think I'll smile like the heroes in your romantic *manga* comic books?"

"A *manga* hero? Is that how you picture yourself? Driving fast cars, hiring assassins, wearing sharp Paris fashions? You are very childish, Akio." She had first told him this when they were seven.

"Oh?" he replied as he had then. "You give me permission to be childish? Why not? In that case I am a giant robot striding over the city, fighting monsters with my death ray, killing opponents with a special karate chop. And in my chest is the control room where the humans sit. You open this little door and there you are!"

"Me?"

"Yes, I've captured you and taken you off to my lair."

"You're a robot, not a lion."

"It doesn't matter, I can have a lair."

"And what would you do with me when we got there?"

Akio's blood was up. In his mind he actually had her at his mercy. "I don't know whether to have sex with you first, or drug you first and then have sex."

"He's terrible," Sumie complained to Masaru. "You're terrible, Akio."

"But you liked the story."

"I didn't. I think you're crazy."

Akio flashed a look at Masaru. "You're not the only one who thinks that."

While Akio was bantering with Sumie, Masaru had been studying the board. Suddenly he bent over it and made a move that blocked

Akio's stones, pinning them hopelessly. Looking up in triumph he exclaimed, "Want more, get less!"

Akio stared at his defeated men, seeing too late the blind spot in his defenses, the unguarded door through which the enemy poured to surround and humiliate him. The game was over, and Sumie had witnessed a total rout.

Masaru started to explain to her how he was able to win so brilliantly when, with a sudden shout, Akio threw himself across the low table at his cousin and with his hands on his neck began throttling him. The weight of his body propelled them both to the ground. It was a samurai tradition that one must be ready at all times to defend oneself. Dexterity and alertness were part of the code.

Masaru evinced neither quality, but went down like a collapsed building. Sumie had to pull Akio off him. "What's the matter with you? Don't you know how to lose?"

"No. And I'm not going to learn because I don't intend to lose again."

"Oh, really?"

"Really. We robots are going to take over the world."

⛩

Masaru was coming up for the fateful university examinations. Once taken, the race for life is over. The person one will be at forty is determined by the outcome, his future salary, even his home and his wife.

The competition, assessing twelve years of schooling, cram school, and tutors, was bearing down on Masaru, who was feeling the weight of it. He stayed away from baseball games to look up references and took a book to bed with him nights, reading by flashlight.

Akio shook his head over this. He never studied in order to answer questions, but because he lived in the world and was entitled to all the knowledge that men had acquired. He looked on it as his inheritance, the only one he had. Mathematics was easy because he thought of it as a language. And Japanese was easy because he looked on it as a secret code. In a way it was, since only the Japanese themselves seemed able to master it. But having done so, other languages were almost rudimentary. "Why are things so easy for you?" Masaru had complained since elementary school.

By the time Akio was in middle school he had the answer. "It's all a go game. You play to win."

But Masaru didn't see it that way; to him it was drudgery. Akio attempted to put it in terms that would appeal to Masaru. "Take baseball. It would be pretty dull if all you saw was the guy up at bat, if you didn't know why he hit the ball or what the possibilities were. That's how it is in every subject."

Masaru shook his head. "What's baseball got to do with it?"

Since passing from elementary school to middle and then high school was predicated on a battery of tests, it had been Akio's job to act as Masaru's coach and get him creditably passed. He accomplished this where innumerable tutors had failed. *They* spoke in lofty terms and generalities, but *he* spoke to Masaru.

Juku school had not accomplished what it should. After an entire day at regular school with just minutes to catch a bite to eat, it was numbing to be sitting once more absorbing facts and memorizing figures, when outside the day called and the protean being inside Masaru wanted to run and stretch and participate in it. By the time *juku* school was finally out, it was evening and the two would make for Kabuki-cho in the Shinjuku district near the subway station to play the machines in tawdry Pachinko parlors, exulting in the glitzy lights and raucous bells and buzzers as they pulled levers. They usually finished the day by buying snacks and drinks at an army of colorful vending machines. Munching hot dogs and octous takoyaki they visited bookstores stocked with Hemingway, Shakespeare, and copies of Kawabata's *The Three Sisters*, as well as porn magazines. They ignored the classics and stood turning pages of beautiful nude blondes trussed up like turkeys for torturing. These females were depicted in fascinatingly contrived positions, hung from hooks, spread-eagled or ingeniously bound, raped by knives or any tool available.

The woman always suffered, the male seemed never able to revenge himself sufficiently for his dependence on her. Relief being temporary, a powerful sexual drive led him from one sadomasochistic experiment to another. It was essential throughout that the woman suffer, sometimes humiliation, sometimes agony, sometimes death. What she suffered was incidental, the important thing was that the vagina be acquiescent and the phallus rise triumphant.

The *Nikkan Gendai* was simply one of many tabloids. It sold a million copies daily and ran three hard-core porn serials, plus a cartoon strip featuring riotous adventures. On the back page were reviews of what amounted to houses of prostitution. They were rated in thinly veiled prose, as other, more legitimate papers would critique theater, opera or ballet.

The boys lacked the money to do any verification on their own, but they perused these articles attentively.

One evening they stood before a local movie house reading the posters when the show let out, and there in the crowd was Sumie. She was with girl friends. She waved and they giggled and whispered behind their hands. Then, with her friends egging her on—perhaps it was a dare—she came over to them. "How come you never call me, Masaru-san?"

"I—I've been busy," he stuttered.

"We could play tennis sometime."

"If he doesn't call you," Akio said, "I will."

"You have to grow up first, Akio."

"I seem to remember we were in the first grade together."

"I'm not referring to chronological age, but to maturity. Explain it to him sometime, will you, Masaru?"

Masaru laughed.

"Be sure now." And she was gone, blending into a flock of pastel dresses.

"She's an unusual girl, isn't she?" Masaru said, looking after her.

"She thinks she's a boy," Akio said. "She doesn't know what's going to happen to her."

Masaru looked at him sharply. "You don't believe all the crap you read, do you? There's such a thing as respect for women too, you know. And haven't you ever heard the word *love?*" He used the form *ai*, real love.

"You're in love, then, are you?" Akio asked.

The tone of voice was wasted on Masaru. "She's the kind of girl who could entertain guests at a *cha-do* party displaying one open flower. . . ."

"*La Dame aux Camélias,*" Akio scoffed.

During the rest of the week Akio was left to his own devices. When he wasn't cramming, Masaru practiced his serve and at the first opportunity asked his father why they didn't belong to the tennis club in Yokohama. He had never before invoked the authority latent in him as heir presumptive, and Akio had to fight his resentment.

When Masaru did spend time with him, it was to talk about Sumie or ask him to fix up a line of poetry so it scanned.

"Does she write haiku back to you?" Akio wanted to know.

"Of course. She is very talented. Do you think it would be possible to get hold of some not-so-well-known haiku that I could sign my name to? Working on them doesn't leave enough time to prepare for the exams."

"Good idea. It will impress her a lot more than this junk."

"You'll do it?"

"Of course. But it will take time to research little-known ones. You'll have to pay me."

"Oh."

"Come on, it's worth it."

They settled on a fee and Masaru asked curiously, "What are you going to do with the money?"

Akio fobbed him off.

When Masaru arranged to take Sumie walking, Akio arranged a visit to Azuma. He had hunted for her address and finally discovered it in Ryoko's sewing basket, along with a receipt book. Checking the ledger, he saw that an emerald ring had been added to the trinkets the girl had extracted from his uncle.

On the telephone she pretended not to remember him.

"The Hawaiian restaurant," he prompted.

"Oh, one of Shigeru's boys? You must be mad to call me. Of course you can't come."

"I'll be right over."

Azuma's six-mat apartment was in the Kabuki-cho section of Tokyo, lined with *snakku* bars and noodle shops where students caroused.

Azuma was dressed to go out. She answered the door with the question, "Have you any money?"

Akio reached in his jacket and, taking all his earnings out, put it in her hand.

She glanced down at the jumble of yen. "Is this all?"

"Yes."

"Well, let's go have a drink, then."

"I thought—"

"I know what you thought. Look, Akio, I don't give it away. This entitles you to drink with me. And when the money's gone, you're gone. Okay?" She closed and locked the door and then took his arm in a gesture he remembered, reminiscent of a Hollywood film star. They went downstairs and into the noisy neon-lighted streets blinking and shooting their colors into the night. Halfway down the block she turned into a place indistinguishable from the others. A blast of Western music hit them. He could barely see because of the cigarette smoke, but as his eyes grew used to the low lighting he made out forms gyrating on the dance floor. Azuma preceded him; she turned and gave him a big grin. "Like it?"

"Yeah, it's great."

She found a table almost on the dance floor. A girl with a female nude painted on both sides of her uniform, but in reverse, took their orders.

"Stop staring," Azuma said.

"Well, it is unusual."

"Let's dance."

He found himself pulled into a slow number, which he danced with his hand inside her blouse. "You feel good," he whispered.

"So I've been told." She pressed her torso against his, and did a couple of slow grinds.

"Again," he said.

She laughed.

"Do that again."

"Not likely. You're apt to come right here on the floor."

The beat changed, syncopated, charged, wild. Azuma threw back her head and, dancing in front of him, mimicked doing it.

"Let's go back to your place," Akio yelled into the din.

"Our drinks are ready." She led the way back to the table. He liked the idea of a table. As they sipped a frothy pink concoction in tall glasses, he found it easy to push the narrow crotch band to the side and work the target area.

They kept drinking and she put down more money than he had supplied her with.

"Have you ever done it before?" she asked him on the way back to her apartment.

"Of course."

She laughed. "Liar."

⛩

It wasn't earth-shaking, but it was a lot of fun, a frolic and a grasping of indecent parts, after which they lay panting, half on and half off the futon. When they caught their breath, Azuma helped him shower, washing him under cascades of soapy water, and they did it again. After which she threw his clothes at him and pushed him out the door.

Akio thought of his cousin who had gone with Sumie to Mount Takao to see the maple leaves in their fall foliage. He wondered if, on the way home, he had gotten up courage to perhaps hold her hand. He was glad he hadn't taken that detour.

He was especially glad when he saw how obsessed Masaru was. Akio concluded that the less a woman gave, the more power she possessed. Since Masaru lay next to him at night he could not escape listening to minute analyses of not only what Sumie said but her into-nation and Masaru's interpretation. His cousin would stop to ask Akio's opinion of how the romance was proceeding, and then rush on without waiting to hear it.

The family's membership in the Yokohama Tennis Club was under consideration and they had been issued guest cards. Masaru compro-mised with his conscience, leaving his studies one day a week to spend the afternoon playing tennis. After the first such excursion he whis-pered across their futons that he had seen his chance. As they walked back to the clubhouse he had pressed Sumie against the bushes by the edge of the lawn and kissed her. "Do you think," he asked Akio, "that I've damaged my chances with her?"

Akio smiled slightly, remembering his own more acrobatic con-quest. Respectable women must be an awful bore.

"I don't know. Was she angry?"

Masaru was uncertain. "She didn't push me away. That's a good sign, isn't it? I would call that a good sign, wouldn't you?"

"Masaru, go to sleep."

Masaru turned on his back and stared at the ceiling. "It's not really Sumie I'm worried about, it's her family."

Her family. Masaru was serious, then. Quite dispassionately Akio appraised his chances. Her father was on the board of directors at

Mitsui, a powerful man. The eldest son worked for MITI. The second son was in politics and the youngest at Tokyo University. He thought there was a son-in-law in the foreign service. To stack up against that, Masaru would need to pass his examination and be admitted to a top school.

"Sometimes," Masaru said, "I think I'm shooting too high."

"Not if you stop spending time at the tennis club! You have to buckle down."

"I know. Once I pass my exams I'll be in a better position. Then I'll be son-in-law material. I *will* pass them, there's no question is there, Akio? You've always gotten me through before."

"Go to sleep," Akio repeated. But he did not sleep. It occurred to him he was the *kami* of Masaru's future. Supposing, just supposing, he did not pass. He would, of course, no longer be considered a suitable prospect by Sumie's family. But it went beyond that.

If Masaru failed to gain a place at a university, Shigeru would not place him in charge of the company; he couldn't afford to. Following this line of reasoning, Akio grew cold under his blanket. If Masaru failed, he would not be appointed to an influential position, and for honor's sake he could not be hired in a lesser capacity. Heir or not, he would be out of the picture. Who would take his place? Obvious. Shigeru would be open to criticism if he chose anyone outside the family to run the company. The true heir would be getting back what should have been his.

What about Masaru? He would still get the house, plus whatever monies Shigeru had accumulated. This might be considerable because during the Korean War the Americans had placed large orders for the company's guidance system, the same they had imprisoned his grandfather for designing. They charged him as a war criminal but didn't mind using his invention, in fact paid very well for it. . . . Other times, he thought, other places. Look at the terrible losses suffered over the string of Pacific islands. Nobody wanted Corregidor or Iwo Jima today. They were only momentarily worth dying for. Afterward they were useless.

By placing trivia and speculation at the forefront of his brain, he kept from thinking about Masaru and the choice he had to make. There was an ancient saying, "A composed soul will last a thousand years." If that was true, his soul was doddering around on its last legs.

He was extremely jumpy and irritable. It seemed to him he was under continual surveillance, that his grandmother watched him constantly.

He visited Azuma again. She was not in, but he got the key to her apartment by saying he was her brother from Shimonoseki. He sat on a *zabuton* and read magazines. Women's magazines were filled with pictures of deformed babies and aborted fetuses. He studied the nude body of a murdered prostitute with interest, and glanced at mangled corpses resulting from a head-on crash. A coroner's photograph of a suicide presented a gruesome sight; the head was some feet away from the body owing to the bizarre method he had chosen of exiting this life, placing his neck on the railroad track of the Tokyo express.

When Azuma finally came home they had a fight. She let him know she had been having afternoon sex at the Sanogawa plant office with his uncle.

"I don't want you to see that bastard again!" he shouted.

Azuma laughed. "Listen to the precocious fifteen-year-old. Are you going to pay for the rent with your allowance?"

Akio stared at her with all the old fury. She backed away from the *oni* she saw in his face.

With difficulty Akio turned his fury into speech. "Okay. Okay. He's the one on top of you now. But in five years—five years—he'll be out. I'll have taken it all—you, the factory. He'll have zero."

Azuma knew better than to laugh or even reply. Besides, she believed him. Some power in this boy had broken out and taken control. They had sex and he asked her to do things even she had not done. It was exciting and she felt revved up. At the same time an instinct told her to watch out for this kid, to go slow. But there was something titillating about the whisper of fear. "You can forget about Shigeru," she told him. "He's just the guy who pays the rent."

But he refused to back down. "Five years," he said again. "You can mark it on your calendar."

Returning home by way of the high school, he thought he recognized the figure on the tennis court. Pressing his nose against the chain-link fence, he watched Masaru. The equipment at the school for extracurricular activity was nil. Masaru played without a net or balls. Actually, what he was doing was performing a pantomime, stretching his racket high, employing a backhand stroke. An inner rhythm and grace suffused everything he did; it was just more pronounced on the court. God, he's beautiful, Akio thought, loving him for it, hating him for it. As he watched, Masaru shifted his racket and rushed the net.

"Hey!" Akio called.

Masaru looked over at him, wiped his forehead with his sleeve, and came to the fence with a loping motion.

"I thought I marked some stuff for you to go over."

"That's right."

"Well, then, what are you doing here?"

"I finished early."

"The man who goes after two rabbits gets none," Akio quoted at him.

Masaru walked along his side of the fence to the gate and joined Akio.

"So, did you look over the chapter?" Akio asked.

"I did. But there's so much material it's not possible to memorize everything."

This was the moment, although he didn't realize it, when Akio made his decision. "I will go over it and mark the questions sure to be on the test."

The way was now open to marking those things that would *not* be on the test. But the mind can hide from itself and fool itself, and Akio was not yet ready to admit to himself what he planned to do.

Before buckling down in earnest, Akio proposed that they make a pilgrimage to the Tenmangu Shrine in Kyushu, which memorialized the great Michizane, a teacher revered as a god for the love of learning he imparted to his students and the high regard with which, because of his influence, the Imperial Court came to look upon the world of academe. It was a widely held belief that a visit to the Tenmangu Shrine brought good luck in the university entrance exams.

Masaru asked why they couldn't visit the Yushima Tenjin. "It's also in memory of Michizane, and it's right here in Tokyo."

"There's more merit," Akio said loftily, "in making a journey."

Momoko protested mildly that it would be better if Masaru spent the time in study. But Akio reminded her that Zen teaches there are many paths. If his cousin decided to walk this one, he would walk it with him.

Momoko sighed. She was a million miles away from understanding her son. Akio, she felt, was her worst failure. She didn't know exactly why she felt this. He was bright, well-spoken, handsome, a son she should be proud of. And she was proud of those qualities, but that was the *omote* side of him. He kept himself on a leash, she was sure of it, sure the *oni* still lurked in him. She was waiting for something to happen, something terrible. But she'd no idea what it was.

The shrine was an overnight train journey. By the time they reached their destination they were glad to stretch and stop at a wayside booth for breakfast. The plum blossoms that lined the entrance to the shrine were in bloom. They entered and put two hundred-yen notes in the box. Pulling the prayer rope, they summoned the *kami* by bell tones and, bowing deeply, begged the spirit of the great teacher to look with favor on Masaru's effort.

On leaving the shrine Masaru said, "If I fail I will eat raw fugu fish and let the gods decide whether I live or die."

Akio nodded; there was not much danger of dying from the toxic organs of the fugu, which were meticulously cut out.

Rain pelted them lightly, and on the way back Masaru talked interminably of Sumie. He had seen her in kimono at a family celebration with her hair Japanese style, swept up, full and high in front. She moved soundlessly on velvet feet. And her kimono held splashes of cherry blossoms and opening buds. Clouds of good omen, turtles, and cranes were folded into her obi. Her beauty was like the slender stalk of iris she arranged for the *tokonoma*.

When they reached home, Akio got out Masaru's books and his own writing materials, which he placed at his elbow. From the instant his pen touched paper, he did not hesitate, but wrote fluently. His hand had known what it must do. But who had given the hand its command?

Zen taught: No hindrance is tolerated in seeking the light within yourself. He marked the passage that stated: Every obstacle must be cleared from your path. If you meet Buddha on your way, kill him!

Every evening Akio continued laying his false trail. And Masaru faithfully copied the material he had written out, committing it to memory.

How could he be such a fool? Akio thought angrily. It was bitter to watch as he entangled himself and struggled. He was already a corpse and didn't know it. Into Akio's mind flashed the story Shigeru had told of the dead officer who completed his report. He put such peripheral thoughts out of his mind.

But thoughts of Masaru were not so easily disposed of. Akio was increasingly angry at his denseness in not catching on. Why didn't he realize what was happening? How could he remain unsuspecting? For a while he was convinced Masaru would come to him and say, "What the fuck are you doing?" But he didn't. He went on studying with pained concentration the superfluous, superficial passages he had indicated.

· What torture. Akio could hardly stand it. He felt like screaming out loud as he had when he was seven and they had taken him to the Shinto priest at the end of a rope.

In the circle of obligation his family must come ahead of Masaru. Besides, there were levies against Masaru:

1. He had supplanted him as heir cousin.
2. He had rescued him countless times from beatings, thereby making him owe unwarranted *on*.
3. He had humiliated him by beating him at go in front of Sumie.
4. He had been preferred by Sumie.

These insults must be redressed. Akio must act to restore his name and family. He owed this to the Oka fighter.

That evening Akio went into the garden and, taking the path to the *koi* pond, knelt and sifted the dirt with his hands until he was certain he had the right spot. He began digging. He shivered and his hackles rose. It was a desecration, like digging up a body.

At last he came to the small package buried eight years ago. He bowed to the *National Geographic* before unwrapping the decayed and rotting cloth. The oiled paper was intact, however, and the pages flew open to the article on the Oka bomb. He stared at it, although it was too dark to read. What a fuss the missing sake cups had made. Fusa swore they had been stolen, while his mother turned the kitchen upside down to find them. He lifted them, cleaning off the dirt with his fingers, and held them up to discern their blue and white pattern. . . . Brothers. Arrows bound together.

In a sudden gesture he smashed the two *sakazuki* against a rock. Still on his knees he began groping in front of him, collecting the shards, which he wrapped with the magazine for reburying. His face was stern, but his hands shook as he covered the shallow grave.

He stole back to his bed. "Father," he told the Oka pilot as he lay sleepless, "you were Shimpu. Your son shall not be less, I smashed the sake cups." He could not sleep, but created pictures of what would happen when Masaru finally knew; at first the *ura* of his heart would take in only the fact that Sumie was lost to him. Before he learned to accept that, the rest would come flooding in on him. There would be no old and honorable company, no position of worth. He would be relegated to a second-class life. He would not be in want, he would get by, even marry, but not a woman of family. He would be transparent, a transparent man. People would look through him as though he weren't there.

At this dour picture, Akio began arguing with himself. He would climb high enough for both of them. He would see to it that Masaru was given an ambiguous title of some kind so there would be no shame.

He couldn't do anything about Sumie, of course. Her family would never permit marriage with a man who had failed the university examination, a man with no prospects.

If he could only make Masaru see that while human feeling was charming, it was a digression. All women had the same equipment. Some were better tempered, some better to look at. But the real difference was in the imaginings with which you invested them, the fantasy.

One did not bother to make dreams about a girl like Azuma. But he recognized it was more complicated with women of good families. They were cultivated like flowers, trained in the arts of *cha-no-yu* and *ikebana*, and often music as well. Sumie played the piano and was schooled in Japanese history. She handled the language with subtlety, and she knew English. It was easy to imagine she had more dimension than a simple girl like Azuma. But it was illusion. Masaru thought of Sumie as the female counterpart of himself. It would be good to wean him from these extravagant notions, replace them with a sense of reality. Of course, when the dream smashed, they would no longer be friends, and that would shadow both their lives. He even considered the possibility that his cousin might kill him. But the picture of the deed would not form. Akio might kill. Not Masaru.

When he considered his own prospects, Akio was dazzled. He had always known that when his turn came for the university competition he would do well. Where he had been limited was in not having a ready-made position to step into. Without this, the best he could hope for was to be a salaryman, catch the commuter train at 6:00 A.M., wear a company badge, learn a company song, work ten or twelve hours with a break for calisthenics and a pep talk. Then evenings drinking with the team—beer and sake followed by brandy and sake. Reeling home for four hours sleep. The prospect was unattractive.

Now everything was different. He would start high and go higher. His career was assured. His future included any pinnacle he dared reach for. He would be *jinbutsu*, a leader of men with a well-placed wife, someone like Sumie with the best possible connections.

He was not mistaken, his grandmother was watching him. Perhaps the old woman, closer to the grave than most, had powers of perception that others did not. Akio felt uncomfortable and avoided her.

In the middle of the night he sat bolt upright. Sweat stood at the follicles of his hair. The Buddha taught: Man is responsible for the most marginal consequences of his acts. It was impossible to guess what the expanding circles would touch. All effects could not be seen, perhaps not most.

This was a sobering thought, and for a while he contemplated turning back. There was still time. It was still possible to copy out and instill in Masaru the correct passages, those he would need to pass.

Masaru again surprised him with his indifference to geometry.

"Masaru," he exclaimed, at the end of patience. "Today, roads and bridges spring from fountain pens that know geometry."

Masaru shrugged. "Come on," he said wearily, "let's get on with it."

"You should practice *shushin*, moral training, to prepare for what lies ahead."

Masaru looked up sharply. "You mean in case I fail?"

"Yes."

Masaru seized him by the shoulders. "I can't fail. You'll see to that. I can't, you won't let me."

Akio pulled himself roughly from Masaru's grasp. "In the end it rests with you."

"Then I'm lost. I don't understand any of it."

"That's absurd. You need to concentrate. Don't depend on me or *juku* school, or anything outside yourself."

"Fuck you," Masaru said. "You're trying to get out of helping me."

"If you choose me," Akio said, "then you choose me."

"I chose you long ago."

"You must choose me again."

"Okay. I choose you. Are you satisfied?"

Akio went into the garden for water contemplation. On the way he passed his mother.

"I am happy you are helping your cousin prepare for the examinations," she told him.

Akio smiled crookedly at her.

Momoko sighed. Why did her son hide his heart from her? Brushing past her, Akio sat on the stone bench by the pond and stared at its dark surface and half-seen depths. After a long time he thought he discerned the ideograph for "man": powerful in battle.

Hour after hour and day after day Masaru plodded through the material Akio set before him. He took to wearing an *omamori* under his shirt. Its good-luck characters pressed against his skin. He gave himself only one break from his studies, and this was the afternoon he was slated to play in the men's singles at the Yokohama Tennis Club. They were now members in good standing, and the whole family attended.

Masaru had perfected his backhand and covered the court with amazing agility. He followed up a powerful American-style serve with a deep cross-court shot. He's beautiful, Akio thought again, and yelled encouragement from the stands. Sumie was there too, flushed with excitement. She followed every movement and also called out to Masaru.

Masaru won the match, and everyone crowded around with congratulations. But it was Sumie's words he drank up, and they went off together for refreshments.

Akio caught his mother's glance resting on him. It was full of concern. She thought he was jealous. He wished it were such a simple emotion. He had an impulse to rush after his cousin and ask forgiveness.

Which only proved he had not forged his warrior's spirit in a pure enough flame. Besides, it wasn't his fault. It was a decision made by Masaru quite freely.

The latter part of February was examination time. The home shrine was decked with fresh white streamers and a small wood plaque bearing Yasue's name. The women called good luck down on their house with incense and offerings.

Masaru purified himself with fasting and gave up tennis. He did not watch baseball on television, and got on Akio's nerves by ringing the bell before the small Buddha on the portable *butsudan* whenever he passed it. As a further pledge of wholeheartedness he gave up seeing Sumie until after the examinations.

Akio watched Masaru's renunciations cynically. He thought of Western cultures and their belief in Satan. Satan was a great luxury. One could heap everything on the devil. . . . How convenient. But unfortunately no Satan existed in Japan, and each person was responsible for everything in his life. While Westerners are born in sin, the Japanese is born pure. There is no excuse if he doesn't remain that way.

Reason told him his decision was both good and honorable. Why, then, did he feel so bad, why were the days a torment to him? Why could he not bear to look at Masaru? Why did he avoid him? He had every right to take his proper place, indeed he was obligated to. *Ko to* his father demanded it, and *ko* to the whole male line from whom he descended, stretching forward to generations yet to be, to his son and his son's son.

Still he found it hard to watch Masaru. As farmers at New Year's clean and bless their tools in Shinto ceremonies, so Masaru sharpened and prepared his pencils and erasers. Many times during the day he approached the *butsudan* reverently. He was following the way of the arrow and the horse, training as *rikishi* train, repressing his feelings, making his mind and his body pure. He bathed only in cold water, ate sparingly, sat many hours in contemplation, practiced cold austerity, and rang the damned *butsudan* bell.

Akio watched this. And he saw its futility. It wasn't going to help, nothing could help. Masaru had not studied the questions that would be asked. So what did that say about prayers and the way of *bushido*? Quite plainly it said . . . what shit.

The day before the examinations, something happened that tore Akio's soul out of him. Masaru spent most of the night attempting *satori*, and early in the morning touched Akio to wake him and indicated he was to follow him. Akio was instantly alert and his senses uneasy. His cousin led him into the garden, to the pond where his mother died. It had in recent years been stocked with *koi*, which flashed and dartled many colors.

On the stone bench were two cups, one empty and one of sake.

Masaru stared at him intently. "I dug up the old ones, but the weight of the earth shattered them."

Akio returned his look steadily.

"It doesn't matter. I am dedicating myself today in the same way as when we took our oath."

"What do you mean?"

"Our soldiers in the Pacific War often conducted their funerals before going into battle, promising themselves to fight until they were dead. I have elected to do the same. I look on the examination as the ultimate battle of my life. If I am unfortunate enough to fail, I do not wish to survive the failure."

"No!" The word slipped out; Akio didn't know he had said anything.

"This forces me to win a place for myself. It will force me to succeed. And so I cannot renege, I call on you to witness my dedication."

"Wait. No, this is wrong."

"Wrong?"

"I mean, I think you have twisted things, Masaru. I don't think you should do this."

"Why? Do you doubt that I will succeed? You've prepared me."

"No, of course not. But nothing's certain. It's possible that . . . that . . ."

"I might fail? That's the reason I'm dedicating myself. So I can't." He filled the second cup with water from the pond where Yasue had died, and stood a long time staring into it, looking for a sign. Having found his soul in the water, he set down that cup and raised the one of sake, holding it out to Akio. "You are my witness, Akio. I pledge my life to succeed. If I fail, it is forfeit."

Akio fell to his knees and beat his forehead against the ground.

Masaru lifted him up and handed him the cup. "Drink."

"I can't."

"Drink, you are my witness."

Akio took the cup in both hands, as though it were too heavy for one.

Masaru drank in his turn. "This is between us, cousin."

If this were a game of go, Akio would have thrown his stones on the ground and conceded defeat. But in this game they themselves were the stones. He did not have to be afraid, as he had been once, that he was a pawn in another's game. It was a different fear now that settled over him; he feared it was he himself who controlled the pieces. He had made a move that could not be taken back.

From that time until he left for the *todai* examination, Masaru was like one in a trance. He had decided to take the test as though already dead. That was the best way to face the ordeal. The dead are unable to feel. Only afterward would success or failure be borne in on him.

He returned home to wait for the posting of the results. The family also waited. They treated him as though he were ill. Everyone was excessively polite and thoughtful. His favorite food was served, his tennis racket restrung, and his opinion sought by his father, who usually ignored him. No one asked how it had gone; that would have been a breach of form, opening the door to bad luck. Besides, he didn't seem to know how he had done. The examination was a blur in his mind. He had been numb the entire time.

The respect rules within the family were carefully obeyed. The pretense was that a favorable outcome was a foregone conclusion. But even that optimistic possibility was not verbalized. Masaru kept to himself, wrote in his diary, did some reading, watched television, and in general lay around.

Yoriko plied him with tea, that universal panacea. She had unearthed a treasured volume containing an ancient treatise on tea translated from the Chinese. On an almost transparent sheet of paper tucked into its pages, Noboru had copied the paragraphs that enumerated the essential properties of tea: manganese, which kills microbes, and iron, which purifies the blood. It went on to describe the alkaline base that counteracts acid found in fish and poultry. The conclusion of the article was that tea was conducive, indeed vital, to good health. Yoriko nodded with satisfaction. She had always known this, but it pleased her enormously that Chinese erudition agreed with her. More than that, it pleased her that Noboru had again reached out to her, as he did in every important juncture of her life. It almost seemed to her that she had had a friendly talk with him and he had told her things would work out for the good of the *ie*.

Masaru listened to her with patience, accepted the tea, accepted everything.

Akio avoided home. He too was at the end of the school year and taking examinations at his level. He did not take them as one dead, but in the spirit of combat. Yet the gusto of other years was absent. Though he responded combatively, only part of his mind was engaged. He walked under the cloud of his decision, waiting for Masaru to know. It would happen any hour now, any minute.

His plan was to behave casually and not let Masaru guess that he gave any credence to the dedication he had been called to witness. At the same time he must not allow his cousin out of his sight. In the spirit of *tatemae*, Masaru might carry out his threat and attempt to destroy himself.

How was it possible that a right-seeming action could result in the death of his brother? The expanding ripple spread.

The question was, could a person be watched every hour of every day . . . and for how long? If Masaru was determined, then at best he could wage a delaying action.

But he saw hope in the fact that at seventeen you wanted to seize the world with mind and body, wanted to walk it, breathe it, climb it, sail it. You wanted to worship and violate, throw yourself into its oceans, lie on its grasses, see, touch, feel, have, rape . . . test your body and your mind. At seventeen it was before you, all of it.

Masaru couldn't throw it away, couldn't blot it out before he had tried himself. It would be not a suicide but an abortion, because he hadn't yet lived. Still, *bushido* teaches that the way of the warrior is revealed in the act of dying and that the instinct for life is not to be trusted. When the equinoctial winds of disaster blow, the ancient moral training of *shushin* recommended that too much importance should not be attached to life, and when there is a decision to be made between life and death, one should choose death, for those who cling to their lives lose self.

Akio wrestled with these concepts. "Think of your death constantly," the fourteenth-century hero Masashige advised. "If it is well done, it can validate your life." His father had known that, and Masaru seemed to sense it as well. It was part of his nobility and greatness of soul. But Akio could not surmount the illusion of life and self. He would not let go of Masaru. He was his brother. In spite of the broken cups, he refused to lose him. If he had to watch his cousin waking and sleeping, then he would. He wouldn't let it happen. He couldn't get along without Masaru.

A day later world time, and just hours later Japan time, Masaru read the posted lists. A loser in these nationwide competitions is said to wear a mask of shame. But Masaru kept any sign of defeat from his face. In fact, if one were to read his face it would almost seem that he had won.

He adopted a brittle manner, inviting himself to join his father's drinking.

Akio sat quietly in a corner and watched his cousin get drunk with Shigeru. Kenji passed back and forth in the hall, looking in on them. Although he drank a great deal, Masaru seemed unable to become drunk. Akio waited until Shigeru stumbled off to bed and then approached him. He hadn't meant to but he started to cry.

Masaru looked at him, and only with an effort seemed to recall why he might be standing there crying.

"I'm sorry, Masaru."

Masaru gave him a long invasive look, penetrating him.

Akio felt he had been run through with a sword. . . . He knows.

A spasm passed over his cousin's face. "You're smart, Akio, but you're not smart enough for two. So forget it."

"I'll make it up to you."

Masaru laughed. "I can't count how many answers I got wrong, but I know how many I got right. Want to hear? 'Category: late-eighteenth-century novel.' Answer: *Yomihon*. 'Category: comic novel.' Answer: *Kokkeibon*. 'Category: the genre novel.' Answer: *Sharebon*. And one or two others." He got up abruptly. "I'm turning in."

Akio returned to his corner. His eyes were soul-sick. He was afraid to go to bed. He was afraid of the sequences his thoughts and dreams might play out. His grandmother passed him with a small smile on her face. She whispered, "So you listened to your old grandmother after all."

Akio caught his breath sharply at what she said. On her return trip through the room he was ready with his reply. He said evenly and under his breath, "There is a mountain, Obasuteyama, for throwing away old women. Go to that mountain, Grandmother."

Air hissed through Yoriko's teeth and she put out a hand to steady herself. "Akio, what are you saying?"

"Please die, Grandmother. It is best that you die."

She raised an arm as though warding off a blow, and her neatly piled hair fell down in gray coils. She scuttled away on padded feet.

A little later Momoko came up to him in his corner. "What did you say to your grandmother? She is very upset."

"I don't believe," Akio said carefully, "that my tone was offensive."

His mother continued to hover uncertainly. "Akio . . ."

"Yes, Mother?"

"You did your best, of course, for Masaru?"

"I did my best in following *ko.*"

Momoko sighed. "He worked so hard and did so poorly. I don't understand it."

"Don't upset yourself, Mother. I'm sure everything will be all right."

Although far from convinced of this, she too went upstairs.

Akio placed his futon beside Masaru's and took up the watch.

He understood his cousin. The mask of light-heartedness protected him from the kindly sympathy of the family. Of course he smiled, of course he got drunk. What else could he do?

He woke several times to make sure Masaru was beside him. Then he woke and the mat next to his was empty and, when he put his hand out, cold.

He knew where Masaru was, and his mind was there instantly . . . the garden pond where his mother died, where he took his oath. To him it was the most holy place on earth.

Akio found him face down in the water. He waded in and, putting his arms around him, lifted his head and dragged him out. He laid him on the moss and turned his face, closing his nose with his fingers and bringing his own head level with Masaru's. He breathed into his mouth rhythmically, breathing for both of them, stopping only to push against his ribs.

Water was expelled in a sudden rush, and Masaru moaned slightly. Taking heart, Akio continued his efforts. When he was certain Masaru lived, he called for help.

The family straggled into the garden, shocked, sleepy, not immediately taking in what had happened. It was Momoko who called the doctor and an ambulance.

Akio tried to anticipate Masaru's reaction to being alive. He thought he would accept it. He had kept his pledge, and would now accept that his destiny lay in life.

The news from the hospital was disturbing. Masaru had drowned. Air had been cut off to the brain, no one knew for how many seconds. It was too early, they were told, to assess his condition.

Then came a further report. It was carefully explained to the family that, owing to oxygen deprivation, Masaru was brain-damaged.

Akio discounted the doctors. If his brother lived, he was Masaru and nothing could change that. He went to see him. Masaru was sitting up in a neatly made bed, staring in front of him.

There was a sudden thudding in Akio's chest, as though the wall itself had fallen into the cavity. "Masaru . . ." he said.

Slowly Masaru turned. His face held a puzzled expression. "I know you." Those were his words.

Akio fell on him, shaking him by the shoulders. "It's me, don't play games. Don't play games, please, Masaru. Please. Be all right, do you hear me?" He sobbed and sobbed and Masaru, lifting his hand, patted him.

1965

In the spring of 1965, when he was twenty years old, Akio's mistress gave birth to a daughter. When Miko was born, Azuma farmed her out. Akio was not pleased at the arrangement. He didn't like giving up anything that was his, and he resolved to rectify the situation as soon as possible. He planned to do this through Shigeru.

Under Shigeru's management the factory was retooled with a more modern electronics division. The rapidity with which the company grew ensured the bank's willingness to lend large amounts.

For several years Akio found time to assist his uncle, even while he still took classes. He worked in all sections of the plant and didn't consider any of it menial or beneath him as heir cousin.

Of particular interest to him was the bookkeeping. Once money was generated he liked to follow it, see where it ended up and what it contributed to the family.

It didn't take Akio long to be aware of some of the shoddy practices that went on. He discovered that Shigeru had a tendency to skimp on the quality of parts. If he could make use of a fitting from somewhere else, it didn't bother him if it was of an inferior alloy. As a result, problems kept cropping up. Akio didn't bring any of this to Shigeru's attention, he didn't criticize, he just made mental notes.

He himself perceived a much larger picture. From toys and electronics it would be a relatively easy matter to expand into robotics, for which there was a new, rapidly growing market.

Shigeru, he decided, was a plodder who didn't look beyond his nose, and whose greed for cutting corners he saw as a weakness. Akio sensed that time was running out for his uncle, and all he had to do was wait. He was not wrong in this assessment.

Guidelines were handed down by MITI, after a particularly tragic accident involving the death of children. All factories were henceforth required to follow new fire regulations.

Shigeru complained vociferously about the new law, which he felt had been promulgated solely to cut into his profits. Akio, listening to this tirade, said, "If I were you, I would implement these new rules as far as your main products are concerned. But they're not going to check everything, certainly not the smaller, cheaper items."

Shigeru didn't reply, but he looked thoughtful. A few days later he brought the subject up again. "I wonder if you're right about our secondary line. . . ."

Akio said nothing, he didn't need to. Shigeru was a fish, unaware that it already swam in a pot.

But when the inspectors closed down the Sanogawa factory, Shigeru reacted not like a silent fish, but like a stuck pig, bellowing to Ryoko, to Yoriko, to Momoko, to anyone in fact who would listen to him, that it had been a mistake, an oversight. He had intended to comply throughout his inventory; he thought he *had* complied. He begged Akio to intervene for him.

Akio intervened, but not for him. He was on track and on schedule. He was selected by the board to take over the entire operation. There was not a dissenting vote. The seven-five-three ceremony that initiated him into the ranks of the Sanogawa males was nothing as heady as this. He had initiated himself into his own manhood, set his own course, and tasted the result. The tempo of his life stepped up, slipped into high gear. From now on nothing would stand in his way, nothing impede him. "Lose to win," his father's mother used to tell him. How simple the childhood formula: he had humbled himself before his uncle, accepted whatever menial position Shigeru placed him in, and lost face before his family. It didn't matter. He had kept his eyes on the goal. And won. The exhilaration he felt oxygenated his blood and lent zest to all he did. Shigeru's tumble from control illustrated the old adage, "Feeling secure is the greatest danger."

His uncle was plucking at his arm. To his query, "Well, how did it go? Did you change their minds? Is it all right?" Akio replied almost indifferently, "It's all right."

"Oh." Shigeru took out a handerchief and began mopping his forehead. "Well, that's good. A small infraction to make such a fuss about. But it's okay now? You're sure?"

"I'm sure. I'm sure because I was put in charge. I'm running things now."

Shigeru stared at him. He tried to say something, but he only spluttered.

"Don't worry," Akio spoke offhandedly, "I'll find something for you to do. I'll keep you on."

Shigeru seemed struck dumb. He didn't even protest. He muttered to himself for a while and then looked at Akio with dawning comprehension. He saw the route that had been plotted. "You did this. You!" he cried.

Akio regarded him mildly, his eyebrows lifted a bit.

"You advised me to flout the new law."

"I'm inexperienced, Uncle, you should have known better than to listen to me."

"And now the factory is yours. You stole it!"

"I could hardly have stolen what belongs to me."

"You stole it!" Shigeru bellowed again, and came at him as though to strike him. Akio didn't even bother to raise his arm. He knew Shigeru would not attack him.

The fight broke out again, this time as a coda between Ryoko and Yoriko. Neither knew exactly what had happened, or what the facts of the case were. Ryoko simply complained that Akio had taken advantage of her husband. Shigeru had placed him in a position of trust, and he had betrayed him.

Yoriko was incensed. "If Shigeru is in trouble, it's his own fault and has nothing to do with Akio."

Momoko did not take sides in this squabble, for it could not be denied that the games Akio played were no longer childish. He no longer threw to displace a tile, but to displace his uncle. He had taken over the factory. She understood why he had been so meek in accepting the hard terms and small pay of his apprenticeship. "The toy factory was your uncle's whole life," she remonstrated with her son. "It's a blow I doubt he'll recover from."

Akio answered her with a bit of sophistry. "We all have the seeds of our own destruction in us."

"Are you saying it was his greed?"

"I'm saying that the five years are up."

"I don't understand."

It wasn't necessary that she should. Azuma understood. She watched his marriage to the beautiful Sumie on television, diluting her gin with tears.

Akio had thought about the possibility of marrying Sumie for years. Besides being attracted to her, he thought her presence in the house might stir some response in Masaru, and at that point memory would flood in. He made a solemn vow to his cousin. But it produced no change whatever in Masaru, who didn't recognize anyone but Akio.

He's right on schedule, Azuma thought bitterly. The marriage enabled him to pyramid toys, electronics, robotics, real estate, into phenomenal success, into the miracle of Japan's trade conquest.

BOOK
TWO

1989

A HAWAIIAN SUN WAS SINKING AND DEFORMING AS IT SANK INTO THE ocean off Waimanalo's white sand beach on the east side of the island of Oahu. It silhouetted two men sitting on a terrazzo patio lush with mangoes, papayas, and the heavy fronds of the frangipani. The roots of the tree ran along the ground like the humped back of some jungle creature. In the house several yards distant from where the men sat, lights came on and there was the sound of voices, but on the patio a hushed silence continued.

The men had a go board open between them and were intent on the game. But only one man moved the stones. He placed a black on one of the three hundred sixty-one intersections, then countered with *takamoku kakari*, the most vigorous response. The variations of the game are said to be more than the number of atoms existing in the universe. It is a game that can be played on many levels. It is both art and philosophy.

The game played by Akio and Masaru had continued for almost thirty years. Invested with ritual, it was something more . . . an affirmation. Each time Akio moved for his cousin it was a statement of faith. One day Masaru would reach out and move for himself.

Of the two, Akio had changed least; his features held a rigidly inflexible cast. Masaru watched the board with a foolish grin on his face. He loved this period at the end of day that Akio devoted to him. He relished being told that he had won. For while Akio did well by his own stones, he employed a stunning mastery in placing the black for Masaru.

Masaru's grin was foolish but it was happily foolish. Akio never smiled and no one would call him happy. Although he owned this palatial beachfront home, as well as hotels, office buildings, a bank, a robotics installation, and a newly acquired high-definition TV plant, he still kept the old home in Tokyo as his principal residence. To this he added another in Malibu, and a third in Beverly Hills. These he considered combat decorations.

Akio customarily reserved this hour at dusk to go over his holdings and plot new coups, whose consequences he played out on the go board. The goal behind other goals was to win a return of Japan's Northern Territories, appropriated by the USSR in 1945. Known as the Kuril Islands to the entire world, Akio doggedly refused to call them anything but Chishima. He had focused on these barren islands because they were of little or no material value. He equated them with his father's death, which also had no material value. But each had hidden values: in his father's case, a strong moral precedent; in the matter of the islands, they had been the staging area for the Pearl Harbor task force. Today, the modes of such conquests had changed. The swords of the samurai were replaced by the spreadsheets of double-entry bookkeeping. To put Clausewitz's maxim into modern terms: "Politics is nothing but the continuation of war by other means." Toward this end Akio manipulated his black stones and his white.

His power base was in his own country, but, capitalizing on the strong yen, he'd taken his investments offshore to the four "little dragons," Korea, Taiwan, Hong Kong, and Singapore. Next he moved on California. He had a timetable and he adhered to it. The weak American dollar facilitated his acquisitions, resulting in more profits than even he anticipated. He used this considerable leverage to invest in microelectronics, which he dubbed the rice of the new technology.

When he stood on the promontory at Pearl Harbor, looking down at the drowned *Arizona* with her entombed sailors, he exulted. It had been given to him and his generation to add a new chapter to World War II. He attacked with fresh cohorts, money. His generals were engineers who "reverse-engineered" patent after American patent.

He fortified his position with a ceaseless supply of yen. It was a formidable approach. The American lines wavered before him and broke rank. The retreat turned into a rout in 1985, when Washington, to make their exports more attractive, sent the yen into the stratosphere. That was the point at which Japan became a heavyweight global investor and lender. The trade war of the last decade was only a preliminary skirmish. He was now poised to launch a financial war. The ten top banks in the world were Japanese. Besides cornering eighty-five billion in U.S. securities, buying thirty percent of all U.S. Treasury bonds, and owning one and a half billion dollars' worth of New York real estate and 4.6 percent of prime property in Los Angeles, Japanese investments in Hawaii had reached the saturation point.

The game didn't end there. There were more stones to place. It was the Occupation all over again, but now it was the Japanese who bankrolled the increasing U.S. debt. With Japan's ninety-billion-dollar trade surplus it was a candy store. And Akio was constantly adding to his shopping list.

Money was not what Akio was after. There was a Shinto shrine on the roof of his office building in Tokyo, and he had another built on his Waimanalo property. He visited it regularly and, bowing, pulled the bell rope. "Father, I fulfill my obligation," he said to the frightened boy sealed into the body of a bomb . . . a boy younger than his own daughter, Miko, as young as Juro.

Working through MITI and the big four—Mitsui, Mitsubishi, Sumitomo, and Yasuda—in Washington, D.C., Akio's representatives outspent the other PAC contingents. There were enough congressmen with yawning pockets to see that his interests were served. Even senators were beginning to dance to his tune.

This financial blitz only set the stage for his true objective, the return of the Northern Territories. Territory was what it was all about. His father had given his life for the integrity of Japan. But it rested with him to see that the islands were returned.

Negotiations had reached a delicate stage, settling into a tricornered ploy involving three nations, the kind of situation he knew how to exploit. Each player wanted something one of the others had. A tempting position for one experienced in go.

The Russians held the Northern Territories. The Americans held
a patent on a silent submarine propeller but were unable to go ahead
with it, as the lathe-cut patterns required Japanese computer-controlled
fabrication. He proposed to finesse the situation by having the U.S.
underwrite the sale of wheat to the USSR at a substantially reduced
price and dangle "most-favored nation" status as a possibility, on condition she return the islands. The payoff to the Americans being the
milling of their propeller blades.

Akio chuckled to himself. In a way it was too easy, like playing
go with an adversary who doesn't know the game, let alone the moves.

This larger strategy entailed a number of smaller decisions. He
had sent his son, Juro, to California to keep tabs on the on-going
operation at the Toshiba plant. But the communications received from
the boy were cursory, superficial, and, to his mind, quite unsatisfactory.
He admitted to himself that it had probably been a mistake to entrust
anyone as young and inexperienced as Juro with so vital a mission.
But he hoped that responsibility would grow him up. He could not
help comparing his son with himself; at twenty he had controlled three
companies. But he should have realized this was too important to
entrust to a novice. In any matter of consequence there were many
opposing elements working beneath the surface. One had to be vigi-
lant, and he had decided to double-team the project by sending his
daughter, Miko, to California. She would stay with her brother at the
Malibu place or, if she preferred, the *pied-à-terre* in Beverly Hills. Miko
was older than her half brother, had graduated from Stanford, and
understood the hearts and minds of Americans as he never could. She
was Azuma's girl, born of his early indiscretion and adopted. She had
been carefully reared, and now held a respected position in his operations. However, Akio considered her too much the modern woman.
She seemed far too Westernized to him, and he suspected there was a
wayward element in her. His son, on the other hand, was all that a
Japanese young man of good family should be, well educated, intelli-
gent, and obedient. His only handicap was youth, but Miko could be
counted on to look after him. Akio leaned forward to place another
stone.

He pressed the buzzer that summoned the closest servant. "Telephone," he said when the man appeared.

It was brought. He typed in Miko's code number, and the automatic memory kicked in. "Miko, how are you? Can you talk?"

In her smart Tokyo apartment, Miko covered the mouthpiece. She was not alone in the large, tumbled bed. "It's my father," she mouthed exaggeratedly so the young man would not betray his presence. He threw back his head and laughed in pantomime. She tossed a pillow at him. "Of course I can talk. Is everything all right?"

They spoke in Japanese, he preferred it. Miko preferred English.

"I need you in California," Akio told his daughter.

"When?"

"At once."

There was a pause at her end.

"Well?"

"Of course."

"I have you booked on a seven-thirty ANA flight. You'll have both the Malibu and Beverly Hills accommodations at your disposal."

"Lovely."

"Kenji will drive you. He has sealed instructions and your ticket."

"Fine."

"And Miko—"

"Yes?"

"I'd like you to speak to Juro. Emphasize the great trust I am placing in him. Bring home to him that I want to know the ins and outs of any complication that may arise."

"I'll do my best."

"Good-bye then."

"Good-bye."

That was his way, no extra words, certainly none of endearment. But Kenji would arrive with a gift for her. Last time it was a Rolex Oyster Cosmograph. Akio paid well; her life was strewn with Hermès scarfs and Lanvin and Gucci baubles.

His mention of Juro meant that she was right about this trip, it was in connection with his plan to retrieve the Northern Territories, which he had discussed again last week over lunch, bringing her up to speed on its progress. He must have an extensive spy network of highly placed executives to which Juro had been added. And now herself. She was insurance. This was how he worked. He had known, for instance, about the Cambridge Report before the ink was dry. He had filed a hundred patents on the new high-temperature technology before the Americans had so much as researched the literature. When she congratulated him, his reply was typical: "Yes, it was a good move, especially as the earliest work in the field was pioneered by Americans. They have become our Manchukuo."

With her father it always came down to that. Singlehandedly he continued the war. It was insane, but how well it worked.

She permitted the young man to mount her, and afterward took him to dinner. They went to Happo-En and had *kaiseiki ryori*, the multicourse dinner for which the restaurant was famous.

Miko dropped the young man off early. The packing would take her no time; it was her thoughts she wanted to get into some kind of order. She could do this best by talking to Oba-sama, her honored grandmother. It was late, but she had to say good-bye. There was a considerable pause while Momoko was summoned to the phone.

"Grandmother, did I wake you?"

"No, of course not," Momoko replied stoutly.

"I did. I know it. I'm sorry, Oba-sama, but I had to call. Father has asked me to go to California for him in the morning."

"California? So suddenly?"

"You know how he is, Grandmother."

"Sometimes I think I know, but too many times I am wrong."

Miko laughed. "Me too."

There was a pause, as Momoko had never learned the art of a telephone conversation where sentences are batted back and forth like balls in a tennis match.

"I want your blessing, Oba-sama, before starting out."

"I will keep your name before the *kami*. . . . Miko?"

"Yes, Grandmother?"

"Do not forget to be Japanese."

"I won't, Grandmother." She hung up. She was four years old, and the house she had been taken to was very large and grand. The room she was left in was furnished in the foreign style, with great heavy pieces such as one saw sometimes in store windows. The servant who had brought her here returned with a woman who did not match the room, for she wore kimono.

The woman bent down to her height and looked into her face. "I'm glad you have come, Miko."

Very slowly Miko raised her eyes to the woman's face. Her face, like the voice, was gentle and reassuring. There was an infinite quietness about her, and her eyes smiled.

"I want you to be happy here, Miko. This is your home, and I am your grandmother. Do you understand? Come, put your hand in mine, I have a surprise to show you."

The hand that grasped Miko's was not much larger, almost like that of another child. She was led out into a wonderful garden. It seemed to be its own world, a world of shaded bamboo clumps and miniature pines. A world of flowers and stone pagodas, and there was a pond with a moon bridge.

The woman who was her oba-sama took her to the edge of the water, where a stand of purple iris grew. "Look below the surface," her oba-sama said. "Tell me what you see."

Miko caught her breath, for in the clear depths flashed *koi* in amazing colors. "I see fish."

"And one of them is to be your very own. Which will you choose, the one with red and gold patches, or the big black and gray? Or the pink who swims so swiftly, or the salmon-colored one who comes and drinks air?"

"Yes, that one. He is trying to kiss the top where we are."

"I like him best too. You have chosen well, Miko."

They stood and watched Miko's special *koi*.

"What will you call him?" Oba-sama asked.

"I can give him a name?"

"Of course, he is yours."

"I didn't know I would ever have a *koi*."

Momoko smiled. "I didn't know I would ever have a Miko."

"Does it make you happy to have me?"

"Very happy."

The child studied her, taking in each feature. "I didn't know I would ever have an oba-sama. And I also am very happy to have you."

And she was still very happy to have her. Oba-sama had been hers, all through her growing up, belonging to her in a special way. Oba-sama was her family. Very early she had been taught to bow before the picture of a young man in a flight lieutenant's uniform, wearing a *hachimaki* around his head. He too seemed to adopt her.

From the first it was Grandmother who looked after her, Grandmother she brought her troubles to. Grandmother was the good-fortune divinity pillar of her life, that held everything up. When the time came, it was Grandmother who helped her pick a college in America. That was where the dislocation occurred. In America she had not known when to be happy and when to be sad, for a person can only

be free of conflict as long as that person stays within accepted bound-
aries. She had ventured out, gone into the world, and lost the harmony
that women of other generations knew.

Her grandmother sensed this. It was, Miko thought, the reason
she wanted to see her married. She came from a time when life was
guided at every step by rules, and an unmarried woman was a lost soul.

It must have been hard to live then, but at the same time . . .
easier. The truth was there was no one she wanted to walk ten steps
behind. Of course, in this generation of New Humans that was only
figuratively the case. But she did not think of herself as a New Human,
or, as the Americans called them, a Juppy. Her brother, yes. He was
definitely part of the new ethos that had it all and looked for more.
She was five years older and fit into no category.

She didn't know the details of her birth. She had tried many
times to worm the facts out of Oba-sama, but had never succeeded.
She knew she was fortunate her father had adopted her. Men in Akio's
position frequently adopted illegimate children if they were male; a
female was rarely accorded such a privilege. Luckily, Akio did not
think like other people. What belonged to him belonged to him, and
he would have it.

There were memories of a before-life, but they were vague. There
were recurring recollections of a rice paddy that was golden in autumn,
of fireflies, of a rice bowl that was never full enough at mealtimes. But
in many ways it was simpler than life in the great house. The years
lived under her father's roof were filled with tensions strung like invisible wires. Sumie lived in another part of the house, the Western part,
with a battery of nurses, nannies, servants, and her infant son. Sumie
was a glamorous figure in those days, who made it a practice never to
speak directly to Miko. She seemed to enjoy pointing up her ambivalent position in the household.

It was still ambivalent. Unanswered questions were piled in her
mind from childhood. Why did her stepmother keep the door of her
Western-style bedroom locked at night? And why did her father submit
to this, why didn't he break it down in righteous indignation? It was
part of an impossible maze. To untangle it one would have to penetrate
the significance of that pathetic creature whom she had been taught
to call Uncle Masaru and the endless games of go her father pretended
to play with him. Somehow it was all tied together. It had proved too
much for her in the past, she didn't hope to solve it now, only to

determine what her place was, what her father wanted of her, and what she wanted of herself.

In the short term, of course, she was Akio's *shosha*-man, the person he trusted to evaluate his various operations, to recommend which to continue to fund, and where to look for fresh prospects. It was the part of her life she felt confident in. But another dimension was being added.

In the morning the alarm clock woke her with the fresh aroma of a pine forest that turned to a preprogrammed lemon scent as she showered and dressed. By the time it switched to jasmine, Kenji was at the door. Akio had taken him on years ago as his driver. He also piloted Akio's private plane. He had, in short, made himself indispensable and served as her father's principal factotum. It was generally assumed, and assumed by Akio himself, that the man was devoted to him.

Miko wondered. The light eyes disturbed her; they disturbed everyone, they were too unexpected, they fit no other feature. There was no way to imagine what went on behind them. Also there was a distinct resemblance to Masaru, which dismayed the entire family. Miko brushed aside thoughts of Masaru, no use venturing into that minefield.

Kenji presented her with an *o-miyage* from her father, done up in embossed white paper with gold tassels. Kenji was obviously disappointed that she did not open it at once. He would have liked to know what had been given so he could lord it over the servants with his inside knowledge. Miko took a perverse pleasure in thwarting him.

With a quick, final look around the apartment, she rang for the elevator. So she was going on another *shugyo*, this time to America. She was divided in her mind about America. While she was still in school she had taken it as her model, demanding for herself personal freedom. With that decision she had cut herself off from the Japan of other generations. And she worried about Oba-sama's admonition to be Japanese even in America. She wasn't sure how Japanese she was right here in Tokyo.

The chronically jammed expressway between the city and the airport was worse than usual, and the ANA flight was ready for takeoff when she ensconced herself in her seat. The maintenance crew on the ground were bowing them off when she opened the sealed envelope. Her instructions were to continue her usual activities—checking out the work being done in superconductivity; visiting universities, think tanks, and industrial plants—but her real purpose was to keep herself conversant with the silent propeller blade that was being lathe-cut by computer and milled at the Toshiba plant in San Clemente, California. Miko folded the letter carefully and returned it to its envelope. It was as she had thought, the objective was the Northern Territories. She found it interesting that there was no mention of Juro. Long ago she had given up trying to second-guess her father, but she didn't much like the idea of playing nursemaid to her half brother.

She was fond of Juro. Everyone was fond of Juro. He was charming, amiable, good company, and extremely handsome by any standard, with cross-cultural good looks. They thought so in Tokyo, they would think so in L.A. Although not as beautiful as her brother, her own appearance satisfied her. The characteristic Japanese eyelid fold had been surgically altered when she was eighteen. The result was an exotic cast of feature, with exact ethnicity not readily discernible. Miko considered herself an Eastern woman who wore Chanel suits extremely well, and that depressed her considerably. Then too, her feelings about California were mixed.

The prejudice against the Japanese lingers on, Miko thought. At Stanford, she had been insulated by a coterie of friends and rarely had to face the outside world alone. But there were moments. . . . A date telling her, "My uncle died on Bataan." Or the word "Jap" uttered in the dorms and cut off as she entered. She remembered the second that followed of self-conscious silence, the American kind. To them silence was an awkward void to be filled at all costs. They didn't understand it as she did, as any Japanese would, as communication.

She reminded herself it was a game within a game. That much she had absorbed from her father. He took over in the mid-sixties, appropriating the factory. Very early Miko understood the importance of great-grandfather's toy factory. Diversification was the key. Old records showed that Akio had borrowed against eighty percent of the firm's capital for acquisition of real estate on a global scale. Buying into a bank, he lent himself money at low rates of interest to invest in fleets of oil tankers that plied the Persian Gulf. This move was quixotically patriotic, since oil was vital to the economy. At the same time she did not doubt its profitability. Then, when the memory chip was first produced in volume, he flooded the market with them. They became so numerous that the bottom fell out. At first the American producers hung on, taking a beating. When losses reached an annual two billion, they threw in the towel. As frequently happens in go, the master allowed them to defeat themselves—or, more accurately, allowed their system to defeat them. American commerce was built on accountability to shareholders and a never-ceasing demand for profits. They were inherently unable to sustain even short-term losses.

Her father, on the other hand, was backed by MITI, an arm of the government. Now, a few years down the *michi*, with the competition disposed of, the industry realized a profit of ten billion a year.

U.S. Memories was the last American bastion; when it fell, the battle of the semiconductor was won. Even so, Akio liked to keep checking. That's where she came in. Miko prided herself on being his point man, whom he sent to scout new advances. He explained to her that the arsenal he counted on was technology. And the culmination of all these ventures? It came down again to the return of the large islands Kunashiri and Etorofu, which, together with Urup, Shinshiri, and Paramoshin, made up the Northern Territories, and were the prize for which he manuevered. These lost territories, which lay off Hokkaido, had gone to the USSR at Yalta, and their recovery had been consistently pursued before the UN. The government regarded them, as well as the smaller Habomai and Shikotan chains, as an integral part of the nation. In 1960 Japan refused a settlement returning the two southern chains, insisting that the Russians return them all. Instead the offer was withdrawn. The punitive aspect of this was not wasted on Akio. And all these years later, he set himself the task of single-handedly bringing about the return of all territories.

This position seemed extreme to Miko. But she reminded herself that the year of her father's birth was the year of Japan's surrender. He fought in every fiber of his being to eradicate the humiliation.

It was made easier by the American posture in regard to Japan; they failed to notice when she stopped being a client state and started making it on her own. They failed to notice when she stopped copying and began innovating. Finally they were alarmed, recognizing too late their dependence on their old enemy and ward. How many strategic parts in how many U.S. fighter jets were of Japanese manufacture? For her father this was the first wave of a frontal assault.

She did not share his preoccupation with the past. The war was a dead issue. It lay in the dust of yesterday, along with the Meiji and Tokugawa eras. It had nothing to do with her.

What had? It was time to find out. She was twenty-four years old, which was already old to catch a husband. What was worse, she had no inclination to catch one.

Miko made an attempt to start the paperback she had brought with her, and then, remembering her *o-miyage*, decided this was a good time to open it. Yves St. Laurent's Opium. She opened the bottle and sniffed. The gift reminded her of her brother; he spent a good deal of time coordinating fragrances with his wardrobe. She worried about Juro. Somewhere along the way he had decided it was hopeless to compete with the dynamism of an Akio.

"I don't want to be a hi-tech coolie," he'd told her, "with my 'golden week,' my six days a year arranged by a section leader to be taken with the entire work group, all wearing company badges and quoting company slogans. No, thank you."

This was in response to her father's initial idea, which was to have him work his way up through the corporate ranks. Juro did not outface his father, but stormed to mother and sister.

Akio, inflexible in all else, was easily persuaded where his son was concerned. He decided Juro would skip the salaryman stage and assume a managerial post more in keeping with his position as heir.

This was only slightly less onerous to Juro. "I can see it. In my office by eight sharp, with nothing to do the whole morning but arrange my golf schedule. Attending meetings whose outcomes have already been decided. Writing an occasional Telex and a few memos, drawing up budgets, downing a stamina drink, persuading myself that nothing is as much fun as a good long day at the office. Looking forward to the close of business, so I can get drunk with the correct group of junior execs, all clones of me. I tell you, that idea sucks!"

Again he worked by indirection, through his mother and Miko. And once more Akio gave way. He had a blind spot where his son was concerned. Reaching into traditional literature, he borrowed samurai virtues to invest Juro with. A son was automatically fierce in loyalty, stalwart, brave, and born with the cleverness to make him a leader. He would leave him his wealth and his empire, and Juro would return him *ko*.

Miko had known for a long time this would never happen, but she dreaded her father discovering it, and it had been her long-standing habit to cover for Juro. She needn't have worried, Akio refused to see.

He gave Juro a block of stock and a separate allowance for investment, and watched with interest, evaluating his handling of it. Miko smiled her rueful, upside-down kind of smile. She was the one who managed the fund and ended up writing reports signed with her brother's name. It was her view that the role of Japanese women was to support their men in all things. This might be one of the reasons she was still single; she really didn't want another person to coddle and look after. She had her hands full.

Miko had gotten into the rhythm of the flight. She didn't mind that Japan was at the end of the earth, making this an eleven-hour ordeal. Between sleep and occasional attempts to get on with the novel, she allowed herself to muse. Though she was only five years older than Juro, they were of different generations and totally different in their upbringing. She had gone to high school with the daughters of the leading *zaibatsu* families, for her father had caught up with these old-line houses very quickly, learning to achieve the requisite consensus, while in reality pursuing his own agenda.

The name Mitsui became prominent in the seventeenth century. Toward the end of Tokugawa rule, Eichi Shibusawa, a member of a prosperous peasant family, left a government position to venture into the cotton-spinning industry. From there the family went into banking and then agriculture, indigo, and miso, a fermented soy bean paste, which became a dietary staple. With success and the wealth that accrued to them, the Mitsui family bought samurai status and within generations went global.

A century later, in the province of Tosa, a young man, Yataro Iwasaki, of impoverished samurai stock, managed to become purchasing agent for the daimyo. In 1870 he established a coastal mail service plying between Tokyo and Osaka. He built his small shipping concern into a trading company that eventually won major government mail routes to China and the United States. A network of foreign contacts was developed, and he began doing business abroad under the name Mitsubishi. For the Formosa campaign of 1874, Mitsubishi was able to provide the government with funds in addition to armaments, creating a Western-style system of centralized banking based on the Belgian model. Currency was made uniform, and the yen adopted as the unit of value.

But the real coup occurred fifteen years later, when Iwasaki purchased from the central government a swampy tract of eighty-seven acres adjacent to the Imperial Palace in Tokyo. Today it had a book value of five billion dollars and encompassed the business districts of

Marunouchi and Otemachi, making it the most valuable real estate in the world.

When Mitsubishi merged its shipping interests with Mitsui to chal- lenge Western shipping lines, government ministries began accusing each other of being pawns of either the Mitsui or Mitsubishi cartel, for while they combined against outsiders, there was great rivalry be- tween the two houses regarding their respective influence in the Diet and national affairs. Like the rest of corporate Japan, Mitsubishi was an integral part of the war machine, building the Zero fighter plane and the *Musashi*, the world's largest battleship.

Breaking up the immense wealth of the *zaibatsu* was high on the purge list of the American Occupation. Their assets were seized and placed in government-run banks. Their personal wealth was curtailed by a ninety-percent levy on income and inheritance taxes. An edict was issued prohibiting Japanese ships from travel in the open sea. By any standards known to the Americans, these prohibitions should have spelled an end to further *zaibatsu* influence. But what the Americans did not realize was the pervasive structure of the companies, whose tentacles reached into all aspects of the economy.

The large banks were not broken up, as the Occupation forces deemed them necessary for the reconstruction of the economy. Of course these were but another arm of the *zaibatsu*. And bit by bit the seized funds were funneled back into the commercial and industrial projects for which they had originally been destined—in short, back under *zaibatsu* control.

During Miko's school years Akio penetrated these august preserves, winning the respect and confidence of the established firms, who shared his belief that industrial development was too important to be subject to the haphazard laws of supply and demand, but must be regulated by the government. Of the old Confucian school, the *zaibatsu* were conservative as far as personal values went, and their morality almost feudal. They did not go in for villas abroad, yachts, or Swiss bank accounts. The great wealth that had only been punctured by the Occu- pation was quickly reconstituted and plowed back into their expanding multinational enterprises. The families, however, were such undercon- sumers that the extent of this wealth was not generally appreciated outside Japan. The women continued to pour tea, arrange flowers, and wear the kimono, at least within the home.

It was this tradition Miko grew up in. But the fabric tore apart when she encountered America. Old ideas were exploded, the old ways gone forever. It was her grandmother who suspected how very bright she was and, in her old-fashioned innocence, not foreseeing the results, had insisted on the kind of education it was impossible for girls to receive in Japan. Four years later, when Miko returned, she found that her contemporaries were embarked on a spending spree such as the emperors of Rome might have indulged in.

Juro was initiated into this lifestyle almost from birth. For him, champagne spouted from golden faucets in gold heart-shaped tubs. The most famous of these golden spas was in the shape of a chicken, Le Coque d'Or, and the cost to romp in it was five dollars a minute, or fifteen hundred yen. It wasn't enough to bathe in gold; the New Humans wanted their sushi wrapped in gold, their hair sprayed with it, their golf clubs made of it, and their business cards embossed in 14 K.

The exclusive New Ginza Hotel was the first to cater to their wildly extravagant whims. Beds were turned down, a favorite flower appeared on the pillow, and room rates jumped to the stratosphere. For a melon out of season they paid a hundred twenty dollars, while fresh strawberries in February were almost beyond price. The young madcaps adored a sparkling mineral water bottled in France, flavored with pungent truffles that had been nosed from the ground by French pigs. A ten-ounce bottle sold for upwards of nine hundred fifty dollars. Nothing was too much. Instant gratification was demanded.

The financial miracle, the *yen shokku*, had occurred, and they haunted the boutiques and smart shops of the Roppongi. Traveling abroad, they bought out entire counters at Harrod's and windows on Rodeo Drive, besides acquiring a third of the world's Post-Impressionist paintings. Picasso's Blue Period was especially in vogue; *Acrobat and Young Harlequin* went for thirty-eight and a half million dollars.

The work ethic of their parents was derided and became the subject of countless jokes. The old folks had never heard of the Southern All-Stars or Michael Jackson. They were heart-and-soul company men, fixtures like their own desks. Their social life was lived at after-hours bars with fellow workers, their vacations consisted of a week at a local hot spring. It was all ordered, controlled, standardized. In revulsion the New Humans disassociated themselves, kicked over the traces, dyed their hair brown and permed it—the boys, too. They realigned their teeth and bite and jawline with the newest dental techniques and recast their features with plastic surgery.

The New Humans were beautiful and glamorous and did not look Japanese. Of course, they did not look Western either, but more as cartoonists draw handsome aliens living in the midst of unsuspecting earthlings.

It troubled Miko that her attitude was censorious. She censured both lifestyles, the traditional one *and* the new, self-indulgent one, although she had nothing to replace either with.

At times she enjoyed the high living and the same luxuries her brother did. The difference was, she could let go. In fact, she had to let go. Extravagant indulgences weren't essential to her well-being or to tell her who she was. Her tastes ran closer to her father's. She could bury herself for months at a time in a project. But was it a satisfying life? Perhaps if you were Akio and convinced yourself you were plunged into a war where tactics and strategy meant a win or a loss on the field of battle, perhaps then.

But she was too sensible, too modern; her Western education had taken too great a hold. An attitude such as her father's seemed totally irrational. How could a man persuade himself of the truth of such patent myths? And of how much more did Akio persuade himself? Because Masaru was the other myth. Not his wife, not his children, not a mistress or even friends . . . only Masaru was always at his side. He kept him with him, whether it was in America, Europe, Japan, one of the "four little dragons," or Hawaii—Masaru was there. And at night, whether the Emperor died, earthquake struck, or the Nikkei fell, the game of go was set up between them, with Akio placing the stones.

"He's mad," Sumie said, and believed it.

Miko wished she herself were a little mad, or at least not quite so sane. The mad, those who persuade themselves their actions are part of a grand scheme, or even that they counted at all, lived intensely and completely, using themselves up. She envied that. Her father had an absolute disregard of self. No, this analysis was faulty. How could a man who owned a private jet, a Citation with custom interior, who drove an Aston-Martin Volane in Tokyo and a Rolls Corniche convertible in Hawaii, how can it be said that such a man was disregarding of self?

That was the amazing thing about truths, they don't necessarily jibe with each other. Both sets of truths Miko felt were true of her father.

The lights of LAX and the far-flung checkerboard of Los Angeles were below them. Miko hoped that by dropping into this world and its culture, the signposts of her life would no longer appear as intricate *kanji* characters, but be written in simple English, and that after a while she would know what to do about Miko. She really had never liked going to bed with beautiful young men who used the same perfume she did, and she hoped that America would show her a better way.

꠸꠸ ꠸꠸

That her father considered her assignment top priority was evidenced by the Lamborghini that a paged white telephone informed her was ready for pickup. She collected the keys at Traveler's Aid, allowed a moment to take in the sleek, futuristic lines, and took off. This was a serious present. She seemed to enter a jetstream. She held it back as one does a thoroughbred horse, and was still flying.

Forty minutes later she was approaching the residence in Malibu. Miko didn't know what she had expected, but certainly not this. Lights streamed from every window and the walls vibrated with sound. Juro was throwing a party. Her first reaction was annoyance. Then she realized their father might not have notified him of her arrival. It was quite possible Juro did not know that she was joining him. One thing was apparent: any meaningful conversation would have to be postponed until tomorrow. This was just as well, because she was still operating on Tokyo time, and only beginning to feel how tired she was.

She parked her new acquisition carefully and took her flight bag, leaving the other luggage in the car. The music was loud and the dress, she saw, informal. Designer jeans predominated, with both sexes wearing necklaces and earrings. She stood just inside the door, looking for Juro. The crowd swirled and milled and jived around her. It was brought home to her why she and Juro moved in different circles. This was too funky for her. She backed out, threading her way through merrymakers, and headed for the boat house. It was the only place she could think of where she could get a good sleep and defeat the circadian rhythm her brain had established. All necessary keys had thoughtfully been inserted in the car key ring, but she discovered the door open.

A young man was standing before a panel that diagrammed the electrical circuitry of the house. At first glance she assumed he was American; his build was American, tall and rangy. But when he turned around she saw he was of her own race.

"This is amazing," he said, as though it were an ongoing conversation. "It's a smart house. You can set it for the most incredible things. Doors open as you break the infrared beam, lights switch on as you approach and turn off when a room is empty. From your car you dial up a bath, or a TV show, or to have the coffee perking. Just take a look at this display panel, it's like the instrumentation on a 747." Then, jerking himself up, "Sorry, I'm Doug Watanabe," and he extended his hand with a grin.

Miko returned him her upside-down frown of a smile. This young man was standing between her and a hot shower. "I'm not part of the party," she said.

"Of course, the flight bag. I should have realized."

"I'm Miko. Juro's sister."

"And you came out here to escape the party."

"Actually to turn in. I've just had an eleven-hour flight and I'm beat."

"Well, look, I'll disappear. I've got no business here anyway, other than curiosity."

Before he could act on this, the door burst open and there was Juro with his arm around a blond starlet type. On seeing Miko he stopped in mid-motion, almost comically nonplussed. Miko realized her guess had been correct and that he'd had no idea she was coming. "Miko, I can't believe this. When did you get here?"

"Well, I'll be getting along," Doug said, and on his way out separated the blonde from Juro and took her with him.

"Did you meet Doug?" Juro asked. "He's Sansei, a crazy kind of guy, an inventor. So what are you doing here? Why didn't anyone let me know?"

Miko laughed. "I guess Father wanted me to discover you in your natural habitat."

"Well, you sure did. This is great, isn't it? I love California. I'm crazy for blond women. They're all blond here."

"I hope, in between parties, you are keeping track of that propeller blade."

"Of course. I think I'm developing a flair for business."

"Monkey business," she teased, then added quickly, "You must be serious, Juro. You mustn't disappoint Father."

"Why? He loves it when I disappoint him. Everyone else is so damned obsequious. Don't mean you, of course."

"Yes you do."

He came closer, his gaze intent. "Level with me, Miko. Did Father send you to spy on me?"

"He sent me," she admitted, "but to back you up, be your ally. He's a bit on edge these days, completely focused on this whole thing with the islands. It's a real chance for you to come through for him, if you'll buckle down."

"That's your role. You do it so well." Then, seeing the expression that crossed her face, "Just kidding. Everything is proceeding smoothly. Say"—he took her hand—"you weren't intending to hide out here? There's a dozen people I want you to meet."

"No. Really, I don't think so."

"But the party is in high gear, I want to introduce my sister to everyone. And when I say everyone, that's what I mean. Movie moguls, big-shot directors, stars too. They're all here, even the so-called captains of industry, with a sprinkling of Washington power brokers, a senator and two congressmen."

When he set his mind to it, Juro had a penchant for melting away her resolve, and she allowed herself to be led back to the party. He put a drink in her hand and, as good as his word, introduced her to so many people that after a while she made no attempt to remember names.

Juro was in his element, charismatic, generating the spirit of fun.

"He's the boy wonder of the business world—worth billions, I'm told," one young thing gushed to Miko, unaware of who she was. The next moment they were introduced and she simply laughed. "Boy, was that ever a blooper."

Miko looked around for Doug, the American-Japanese, but he didn't seem to be there. Juro claimed her attention once more; he was obviously high, more on excitement than liquor. He was the center of fawning adulation from both men and women, receiving extravagant compliments that he shrugged off with a newly acquired, charming humility. He was enjoying his own party so much that everyone else enjoyed it too. He was continually surrounded, never permitted to finish a dance, and rarely a joke or story, before being taken over by another group or person, who would start out, "Oh, there you are!"

She moved to one of the Doric columns to observe him better. He wore a T-shirt whose logo read "Lonesome Cowboy." Lonesome was something that, if tonight was any indication, he had not been since reaching the United States. His guests seemed to find his unabashed love of the spotlight irresistible, and his high good humor affected them all. It didn't hurt that he possessed the beauty of an Asian Adonis. In fact the element of the exotic seemed to strike a pleasing chord with the Hollywood crowd. Prominent cheekbones enhanced the line of his face, to which the slightly aquiline nose lent strength. Had his eyebrows been circumspectly plucked, she wondered, or did they naturally resemble the wings of a swallow in flight?

There was no doubt that her brother was the center of attention, the momentary darling of this notoriously fickle world. Seeing the flush on his cheeks, the heightened sparkle of his eyes, she worried that he had been swept away by people who were not his people and whose ways he did not know.

That worry was yoked with a second. Had he really kept on top of things, as he claimed, or had he been distracted by the glitter of the life he was living, which, if she could judge by tonight, was even more frenetic than he led at home? The women, as he said himself, were all blond.

Miko slid back the heavy drapes to frame an ocean. It was the same ocean, of course, but how different this side felt. Last week, when the plane set down in Los Angeles, her Japanese mind had jammed like a gear box. The fact that everything was happening in English sent her into a momentary paralysis. But she quickly adjusted her thought and tempo, turning the LED in her brain to read *America*.

In much the same way, the sprawling beach house attempted the impression of an English manor. Five-sided Turkoman camel trappings with ivory backings hung in the study. Sumie had acquired them after learning they were used in wedding processions. She insisted they gave the place a country-house ambience. Actually they represented a triumph in collecting. Her pastime had become a passion. The lordly mahogany breakfront bookcase of neoclassical proportions, replete with pedimented top, represented another coup. The Chippendale dining table with its spider-backed chairs made her happy for a month. An upholstered Regency chair with Egyptian motif, for which she had outbid the Emir of Oman, was especially prized, as was a small circular table inlaid with burls of white ash.

Juro added his talents to the decor. Obeying his pixie impulses he bought up calendars of dogs, which he had carefully mounted in heavy gold frames with nonreflective glass. They were hung throughout the mansion in lieu of the usual English ancestors.

Brother and sister had long ago developed their own brand of rapprochement. They were not close in the sense of sharing confidences, but they enjoyed palling around. When Juro was about ten he had tried to gain ascendency over her by virtue of being the boy and because her antecedents were what his mother called "questionable." But he discovered she could be a useful ally, so in spite of Sumie's efforts to the contrary they became friends.

Miko sat down with an old address book from her college days, and spent the morning telephoning. Two numbers no longer answered, and the third try produced the information that the party she was attempting to reach was on vacation. And in a somewhat disappointing conversation with Irene, whose face she could no longer recall, they professed themselves delighted to be in touch, but, owing to conflicting schedules, left any future meeting vague.

Miko dealt next with the servants. Giving them the day off, she proceeded to fill the fridge with goat cheese, pizzas, stuffed prawns, beluga caviar, Breyer's ice cream, and bottles of California Chardonnay. The kitchen would take a day or two to become acquainted with; it bristled with a pasta machine, a cappuccino dispenser, and a gourmet coffee machine for pressing premium Arabica beans and Jamaican Blue Mountain flavored with vanilla. There was also an intimidating food processor, an automatic bread maker, a restaurant-size freezer, and an industrial range with built-in microwave. Miko wondered if the Mexican servants knew how to operate any of this. She tied on a flour-sack apron, and, when Juro came in, made him a spectacular meal.

"Close your eyes," she told him, "you're near the Roppongi Cross-ing at the Hard Rock. Try the pizza with duck, sausage, and green chili. Or how about roast lobster?"

"What is this, *green* butter?"

"It's Thai. The curry turns the butter green."

"I'd like the old-fashioned yellow kind, please."

"Your taste buds are so pedestrian I can't believe it."

To redeem himself, Juro opened a bottle of Chateau Petrus, which they sipped on the porch, watching the waves purl onto the sand.

He was good about saving time for her. They played tennis at the Palisades Club their father had just bought. He even rearranged his social schedule to attend the Bolshoi and took in a play at the Music Center with her. But the walks on the beach she took alone. The expanses she gazed into were beyond human life spans; their being was in some other time reference. Looking out at their immensities, she was reminded of Sung Dynasty paintings, those marvelous monochro-matic scrolls showing nature in waterfalls and mountains. Only after staring at the scene for some time did you realize that people were incorporated into it, but on a small scale. Or rather, an accurate scale.

That was what it was like to walk at the edge of the sea. So delusionary are human beings that for a moment she felt she encom-passed the vastness. All of which did not help her solve the unsolved questions of her life. For a woman who was such a good judge of a microchip, why couldn't she read the human heart? Why so many personal failures? Oba-sama told her she had a man's mind in a wom-an's body. Was that the problem? Were men afraid of independence in a woman? For she had to admit to herself that she did not have a good track record with men. In recent years she'd kept them at an emotional distance. No one got close.

In a sense her involvement at the San Clemente plant offered a respite from her own problems. At the highest level she was wined and dined, and her request for a tour of the operation granted without demur. The physical setup for producing the submarine propeller blade had been worked out and was under way. She did not neglect the political aspect either, spending a weekend in Washington, during which she saw the Russian ambassador and spent an afternoon with the congressman who was lobbying to see her father's proposal through the House. Phone calls from Akio were part of the peak traffic in high-tech information that traveled by fax and Telex during the electronic

rush hour of midnight between Tokyo and L.A. Memos reached her detailing the Silicon Valley plants she was to visit, and programs at various universities she was to look into. She stayed up to receive them, wishing she could see the grand puzzle her father was fitting together, of which her endeavors were one small piece. Juro had his assignment as well . . . another piece.

Her *shosha*-man role served a double purpose, as her father had recently invaded the high-definition TV market. Its rather frivolous purpose of giving the world bigger and better TV viewing masked the real objective, which was military. An HDTV in the cockpit of a fighter or the console of a tank would reveal, in completely accurate imaging, installations many miles distant. It would also revolutionize medicine, especially X-rays and computer tomography, while technology developed along the way would become part of the mainstream of science in the twenty-first century.

Miko's scouting expedition took her to USC, Cal Tech, UCLA, the Hughes think tank in Malibu, and north to Silicon Valley to view new high-resolution monitors at Hewlett-Packard. From there she went on to Berkeley. She made copious notes sitting in on lectures, talking to grad students and principal investigators.

At one facility they were experimenting with light instead of electricity. The race was on to etch ever-smaller microchips. A see/hear chip was being developed that converted light patterns into sound, while sensors were automated to recognize visual systems.

Miko knew she had looked at the future. She wrote a long report that she faxed to her father. Then she cast about for Juro. He had left phone numbers, but no one at any of these places had heard from him. Growing worried, she phoned the Toshiba plant, only to be informed that he had not been by for a week. She tried the Palisades Club next, but he had not shown up for his last three tennis lessons.

She tried to remember the name of his friend from Toshiba, but couldn't recall it. Finally it came to her, Yawata. But it turned out his number was unlisted. Miko continued her walks on the beach, wondering, now that all her conversations were in English, why it was that she still dreamed in Japanese. As she stared out at the demarcation of water with sky, a line of Yeats's floated into her mind, an airman's poem:

A lonely impulse of delight
Drove to this tumult in the clouds

She speculated on her kamikaze legacy and a boy Juro's age, sealed into a sky-tossed death capsule. No impulse of delight there—but the tumult, that had surely been present. And in some way she didn't entirely comprehend, it impacted her life.

The large home that occupied bluff and beach seemed too quiet. She no longer enjoyed preparing gourmet treats, but ate out at fast-food places. She wondered if Juro's mission was on track. She had the feeling that he looked on her assignment as being in competition with his own. Or at least in competition for their father's approval. She hoped she was wrong about that. She thought of asking her father if Juro had checked back with him, but her brother would be sure to misconstrue such an inquiry. What seemed most likely was that he was having a fling, and when it was over he'd be back.

She stocked up on old movies and foreign films to watch at night on the VCR, and settled down to wait. When the phone call came, it was not Juro.

"Hello, is Miko there?"

"This is Miko."

"Well, look, I'm Doug Watanabe. We met at your brother's party. Actually, I'm phoning about him."

"Is Juro all right?"

"No. No, he's not. He flipped out. I think you'd better come get him."

"My God." She was already scribbling the address.

It was a trailer at Paradise Cove, past the pier on the sand. It seemed familiar to her; she thought perhaps they had shot a TV series here. She climbed the steps to the porch and knocked.

"It's open."

The door swung in at her touch, and she looked into a twelve-foot-wide area that served as living space. Juro was on a couch, pinned there by Doug.

She was shocked at Juro's appearance. Where was the proud look of this Oriental Adonis? His head jerked about, his eyes rolled, he was laughing inanely, and there was spittle at the corner of his mouth.

"Do sh'ta no?" The words came out in Japanese, the first Japanese she had spoken since leaving Tokyo.

"Sorry, you'll have to speak English."

She shot him a curious glance. *One of those,* whose parents or in his case, grandparents, came to America. Her first assessment was cor-

rect, he *did* look American, even moving with the athletic ease of young American males. Juro began flailing about and reciting what sounded like a racing form. Again her heart thudded against the wall of her chest. "Have you called a doctor?"

"Not yet. I didn't know what kind of trouble he'd be in if this got out. Besides, I think we can handle it."

"But what exactly—"

"He took one hit too many."

"I see." Her voice was frosty.

"I didn't give it to him. I wasn't here."

"Whose place is this, then?"

"Oh, it's my place. But I've been out of town. I lent my pad to a friend."

"You mean to Juro?"

"No. I didn't know he'd be here too. They must have been partying since I left."

"Did his friend—this friend of yours—just go off and leave him?"

"He wasn't in much better shape. He took off when I came."

"My brother could have died."

"Look, I'm not responsible for your brother."

"I know. I realize that. Forgive me, I'm upset. So . . . what can I do to help? Get some coffee going?"

He looked at her with a tolerant smile. "Coffee's no good with crack. See if there's a Valium in the medicine cabinet."

Miko nodded. There was only one direction the bedroom could be and the bath was off it. A book was propped against the cabinet. She removed it and checked the shelves. There were books all over, in unlikely places, one propping a window open, another with a razor as bookmark.

She checked out the cabinet. "No, nothing like that."

"Okay, we'll try liquor."

"Are you sure?" she asked, coming back into the room. Juro was mumbling excitedly in Japanese, both asking and answering questions in a strident high-pitched voice.

"It's in the kitchen."

The kitchen was created by a counter separating it from the living room. "To the right of the glasses," Doug directed.

She removed another book. "Yes, here it is. It's Absolut, is that all right?"

"Add a splash of orange juice."

She brought the drink in and held it out for Juro, but he was unable to focus.

She placed the glass against his cheek to make him aware of it. "Juro, Juro. It's Miko. I've fixed a drink, it's vodka. I want you to drink it. Go ahead, drink it, it will make you feel better." She brought the glass to his lips, and the swallowing reflex took over. At first he gulped, then, more steadily and with more control, began to sip.

A violent, spasmodic jerking seized him and the drink spilled on the plaid couch.

"Give it to me," Doug said. "I'll get it down him." He took the glass from her hands and looked at her quizzically. "You're shaking."

"I'm all right."

"Better fix something for yourself."

Miko shook her head. "I just want to get him home."

At that moment Juro's eyes flew open. He took in Miko, the place, Doug Watanabe. "Shit. I did it this time."

This reasonable comment reassured Miko. She turned to Doug. "Would you help me get him down to the car?"

"Are you sure?"

"Yes. Thank you. I really do thank you. I can manage from here."

Juro had sunk into a dissociated state; he was hauled to his feet and his steps directed onto the porch and down the stairs.

Doug Watanabe stopped at the sight of the red Lamborghini Countach. "Jesus! This is yours?"

She nodded, guiding a suddenly cooperative Juro into the passenger seat. The shutting of the car door triggered a bizarre reaction; Juro began clawing at the dash and screaming.

"Oh, my God," Miko said under her breath.

"This won't work." Doug maneuvered Juro out while keeping a tight grip on him. "I'll drive you back. You get in the passenger side, and we'll try to squeeze Juro in beside you."

She ducked into the car and reached for her brother. "It's not far. Just put him on my lap."

Doug tried to comply, but Juro began to struggle. Straining, Doug pushed him in on top of her. "Hold his hands so he can't grab the wheel. Shit! We've got to get him calmed down. Do *you* have something in *your* medicine cabinet?"

"Like what?"

"Prozac."

"I don't think so."

"It's probably just as well. After the jolt we gave him, I think he'll sleep it off." He withdrew his head and shoulders from the window, and, closing the door quietly this time, walked around to the driver's side.

Juro flung himself against the other seat and his body stiffened. It was almost impossible to move him. They pried his hands from their hold. "Don't be afraid," Miko whispered, "what are you afraid of?" she continued, murmuring reassuringly in Japanese while Doug slid behind the wheel of the fire-breathing supercar.

"I understand that these cruise missiles sell for four hundred thousand above sticker price, if you can get them."

Miko pressed Juro's head to her shoulder. She didn't answer.

Doug put the Countach into gear. There was the roar of a fast start. Juro contorted, arching spasmodically. He thrashed from side to side. One leg now somehow stuck out the window.

"Have you got him?" Doug asked.

She nodded. The breath had been knocked out of her, but she had him in a stranglehold. In thirty seconds the car was a mile down the Pacific Coast highway.

"Phenomenal!" The word exploded with Doug's breath. The two tons of ultimate art in motion rocketed on until Miko pointed out the turn was ahead. No antilock brakes, no power steering, no multilink suspension. "Whoa!" he exclaimed, as the car came close to swapping ends. "The monster is horrendous."

"It's a serious car," Miko agreed.

The electric gate clanged behind them. "Well, we got him here," Doug said. Then, turning toward her, "Say, that was something. Its top speed must be close to 200 mph." Doug put the Lamborghini in park. "This is probably the fastest thing on four wheels." He regarded her with fresh appraisal. "It's spartan, though. No creature comforts."

She shot him a cryptic smile. "You're saying it's no car for a woman."

He looked uncomfortable, and she laughed. "I admit it's user-unfriendly, but you get addicted."

Lights went on at the door of the mansion and at several windows.

"Do we leave the car here?" Doug asked.

"We could invite it into the parlor."

"If it were mine . . ."

They disentangled Juro who was now quiet and went docilely into the house. Miko led the way. "If you'll bring him upstairs—"

"Aren't there servants that go with a spread like this?"

"Yes, but I'd rather not call them. They work for my father, and I don't want him getting wind of this."

"I see. Yes. Very sensible. Come on, my boy, we're taking a little trip upstairs."

Miko led the way, turning at the landing. "The bath is over there, through the dressing room. If you can manage to get him in the shower, I'll lay out pajamas for him."

Juro meekly allowed himself to be led away. In a few minutes she heard the sounds of a skirmish, then the shower running and shouted protests in Japanese.

She brought the pajamas to the door of the bath. "I'm leaving the things out here," she called.

The door burst open. Doug had apparently taken the shower with Juro; his hair was wet and slicked back, his clothes in a pile on the floor, and a towel around his waist. Juro broke from his grip and ran into the bedroom. Miko followed, and the two of them wrestled him into his pajamas.

Miko turned down the covers. Her brother suddenly stopped shouting. He seemed glad to get into bed. He closed his eyes and passed out. She stood watching him for several minutes. As sleep settled over him, the wild, out-of-control look vanished. In repose he was once again beautiful.

Doug was in the bathroom, getting into his clothes. She beckoned to him, and he followed her downstairs. She went to the side table and poured two drinks. "I can't believe it, I had no idea Juro did drugs."

"Maybe he doesn't. Maybe it just happened."

"I suppose he should be seen by someone, but it would have to be done without Father knowing."

"I imagine that being circumspect is routine around here."

"Juro is the only son. My father counts on him."

"I see."

"No, you don't see. Not if you're not Japanese."

"I know something of the tradition."

"With my father it's more than that." Miko looked across at him, and, in an attempt at an apology, said, "Usually at a first meeting people try to make a good impression. You've been plunged right away into a family scandal."

"We do seem to have dispensed with formalities. However, I see that you need to tread carefully where your father is concerned. I mean, you can't pick up a copy of *Fortune* or *World Report* without reading about him. I know I hope to be able to get to him—well, probably not him, but someone in R-and-D."

"You have something you're trying to market?"

"Yes. I'm an electrical engineer. I have my own company, small potatoes, but we produce computer circuitry. And I've been fooling around with lasers, packing more and more data into gallium arsenide wafers."

"They're hybrid, right? Part silicon for low cost and proven reliability, part gallium arsenide for speed?"

He looked at her in surprise. "You've got it."

"Gallium arsenide comes in fairly large crystals. How are you able to splice them into silicon-based circuits?"

"Well, I hold a patent on the method. It's sort of like steaming a postage stamp off a letter. We're able to get thin strips of the material and splice them in."

"You must use some sort of acid to eat away the excess material."

"We do."

"You're right, my father would be very interested in your process."

"Of course, more work is needed to incorporate the wafers into chips."

"If it works, it's a big step."

"In theory it works."

"That's why you were out of town, to arrange financing?"

"Yes, but I didn't have much luck."

Miko thoughtfully revolved the ice in her glass with a swizzle stick. "So what are the hurdles?"

"Well, we need to get a handle on the temperature. At present the circuitry is overheating."

She nodded.

He regarded her with quiet amusement. "They really are inscrutable, the Orientals."

"Why do you say that?"

"Because I can't read you. You seem to follow all the technical stuff, but I've no idea whether you intend to mention it to your father."

"Of course I will."

"Really? That's wonderful."

"I'd have to visit the premises, take a look at your operation."

"Would you? Here's my card."

Miko laughed. "That's the first Japanese thing you've done, hand me a *meishi*. It's sacred ritual in Japan, a way of suggesting how low the other guy should bow to you."

"Lady, I'll bow as low as you like."

"I'll ring you at this number." She stood up, obviously the cue for him to leave. He found that he wasn't at all anxious to go. By Western standards she was diminutive, with the smooth oval face of a child. But she was conversant with DRAMs, fiberoptics, and God knows what else. "If I can be of any help as far as Juro is concerned . . ."

"Thank you." It was a dismissal.

A week later he escorted her through his somewhat makeshift plant. She was full of questions, criticisms too. "You need to completely computerize your assembly process. This stuff is much too delicate to be handled."

"Yes, that makes sense, but robotics is expensive."

"Not if you own the robots."

"Could we," he asked, "talk about it—or not talk about it—over dinner?"

Miko had lectured herself on this eventuality and promised herself she would not become involved with any more good-looking but quite ineligible young men. That was one of the freedoms she had bestowed on herself. Once she had decided to be her own person and not marry right away, it had seemed logical to take lovers, Western and logical. Only it hadn't worked out. And many times she had gone to the theater alone. The theater was the one place where it was acceptable to cry. Heroes had sad fates, and she could weep openly for them, knowing it was also for herself. She straddled two worlds brilliantly, successfully, ask anyone. Or not quite anyone. Her grandmother looked at her often with eyes full of concern.

As for Doug, he was Sansei, which made him totally unacceptable. After all, who were the Japanese who had come to the United States in the early 1920s? Poor dirt farmers, mostly from Hiroshima-ken, who couldn't make it at home. The grandson of such people would not be suitable in her father's carefully kept books, where everyone had his proper place.

Having predecided all this, on the spur of the moment she said yes. He took her to the Beaurivage and she told him of the trendy spots in Tokyo that were duplicates of their American counterparts.

"The Japanese, as you know—as everyone knows—have a talent for imitation. The rest of the world tends to scorn us for this. Personally I think it can be pretty funny. For instance, America-in-the-fifties is a current fad. In Osaka they've opened a diner that serves meatloaf, hamburgers, and malts. The waitresses wear bobby socks, saddle shoes, and swing skirts, and have bows in their hair. There are at least two hundred McDonald's in Tokyo. Denny's has caught on too, but it's a bit more upscale. Then there are the really posh places like Spago's. They copied everything from the L.A. original. I mean *everything* is the same, the wood paneling, the tables and chairs, all complete replicas, even to light fixtures and the exact paint tones. Anyone else would have been satisfied, but they had to carry it a step further. Being Japanese, they were compelled to. So Spago's in Tokyo has the same phone number as the L.A. Spago. Marvelous, isn't it? But I'm afraid it carries on the old cliché about us."

"Us?"

"As Japanese. Oh, I forgot, you're American."

"That's right."

"Are you really? I mean, do you feel American?"

"Of course. I went to Berkeley, worked as a lifeguard summers. I root for the Rams. I climbed El Cap. How American can you get?"

"Well, you could have freckles, red hair, and a turned-up nose." Then, to see what he'd say, she added, "You could have parents who weren't interned during the war."

"Those were my grandparents. And they weren't interned. They opted for Colorado. The government didn't want Japs on the West Coast in case of an invasion. I don't fault them for that. My great-uncle fought at Salerno in the 442nd, and won the Distinguished Service Cross. Sure I feel American."

"Do you ever run into discrimination?"

"Only since the Japanese have been buying up L.A. The power of the yen is resented, you know. I resent it myself."

Miko laughed. "I really believe you *are* American."

"Ask me anything you want on the Civil War, and I'll tell you."

"But how are you on the Meiji Restoration?"

"The what?"

"Don't you know any Japanese history?"

"I know that Perry landed in 1853, and Lord Ishido was buried alive with only his head sticking out, because I read _Shogun._"

"Don't you feel any affinity at all with the people or the culture? Don't you feel part of it?"

"Quite honestly, no."

"I think I would feel at least curiosity. What do you think of Japanese women?"

"I dated daughters of family friends when I was growing up. Generally they weren't too much fun, I suppose because we had two sets of parents looking over our shoulders. In college I went out with Occidental girls and married one of them."

"Oh, you're married. I didn't know."

"_Was_ is the operative word. But to get back to Japanese women, they're exotic, and a bit mysterious."

"I think you're hung up on inscrutable."

He laughed. "Well, I'm easy enough to read. I'm thinking that a walk on the beach would go nicely after dinner—if you've the time, that is."

Miko hesitated. That was one of her private things, something she did to commune with herself. But once again she found herself agreeing.

The spume rolled up on the sand in circular lacy swaths. Its rhythm allowed them to get in touch with the rhythm of their own bodies. "I've been thinking about your smart house. It's not surprising that it's owned by a Japanese."

"We're ahead of the rest of the world, hadn't you heard? At Miyazaki they've done a mockup of a levitating train. They've got four miles of superconducting railbed in place. It cruises at three hundred miles an hour. The U.S. gave up on the idea in 1975, but we're ready to go commercial with it."

"I've been reading about your smart streets and smart cars too. We're just beginning to work on that. Santa Monica, for instance, has fifteen miles of coordinated sensor information that will relay delays, detours, and accidents via cellular phone to twenty-five specially equipped Olds Deltas. In another system, tiny road chips communicate with on-board navigation devices. So you've got smart cars talking to smart streets."

"Of course the ultimate would be automated stretches of freeway," she suggested, and told him that advances in HDTV would eliminate the need for windshields.

"You're saying you no longer see the road but watch it through your TV screen? I think drivers might resist being taken out of the loop. They like to see with their own eyes and put their foot on their own gas pedal."

"That's right. In cars it doesn't make a great difference. But apply it to a supersonic aircraft, and the Stealth bomber becomes as old-fashioned as a covered wagon."

"It's all old-fashioned. Technology that depends on massive amounts of this world's ores and minerals is obsolete. The future is *micro*, dancing sparks of electrical energy connecting minds and ideas. Why get on a levitating train at all? Or into a smart car, or any kind of car for that matter, even your Lamborghini?"

"Yes, I see. You bypass all that. Everybody stays home and plugs in."

"Exactly right. That's why the chip is the future. The future only exists because of them. The chip in its purest form is hooked into thought."

"You might plug into some rather peculiar minds. For instance, a colleague of my father's carries out a monthly ceremony attended by all his engineers to commemorate the deaths of thousands of hamsters whose lives were taken in experiments on a cure for leukemia. And Sony has two robots who are union members in good standing."

"That seems a little weird. But we can't quarrel with the results."

The lights of Point Dume came on, cradling one arm of the bay, and the ring that formed Santa Monica outlined the other. He was aware of her in different ways, as though there were two or three Mikos. "Are many Japanese women as well educated as you?"

She nodded. "That's not the problem. I have an outlet for my education, most Japanese women don't. Eighty percent of working women in Japan are OL's, Office Ladies. They're trained in bowing. Quite literally. At one of my father's plants he has a stainless-steel machine. Gauges are set for the various respect bows, and the trainee harnessed into it. They are also given instruction in how to pour tea. No business meeting in Japan can start before the amenity of tea.

Mostly, young women sit at desks in front offices looking decorative. And then they marry."

"You make it sound as though that's the end of the road."

"It is. They surface again as 'education mamas,' living through their sons, seeing they get into the best schools, pushing them to succeed."

"You're not married?"

"No, I'm an Old Miss."

"An Old Miss . . . old maid . . . you? Come on."

"I'm twenty-four. What you'd call over the hill."

Doug laughed. "May I dispel such an illusion?" And before she understood what he meant, he had kissed her. He bent down to do it, having to half-scoop her up in his arms.

When he set her down she remained with her head tilted back and her eyes closed.

"For an Old Miss, you're something." And he folded her again in that enveloping embrace.

"Doug, I liked that."

"So did I."

They went to his place. He found her delicate and small. "But the package," he told her, "is all there." Her breasts were high, giving the impression of a nubile girl rather than a woman. She showed him the wet love of the Japanese.

Afterward she nestled comfortably in the crook of his arm, deliberately ignoring the fact that she had once again left the safe shallows and plunged in over her head. Or maybe not. They continued to explore each other. "What are the coordinates of Doug Watanabe?" she wondered out loud.

"Right now? Your right arm and the left leg you have draped across me. I never saw such tiny feet." He leaned over the edge of the bed, and picked up a shoe she had slipped out of, turning it in his hand. "Is this for real? My hand is bigger."

She laughed at him. "You're Japanese and don't know it."

"Why do you say that?"

"There's quite a foot culture in Japan. Many men are turned on by a lovely foot. It must be in your genes. But I want to know more about you now that we're lovers. We are lovers, aren't we? I mean this isn't a . . ."

"One-night stand? No, we're lovers. But you got the cart before the horse. You should have asked to know all about me first. Suppose you don't like what you hear?"

"Well, then I'm stuck, nothing I can do about it." She watched him while not seeming to. "The first question is why, given all the things you might have been, are you an electrical engineer?"

"Well, I didn't want to be a fireman or an Indian chief. And I have just one thing going for me. I don't believe the impossible *is* impossible. At school I was told I had no common sense. That's right, I haven't. That makes it easy for me to identify with things like two electrons at opposite ends of the universe who have some kind of superluminous connection that enables them to communicate faster than the speed of light."

She rolled away from him, taking the sheet with her. "And you want to inscribe it all into your wafers." She sat up. "What about your wife?"

"We're divorced."

"I thought that's what you said." She shook her head. "But don't worry. It's a prerequisite with me that I fall in love with men I can't marry. My father would never consent to my marrying a Sansei. So it doesn't matter to me whether or not you're available."

"That sounds odd to hear from a modern woman. 'My father would not consent.' "

"That's because, after all, you are American, you don't understand us."

"Do you understand yourselves? Why, for instance, have the Japanese taken to celebrating Christmas?"

"That's easy. Because it's a present-giving holiday. We love giving presents. And we love holidays. We are just starting to celebrate Halloween. The last few years the stores have been full of costumes, witches, and pumpkins."

"How about Thanksgiving?"

"That's being added, but just as a feast day. We haven't figured out how to incorporate pilgrims and Indians."

"The Fourth of July?"

"We're working on it."

"Bastille Day?" They rolled over on each other, laughing.

The times she prized most were those evenings they tried to figure out who she was and who he was. She found herself telling him the stories that were part of her growing up, especially those Oba-sama told about her grandfather Noboru. "I always thought it was odd to have a young grandfather. Everyone else's grandfather was old. But mine was twenty-two, dashing in his flight uniform, a *hachimaki* around his head. He was very good-looking. I used to be in love with him. Until I got too old for him," she laughed.

"Was he the kamikaze? I've never understood that. I mean, if you have a chance, any chance at all, that's one thing. But to deliberately sign on for a one-way mission with no possibility you'll come out alive. I don't see it. Especially by then the war was over."

"That's the very reason. Just because the war was lost. He did it for what came after. He did it for us. I always thought he did it for me."

Doug shook his head. "I don't get it," he said again.

"I even think," she added, "he did it for you."

⛩

Miko came in from an evening spent with Doug. They had made love at the beach trailer, watched a foreign film on the VCR, and drunk good champagne. Her mood was glowing and she smiled as she crossed the atrium and started up the stairs.

The sound that reached her was not loud, but it caused her to turn and listen. The small scratching noise seemed to come from the study. Switching on more lights, she went back down. The door to the study was ajar. She pushed it open.

Juro sat on the polished wood floor, staring at the fireplace, which at this time of year was swept clean. His right hand scrabbled in a persistent manner against the floorboards, removing the wax sheen and digging into the wood, leaving a small groove.

To her horror she saw blood from Juro's fingers dropping into the scarred area. "What are you doing?" she cried in consternation.

He didn't move; there was no indication that he knew she was there. "Oh, Juro." She sat down on the floor beside him. It was evident, what should have been evident at the beginning, the problem with Juro was not going to go away. She watched him uncertainly for a moment. Finally she said, "Let me see your hand." She took it and it lay unresisting in hers. A thin sliver had embedded itself under the

nail. "I'd better get that out. I think I have a tweezer in my purse."
She rifled through it, then dumped the contents out. "Yes. Look, the
end is blunt, I think I can get it with this." She bent over his hand.
"Tell me if I hurt you."

He jerked away. "It's not the hand. It's the fucking fireplace. Did
you ever see a fireplace shrunk to the size of a postage stamp? And
that's just the start, I mean it started with the fireplace, but everything
is getting smaller. You can't actually see it happening, but just look
away a moment, then look back. There! You see!" His voice rose to
a shout. "What did I tell you!" The irises of his eyes were without
rims and fixated.

Miko took his head between her hands. "Juro, you know you're
talking nonsense. Calm down, take a deep breath. That's it." She
continued soothing, stroking, reassuring until gradually the tension
went out of him. But the fight went out of him as well. "Miko"—his
voice was almost inaudible—"I'm falling apart. I don't know what's
real anymore. I stand in puddles of terror and the world doesn't obey
Newton's Third Law. Inanimate things have power over me, tables rise
up against me, chairs battle me. Windows smile and beckon me to
jump out of them. And the thing that holds me together, the faint
memory of sanity, keeps getting fainter." He reached for her, his grip
tightening spasmodically. "Miko, help me!"

She pried his hands from her collar. "I will help you, but you
have to help too. You have to agree to help yourself."

He crumpled into her lap.

"Juro," she whispered, "I can't manage this kind of thing. You
have to have professional help."

She felt him stiffen. Even in this abject state he was resisting.

"It's the only way," she insisted. "We've run out of options."

He sat bolt upright, his eyes bright, focused, and hard. "You want
to lock me up."

"There's a place in Orange County, a private sanitarium. It can
all be handled. Your files will be confidential. Father won't know, I
promise you. You have my word."

⛩

On the drive to Greenfields, Juro was silent and hostile. Miko made apologetic attempts to reach him. "You know it's the only way, Juro. If you don't get clean your whole life is ruined."

"I remind you whose life it is."

That was the trouble, when he was off the stuff he was reasonable, even persuasive. But how long before he would be screaming, sobbing out the hell of a bad trip? Last night it was the fireplace; before that he had been swept off the earth while a world of endless space lapped at him.

At such moments it would have felt right to put him in rehab. But it required all her resolution now, when he was rational. She was used to acceding to him as the boy of the family. It took a great deal of resolve to flout him.

He broke his haughty samurai pose long enough to ask, "I have your promise about Father?"

"He'll never know, I swear it."

His dread of his father was as great as his fear of madness, and it was that more than anything that kept him in line.

Greenfields had the ambience of a posh country club; there were golf links, several tennis courts, and the attendants did not wear white coats but mingled with the guests.

Miko pulled up in a slot designated Guest Parking. Juro, who was quite taken with the Western custom of public kissing, reached over as though to give his sister a farewell peck on the cheek, instead he bit her. Miko uttered a small cry.

"I'll get you for this, Miko. Remember, the world tilts. . . ."

He used to say the same thing to her as a young boy whenever she crossed him: *The world tilts until the wrong is righted.* And he always kept his word. When she had forgotten about the threat, she would find that her regrets had been phoned in for a wedding she expected to attend, or that she had canceled a theater party, or that there was trouble with Sumie over some made-up tale. Miko never could imagine what form Juro's revenge would take, but as in *The Tale of the Forty-seven Ronin*, it would be arranged. This time, however, she found she couldn't be angry, he was so confused, so frightened, so ambivalent. All that was left of happiness were shards that cut him like knives. It broke her heart to see that he mistrusted her, for who else was there to stand by him?

᛭ ᛭

Momoko woke up feeling happy and not at all surprised to find a morning rainbow spanning the bellflowers and bush clover. When seen in the morning a rainbow was supposed to be a harbinger of rain. But she didn't believe that. There would be no rain today, it was Wednesday. And like a young girl she counted the hours until they would be together.

It was a love that all these years she had kept to herself and told only to the wind. But it was this that nourished her spirit. When he embraced her it was with his whole being. And her love for him was no tame thing, no cultivated garden plant, but a wild growth. Once she had fought these feelings, but can you fight the sudden storm of your heart? It is part of your body, it is you.

And the years proved this right, for with him downstream was the same as upstream; he had loved her when she was young, he loved her now when she was old. She felt safe with him. She felt other things as well, an over-the-moon happiness when she was with him that the remainder of the week kept her humming about the house and serene in facing difficulties. It was true that she had to mask her feelings and speak many lies to account for her absence each Wednesday. But they were lies based in truth, the *ura* side itself had an *ura* side. After all, she must exist in the same *dohyo* as the rest of the family. And the few hours set aside on Wednesdays did not subtract from her contribution to the household. She reminisced with Yoriko about the past, the war and all that it had taken. She attended to Masaru's needs, kept in touch with Miko, was conversant with Sumie's life and to some extent Ryoko's, worried about Juro, and from a distance uneasily surveyed her son's enormous success.

Besides all this, she picked fresh flowers and arranged them daily, worked in the garden, and in no way withheld any part of herself from the family . . . except on Wednesdays. An inauspicious day on any calendar, for her it crowned the week like a string of gems stretching back over the years.

And this morning another pleasure awaited her, a letter on her breakfast tray. The writing on the envelope was Miko's, and she smiled, remembering a little girl's first childish attempts to form her letters.

She read the note through quickly for news: Akio's project was going well and kept her busy traveling between Malibu and San Clemente; she and Juro had seen a play; she loved living at the beach and took long walks by the sea. Momoko pursed her lips at this account. This was what Miko wanted her to hear, but it wasn't what the letter said. Momoko read it again, slowly, with knit brows. The letter could not repress the happiness that permeated each unrelated incident: the job, the play, Juro, the sea, the walks. Only with the mention of Juro did she sense that Miko was touching earth. For the rest—a dangerous happiness.

The danger was that Miko was in a land among strangers, and had chosen one of them. She herself had given the initial spin to the top that was almost certain to waver and topple over. The education she thought would free Miko had thrust her into a male-dominated world, and Miko was vulnerable. The ties of her own tradition were loosened, and she was not comfortable with those of the West. She was, Momoko thought, adrift between earth and sky. She sighed for Miko's happiness, wishing it could be as secure as her own, but at the same time realizing that each person opens the door and invites his own misfortune in. She folded the letter carefully and tucked it into her stationery box. What could one say to a woman in love? It was too late for "Be careful."

The *ofuro* soaked away the small cloud she had been served with breakfast. Wednesday! said the flowers nodding in the garden. Wednesday! called a house swallow. Wednesday! a patch of bright sunlight on the tatami proclaimed. She made out a long shopping list for Kenji, and suggested, as she did every Wednesday, that afterward he go home and have lunch with his wife. Kenji was the only one who knew about this day, but even he didn't know where she went. Of course he realized he was part of some larger scheme when each time she took the basket of food from him, pretending she had purchased it herself. Yes, Kenji knew in a general way, but he didn't know who it was she met. She never went directly, but by circuitous routes, worked out and changed every few weeks. They had thought this wise, because too many people would be affected if their relationship ever came to light. She had a family, he had a family—it would be a disaster. But being aware of the risk, they did every sensible thing to guard against it. This day she happily took the express train for a fifteen-minute ride out of the city and back, before starting for their house.

Yes, they had their own house, an ordinary little house in a street of ordinary little houses. It was simple, neat, and opened to a garden, the garden she had dreamed of as a girl. Every plant she had put in herself, spending some of the happiest hours of her life there. She hastened to it each time with the same expectations. As she reached the house, her heart beat a bit more quickly.

Takeo opened the door. He had arrived first and shooed the servant into the kitchen, where she prepared tea. Their meetings were never casual; each time was like the first.

He thanked her for coming, as though she had not come every Wednesday for thirty-five years.

"One hundred million," he said, taking her hand and leading her into the garden, "and one heart." Meaning he would set the feeling in his heart against one hundred million others.

They sat on a stone bench, sharing the brightness of the garden and the day. "You look especially lovely this afternoon, Momoko."

She smiled, he told her that each time.

"To describe you," he went on, "is not possible. One might as well try to catch the wind in a net. But," he added, "I think I am wrong to praise you, it is praising myself. You are myself."

Love-words and a delicious silence, during which they munched sweet bean jam and rice cakes. Momoko poured the tea; she was the hostess here, not Sumie or Ryoko, but she. This was their house, their garden, their tea, and the oshiruko had never tasted better. How could she explain the contentment of sitting here with him? It would be like explaining a dream.

Afterward they went into the six-tatami mat room and closed the door. "You give me," he whispered to her, "the strength that only a woman can give a man." She placed a finger against his lips, and they completed each other. Afterward, when they had dressed and were preparing to leave separately, she said to him, "Without you I also have no self."

⛩

Geisha entered from the garden, a stately pine, a slender, yielding bamboo . . . gracious, balanced on gold geta whose bells tinkled as she stepped out of them. One attitude blended dancelike into the next.

Akio had looked forward to this night with geisha. But the episode at home left him unable to react. His soul was sick. Even Setsuko's approach, sliding one foot pigeon-toed in front of the other with knees slightly bent, failed to move him. Taking several steps in his direction, the geisha bowed, and the wayward strands of shining locks that had escaped the fullness of the chignon fell forward; she wore the elaborate *tsubushi shimada* for his delectation. Unclasping her hands, she took sake from a low table, handling it as though it were a vial of holy water. He noticed the barely perceptible slope of her shoulders.

Setsuko was a rare orchid of the flower-and-willow world. He had met her three years before when she performed Kamo River dances at the National Theater. In the traditional *Pine and Bamboo*, he had cried *"Mameyuki!"*

When she danced *The Journey of the Butterflies*, the artistry with which she captured the suicide love pact touched him. He had never witnessed such perfection of movement. He sent a note backstage.

His limousine waited for her at the alley door. She entered it, holding the hem of her kimono in her left hand in a typical geisha gesture.

That night he learned two things: that the art of life can transcend the art of the stage and that Setsuko did not grant the pillow.

He had played with geisha before, but only she had the ability to erase his life and cause the world itself to fade. She substituted for it a timeless water world.

That was what he needed now, tonight, to be taken from himself, lifted by her art to some other realm. If she could work her magic on him tonight, she would be a sorceress indeed.

That evening he and Masaru had arrived back in Tokyo. After bathing and dressing he went to retrieve Masaru for their nightly game. Obviously he came before he was expected, for he witnessed a scene that shocked his soul. He knew, of course he knew Masaru was incapable of tending to himself. But at the same time the details had been carefully hidden from him.

He stood still, out of sight, pressed against the far side of the half-open rice-paper screen, watching as Momoko, with soothing noises and small exclamations, managed to get the *hashi* of noodles into Masaru's mouth. Many of the threadlike *somen* and much of the sauce was smeared on his face, which she kept wiping, reproving him as she did, speaking as one would to an infant, telling him to open wide, chiding him when he turned his head.

It was horrible to see. Akio was frozen to the spot, unable to go away or even make a sound.

Masaru messed himself and Momoko pushed him down on the tatami and undid his trousers, then removed the *fundoshi* he was swaddled in. Following what was apparently an old established routine, she dipped the ends of a paper towel in water and began to clean him, spreading his legs with her hand and wiping the feces from the crack between his buttocks, moving the towel to cleanse his scrotum and forward to flick traces from his penis which changed by the rhythm of her hands from flaccid to erect.

"No, no," she chided him, slapping down his hands, which reached for her. "Be good now. Be a good boy."

The forty-six-year-old man babbled at her and obeyed.

Akio backed away. He went to the toilet, not part of the bathroom but enclosed in its own cubicle, and there threw up repeatedly.

His whole life was a denial of what he had seen.

Masaru, fed, cleaned and changed, was brought to him looking manly and beautiful for their go game. He realized he insisted on this deception. Masaru was Masaru, his brother, arrows in one quiver and all the rest of that shit. He chose to forget he had smashed the cups. He remembered selectively, editing, lifting up only certain threads for examination, letting the rest lie buried.

The entire household cooperated in the farce. What must they think? His special truth had to be cleaned up before he could look at it, his brother made presentable before he could love him.

Tonight he forwent the go game. Tonight he could not stand any more doses of reality. He doubted he could ever play go with Masaru again.

Setsuko held her fan with the thumb on the inside and moved hand and wrist in a languorous gesture. *Iki*, style. Style was everything.

He was pleased that she wore a formal *homongi* for him, with its puddle of drapery on the floor, trailing and rustling provocatively as she walked. The sleeves fell to her hips, revealing a motif of willow shot through with gold strands. The flowing line contained the magic of twelve hundred years, emulating the folds of jasmine. The obi was tied daringly low, for the higher it is positioned, the more virginal the woman. The knot was stitched with clouds. Under it, suggestively erotic, was the barest glimpse of the *obi-age.*

The line of kimono was not spoiled by a line of underpants. Geisha wore none; only the finest of silk *koshimaki* was spread for a width of two feet across her belly. Setsuko had told him once in a confiding mood that she studied with a famous *onnagata*, the male impersonator of women in Kabuki theater. He taught her *sambaso*, the votive Shinto dance, and the finer feminine arts, such as where to apply perfume.

Setsuko placed the cup in his hand, and decorously began *oshaku* or "pouring." She sat beside him, keeping her back straight, tucking her feet under her. Her kimono swirled into classic lines. Clothes, he realized, revealed geisha. Akio lolled with his drink, attempting to relax. He watched her hands as she poured another sake. In even the simplest motions they were birds on the wing.

She reached for her samisen, which leaned against the wall, arching her back as she did so, revealing the nape of the neck, lustrous, pale, and seductive against the black hair and the wayward lock that escaped her perfect coiffure. She plucked the lute-like strings and sang *nagauta*, love songs. Her voice enticed, murmuring softly. She bent over her instrument in a pliant, coaxing way and the sleeves of the kimono fell from her wrists.

Akio reached a hand under her brocaded robe and grasped a folded foot, which he dragged toward him. Her body uncurled and slid close. He smelled the artificial smell of the thick white makeup and heavy rice powder with which geisha cover their faces.

"I have acquired geisha taste," he said. "No other woman can make me happy."

She stretched out her leg and let her small, high-instepped foot climb his chest until it rested against his face. Each toe was exquisitely chiseled, like the tiny shells one finds at Enoshima beach. The heel was a pearl-like mound, soft, as though it had been bathed in limpid spring water. He caressed it many minutes before pressing it against his genitals in erotic massage. He imbibed steadily, fondling the foot and allowing himself to be fondled in turn.

"I like a man to be well-hung. Such a man responds to the games I play."

"Play away," he said, alive only to her touch. "Is it true," he asked to tease her, "that geisha use unguents of nightingale droppings?"

She laughed. "Would you rather we used some other kinds of droppings?"

He tucked his hand inside her kimono. "My head is in mists. Swirls of mists like the base of Fuji. What aphrodisiac do you use?"

"A man's own juices."

"What was in the sake, charred eel and lotus root?"

She only laughed, the barest tinkling of some distant bell.

He liked the sensation of being mildly tipsy and the license it gave him to put his head between her thighs and push them apart.

She exchanged sake cups with him and, rising slowly so as not to displace his hands, danced above him while he clutched her clipped pubic hair, feeling both mound and damp slit. Knees pointing outward, she stooped, allowing his mouth while from her sleeve she took the diced rings of a sea slug and fit them on his penis like a French tickler. It was the ultimate geisha game. The customer expressed his sperm and quieted.

He had played with geisha. They took formal leave of each other, not touching.

Akio stepped out of the inn into the maze of lights and signs typical of downtown Tokyo. The twentieth century thudded against him. His bodyguard fell in behind him; the garish neon stripped him of the protective haze in which he had been indulged and catered to, which had wiped out time and place and the sight of Masaru fouling himself.

He had once seen a puppy being tortured by a group of children who rammed a thorn into its eyes, blinding it. In this fresh burst of agony, Akio wished for the thorn. But it would do no good. He wasn't seeing through his eyes. To be effective the stake must be driven through his mind, for it was there he saw Masaru.

He urinated against the side of a building. He urinated on the twentieth century, on the couples that passed, on the Americans. He thought of having Kenji fix him up with some college kid who prostituted herself as a sideline, collecting money for a trip to California.

But he needed more distraction. His own car was too conspicuous, so he took a taxi. The driver, in cap and white gloves, drove him to Mother's Place, marked by a red lantern. It had been bought by him and given years ago to Azuma. Her trademark was the row of individual bottles of Remy Martin VSOP cognac, which set it apart from the other *bottoro-kipu* bars that kept bottles for special customers with their names penciled on the label. She also served good sushi. But it was the clientele that attracted, that made it one of the in places, filling every night with *talentos* and TV *onapets.*

It was already late in the evening, and a group of salarymen were playing "shallow river" with a girl so young she had drawn hairs with eyebrow pencil on her mound. To the accompaniment of a shrill horn and drumbeat, the men formed a knot around her, demanding another glimpse. At the beginning of the game the skirt was only raised inches, but as the music and the lust quickened it was all the way. But the men had been ladder-drinking and were too far up the rungs to do more than laugh and joke and dare each other to wade in the shallow river. Someone mentioned *mizu-age*, and this brought derisive giggles. Yolks and whites of egg were used at one time to deflower a virgin. The man swallowed the yolks and rubbed the albumen between the girl's legs every night for seven nights. By that time she was relaxed and unsuspecting and penetration took place. Who had time for that kind of nonsense today?

Seven nights, shit!

Akio went past the champagne-and-oyster bar into the Peony Room, looking for Azuma. She was at one of the back tables, telephoning, but hung up when she saw him and rose, bowing, then rushed to embrace him.

"Akio-san." She pulled back slightly. "You've been drinking." Azuma was the one person who spoke out to him.

"Yes," he said, "and I plan to continue."

"In that case . . ." She ordered a specially blended Vieille Réserve cognac, which appeared almost instantly in a Baccarat crystal decanter. "I wish for you," Azuma leaned toward him, smiling, "that all your far-flung business enterprises, your multinationals and holding companies, banks and factories, do as well as this little bar of mine." She looked stunning in Western dress, sleek and sophisticated; one would never guess her gutter origins. She had aged well. Collagen treatments, retin-A, and the skilled hands of a masseuse kept her skin firm. She had developed an informed and cultivated taste in food, decor, dress, and judgment. In short, she made herself an invaluable member of Akio's team. Of course, she made a good thing of their relationship as well. It ceased being sexual years ago. Akio had his pick of young girls, starlets, singers, actresses. But Azuma was useful to him, and as a result lived in an expensive apartment and was driven about in a Lincoln

Town Car. These perks were in addition to the bar and restaurant. She was his conduit. Akio made it his business to know of deals in the works, of mergers before they happened, which foreign firms were weak and primed for takeover. What better way than through a still-handsome hostess who nightly listened to the drunken aspirations and disappointments of highly placed executives and political figures.

"Azuma, I have a new assignment for you."

"You know I will do my best. Who is to be the subject of this new project?"

"I am."

"You?" She looked at him in astonishment.

"Yes, me. I have all my life thought how lucky I have been. Everything I touched seemed to work out for me and to lead to other, equally profitable ventures. I always thought I was born under a fortunate ascension of stars."

"You are brilliant, Akio-san, you made your own luck, your own fortune."

He held up his hand. "Something happened earlier this evening, something I saw on a daily basis but never looked at. It started me thinking. . . . One accepts good fortune and questions bad. Only if things go wrong do you ask, 'Who did this to me? Who is responsible?' Isn't that right?"

"Yes, I suppose so."

"I have always been proud, perhaps too much so, of my accomplishments. But—and this is what has just occurred to me—when things go smoothly you tend to say to yourself, 'My facts and figures overwhelmed them.' Or, 'I was able to dominate by sheer force of will.' Or, 'I had additional voting shares.' Or, 'My vision was more penetrating, more long-term, more correct.' In other words, you convince yourself the good luck doesn't need looking into. But, and this is what I learned tonight, it all needs looking into, it all needs to be questioned."

"I don't understand you, Akio-san. But in that I am like the rest of the world. Tell me what you want me to do exactly."

"Treat me like any subject I ask for information on. Research my life, look at the various decisions I made, the companies I acquired, the financial deals. Research everything meticulously and then give me a complete report."

"On yourself."

"Exactly."

"You're drunk, Akio-san."

He shrugged. "I expect interesting results."

"What happened that makes you want to question everything?"

"Something that made me sick, physically sick. I threw up. But the soul has no release mechanism. It's stuck with all the crap."

"You talk in riddles, like a Zen monk."

Rallying a bit, he replied, "Why should I make your research easy? You are to find out everything about me, who I am and why."

"Are you drunk, Akio-san? Or do you really want me to do this?"

"I am drunk, and I want you to do this."

"You won't get angry with me?"

"I have a feeling it will be myself I will be angry with." He sat morosely for a while. "I went to geisha tonight."

"You did? Before coming here? I could have told you geisha are old-fashioned, out of the know. You had to come here to set things right."

"Geisha is old-fashioned, yes. But she has her place. Simply because she is from another time she gives you perspective and makes you remember something important . . . that you are Japanese."

"You never forget that, Akio-san."

He ignored her interpolation.

"I've brought the big guns into position. The Northern Territories are to be the ultimate battlefield on which to confront the brain-dead Americans."

"Brain-dead, the Americans? Why do you say that?"

"What is their reaction as the dollar slides? 'Don't worry. Be happy.' " He turned toward the bar to watch one of the customers seize the microphone and do a takeoff on Sammy Davis, Jr. But he only appeared to be watching these antics. In his mind he continued to unravel the thread. Brain-dead was exactly what they were. Concentrating for the last forty years on the USSR without ever reevaluating the situation, America hemorrhaged trillions into defense while gutting itself in R-and-D. And the record reflected it. The U.S. market in phonographs dropped from ninety percent to one percent, color TV from ninety to ten percent. Her consumer electronics manufacture skidded to below five percent. They'd nothing to sell anymore, not TVs, not radios, not VCRs, machine tools, microwave ovens, or cameras. So what do they have?

The power base of America is armaments, and *perestroika* pulled the rug out. They couldn't let go of the old fictions.

A new democratic Europe would make her big move with the European Community. Japan had made hers. Only Uncle Sam, that outdated old uncle, will not take off his blinders, wipe his eyes, and step onto the world stage. He can't. The EEG is flat. There are no signs the patient can be revived.

Banzai!

Azuma glanced sideways at Akio's vacant expression. She was used to these lapses when his eyes glazed over like a cat's.

He was thinking of Venice, Italy. In the fifteenth century a stiletto was designed, the blade of which was so thin that a man stabbed on the Grand Canal, though dead, had time to reach St. Mark's before he knew it. That was the condition of the Americans. The question was, when would they realize they were dead?

He knew the answer. When the nations of the world no longer accepted an unstable dollar as universal currency. The global community was awash in dollars. He'd recently made a business trip to Sweden. The timing had been crucial; the Swedish government was preparing to float a large international bond issue. As a result of his visit they'd brought out their issue not in dollars but in yen, starting a trend that would only gain momentum.

A fifty-billion-yen offering, and it was gobbled up by international investors. Were the Americans finally shaking in their boots? Not at all, they didn't even notice. The Swedish incident rated a mere mention on a back page of The Wall Street Journal.

But the dike had begun to trickle. There was worldwide reluctance to hold dollars. Tokyo's Ministry of Finance was pressing the U.S. Treasury to issue a hundred million in ten-year yen-denominated bonds through the Long Term Credit Bank of Japan.

"It's started," Akio said, suddenly verbalizing his thoughts.

Azuma was attentive. She always listened when Akio spoke.

"In Europe, economists have pegged everything to the EMS, the European Monetary System. Which really means tying it all to the deutsche mark. But it won't work. It can't. The European plan is unworkable because it ignores the power of the yen, which already outweighs their ridiculous EMS basket. The Pacific Rim will be the first yen bloc. And the twenty-first century will see a yen-dominated world. Think what that means! The yen will be the coin of the realm. It's a pincer movement—on one side the economy, on the other real estate. The return of the Northern Territories rubs out our great defeat and puts an end to the most protracted war in history."

"I don't know about all that, Akio-san. You'll have to explain to me one day about the Northern Territories. The one thing I know is that I am going to put you to bed here. You're in no condition to go home."

Akio, who a moment before had controlled the world, was docile under her hands, allowing his toenails to be cut, his ears cleaned with a cotton swab, and the hairs clipped from his nostrils while soup heated on the hibachi. After all, it was the duty of a servant or Azuma or his mother to see he was given a bowl of miso soup, groomed, and put to bed. It didn't matter who performed these services. In Akio's mind women were interchangeable. Azuma gave the best back rub. But with her head for business and intrigue and her never-failing sense of what was best for Azuma, she lacked the ultimate feminine quality of soft acquiescence.

His wife, who should have attended to these needs, did not. He often looked at her, seeing the girl in the middy blouse leaning her bike against the wall. It was twenty years—not since Juro's birth had Sumie ministered to him. He had made that impossible, he had made everything between them impossible.

It had all stopped abruptly, the warmth, the confidence, the intimacy. He had destroyed it. He'd had no choice. It was necessary to repay the *on* he owed Masaru. When he'd made the pledge he'd not yet married Sumie and had not known that an understanding would grow between them, expressed as much in comfortable silences as in wet love. But there was no question that the pledge must be fulfilled. Juro was born, his line established. There was no longer an excuse to defer his obligation.

He entered Sumie's quarters, leading his cousin by the hand, and took him to the edge of her tatami.

Sumie looked up at him, startled. To overcome the rush of human feeling, Akio spoke brutally. "I owe Masaru. He has my promise."

It bewildered Sumie to see the two men standing there. "You promised him—what?"

He didn't reply.

Some intuition woke in her. She backed away from them into a corner of the room. "Akio, no!"

"I can never pay the *on* I owe him. But I must pay what I can. Sumie, it may kindle some memory."

"Do you know what you're asking?"

"It's promised," he said again.

"You'd no right. Besides, it was promised to an idiot who doesn't know, who can't remember."

"*I* know and *I* remember."

"Akio . . . he makes my skin crawl."

"He loved you."

"Look at him. He's an imbecile."

"He was present at my seven-five-three ceremony."

"Respect me, I'm your wife, the mother of your son."

"I do respect you, Sumie."

"Then take him away. Now. Take him out of my room, away from me."

Akio did not move.

"You must, Akio-san. I couldn't stand it."

"It's no use. We are caught in the same *giri.*"

Sumie became calm, she stopped pleading. "I'll never forgive you."

"I know that."

She searched his face and, seeing no reprieve, obediently lay down on the mat and closed her eyes.

Ryoko and old Yoriko had been waiting with Masaru. They undressed him and massaged his body with sweet oils until there was understanding in him at a physical level.

The idiot covered Sumie, who lay under him like one dead. Her teeth were clenched, and her fingernails pressed four small curved lines of blood into the palms of her hands.

Akio slid the door to, closing out the would-be spectators. There was an excessive amount of saliva on Masaru's face as he pressed it against Sumie.

Akio looked away. He saw the matching sake cups he had stolen when he was seven. He saw his own face in the water, as he repeated Masaru's words.

Brothers . . .

Two arrows . . .

He saw . . . himself breathing into Masaru's mouth, giving him his life.

He turned back. Sumie's eyes were still closed. Masaru was inert beside her. Akio put out his hand. He touched the wall for support. The sound of a sob escaped into the room. One of them was crying.

Although the main house was fitted with shoji panels, the walls erected between the inhabitants were more substantial. Yoriko was dying. The old woman was somewhere between *beiju*, the age of rice, and *hakuju*, the white age. She had no illness but was fading like an old kimono that had seen too many days of sun and rain. She communicated almost solely with Momoko and had forgotten that there had been a time when she was not on friendly terms with her daughter-in-law.

Akio wondered what the thread was, the kernel of being that made her the woman he had known as a child, the grandmother who had given him three *moxa*. He bore the scars still. For Akio the *moxa* were badges of courage.

Did this old dying woman remember? What memories had she? Did she think of her son the Oka fighter? Of her husband indicted as a war criminal, who had died in prison? Had she outlived passion, love, memories? Did the brittle husk of a body that wrapped her retain anything of the past? If not, what spark made her Yoriko?

Even as a child he had never felt affection for her. She kept sweets in her pockets for him, but he did not care for sweets. She showed clearly that she favored him over Masaru, but he did not need her.

Her tight rein as the matriarch of the family gradually loosened and she relinquished her hold, to retire to a ceremonial position in the house, content to have the younger women squabble over what had been her domain. Ryoko continued to consult her out of form, but Sumie did not bother.

Momoko, her friend, stayed aloof from the day-to-day running of the household and the affairs of its occupants. She had put in her time; there was not an inch of floor she had not been over on her hands and knees, no sheet or other bedding that had not known her washing and mending. She made no attempt to assert her influence, but deferred to Ryoko. Was it really so important that winter clothes were lined on a Tuesday or a Thursday? She had never been able to persuade herself of this.

Ryoko, on the other hand, was passionate about managing the house. For with Shigeru's death a dozen years before, her position in the Sanogawa clan was considerably weakened.

The years had not been kind to Ryoko; her tightly drawn skin had yellowed and wrinkled while Momoko still retained the creamy complexion of a girl and the same serene, unhurried manner. She was entering her later years a beautiful woman. Akio, who was exceedingly proud of her, secretly thought it was her consistent refusal to involve herself with anyone or anything that kept her young. Life washed over her without touching her. There had been tragedies, but she distanced herself from them. She did not worry, she did not grieve, she did not get close. And so her lovely face remained unlined.

He was her only child. Yet the symbol of her love, the thing she talked sometimes to him about, was a red silk bunting she made for him before he was born. She had loved the child who wore her bunting. He felt it could have been any child.

And now one link in this intricate chain of relationships was about to snap. His grandmother, who would soon cease to be, requested that he come to her. And although he was a man of forty-four, a chief player on the global stage of trade and politics, he nevertheless felt a sense of solemnity and awe on approaching his father's mother, who stood at the edge of time.

Yoriko was freshly bathed and dressed in a ceremonial robe. Momoko had leaned her against a stack of cushions on the tatami. Beside her a jar of incense gave off its fragrant wisp of smoke, masking the odors of age. The *zabuton* were placed to take advantage of the garden, which was an integral part of the room.

Akio bowed to his grandmother and took a seat at her feet. A servant served tea. The old woman kept silent. The silence permeated his mind. She was believed to be ninety-seven years old but the mask of her face was timeless. She had left the world and the affairs of men to cultivate another garden than the one she looked at.

She startled him by saying his name clearly and distinctly. "Akio."

"Yes, Grandmother."

"That elderly pine at the edge of the garden. Do you see it? I knew it when we were both young. But I wish to speak to you about something else. It is in regard to my son-in-law, Shigeru."

This reference to the dead Shigeru surprised Akio.

"I have been concerned about Shigeru lately. Since the war your uncle has been content to carry on the original family business, the manufacture of toys, devoting himself to the company, to its growth and integrity. Until now it has been extremely lucrative. But Momoko tells me new laws have come into effect that have to do with safety and flammability standards. She tells me that on your advice Shigeru is disregarding these laws, tempted by the larger margin of profit. Akio, I beg you, do not destroy this man. He is Masaru's father. Do not advise him wrongly, Akio." The ancient, frail hands fluttered in agitation a moment before subsiding on her lap.

"Do not worry, Grandmother. I can do nothing to Shigeru. Why should I want to?"

"And the advice you gave him?"

"He is under no obligation to follow it."

"But he could lose the company."

"The company would not go outside the family, I promise you that."

"And Shigeru, what will become of Shigeru?"

"Do not worry about him, Grandmother, a token of him resides on the home shrine."

The pause became drawn out.

"Then it was some yesterdays ago?"

"Yes, Grandmother."

"I will rest now. Tell Noboru to play more quietly."

Akio set down the teacup and withdrew; he had not envisioned such an unsettling interview. He hadn't realized at the time that Yoriko knew anything of what was going on. She hadn't mentioned it to him until now, a quarter of a century later and long after Shigeru was dead.

Was she purging herself for not having interceded for Shigeru? For all errors of omission? Well, it did not lie on his conscience.

But other things were not so easily disposed of. He had not been able to play go with Masaru since the evening he saw Momoko prepare him. He had tried for almost thirty years to give Masaru back his life. But not even Sumie had been able to do that.

There were times when Masaru cried like a child. Usually it was Momoko who comforted him, but it was hard to get him to stop. He knew he was unhappy without knowing reasons. Masaru spent his love on a cat whom he played with. When it died Momoko replaced it with a similar cat.

Sumie? Sumie had locked the door.

The life Akio followed with passionate concern was the life of his companies, the life of the yen, and the progress of his personal war through which he planned to vindicate his father's death. Night after night he worked out his moves alone at the go board.

For long stretches of time Akio lived the life of a monk. Then he would exhaust himself with vacant-eyed *talentos* and fifteen-year-old *onapets* playing body games and indulging in "forget the year" parties.

But he was easily bored, easily disgusted. After such dissipation he would bathe and, in kimono, make a pilgrimage. Kneeling long hours in contemplation, he heard the frogs, the cicadas, the night heron stalking carp in the sunny water of the pond. When he heard nothing he would return refreshed and plunge back into overseeing the affairs that pressed upon him from every continent.

Recently, in the middle of a delicate maneuver, his mind would wander to Juro. He wondered if he expected too much from Juro, who he had always assumed would at the proper time take over from him. Juro's role was inscribed in the tablet of his heart. One day he would succeed him, and, on a further day, pray for him.

He was a beautiful son. Even as a small child he was beautiful, and his mother dressed him like a prince. He was bright as well, clever in school. There were a few lapses owing to high spirits, but they amounted to nothing. He had been accepted at Keio University and, with other young men of his class, lolled his way through the four years.

During this period he gave him a sizable portfolio of investments and shares in some of his holdings, with an eye as to how he did with them. He was gratified in checking them over at six-month intervals, to find that the boy handled his portfolio shrewdly.

In the beginning Juro was guided by his sister. Akio had never regretted raising and educating her, but Miko was a difficult child. She did not fit easily into the household. She tried too hard, demanding affection, but could not believe in it when it was given. An insecure child, whose brilliance no one could doubt. Only Momoko succeeded in penetrating the many barriers she put in the way of love. His mother had mentioned quite pointedly only last week that he should arrange a marriage for Miko. He'd nodded absently. There was some truth in what she said, to be sure, but there was plenty of time. Besides, in her shrewdness Miko was very like her mother and he needed, in fact depended on her.

Akio told himself he must stop analyzing his family as though it were a holding company he was thinking of acquiring. He did not know how to relax anymore. Time away from work was more stressful than overseeing the hundred and one details that crossed his desk.

The call from Azuma came. The message that she would like to see him at his convenience could only mean she had information for him. He found that he was apprehensive. This was himself waiting to be exposed; his life, his intrigues, his envelope passing. How would his hopes and dreams look from the outside, neatly categorized in a ledger?

Reading a folder on himself, would he think, "What a fool?" His typical reaction when studying the briefs of others. He called for Kenji, who appeared so swiftly that he must have been waiting. Although he wore the white gloves of a driver, and it was he who paid his salary, Akio knew it was his mother to whom Kenji owed primary allegiance. She was the only one of the family who took any interest in him. It was she who told him Kenji was married to a Korean woman. He hadn't known. This concern of his mother's was repaid with an almost doglike devotion. He, on the contrary, had always kept Kenji at a distance, partly because he was born under a cloud, and partly because he could not forgive his resemblance to his half brother. Looking at him tonight, he thought of the days he and Masaru were boys together.

Would the Akio of those years feel the same apprehension he experienced now? The very idea was ridiculous. What had happened between then and now to make such a feeling grow in his belly?

Mother's Place had not opened for the evening. The empty rooms, chairs leaning inward against the tables, the long ebony bar unattended, produced an eerie effect. The quiet had an expectant quality about it. One sensed the noisy, milling, laughing, smoking, jostling crowds that would soon spill into it.

Azuma was in her office at the rear. She rose and bowed as he entered. Tea was ready at her elbow; she served and poured it graciously and the ceremony was gotten through appropriately. When the silence had accumulated sufficiently, Azuma broke it to say, "I thought it might be of interest to you to hear the report we have gathered on the subject, although it is only preliminary. . . ."

The subject, of course, the subject. It was typical of Azuma to finesse it. She proceeded, reading a report written in the third person that continued to refer to "the subject." On this impersonal note it went on, oddly enough, to relate the affair with Shigeru and the toy factory.

When they were going to close it down for violation of safety standards he had petitioned to be allowed, as a family member, to run it properly. On hearing the story recounted, Akio nodded—it was pretty much what had happened. But wait a minute, here was something he didn't know. The petition had been approved by one Takeo Kuroda.

Akio's knuckles blanched as he gripped the arm of his chair. Takeo? Why should his stepfather concern himself? Why interject himself? He had married another woman, he had both sons and a daughter. He had no business dispensing favors to him. Did he hope to ease his conscience by approving a petition that undoubtedly would have been granted anyway?

"I won't have it!" he said aloud.

Azuma looked up in surprise. "Is something the matter?"

"Yes, something's the matter. I have worn an *on* to this man since my childhood. I won't be in his debt any further, I refuse."

"It looks to me as though it was a casual thing. The petition happened to cross his desk and there was no reason to deny it."

"No, it was not casual. It was deliberate. He sought it out. He wanted to put me at this disadvantage."

"He must have thought you would never know."

"Not at all. Why shouldn't it come out some day? And when it did I would be entangled in more *on* that I can never repay, even if I wished to. And I've no wish to have anything to do with that man."

"But Akio-san, he has a great deal to do with you."

"What's that? What do you mean?"

"His name appears again and again in this document."

"What?" Akio thundered, and, getting to his feet, snatched the report from her. He riffled the pages. Staring out at him from almost every page was *Takeo Kuroda*. He had interceded for him when the company needed a license to expand into robotics. His name was on a government consent form issued when Akio applied to the Long-Term Credit Bank to borrow against holdings for his real-estate transactions.

It was unbelievable, this man, this betrayer, this enemy, had set himself up as his personal *kami*. Throughout his career, this man had championed every enterprise. It would seem that what he had seen as his luck was, in reality, Takeo, looking over his shoulder, smoothing things for him at each crossroad.

MITI had seen to it that contracts were awarded him over larger and more established firms. In two cases of patent disputes Takeo's had been the deciding vote. In one instance eighty million dollars accrued as a result. It was intolerable!

Things he thought he himself had brought about by clever maneuvering, manipulation, and foresight had in fact come to fruition through the efforts of one man—not himself. Takeo Kuroda.

Azuma made herself small in the face of Akio's anger. His rage was hot lava, moving in a molten stream of invective. "He'd no right! Bastard! At any crucial moment in my life, there he is, this person who injects himself into the equation, who brings his influence to bear when it is unwarranted. Unwarranted and unnecessary. Was it so unlikely I would have pulled off the computer deal on my own? Of course not, but now I'll never know. His constant interference has undermined me utterly.

"Were my successes my own? Or were they simply favors? If the whole way has been paved for me, what have I accomplished? This motherfucking son of a bitch has beaten me at every turn. He has used a screen of kindness to undermine my confidence, make me doubt myself. But if he thought I would be crushed into the dust by *on*, he is mistaken. Like a *rikishi* wrestler I have not yet touched the ground. I can recover my balance."

He turned to the woman crouched in the corner. "There is a new assignment. Takeo Kuroda."

Azuma gasped. "He is very highly placed. He has the ear of the Minister of Finance, and is venerated by all who know him as a Shimpu fighter. The papers call him 'Mister Clean.' There can be nothing against such a man."

"We won't know that, will we, until we look?"

"*Asahi Shimbun* carried an article just last week. Surely you saw it? Someone in one of his offices was caught tampering with the books to disguise the fact that a large sum of money had been siphoned out of the operation. Your honored colleague reacted by personally taking a salary cut until he himself had paid the money back."

"Yes, yes, clever. He got a good deal of mileage out of that. There is no doubt the man is clever. Clever, wealthy, highly placed. All of that. That's the challenge we are faced with. Somewhere there is a chink in his armor. Find it."

⛩

Azuma did not scruple to employ yakuza. She had used them in the past and made no bones about it. They got things done. If their methods were somewhat unsavory, she did not concern herself. If they used intimidation, that was undoubtedly what it took. She was aware that occasionally people were roughed up. But the yakuza produced results. You could depend on them.

She had first availed herself of their services when Akio backed a political candidate. The yakuza saw to it that the opposition didn't speak in the Diet for more than three minutes. At one point they turned off the power to the microphone. On another occasion they threw chairs and created such pandemonium that the chambers were cleared. There was no question as to their effectiveness, none at all.

She found them extremely deferential—swaggering they saved for public appearances. It was part of their mystique, like the Mercedes they drove. If they were surprised that such an eminent person as Takeo Kuroda was their assignment, they were professional enough not to reveal it. He was not the first prominent figure they had tailed. Azuma requested a twenty-four-hour surveillance.

Takeo's conduct appeared exemplary. He seemed to follow the same routine, the same busy schedule, day after day.

Until Wednesday.

By Wednesday the yakuza became bored and grew a bit careless. On Wednesday the subject gave him the slip. Perhaps it was unintentional, nevertheless he disappeared.

Thursday it was back to the same routine, breakfast with his family, chauffeured to his office, meetings till noon. Then to the putting green on the roof in lieu of lunch. The pattern continued, afternoons were filled with more meetings, and he generally paid a call on one or two government officials.

In the evening he repaired with other highly placed individuals from MITI, or the Diet, or his own Finance Ministry, to one of Tokyo's elegant night spots. They dined together and drank in earnest, usually visiting several bars where they were frequently joined by the *mama-san* and a *talento* or two.

As they grew progressively drunk they entertained each other with songs, impersonations, and off-color jokes.

Around two o'clock the subject's chauffeur came in and, prying him loose from a weeping minister of state, delivered him home. And so it went until Wednesday.

The yakuza, aware that last Wednesday he had been given the slip, was especially alert. In spite of this it happened again. The subject was in the men's room and then he wasn't. The yakuza could not discover a trace of him or where he had gone.

It seemed improbable to him that the subject knew he was being followed. It was more likely a habit of long standing to be particularly careful on Wednesdays.

The third Wednesday the yakuza was led a merry chase. Again he was confident he had not been spotted. Whom was he protecting that made his quarry so careful? The wife of a colleague? A movie star? A great lady of a famous house? The yakuza found himself indulging in unprofessional curiosity.

The subject left his limousine and took a cab. The cab after a short detour parked in a lower middle-class residential district. The subject paid the driver and started down the street, walking briskly. Which indicated he knew exactly where he was going, since houses are numbered in the order they were built and the addresses have nothing to do with location. Sure enough, he turned into a modest house in the Japanese style. An aged servant opened the door and with deep bows admitted him as though he were expected. The yakuza grunted with satisfaction. This week, for the first time, there would be something of interest in his report.

⛩

They met with smiles, but for different reasons each had a heavy heart.

Takeo, always perceptive where she was concerned, turned her face up to his. "You are touched with sadness today, Momoko."

Momoko felt when his arms were about her that he could ward off autumn, the season before death. "I cannot stay long today. Mother-in-law has weakened very much. I think the life wind will soon be stopped."

"She is old, but, still, Death keeps no calendar."

"I have been close to her. My feeling is it will happen at any moment."

"You always puzzle me, Momoko, which is one reason I love you. But I find it strange that you grieve in advance of death for someone who was cruel and unjust to you, someone who came between you and Noboru and ultimately drove him to enlist in the Divine Wind."

Momoko was quiet a long time. He felt her heart against his chest. "Mother-in-law shed a tear for me when Akio was born."

"So you forgave her everything."

"Not forgave, understood. Her tear was not only for the pain of birth, it was for the pain of death. It was her duty to tell me of Noboru's death. I think of it this way, Takeo-san, that life punishes us enough, we don't need to punish each other. Look yourself at how life stripped her, first Noboru, then Tomonori, and finally Yasue. Today she is surrounded by family, yet alone . . . except for me. Besides," she continued more lightly, "I must have been very spoiled in those days. She used to tell me that I had been brought up under a painted parasol."

"And then came the hardships of the war."

"Yes. Afterward, during the Occupation, I saw newsreels of Americans waving and cheering their soldiers off to battle. How different with us, do you remember? Large crowds standing in silence."

"I remember, and I wish I did not. I wish you could have continued under your parasol."

"If I had, I doubt you would love me."

"It is true, the one a samurai loves must know the spot in the throat to plunge the dagger in. She must be strong."

"Mother-in-law used to say, 'If you fall down seven times, you must get up eight.' "

As they talked their voices became softer and then stopped altogether. His hands soothed her and soon there was no gravity, no up, no down. It happened somewhere outside time.

Slowly the room returned, and the world. Even then they didn't move, but watched the shadow play of morning-glory on the screen, watched it sway and tremble. "Momoko, you must be very careful coming here in the future."

"Something has happened?"

"I'm not sure. I'm being followed. I think he's professional, a yakuza."

She caught her breath sharply. "A yakuza? But why?"

"I don't know. I have political enemies, of course, but why they should spy on me and have me followed I can't imagine."

"Have they found out about us, about our Wednesdays?"

"I doubt it. But the only reason I can think of to have me followed is for the purpose of blackmail, perhaps to force me to vote differently on some issue before the Diet."

"You couldn't be mistaken?"

"About being followed? No. I don't think anyone has uncovered anything. More likely, it's the other way around. My private life is being pried into to see what can be brought against me."

He had been right, you must know at what spot to plunge in the dagger. "Do you think," she asked, "that we should let a week or so go by before we meet next?"

"And give my enemy that satisfaction? No. I cannot stop breathing when I wish to, and I cannot stop seeing you even for a short time." His arms tightened about her, and she had the illusion of safety. Still, when it was time to leave, he worked out a new route for her to come by on their next Wednesday.

That same week Akio had his secretary schedule a meeting with Takeo. They both served on the committee formed to look into the question of the Northern Territories. And now that the propeller blade was in actual production it was time to bring in political cohorts. Negotiations had reached a delicate stage, settling into a tricornered play involving three nations, the kind of situation he knew how to exploit. Each player wanted something one of the others had. A tempting position for a go player. At this point, if he could persuade Takeo to lobby the Diet and line up solid support for the project, he felt success was virtually certain.

Akio was a few minutes early for his appointment, so he stopped at the roof shrine. There were no prayers in his mind. He had a secondary motive for being here, an overpowering desire to look Takeo in the face and assess the man who for a brief while had been his father, try to figure out why he was meddling in his life. He sought composure. He needed to attain a calm state. Personal anger was a form of self-indulgence that he must rein in. All energy must be concentrated in ensuring the ultimate return of the islands.

Akio walked past the putting green and driving range enclosed by enormous wire fencing, and continued along its perimeter to the elevator, which requested that he turn front and wished him a good day. The electronic voice, he decided, was a mistake; actual bowing girls with voices pitched artificially high, like birds chattering, were more pleasant.

He did not wait in Takeo's reception room, but was immediately ushered into the office.

Takeo rose from his desk, bowed, and approached to shake hands in the Western manner. He was still, Akio thought grudgingly, a fine-looking man. His eyes were alert behind a face in repose, a sensitive face, the face of an artist rather than a civil servant. The face fascinated Akio.

It was the face of his enemy.

Disturbingly and unexpectedly, it was the face of his father. Memories crowded in, memories he didn't know he possessed . . . of an outing in a boat with his mother laughing and singing songs . . . of Takeo leaning toward him, throwing a slow ball that he would be sure to catch. He remembered something else. As a small boy of five he had been dressed in samurai robes and Takeo had set him upon a go board, explaining it was the battlefield of life, and through play and practice he would come to understand the root of the universe. Frequently after that Takeo allowed him to set up the pieces and make a few simple moves. He remembered that their last session together with the black and white pebbles had not been finished.

By an effort of will Akio took himself in hand. The polite words he was using floated as in the comics, over his head in a helium caption. Underneath he struggled with memories, with anger, with a distinct desire to break down and cry like a child.

This man who had been his guardian and his father was having tea served. Akio felt uncomfortable sitting in an armchair drinking tea. He always felt uncomfortable when the cultures mixed.

Takeo gave the appearance of total relaxation; his movements were slow, measured, and graceful. He was a graceful man. Because he was a survivor of the Special Attackers, a member of the 201st, a mystique surrounded him. But it seemed to Akio there was something

ignoble in returning from a mission no one else returned from. His
father had not returned. His father had been incinerated carrying out
what should have been Takeo's attack against the Americans. Why,
then, did Takeo enjoy this undeserved reputation? People who worked
for him revered him. There were many stories of his kindness, his
largesse, his taking time to simply talk to someone in his employ as
he would to a son or daughter. Among his peers at the Ministry he
was considered in another light, a man to be reckoned with.

His host greeted him warmly. "It does me good to see you, Sanogawa-san. I follow your illustrious career with great interest."

Inwardly Akio winced. With these words Takeo unsheathed the
sword of the samurai.

"May I inquire," Takeo continued, "as to the health and well-
being of your esteemed mother?"

"She is well," Akio said curtly, consciously keeping his fingers
from clenching. He proceeded to admire the glaze of the tea bowls.

His host inclined his head.

They sipped in silence.

Finally Akio said, "We serve jointly on a committee that is critical
to Japan."

"You refer to the committee on the Northern Territories?"

Akio cleared his throat. "The impasse that has stalled our efforts
for months is that Russia claims we renounced the islands in 1960,
when we refused to accept the return of Shikotan and Habomai. But
we both know they are hardly more than rocks. I think we are agreed
that they must return *all* the islands, Kunashiri, Etorofu, Urup, Shinshiri, Panamoshin, *and* Shikotan and Habomai, the entire group. Especially as they were seized after the peace treaty with the United States
was signed."

Takeo allowed a silence to close about them before replying. "The
USSR cites a secret provision in the Yalta agreement of the preceding
February. Be that as it may, our claim for normalization and restitution
has been on file with the UN for over thirty years."

"And would be for another thirty if not for a fresh development."

Takeo regarded him with interest. "Which is?"

Akio leaned forward. "Do you remember the silent submarine
propeller blade designed initially by the Americans?"

Takeo nodded. "I seem to recall that the whole thing erupted in
scandal."

"That's correct. There was an infringement of patent rights. It was dropped by all sides. However, since then the Americans made a design improvement, different enough to allow them to take out a new patent—in the U.S. But they are unable to go ahead with the milling without our complex lathe-cut patterns, which require computer-controlled fabrication. In short, they need us."

Takeo touched the tips of his fingers together.

Akio continued. "It's an interesting situation. They want the propeller blade badly. We, on the other hand, badly want the return of our Northern Territories."

"We'd have a quid pro quo," Takeo observed, "if they belonged to the Americans. Unfortunately that is not the case."

Akio was prepared for this objection. "As I see it, we are setting up a go contest with opponents unaware of the ramifications of the moves. Simply by finessing matters in such a way that the U.S. agrees to underwrite the sale of wheat to Russia at a slightly reduced price, and dangles Most Favored Nation status on condition that she return all disputed territory, we force Russia into a *sente* where she must move against herself."

Takeo nodded slowly. "The payoff to the Americans being our technology for milling the propeller blade?"

Akio smiled across at him.

"It's an ingenious plan," Takeo conceded, "and I would give it my personal endorsement but for the fact that I have a strong intuition it has already been implemented."

Akio inclined his head. "You are correct in this as in most things, Kuroda-san. Our Toshiba plant in California is in the process of manufacturing the blade. Not only is it in production, but I approach you now because I am assured that there is no doubt of the success of the operation. Within a matter of months we must be ready to negotiate at a political level."

"I see. Would you propose approaching the Russians ourselves, or dealing covertly through the Americans?"

"I think the deal should be struck by the Americans, who are ready to fulfill their end of the bargain, and who basically don't care who holds the islands."

The pause between the two men lengthened. At last Takeo spoke. "And I am to exert whatever influence I can bring to bear to coordinate things and see they proceed without a hitch?"

Akio said smoothly, "As you have done so many times in the past."

Takeo glanced at him sharply. Again silence settled between them. "I wonder if you do not place too much confidence in my abilities?"

Akio outfaced him. "I don't think so. Not when our intelligence states there are presently ten thousand Russian troops stationed on the islands, forty MG-23 warplanes, along with tanks, attack helicopters, and missiles. We must prevent them from making a fortress of the region."

Takeo revolved this in his mind. At last he said, "Your proposal seems to be extremely sound, Sanogawa-san. Of course the matter must be laid before the other members of our panel."

"Of course."

"However, you have my assurance I will do my best."

Akio was forced to thank him. Although absolutely necessary, the interview had been difficult. He needed Takeo at this juncture. Yet, even with Takeo cooperating, he knew him to be an opponent. It was easy to be put off guard by his courtesy and charm. When he spoke to him of a go game, he wondered if the same picture flashed before Takeo's mind. . . . Yes, it had been easy to love him, which made his defection the more cruel. It was ironic that he was the man who, with his intimate knowledge of the workings of the Diet, could best serve him now.

It had always disturbed him that his mother refused the emotions of pain and anger that attacked him regarding Takeo. After the divorce she carried on as serenely as before. Perhaps she had not loved him as he had. And yet . . .

He tore his mind from the past. The meeting had been positive. Takeo would lobby for his proposal. That was where he wanted him, in the open where he could watch him. And he wondered again what Azuma would bring to light.

In this unquiet mood Akio decided to return home and spend an hour under the ministrations of his acupuncturist.

As he entered his house gate he heard sutras for the dead. The sacred death water had been administered by the family, each of whom in turn applied the brush to the dying woman's lips.

And now Yoriko was gone. It struck him as black comedy that he should be upset by the death of his grandmother. Especially since, according to his mother, she had entered the white age. Perhaps it was not her death that upset him, but that the ranks were thinning. His own mortality must be acknowledged, the day sutras would be intoned for him.

The women of the family wore kimono and he himself bathed and changed. He donned the color of mourning, listening as he dressed to the striking of a bell, the tone of which was deep and mournful.

Death had its *omote* and *ura* aspects. It was release from the sad world; it was also an intruder. The word *death* had connotations of "misfortune" and "abnormal." The shrines refused all contact with the dead, holding no rites for them. Death was given no place in the world of living men. It was an evil to be expelled with the sound of bells and cymbals, with fluttering strips of white blessings, and sprigs of sakaki. For comfort, the family must turn to the Buddhist temples and the sutra.

Akio rinsed his mouth and spat before going in to view the remains. They were all assembled in the room where the body reposed, Masaru too. He had been freshly groomed and also wore kimono. It was Akio's standing instruction that his cousin attend all family functions. He bowed to him gravely before approaching the body of his grandmother.

If there had been death throes there was no evidence of it; the corpse, draped in white, lay simply, hands folded together in prayer, looking waxen and unreal. Akio bowed to the still form of his grandmother respectfully.

Yoriko had eroded in life as much as a living person can. One so aged must have been part of the other world for some time. Now she would join her son, Noboru, and her husband, Tomonori, on the home shrine.

The flowers for this death were set about in trays, starkly indicating the heaven line, the nature line, and the man line. Ryoko was weeping although she had not loved her. Momoko seemed to have no tears, at least none that she could shed. With Yoriko she lost the last witness to her life. In her turn she approached the body, holding slippers in her hand, which she left beside Yoriko for her journey.

Akio consoled her, saying, "She left many footprints."

Momoko lifted her face, it was without expression. She did not tell him about Masaru's cat, who had somehow gotten in, jumped on the corpse, and walked across her open eyes.

"Mother," Akio said to her, "you are to prepare the home shrine to receive her. Just you, no one else."

"Thank you." Momoko bowed before her son.

The members of the family, Sumie, Ryoko, even Kenji, one by one approached the altar and burned incense to the spirit of Yoriko. Masaru, to everyone's surprise, joined them. When it came his turn, he stared down at the smoldering stick a long time. His face was in repose; the foolish grin that so frequently sat on his features was gone.

Masaru turned and surveyed the others. When he came to Akio he paused. Akio returned his look in a searching way.

Everyone present was riveted. An event was taking place in this room filled with a silence so strong it held action and speech in abeyance. No one moved, it seemed almost that no one breathed.

Into this silence Masaru spoke the first intelligible words he had uttered in thirty years. Looking directly at his cousin he said distinctly, "Plum blossoms."

The spell was broken. Akio leaped to his side. He grabbed his hands. A great smile broke through him appearing on his face along with tears. "Yes, yes, Masaru. Plum blossoms. Go on."

Masaru's expression did not change. It continued to rest benignly on Akio, but he said nothing more.

"Plum blossoms. Of course, the plum trees were in bloom when we went together to visit the Tenmangu Shrine in Kyushu." He stopped, remembering that was the beginning of their preparation for the Todai examination. But this miraculous happening, this breakthrough into rational speech, could not be allowed to pass. It might be the beginning of a return. His cousin might be coming back to them. He turned to the others. "Plum blossoms. Quickly, tell me what it means to you. Sumie?"

"It means," she stumbled over the words, "February, the month of February."

"Yes," Momoko said, "when the blooms appear. It is the season of renewal."

"But what does it mean?" Akio pleaded with them. "What is the meaning of it?"

"For the sake of heaven," Sumie said, "what do you think it means? Nothing. It means nothing. The man is an idiot."

Akio raised his hand as though to strike her, but it fell heavily to his side. He turned to Masaru. "Plum blossoms," he said encouragingly. "You were speaking of plum blossoms, Masaru."

But the light of comprehension had drained from his eyes.

"Plum blossoms," Akio muttered, "plum blossoms," urging Masaru to repeat the first sensible words he had spoken since the hospital, a lifetime ago. Had he saved them up all these years? Were they a clue to what went on inside him? Was it possible it was a first step toward recovery?

Akio spoke to Kenji. "He must be watched constantly. Day and night. If he says anything else it must be taken down. Do you understand?"

"I understand," and he bowed low.

But Akio turned away. If he recovered, would Masaru blame him? Perhaps in some recess of his being he blamed him now. The words were a result of shock at seeing his grandmother dead. The real question was, were they tied to thought? Did "plum blossoms" refer to that expedition they had taken together as boys? On the journey home Masaru had talked endlessly of Sumie and the examinations, for his hope of her rested on his performance.

Was that it?

Or had it nothing to do with that? Akio had been shown another facet at which he would rather not look. He had assumed, taken for granted, that he would move heaven and earth to have Masaru recover. He had spent fortunes on psychiatrists and psychologists in the past, all of whom had given up, saying a recovery was not possible.

Suppose they were wrong? Suppose there was a gradual return of faculties? He'd told himself this was what he wanted above all else, this was what he prayed for. . . . But was it?

A layer of his soul was stripped away. The question he posed himself now was, Do I want Masaru to recover if he blames me? He glanced almost enviously at the coffin of his grandmother as he left the room.

There was no land to be had in Tokyo at any price. Real estate in and around the city was valued at $7.7 trillion. The cemetery problem was solved with vertical burying. The official grieving lasted fourteen days; it would be another forty-nine before the ashes were interred and the funeral party took an elevator down seven levels to the section Akio had purchased for the family.

Only a few days into this protracted mourning period Akio received a message from Azuma indicating that she had news regarding
Takeo.

Akio had hardly dared hope for a sex scandal. But Azuma assured
him she had definite knowledge of a secret mistress, an affair, she
insisted, that had been carried out for years. Not since Prime Minister
Uno had been brought down by involvement with a geisha had there
been anything that promised to be so big.

This was news indeed. So Mister Clean had played around all
these years! The happy marriage was so much PR. Well, well. He
would be in no hurry to make this information public. First let the
man use his considerable influence in the Diet to forward the cause of
the Northern Territories. Then let the story leak out. The rest would
take care of itself. It had taken Japanese women forty years to begin
to wield their power, but with the advent of Takako Doi and the "Pink
Revolution," they were a political fact with the clout to vote out of
office anyone with a sullied reputation. Perhaps he would be able to
gather the rice while it was still green.

"Keep digging," he told Azuma. "I want to know everything,
every sordid detail." He turned at the door. "By the way, what does
'plum blossoms' mean to you?"

She stared at him blankly.

⛩ ⛩

It was a Cal 20 sailboat. Doug maneuvered her skillfully through the
forest of masts in the marina toward open sea.

Miko covered up with a hat over her face. She watched the swath
the boat cut and was conscious of the breeze riffling her hair where it
escaped the broad-brimmed Panama. It would have been a perfect day
if only it hadn't been so wrong. She didn't know why she had come.
Looking across at Doug lolling on the hatch naked to the waist, making
an adjustment of the wheel with one bronzed foot, she hated him.

She hated his great American build, the fact that he was tall,
slender, well muscled. You knew just looking at him that he did tennis,
racquetball, sailing. Why couldn't she have settled on someone else,
one of those passive types who worked out on a stationary machine in
a corner of the bathroom? Then it might not have happened.

She had been attracted to Doug in the first place because he was totally ineligible. Wasn't that the only kind of man she was ever attracted to? There was no category of human being her father resented more than those Japanese who forsook their homeland for America. She knew he would forcefully oppose any such alliance. It would have been easier for him to accept an Anglo-Saxon American.

Of course there had never been a question of a serious relationship. From the beginning it was swimming naked in the night surf and talking gallates and fiberoptics, the only kind of poetry he understood. Perhaps she should have confronted him, told him she was pregnant.

He might even have married her. But not for her sake, for the sake of being admitted to the Sanogawa *ke*. And she had not been able to give up her pride.

She accepted that she should never have indulged human feelings where Doug was concerned. He was *gaijin*. In choosing him she had gone against the way she was raised and all she had been taught to believe.

"How about breaking out the beer?" Doug called cheerily from the bow.

"Right." She rummaged in the refrigerated chest filled with picnic things and tossed him a can.

"Why don't you come forward?" he asked, patting the place beside him.

"Once we're out of the harbor." The wind blew her voice back. Today was a mistake, she knew it looking into the striated depths of ocean, a bad mistake. She should not have subjected herself to this, she should never have seen him again, but telephoned good-bye in a detached, civilized manner. But no, she had to inflict this wonderful, perfect day on herself. She pulled the Panama down farther over her face.

She had known it would be unpleasant. What a horrid euphemism for the Operation Rescue people who demanded that every unwanted pregnancy be carried to term. She'd read about them, seen them on television, but it was quite a different thing being exposed to them, having to walk the gauntlet. Her heart seemed to have cut loose and be swinging wildly about in her chest. There were hand-lettered signs waved in her face, and the chant . . . Murderess! Baby-killer! This belligerence activated a kind of fury. In that instant she understood *tsuji-giri*, loyalty to the sword . . . the right of her ancestors to test the sharpness of the *katana* by slaying passersby. She felt herself capable of flailing about in this crowd of foreigners. A police officer came forward and strode beside her to the door. Even so the sleeve of her dress was grabbed and a woman shouted in her face, "It's your *child!*"

Inside a volunteer greeted her. "I'm so sorry," she said, "for a while we were rid of them. Would you like a glass of water?"

Miko shook her head mutely. She saw that she was a pawn, only counting insofar as her presence allowed the factions to make political statements. Her distress, her fear, her irresoluteness meant nothing. They were role-playing, the kind volunteer as well as the unruly crowd. Only her Japanese training permitted her to sit impassively and wait.

It was too late to ask herself if she was doing the right thing. She had gone through that last week when she first came to this storefront building and received counseling. The crowd had not been present that day. The interview itself had been the thing to get past. The probing questions were extremely painful to answer, but, difficult as the questioning was, she recognized that the emotion had all been on her side. Her interlocutor was a professional, doing a job. Her final decision was of no interest except to herself.

She had gone over it all week, torturing herself with possibilities she was about to shut out. She felt as though the *nodowa* technique was being applied, that she was in a vise impossible to break. She hoped to punish herself with the pain of the procedure. She hoped to suffer as much as the small life that had planted itself in her.

It was terrible to scrape it off like mud from one's shoes. But she herself had grown up unwanted. That was a worse crime. The knowledge of abandonment was never absent, it was there from day to day and year to year. She refused to subject any living thing to that.

There was a magazine on the table in front of her. She picked it up and blindly turned pages, feeling the smooth gloss of the paper under her fingertips. Finally she was ushered into the surgery.

The midwife moistened pieces of paper with spittle and placed them over the baby's nostrils and mouth. They said it took no time at all.

Miko undressed in a cubicle the nurse showed her, drawing the coarse curtain and putting on a stiff gown that tied at the nape of her neck. There was another tie, but it was broken. The nurse indicated she was to get on a narrow, black padded table. This was where it would be performed. Her feet were guided into cold metal stirrups and she was given an injection. Gradually she became conscious of a strong overhead light. The light grew brighter as everything else became blurred.

A great surge of rebellion against herself and what she was doing traveled like a tidal bore through her, running counter to her decision and her action. "Oba-sama," she said under her breath, "don't let me do this thing." The child was not hers alone, but a gift to the generations, to the family. She removed her feet from the stirrups, sat up, and slid off the table. The doctor looked up from her instruments, the nurse came toward her.

She backed away from them. "I'm not going to do it. I changed my mind." She threw herself at the door, pulling it open, and fled down the corridor, the short white gown flapping about her. She ran through the waiting room, knocking against a table, sending magazines spilling onto the floor. She could see the heavy glass door, the sunshine outside, the bright day—she was almost there—

"It's all right, it's all right," someone was saying, "you did just fine."

She opened her eyes. The nurse was holding her hand and smiling down at her. "You see, there's nothing to it."

"But, but—" She looked around confusedly.

"You're in the recovery room. It's all over."

She remembered now.

She had never reached the glass door.

Physically she was fit almost immediately. She made several decisions; the most important was not to see Doug again. He knew nothing of this and she wanted to keep it that way. She would take Juro out of the sanitarium and return with him to Tokyo, where she hoped they could both resume their lives.

Once she was away from Doug, and the possibility of seeing him no longer existed, she could put all this behind her. Yet when he called to ask her sailing she said yes.

They had been friends as well as lovers, and she felt she owed him this afternoon to say good-bye in. But now she was actually here, out on the water with him, it made no sense at all. Why did she persist in dragging out something that was better ended as fast as possible?

Now he is dead—
that heartless bird Who broke
thought's peace with
His shrill cry. . . .

"Miko," he called, "this is great, from here you get the salt spray on your face."

She went forward reluctantly and sat on top of the hatch.

"Do you want to take the wheel for a while?"

"No."

"In three or four minutes we'll be past the breakwater."

She didn't say anything but watched the glassy swells slip by. It occurred to her that like Kabuki actors she carried around hatboxes with severed heads in them.

"Did you ever think," he said, "that we get on pretty damn well?"

"Ummmm."

Doug made a further effort. "We picked a nice day for a picnic, wouldn't you say? As near to perfect as you can get."

She nodded. "It's lovely."

"Miko, I'm trying to talk to you."

"I'm not preventing you, say whatever you want."

"Well, the other evening I made up two lists. Have you ever done that? One 'pro' and one 'con.' I don't know, it always seems there are more reasons not to do something than to do it. But I intend to disregard that 'con' column and I want you to do the same, because I'm going to ask you to marry me and I want you to say yes."

"What?" She swung on him. Her eyes blazed fury and the color drained from her face. "What did you say?"

"I'm asking you to marry me."

"For God's sake, Doug, don't say another word."

"But why?"

"Why? Can you really ask me why?"

"Let me try to understand." His tone was pseudo-patient. "On a scale of one to ten, family and words like *ko, giri,* and *on* are way up there. But things like love and marriage . . . do they even get on the chart?"

"Human feelings are important, very important, but . . . oh, what's the use? I can't talk to you. I'm going to Tokyo as soon as I can. I'd go tomorrow but I have to make arrangements for Juro to come with me. Look, just put about, Doug. This was a bad mistake. I should never have come out with you today. Put about, please."

He did as she asked, whipping the sail from port to starboard. When he was on course and headed in, he still busied himself with the ropes. How did she know this? She wasn't looking at him, but staring at the alien surface below.

They were in the channel, threading their way back through the maze of masts and boats at their moorings. When he brought the craft in she sprang to the dock and walked away.

He secured the boat to the dock cleats and came after her. She heard his steps pounding the pier, he was running. "Miko, am I supposed to let you go just like this? How are things different from last week when we played tennis and had dinner at the club?" He tactfully left out, *And made love.* "Or the day we drove to the Santa Barbara Mission?"

She stopped and faced him. "How are things different? Since the last time I saw you I had an abortion." She took a small pleasure in the shock that passed over his face. "Your timing is a little bit off, wouldn't you say? Now stay the hell out of my life. I never want to see you again."

He stood there and let her go.

That evening she poured herself a cup of coffee for dinner. She took it with her to television, but found nothing she could concentrate on. She made plane reservations that must be confirmed, and then phoned the sanitarium. The last several visits with Juro, while his resentment against her was still evident, had assured her that he again had a grip on reality. She spoke briefly with the psychiatrist, who agreed to release him on the understanding that she would arrange for him to join a support group. As far as she knew there was no such thing in Japan. But they had both been bruised too much here, they had to go home.

The platelets of time rubbed up against one another and a moment from before blended with the present so that the sanitarium where she sat waiting and the clinic merged. She was waiting now as she waited then, turning the sized pages of a magazine. It was the smell, she decided, not of medication, but of whatever they sprayed to disguise it that was identical . . . a sickly sweet stench.

When Juro came into the reception area, she was struck at once

by his subdued mien. He's very angry, Miko thought. This was substantiated by his silence as he marched out to the parking lot.

"I'll drive," he said as they reached the car.

"Okay." She handed him the keys.

He pressed the code of the door-handle computer. "It's good to
be in charge of something after not having been in charge of anything,
even yourself."

"I didn't know what else to do, Juro."

"Forget it. I understand you're shipping me back to Japan."

"We're going together. I've things to do in Tokyo."

"I bet you have. That's fine with me, but I'm not going."

"Juro. You can't stay here."

"Why not?"

"And run around with the same people that got you into this
mess? Please don't self-destruct on me, Juro. You know it's better if
you go home with me."

He was flying the Lamborghini rather than driving it, but she
refused to ask him to slow down. She stole a glance at his face. It
was strained and determined. "So stay, overdose, kill yourself. Who
cares?" But the pull exerted by this younger half brother was strong.
"Juro . . ."

"All right, I'll go. You'll tell Father if I don't. I want you to know
I know that. As it is, I have to stand by and see you ingratiate yourself
with him. Any time you want you can cut me out completely just by
telling him he's got a doper for a son. Boy, did I ever hand you the
dagger."

Miko was stunned; she could hardly follow the line his invective
took. "Juro, for God's sake, Father has already been generous to us.
Do you want it all? Take it."

He spoke through clenched teeth. "How two-faced can you be?
You're his confidante. You came over here to spy on me."

"It's true Father sent me, but to team up with you, not to plot
against you, Juro. I swear that's how it is."

"You're smart, Miko, but you're smart in a dumb kind of way.
Didn't it ever seem odd to you that Doug Watanabe latched on to
you? I know you've got stars in your eyes, but he's got dollar signs in
his."

"I don't want to talk about Doug. It's over."

"Oh." He shot a quick look at her. "I didn't know. Sorry."

She laughed mirthlessly. "One of those things, I guess."

Their flight was the following morning, so Miko turned in early. In her dreaming Kabuki figures kept rearranging themselves. In the distance a child's voice was calling her Mama. She told it to be quiet, it was dead. Doug wore a mask and faced her father, who was a gold and red lion, while a dragon wove in and out, spitting cold malice that burned her flesh. Oba-sama stood in a corner, weeping bitterly.

Part of the night she lay awake. She kept seeing the expression of shock on Doug's face. A samurai would have beheaded her on the spot, but he was the son of dirt farmers.

She made another effort with Juro at breakfast. "Can't we be friends, Juro? I've tried to act for the best."

"Best for you, you mean. It wasn't convenient to have me around, was it? I was in the way of your big romance."

"So I shut you up in a madhouse?" She spat the words at him. "My God, you can't believe that."

"Oh, but I can." And he burst out laughing.

"How can you be so difficult?" she shot back at him.

"I'm not being difficult, I'm being Japanese. Or have you forgotten?"

He was right. She had forgotten her promise to Oba-sama, she had forgotten to be Japanese. She had fallen off the gossamer bridge she had spun between two worlds. The New Humans wore cotton sweats and Reebok running shoes, which is what Juro was wearing for the flight. But the old concepts, the ancient values, could be hauled out at any time and donned like the obi and kimono.

For the next hour they spoke to those around them, servants, cabbies, ticket agents, not to each other. She couldn't think how to justify this abandonment of the propeller milling to her father. She had never experienced his anger, but she knew it would be intense. Perhaps he would not forgive her, but she had no choice. She had to return.

Their flight was announced, and there was a stir among the passengers as they picked up carry-on luggage, corralled children, said good-bye in many languages, and began to queue up.

Doug was there. She saw him moving against the crowd, buffeted by tides and flows of people.

"You're not going to leave like this," he said as he reached her. "I want an explanation. First of all I want to know . . ." He broke off and glared at Juro.

"I'll board," Juro said. "Do you think you might stay?" he asked his sister.

"Of course not," Miko said. "I'll be there in a minute."

"We don't have gifts," Juro reminded her.

"We can pick them up at the other end, at the Narita terminal."

"Yeah, I guess." He nodded to Doug.

But Doug had just started with Miko; he didn't even notice Juro moving out of sight in the line. "How could you have done it? You didn't say a word to me, not a word."

"What should I have said? 'I'm pregnant and I want you to do the right thing'? Or perhaps I should have gone to my father, he could have arranged a shotgun wedding."

"And now once again you're taking matters into your own hands. You don't give a shit how I feel, you're just taking off. It seems to be a pattern with you. Not, 'Let's talk it over,' not 'We've got a mutual problem'—but to make another arbitrary, wrong-headed decision."

She twisted away from him. Deplaning passengers were being disgorged into the area, and she made an effort to lower her voice. "Why should I listen to you? I'm not one of your damn microchips. I've run my life so far with no help from you."

Doug bent over her, a look of concern in his eyes. "Miko, listen to what I'm saying. . . ."

"What are you saying? What exactly the fuck are you saying?"

"That we're going to get married. There's been enough destruction, enough negative stuff. We're going to look ahead from now on, we're going to build a future. What do you say?"

"I say my bags are on their way to Tokyo."

Doug nodded. "That's better, you're inching toward it. How about a big spontaneous 'Yes'?"

Tears were running down her cheeks and into her mouth. "Yes, yes, yes!"

The ANA flight had just cleared the runway.

⛩

They were married at City Hall on a lucky *taian* day. They were asked to swear and they were asked to sign. And since there was another couple waiting, the whole thing was hurried. But that was not Miko's impression. What she saw was the bouquet of white roses. She put one in the buttonhole of Doug's jacket. His parents were there, a quiet, neatly dressed Japanese couple who beamed on her and kissed and hugged her in the American fashion.

There was no one there for her. The wedding was secret and without her father's consent. She had never imagined she would get married without her family around her. And without Oba-sama's kimono, the one shown her so many times, with pine sprigs, pink-crested cranes, and purple plum flowers. During the war this trousseau had been sold, but later repurchased and folded away between layers of rice paper in Momoko's hand-carved paulownia chest.

They honeymooned aboard the sailboat, renamed *Miko*. She pointed to the corner of heaven under which she guessed the home islands of Japan lay, and Doug secured the lines and set the jib. A newly discovered Miko listened to the slap of the water against the sides of the boat. Gone was that frivolous girl who covered up her anxieties and concentrated on being a shrewd *shosha*-man by day, playgirl of the Eastern world by night. This softer, more relaxed Miko didn't have to excel, didn't have to continually prove herself, she could just *be*.

They made themselves a nest of rain slickers, coiled ropes, and sweaters, and he told her about George Washington. "You see, he is the reason I don't worry about the mess this country is in with its massive debt."

"George Washington? I know about him. He was your first President. He defeated General Howe and helped win the war against England."

"Exactly right."

"But what does he have to do with anything?"

"Well, you see, at the end of the Revolutionary War he faced a debt-ridden economy just as we do now. In fact, in those days the deficit was even worse—fifteen cents to the dollar. And look, we pulled out of it to become the strongest nation in the world."

"Yes," she said, kissing his throat, "and you'll do it again."

"That's right, we will."

"Didn't he have a wife called Martha Washington?"

"He did. And they lived in a place called Mount Vernon that looked out over water."

"Just as we look out over water. More water than they had."

"Much more."

⛩

When it happened now, it wasn't unwanted, but a miracle. There were four months between pregnancies, time enough to realize that one life does not replace another. And she asked forgiveness for her happiness. It seemed to her the pregnancy itself was a token that the *kami* had forgiven her, even though she had not forgiven herself. She went downtown to the Japanese section of Los Angeles and, searching out a Shinto shrine, bought white fluttering strips of blessings from the priests. She had been offered another chance and she was going to do everything right this time.

Miko noted each change in her body with awe, the expansion of her waist, the tenderness of her nipples, the overall sense of well-being. This child symbolized, as nothing else could, a thread of continuity that from now on would run through her existence.

The first few months of her pregnancy seemed something that was between herself and her body. Then she began looking for the right moment to tell Doug. Finally she said it straight out, apropos of nothing.

"Doug, we're having a baby."

He was at the kitchen table, working on his scanning program.

"It's a boy."

He looked up then. "What's a boy?"

"Our baby."

"I thought that's what you said."

"I had an amniocentesis."

"My God, we're having a baby?"

"Are you pleased?"

He scraped back his chair and in one of those quick lightning motions took her in his arms. "Now we're pointing toward the future. I think it's a miracle."

"Really? I feel that too. It's a sign that everything will work out for us."

Doug nailed a *kamidana* to the wall and Miko planted a *Rhodea japonica*, which is green for ten thousand years.

They had been married a year, and she had been able to see the propeller project through to the present stage. There had been several postponements. The journal box kept overheating, and new specifications had to be written. The other delay resulted from a wildcat strike, requiring three-way negotiations between the company, the strikers, and the union. But things were on track again, and the blade all but complete. It was hard to realize that so much time had passed since she had wired her father that Juro was badly overworked, down with flu, and she was sending him home for a rest. Akio had accepted this. And now he would be calling her back. Miko was pondering what to tell him when at this juncture Doug called a powwow. She had never heard the expression.

"Well, I've done it!" he told her. "I can pack the lines ten times closer and etch them ten times faster. The problem was, I was working on the wrong end. I've been concentrating on the substrate, trying to improve on gallium arsenide."

Miko had come to dread these times he called breakthroughs, 'when something clicked for him. For a few heady hours, dream was turned to reality. He saw the world network of communication powered by the tiny chip under his microscope. Juro on drugs never reached an emotional high such as swept Doug at these moments.

Adrenaline charged his speech, and he waltzed her around the room, turning with her in his arms until they fell into a chair.

Even then he wouldn't let go of her. "I tried lanthanum gallate. You remember." He laughed crazily. "I don't know why I kept looking, a hunch I guess. I kept poking around in the monazite residues, and finally came up with this fantastic neodymium stuff, neodymium gallate."

"And that's your breakthrough?" She tried to disentangle herself but he wouldn't let her go.

"Not all of it." His enthusiasm was unstoppable. "I was working on the wrong end. The neodymium is great. But the real breakthrough is in the etching." He broke off long enough to rearrange her so she was sitting on his lap. "You're trying to draw these tiny scratches, okay? But you can only get so far improving the substrate. . . ."

Part of her followed this soliloquy lovingly and part critically. How important all this was to him! Like a kid building with Legos, he built theories enabling him to process sixty-six million instructions per second on a single chip. His dreams were of electron pulses moving without resistance, compounding knowledge in continuous flows. Himself the architect hooking together complex circuitry in a seamless interface.

"You see this ultrahigh-intensity-focused gallium ion beam? I've designed it so it can etch lines three to four nanometers in width on a gallium arsenide wafer coated with resist. Three to four nanometers, that's against ten to twelve for current electron-beam lithography. And ten times as fast."

Doug was drunk on achievement, unable to simmer down. "Do you realize how skinny three nanometers is? We'll be able to make an integrated circuit with such ultrasmall features that we get into quantum effects, where electrons start to behave like waves and pass through solid matter like . . . like thought."

She kissed him gently. The problem was tomorrow—or whenever it was reality set in. She had married Doug without knowing this mercurial side of his nature. He always appeared to be in control, adopting a light, slightly cynical, joshing manner that hid the intensity of the search he was embarked on.

She had ridden out several of these breakthroughs with him, at first experiencing something of his exhilaration. But in each instance there followed a period of concentrated effort, when he checked and rechecked his figures, his sources, his methodology. In this backtracking a discrepancy invariably came to light, which meant, in his vernacular, the breakthrough had crashed.

It crashed and Doug crashed along with it. Everything was its opposite, the high of yesterday the low of today; the hope then, the disappointment now. Worse to her than anything else was the self-doubt. He questioned himself and his ability, dragging in all his failures, even his failed first marriage.

"Why did I think I could do this? It's ridiculous on the face of it. My parents are semiliterate immigrants, descended from dirt farmers. I should trade in all this high-tech equipment and buy myself a wheelbarrow."

So it was with a sinking heart she watched him set himself up again. The first ebullience had passed. He crouched at the desk with his books piled beside him, trying to disprove his own work, looking for the fatal flaw.

She kept herself quiet, out of the way, as she waited for confirmation of another failure.

She fell asleep on the couch, and when she opened her eyes he was still at it. Beside him were scribbled notes, references to look up, and books scattered everywhere. She stole out of the room and made coffee. Oba-sama used to tell her the Way of Tea is attained by understanding morning dew on rice blades. The way of coffee, she supposed, was attained by understanding aroma.

When she brought it in to him, Doug's head was resting on the desk.

She set the cup beside him, afraid to say anything, to ask anything. He raised his head. He looked exhausted, but he smiled, a distant, tentative smile, as though he didn't dare feel what he was feeling or think what he was thinking. "I can't believe it, Miko. I really can't believe it."

"Oh, no!"

"Oh, yes, quite definitely yes."

She put her arms around him wordlessly, and wordlessly he clung to her.

They went to sleep and woke in another day. They made sleepy love, brushed their teeth, had a big breakfast, and were back in the real world.

"The main problem now," Doug said, "is taking our pig to market in Tokyo. How do we protect ourselves?"

They spent many evenings writing a proposal. When he had it in final shape, she was to carry it to her father. It was to be a kind of peace offering. Of course the real peace offering was the child. She had never before in any serious matter gone against her father's wishes. She was afraid to imagine his reaction when he found out she was married, and to a Sansei. What would it mean to their relationship, and to her place in the *ie?* She worried about this while hoping that a grandson would smooth things over.

She had written a hopeful scenario in her mind that went like this: Once Akio knew of a grandson, he would forgive her marrying. He would buy into Doug's company, form a partnership, and start manufacturing, using Doug's process and incorporating the new materials.

If Doug was correct they were at this point now. She was amused at his nervousness in allowing his invention out of his sight. "Are you afraid my father will steal it?"

"Let's keep this general. Anyone can attempt a clone."

"I agree you've got to be cautious. And I'm not naive, I know my father didn't achieve what he has by being scrupulous where other people's ideas are concerned. I think it makes sense for me to go to my father directly and recommend a fifty-fifty partnership, persuade him he needs you to work out any bugs that may crop up once he goes into production. Another point in favor of doing the operation state-side, there are no import taxes if he manufactures here."

"Yeah, once the child is born, you should definitely make the trip. You're too close to your time to do any traveling now." Doug walked back and forth, chewing a pencil. "I think you'll be able to convince him."

Miko found she hadn't convinced herself. "I don't know, what you said about cloning worries me." Her face cleared. "Suppose we withhold a piece of the puzzle?"

"Not give him the complete story?"

"Not at first, until we see how things go."

"But he's your father."

She smiled back at him.

Doug was still troubled. "How will he react when he realizes we've held out on him?"

"I should think he'd respect your business sense."

"You think so?" he asked dubiously.

"Let me tell you one of my father's favorite stories. It has to do with Soichiro Honda, who returned from a trip abroad with smuggled motorcycle components hidden on his body. Even up his . . . you know. That was the start of Honda. And that is the kind of man my father admires."

Doug laughed. "It's a great story, tell me more."

"About Honda?"

"About your father."

"Ahhh. With Akio Sanogawa what you see is not necessarily what is there. He is a man who allows himself to be underestimated. He works through an invisible atlas of personal and corporate *keiretsu*."

"Connections?" Doug asked.

She nodded. "He has made a study of the committee system of

the Lower House and manipulates it like a go master proceeding through the various *dans*. In fact I've often thought . . ." She broke off.

"Was he born into the *zaibatsu*—isn't that what you call the wealthy families who supposedly rule Japan?"

"He is one of them, but at the same time unique. He pays lip service to his chairmen and senior people, listens to every opinion, but it is all orchestrated so that the consensus he achieves is exactly what he planned to do anyway, typical *nemawashi*. He pays his consultants salaries that far exceed his own. The modest salary he allows himself is a smoke screen. He holds stock options—that's the secret of his wealth. But he's careful, he was not indicted in the Recruit scandal or, before that, caught up in the Lockheed mess, although I'm sure he was involved in both. You see, in Japan politics is an integral part of business, a one-trillion-yen-per-year business that grows at twenty percent annually. My favorite Liberal Democratic Party slogan is 'Five to win, three to lose.' Meaning that it takes five million to elect a candidate. If only three million is collected, he will lose. But my father's candidates never lose. The assets of his companies make them in effect *sogo-shosha*, trading houses, banks in their own right. This gives you some idea of the magnitude of his operations."

"And we're going up against a man like this?"

"You forget I'm his daughter."

He pulled her closer to him. "You know, I've been thinking that America has woken up vis-à-vis its position with Japan. Now we know what's going on, my feeling is we won't try to catch up in every area. I mean, why reinvent the wheel? Take high-definition TV, we're at least ten years behind. My guess is that we'll bypass it, render it obsolete with a completely different solution. And in the meantime we sit back and watch your little island country make all our mistakes, a newly acquired taste for spending, for luxury, for lying down on the job, for cutting corners. In other words, Japan is so far ahead and moving so damned fast, she'll go down the tubes ahead of us." Doug loved the prospect and laughed uproariously.

Miko did not join in. "Doug, don't make my father's mistake. It's not a war. That's the whole point. This micro-world of yours can make mankind itself free and independent. For the first time people will have ascendancy over their world. Don't you see, Doug? It's an economy without borders. And it's here right now, if we only have the guts to

recognize it. There are detours like some of the East European countries, who think they want to go back to the nineteenth century.
Culturally that's fine. Sure, everyone does his own thing, goes to his
own church, keeps his own holidays. But economically that spells disaster. It's against the tide, a forward tide where parts are manufactured,
assembled, shipped, and sold in a vast global surge of energy, ideas,
and capital. It's the most exciting and hopeful moment human beings
have ever faced. Cooperation, Doug, on a global basis."

His reply was to hug her, and DRAMs and ion-beam lithography,
borderless economies and quantum effects in integrated circuits all grew
indistinct, lost in long, lazy kisses.

⛩ ⛩

Azuma let the typed report fall from her fingers. She regarded the
document as though it itself was malevolent, perhaps even a demon
from the old mythology. What should she do? She couldn't tell him.
But supposing he found out from another source? Knowing Akio's temper, she couldn't take that chance.

The whole thing seemed so preposterous. They had their own
little house tucked away in the suburbs, and had for years. For years
they'd met there on Wednesdays, nothing was allowed to interfere with
that.

But such an unlikely pair. Takeo Kuroda, an Oka fighter, a leading
figure in the world of finance. He was among the elder statesmen of
Japan, one who guided her destiny. He had married into one of the
first *zaibatsu* families. What was he doing with an elderly lady, a woman
whom he had divorced thirty-seven years ago?

It struck her as bizarre. If he was going to play around he could
afford a geisha—or anyone he pleased, for that matter. He could set
an inamorata up in high style at a world-class hotel or in a chic
apartment. But an old-fashioned house in a working-class neighborhood, how very odd.

It almost seemed to her the report was about two different people,
someone who was not Takeo Kuroda . . . and someone who was not
Akio's mother. How could she escape the misfortune such information
was certain to bring? Her solution was to postpone calling it to Akio's
attention. She was well aware that no one thanked the messenger of

ill tidings. And these were ill indeed. Worse than that, they were ludicrous, exposing those even peripherally concerned to ridicule.

Akio worshiped his mother. Shocked and outraged, God knew what he would do when he discovered the truth. Azuma trembled. With a stroke of the pen he had signed the restaurant and bar over to her. With a stroke of the pen it could be taken away. With her livelihood gone, then what?

Azuma was out of sorts and cross with her help. She fired the dishwasher, and at night lay sleepless trying to work her way out of the trap. When she could not accomplish this, she decided to end the misery and the uncertainty by telling him. She had gone over and over it. There was no other way.

She put on kimono in case he killed her on the spot. After all, it was his mother she was defaming. She placed the call and was put on hold. Akio was speaking to the Banque Indo Suez in Paris regarding a tax shelter in the Cayman Islands, a spinoff from a North American real-estate outfit whose holding company was based in Luxembourg. His object was to avoid a thirty-percent U.S. capital gains tax. When he worked it out to his satisfaction he plugged into the line Azuma waited on.

Her voice was low. "Akio-sama, I have the information."

"Ah, that means there was something. Can you give it to me over the phone?"

"I think not."

"I'll come by."

Before he could get out the door there was a call from the Diet. The morning was half gone by the time he was ushered into Azuma's office. She stepped from behind her desk. He was surprised to see her in traditional garb, and more surprised to see her prostrate herself on the floor before him.

"What is it? Is something wrong?"

"Yes," she murmured, her lips against the carpeting.

"Well, it can't be that bad. Get up, tell me what you've discovered."

Azuma did not move. "Do not be angry with me, Akio-sama."

Akio was already feeling annoyed. What was the matter with the woman? "Come, come," he said, an edge of impatience showing in his voice, "get up and tell me whatever it is you have found out."

She rose reluctantly and had tea brought in. The short hiatus,

which usually relaxed him, added to his impatience. He waited until
it had been served and the servant left. "Now, there is something you
have to tell me about Takeo Kuroda."

"It may be understandable if one recalls their beginnings."

"Whose beginnings? What are you talking about?"

"If one remembers that they were once married."

"Are you speaking of Takeo?"

"Yes, and the woman he sees every Wednesday afternoon. They
have a home, a very modest house. I believe the garden is lovely."

"I don't give a shit about the garden. Who is the woman?"

"Your mother must love him very much, and he her. Perhaps they
never considered themselves divorced, perhaps—"

"My mother? Did you say . . . my mother?"

"Consider, they are two elderly people. It can't be a question of
a passionate liaison, not anymore. By this time I'm sure it is platonic,
and that they are simply dear friends. It is very sweet, really, two old
people who have—"

"Stop your prattling and let me think. There can be no mistake?"
He began to pace the room. No, of course not. It explained why she
was never angry with him, why she would never hear anything against
him. For his sake she went from honorable wife to kept harlot. "Every
Wednesday, you say?" He lapsed into cogitation. Wednesday, Wednesday . . . wasn't that her market day? Of course, yes. The day she set
off with Kenji holding her market basket. How simple we all made it
for her.

The duplicity! The exquisite duplicity. All she had to do was
return with baskets of food that Kenji purchased. How could she have
brought such *haji* on him, on his father's memory, on the entire family?

"Is it possible?" he asked aloud. "Is this thing true?"

Azuma knew better than to reply.

That placid face, so open. Her manner, that of a simple Japanese
woman who kept her house and garden, who raised her son and grandchildren. That was the mask, the façade. Underneath, so brazen. She
played out her role and was admired by all. She was the dutiful daughter-in-law. His grandmother had loved her. She had died in her arms.
And I . . . I . . . His teeth clamped and he sucked his breath through
them.

"He'll pay for doing this to me, and so will she."

Azuma spoke in a small whisper. "She thought you'd never know, Akio-sama, that you'd never be hurt by this."

"Don't dare try to comfort me! Don't speak of her to me, do you hear? Never! You're never again to speak her name."

Azuma spread herself lower against the floor.

For some reason the hit list he had compiled as a boy flashed into his mind. Even then Takeo headed it. What a list he could compile against him now. He sent his friend to his death, then married his friend's wife and took her love. He took his friend's son and told him he had a second father. And when the boy and the woman loved him, he sent them away. Divorced the woman, let the whole world know of her barrenness. And then, as though the harm he had done them were not enough, he made her his mistress.

Akio's anger was too much to contain. "Her life must have become a tissue of assignations and lies. He forced her to live a lie. And for this he must be called to account."

Azuma knew she was not his confidante, she was simply there. She made no outward sign.

Akio had himself under more control, the shock that had precipitated his outburst passed. But this new knowledge must be transmuted into something he could live with.

⛩

Momoko was on her knees in the garden by the newly planted azalea bush, sifting through the soil with gloved hands. The dirt was rich and dark. She liked the smell of it, it was a healthy garden. She approved of the earthworm burrowing its way through it. What weeds there were went into her basket, but there weren't many. The garden, she felt, was the spiritual part of the house. She had worked in it as a girl and she worked in it now. Yoriko had put in that splash of lavender morning glory and the stand of bamboo whose reflection could be seen in the pond. She remembered the day she and Yasue planted the iris bulbs and the hyacinth. She could almost hear Akio and Masaru laugh as they sailed their paper boats.

Although made by many hands, the garden had taken on a character of its own, and one added carefully to its profusion, asking, "Will it contribute to the harmony?" The small azalea bush, she felt, did, carrying out the line of more mature planting.

Into her garden came a figure who, although in modern dress, walked as though he had two swords by his side. He brought disharmony to the garden.

"Mother, I was looking for you."

"I am here."

The serenity with which she regarded him froze the words of accusation. They refused to come. It was necessary to feed his indignation with thoughts of Takeo. "I have heard disturbing rumors," he said finally.

"If they disturb you, why listen to them?"

"Because, Mother, they concern you."

She looked him full in the face, waiting calmly for him to proceed. It was he who became agitated, who developed a twitch.

"Well, son?"

"It has to do with the man you were once married to—Takeo Kuroda."

Momoko patted the earth into place a final time and stood up. "So you know."

"How could you? What were you thinking of? You have brought *haji* to the entire family. It is a disgrace."

"I did not think in such big terms."

"In what terms did you think, I'd like to know?"

She was in no hurry to answer him. She considered carefully what she would say. "Like any woman in love, I thought of him and of us. We only wanted to be together. It meant a great deal to us. And I don't think we hurt anyone."

"How can you say that? You're still seeing him. At your age. Can't you see, if it got out you'd be a laughingstock."

"Why is that? I loved him when I was young, I love him now that I am old. Is that so hard to understand?"

"It's ridiculous. A woman of your years going to trysts and secret assignations with a married man. Oh, yes, I know all about it."

"Did you have me followed?"

"Of course not. I had him followed. Imagine what it was like for me to find it was my mother who was the other woman."

"You must have been surprised," Momoko said mildly.

"Surprised? You don't seem to have any notion of the position you place me in."

"You?"

"Of course, me. I can't afford this kind of scandal. He knows that, he counts on it. But he crossed the wrong man this time."

"Akio, it has nothing to do with you. Takeo has always considered you a son. Circumstances didn't permit him to be close to you growing up. But he promised me that he would always look out for you, and he always has."

"You made me part of your bargain? How could you do that? How could you put me in the position of owing *on* to your lover?"

"I didn't see it like that. I was married to him once, and he was at that time full of plans for your future."

"At that time I was his son. But he got rid of us, both of us. From then on he had no rights over me."

"Feelings don't change so easily, Akio."

"Mine did."

"He understood your anger."

"I don't want his understanding, and I never wanted his help. You have placed me in an intolerable situation."

"I'm sorry." She put her hands together and lowered her head.

"And not just me, the entire family. And of course yourself."

"I'm sorry you feel that way about it."

He stared at her in disbelief. "Is that what you meant just now when you said you were sorry? You are sorry simply at the way I have taken it?"

"Yes, I suppose that is what I meant. I am sorry to have hurt you."

"But you feel no shame for all these years of being a mistress to a married man?"

"No. I was married to him first."

"That has nothing to do with it. If anything it adds to your shame, being cast off. And don't tell me again about his parents insisting on children. I know all about that. Again it reflects poorly on you. You were unable to fulfill a wife's proper duty. It is one shame piled on another."

"We who went through the war don't feel that. There was terrible hardship, never enough food, everyone suffered. I felt sad that because of it I could not bear more children, but not shame."

"It seems to me you have a peculiar way of looking at things. According to you, nothing is your fault and you did nothing wrong. Well?"

"I think I did less wrong than you seem to think I did."

"All right. There's no use arguing about the degree of your guilt. I will be satisfied if you promise me you will never see Kuroda again."

For the first time Momoko was upset. But she did not hesitate in her answer. "No."

Akio choked back anger and tried for a modicum of calm. "I can't believe this. Are you totally without any moral sense?"

"I don't think so." She spoke quietly with downcast eyes.

"Then you will do as I say," he thundered.

"Why? Why should you wish to do this to me? I love this man. Do you wish me to stop being a woman, a human being? Do you wish me to be a stone?"

"For God's sake, Mother. I want you to act with decency and a sense of propriety. Is that so hard? You owe me that. You owe your grandchildren that."

She looked at him a long minute. "I don't think so," she said, and went into the house.

Akio stood staring after her. "Very well," he called. "Very well, Mother. There is more than one way to approach this problem."

Momoko's immediate impulse was to get in touch with Takeo, tell him that Akio knew, and be reassured that it would make no difference. But she decided to wait until their day, until Wednesday.

They had tried before to meet only once a year, at Tanabata, the day no one was allowed to keep lovers apart. But the Sanogawa swords brought them together. Agents of Takeo's tracked them down and retrieved them from an antique shop in Santa Monica, California. They had been kept together as a pair, but what their history was, was impossible to know. With their return, honor was restored and a weight lifted from Momoko.

Takeo brought the swords himself. It was to her he had promised them, and it was into her hands he put them. Their eyes met across them, and his reserve shattered. "Momoko, I can't do without you. Can we meet? Just to talk, if you wish." Though he spoke softly, she saw into the *ura* of his heart. But she shook her head.

"Momoko, listen to me. We are approaching Tanabata, you promised to see me then. I'll wait for you at the temple."

At Tanabata she was beside him, kneeling at the altar.

"Momoko," he whispered, "my marriage is to a good woman, but I do not love her. The marriage is for one purpose, to carry on my line. Must I be punished the rest of my life for following the path of duty? Momoko, you yourself urged me to it. But I find it intolerable without you. I even miss the folded clothes in your old carved chest."

Momoko smiled to herself; forty years and yesterday were not that different. She remembered the birth of his first child, a son. Takeo's happiness was apparent, and she strove to be happy also. They drank sake together and put on music. But when he left she cried herself to sleep because his son wasn't her son.

She fought these thoughts and tried to live her life as Shinto dictated, as one would speak a prayer. Looking back, she realized of course that human beings and *kami* could not agree in all matters.

Wednesday she gave a longer-than-usual shopping list to Kenji and proceeded by taxi in a circuitous route to the small house she called *their* house.

She arrived ahead of Takeo. The old servant brought her tea and she waited in the garden. This garden knew her touch also. It was a single-person garden, not a generational one. It was here she had made her free area. She smiled into the face of a camellia nodding over a bed of primroses at its feet. This is what she had promised herself as a child. The free area of her garden was part of the free area of her life. She mused over the colorful corner in an almost somnolent mood. She would add valerian and perhaps a creeper of some kind.

With a start she realized time had gone by. A lengthening shadow must have alerted her. She glanced at her watch. How odd, over an hour had passed.

Takeo was never late, and on the few occasions over the years when he was forced to be out of town on their day, there was always a note under the Korean dogs at the gatepost of the old house. She called the servant and questioned her. But she knew nothing.

Panic overtook her. Why had she thought it of no great importance that her son knew? He had been terribly angry. Instead of coming to terms with it as she assumed he would, had he directed his anger against Takeo? What had he done? What had happened?

What should I do? she asked herself distractedly. How can I find out what has occurred? She hurried home, forgetting to meet Kenji with the groceries, and went directly to the Korean dogs that surmounted the stanchions at either side of the gate. She felt under them, but there was nothing. She went to the Western section of the house, sat at the secretary, and penned an invitation to Takeo Kuroda and his wife asking for the pleasure of their company at the opera. She looked in the paper to see what was playing. *Turandot.* She wrote that she had tickets for a week from Friday. Momoko sent the invitation by hand requesting an immediate reply. Mrs. Kuroda, whom she had met only casually, would consider it somewhat strange to receive the invitation, but since it asked for an RSVP, if there was anything amiss she would learn of it.

Toward evening the reply was brought. Mrs. Kuroda regretfully declined as her husband had the day before met with a serious traffic accident. He was at present hospitalized with a fractured pelvis and internal injuries, but was expected to recover.

The world spun away from her, a void danced before her eyes. Momoko put her hands to her head but the walls still canted at an odd angle.

She had first been afraid of Akio when he was still quite small. She remembered calling him Little North Wind because his tantrums came on with such fury.

She recalled the dreadful ordeal with *moxa,* and how he had stubbornly withstood it. There was an unreachable core in him that nothing could conquer. She recalled taking him to the priest, pulling him along at the end of a rope with Yoriko helping her. At times he would rush at them, pummeling, kicking, even biting, and once he lay down in the middle of the road.

But after undergoing purification he had quieted, turning to a memory he didn't have, to Noboru. Noboru the war hero, who had dedicated his life. Whatever it was he needed, Akio found in that distant figure.

The other pillar to which he fastened his life was Masaru. Even in those early years Akio's attachment to his cousin caused her worry, a worry she found hard to explain. It was natural, she told herself, that he admire and emulate the older boy. Yet Akio was not one to grow in the shade when another grew in sun. And Masaru in those years was heir to their grandfather's fortune.

The problem, although it was not perceived as a problem then, was that Masaru did not possess the keen mind that Akio did. School was never difficult for Akio. He never seemed to work, yet stood at the top of his class. Masaru found it all hard going. She watched with a sense of disquietude a kind of symbiosis develop between the boys.

Yoriko, who had come to understand her, asked sharply, "What do you fear?"

"I don't know," she replied. "Nothing."

Nothing at least that she could articulate. But she knew the power of the north wind, and that its intensity was never really checked; at times it simply abated. At any moment it might break out with renewed force.

Akio grew up straight and handsome. He was meticulous in following the codes of deportment. He was courteous and properly respectful, but she was watchful. She had borne him, he was her child. She ultimately was responsible.

In spite of being correct in his relationships with people, he was not loved as Masaru was. This, she thought, was because he kept something back, the something that said who he was.

Perhaps he let Masaru know him.

Momoko was not certain when her feelings changed toward her son. She had adored him in his red silk bunting. He had been her little prince. As he grew and ran about the garden, he was the center of her existence.

In the apartment Takeo provided for them he had been hers. But then—and here she bumped up against it once more, the extent of Akio's hatred and bitterness toward Takeo once the divorce took place.

She had and had not been aware of it. It was something she didn't want to acknowledge. But she saw now that it was his chief demon. The priest had not driven it out, simply banished it to an inaccessible place in his psyche. How perverse his demon was, compounded by the trauma of a father he did not have, a war he had never experienced, a second father who rejected him, and two fortunes that each slipped away from him.

These factors molded Akio. He was among those who moved Japan forward and were responsible for the yen shokku, the great economic miracle. Everyone bowed before Akio Sanogawa. And he himself was suffused with a sense of destiny. That was the trouble—ask any bat and he will tell you he is a bird.

How was he able to force his will and his dream on a nation? He practiced on the household. The day Akio and the impaired Masaru resumed their game of go, she shuddered.

This time, Momoko told herself sternly, she must not turn away. This time she must look squarely at the facts. The fact of Akio's anger. The fact that he told her she was not to see Takeo again. The fact of her refusal.

She could not escape the conclusion it led to. Who had driven the car that ran down Takeo? Kenji would not have done it. No, of course not. Besides, Akio would never use a car identifiable as his. Sumie had told her once that he employed yakuza. She thought it amusing. Yakuza disturbed shareholders' meetings, asking ridiculous, long-winded questions until the time allotted for the opposition to speak was up. They served as Akio's bodyguards on trips and ceremonial occasions. Did they also act as his henchmen? It took only a small step to reach this determination. Momoko felt cold. She had never been so cold around her heart.

She arranged with the servants that she would take their place and prepare Akio's evening soup herself.

Momoko waited in the shadow until she heard Akio's steps. They were a bit unsteady. Kenji was with him to slide back screens, turn on lights, and help him up the stairs.

Momoko came forward and bowed deeply.

"Is that you?" Akio asked, surprised.

"Yes, son. I have the honor to wait on you tonight."

Akio grunted noncommittally and dismissed Kenji. Did this mean a torrent of recriminations? Her presence indicated that she knew about Takeo's accident. He feigned more drunkenness so as not to have to talk to her.

Momoko humbly gave him his robe and, humbly offering her services in undressing him, asked if she could clip his nails. He allowed this, still uncertain what to expect.

"Will you have soup, son? There is some warming."

"Yes. Soup."

Her forehead touched the floor and she did a backward crab-scuttle on her knees out of the room.

That meant, almost certainly, that he had won, that she had been brought to his way of thinking.

Momoko returned and served the soup on her knees. "I hope it is not too hot, son?"

He tasted it. "It's all right, Mother. Delicious in fact."

"I am glad you are pleased."

The conciliatory tone, the age-old traditional manner of serving, the very bowl that had been chosen, all told him that she had capitulated. She would from this time live out her days a credit to him, a gracious figure there to look after his needs. Akio smiled his contentment and asked for a second bowl.

⛩

Father and son luxuriated in what had previously been known as a *toruko*, a kind of Turkish bath prevalent in the Asakusa. However, the Turkish government complained officially and the Japanese government requested its citizens to find another name. It was currently called Soapland. Akio had plunked down four hundred dollars apiece for the full treatment advertised to last ninety minutes. This consisted of a bath given by two young girls who bowed to the floor before opening their kimonos to reveal that they were naked under them.

They washed the men in an intimate way, with slow, leisurely strokes, giving a soapy massage that lingered on the male organs. When their clients were sufficiently stimulated, they were rinsed by means of a pitcher, guided into the tub, and instructed to be passive. The girls then began a series of acrobatics involving slow-motion cartwheels in the water followed by sexual advances made to each other, with the men as spectators, offering advice and calling out suggestions.

When the entertainment was finished the masseuses dried and dressed their customers and, bowing politely, offered their business cards. Akio left a handsome tip.

Juro was flattered that his father was spending this time with him. But even though he was extremely affable, Juro found it impossible to relax. Ever since his unexpected return a year ago, he had felt more constrained and uncomfortable in Akio's presence than usual. How could he be at ease with someone who controlled his life and future so absolutely? On the surface his father seemed to accept Miko's explanation without question, and that in itself upset Juro. Had he swallowed the story his sister concocted—flu, run-down condition, homesickness—or had he only pretended to? His father was an enigma to him and always had been. He seemed glad to have him home and had been exceedingly generous, buying him a seat on the Stock Exchange. But Juro waited for the other shoe to fall. When it didn't he proceeded to hook his modem over a dedicated line to Miko's computer in California. This enabled him to manage his accounts to the satisfaction and, at times, the admiration of his father and his associates. Miko, by way of payment, extracted a promise that he would stay clean.

Juro was beginning to unwind and feel this Soapland excursion was intended as a vote of confidence and might even mean another step up the ladder. But he didn't know if a tension-filled evening such as this was worth it. Fortunately, his father was too busy to invest much time in him, and, over the course of the year, there had only been two or three such outings. This one, he told himself by way of a pep talk, was going splendidly.

"Do they have anything like this in California?" his father asked.

"Not that I know of."

Akio laughed. He liked his own country to outdo the Americans in everything. "Come," he said expansively, "we're having drinks at Mother's Place."

Azuma herself waited on them. She indulged in risqué repartee with Akio and steered a TV *onapet* to their table. The girl was quite drunk. Someone had already unbuttoned her dress and Juro had only to put his hand in to fondle.

They were speaking of Miko, Akio commenting that the submarine blades had taken longer to produce than expected. Now they were in the final phase of completion he would be calling her back. Azuma stopped at their table from time to time with jokes and laughter. Juro was describing an American-Japanese, a Sansei, in unflattering terms. "In the dark you'd think he was American. Big, you know? Tall. But his ass is the same color as mine."

"Did he show it to you?" Akio joked.

"No, but he showed it to Miko."

Akio stopped laughing. "Miko?"

Juro was more than a little drunk. He hadn't meant to go this far. But he still brooded over his humiliation in Los Angeles. Time had not softened him but merely deepened the resentment he felt. Besides, Miko needed to be reminded she was only his father's bastard. He'd been on the verge of revealing a few choice Malibu items more than once, but he was frightened of getting in over his head, and had always checked himself. Now he blustered his way through. "Sure. They had a real hot thing going."

"And what is the name of this Sansei?"

"Watanabe. Doug Watanabe. I have a source in California who swears they're married."

"Married? Miko and a Sansei? Behind my back?"

"You wouldn't have given your permission, Father."

"You're fucking right I wouldn't give my permission. I'd have his balls pickled in a glass jar first. My daughter and the son of dirt farmers? She'd lie on her back for that scum? I don't believe it."

Miko was a bright thread in his life. If this was true, that thread had been yanked out and left dangling. With an effort he straightened in his chair. "Well, well." He stared ahead of him, eyes unfocused. . . . He remembered her at five, sitting on his knee, hunting through his pockets for *okashi.*

"Are you angry with me, Father? Perhaps I shouldn't have said anything. Am I out of line?"

Akio looked up with a start. He had forgotten Juro. "No, no," he said absently. "You are a good boy."

Azuma, while staying prudently in the background, had managed to overhear, as she always did when the subject was Miko. She left the club early for her apartment, which she shared with her cat, Oki.

The short-tailed Burmese went well with the decor and had initially been chosen for that reason. However, the cat had gradually become the master and Azuma more and more the servant, changing Oki's water, going out of her way to purchase special kitty treats. Oki ate from a monogrammed bowl and had catnip toys, as well as padded perches, a scratching tree, his own basket, kitty litter discreetly screened off in a corner of the room, and a set of grooming materials. He greeted Azuma with a discordant yowl, arched his back, and rubbed against her legs.

For once he was not picked up for his trouble. Azuma had never interfered where her daughter was concerned. Akio did not permit it. Her agreement with him was that she would keep strictly out of Miko's life.

She had never been a mother. She had never even nursed her child, but located a lactating woman, while her own full, oozing breasts had to be pumped for weeks until they dried.

Men had been her living, but by age fifteen she was no longer a street girl. Shigeru had given her a six-mat cubicle of her own, and she saved every cent, depriving herself, looking to the day she would own her own bar. She was lucky there, for when things began to go right for Akio, he was generous. Not only did he set her up with her own restaurant, but he adopted Miko. What a strange and unexpected man he was. He did not like to give up anything that was his, even a girl child.

But *she* had given her up, paying to have her raised by strangers. It was not easy; after all, she had human feelings too. She felt better about the child once Akio adopted her. And a bargain was a bargain. Even when Miko was eight and had scarlet fever, Azuma did not telephone. On Girls' Day and on New Year's she sent no gift. She gave to her employees, to the barman, the doorman, the *jokyu* girls, but not to Miko.

She had broken over in a small way. Shortly after the child recovered, one of those infrequent notes had come from her grandmother. In it she mentioned a family outing that was to take place the following weekend. That Saturday Azuma stood on a hill in a park and watched a little girl run and play. But she had not spoken to her or even drawn close. She was scrupulous in keeping her end of the bargain with Akio.

Azuma tapped her fingers on her lap. What was she thinking of? She must be mad. She could never go against Akio. It would mean the end of everything.

Still, it seemed only fair to warn Miko that her father knew of her marriage. She could write a letter, give her a chance to think things through, take whatever measures she wished.

Not only did Miko need this chance, she needed it too. It was a chance to be a mother.

Looked at rationally, the impulse was quixotic, perhaps downright stupid. Eventually Akio would know, he had eyes and ears everywhere. She knew. She was one of them.

Suddenly this sophisticated woman, whose eyebrows were carefully shaved and penciled in a high dark arch, whose hairline was plucked into a widow's peak, whose ten fingers and toes each showed a moon, this lady gowned by Dior, breathing Parisian scents, curled in on herself and cried like a child because she could not do even this for her daughter.

Oki came and again rubbed against her. Azuma lashed out, sending the surprised and spluttering animal across the room, but not before his claws had laid open her ankle. She was glad to see a trickle of blood. She was glad to know there was something that could bleed.

⛩

The news reached Akio that the silent propeller blade had successfully passed the sonar test. He suppressed his elation. They had a product! He turned his attention to guiding his plan through the political reefs that lay ahead. Takeo was out of the picture, but in the interim he had cultivated other contacts, and it was these he would send into action. That this second team was somewhat hastily formed did not concern him overly. In a way his life bore out what he had learned from business dealings, that investments held long-term unfortunately produce the more problematic return.

Take the investment one makes in one's children, an emotional commitment bound up in hopes and dreams. These are not the hands-off kind one turns over to a broker or accountant. No, it is an ever-present, often inconvenient kind, requiring constant readjustment in one's thinking and a constant outflow of funds.

When some twenty-five years have passed and you expect to cash in, what happens? You face, as he apparently did with Miko, an un-friendly leveraged buyout.

Of all moneymaking schemes, Akio considered the LBO hijinks the least productive and most injurious. Nothing tangible results. It is money making money by the maneuvering of ledgers. Of course, if it were only moving money around, it might still be acceptable. But the game weakens the company, which, in trying to keep control, cuts back on research and development, lets employees go, and trims the salaries of those who remain. In its effort to escape the threatened takeover the company becomes undercapitalized, makes an easy mark of itself, and is gobbled up. A zero-sum game with absolutely nothing resulting from all the shenanigans.

Akio was a puritan in these matters. He wanted to see an end product. He was committed to a world forging ahead under the banner of the rising sun. But this depended on cash flowing rationally, buying *something*, not simply feeding on junk bonds.

In the midst of gearing up for the next phase of the silent propeller project, Akio received a body blow. Betrayal at San Clemente. The Northern Territories deal was sabotaged. A shock wave passed over him, twisting his gut and suffusing his temples with blood. His generalship in a war that was over at his birth was snatched from him. The respect he hoped to pay his father, the recognition by his country, commendation from the Emperor, a place in history—gone in a second.

Someone of sufficient stature to be conversant not only with the technical end but the political ramifications had sold out. Rage that affected him like an illness, paralyzing even his thought processes, gradually subsided and molded itself into purpose. Several investigatory teams were put on it, who backtracked to the previous summer.

Miko's faxed reports had confirmed that, until the last minute, all was going well. But now, when the blades were manufactured and a resounding, triumphal outcome certain, the whole carefully balanced structure crashed to the ground.

Unbelievably, someone had sold out. The Russians, not the Americans, got the propellers, and not for territories but for money. Useless money that Japan was literally awash in. The Northern Territories slipped from his grasp.

How had it happened? The Americans were all over him in a flurry of abuse. While placating them as best as he was able, he could not escape the fact that his investigation pointed to someone in his own organization. Further inquiry narrowed to those with whom he had personal contact. Both his children were caught in this more finely meshed net. He realized this could turn sour indeed.

He was already greatly disappointed in Miko. Following up on Juro's remarks, he had discovered that she had been married an entire year. At the moment she had no idea he knew this. That confrontation awaited her return. However, there was a difference between acting from feeling and betrayal of country.

The search narrowed again, this time to an engineer at Toshiba, who named his contact.

A series of dates were run through computer scans, which verified what had been alleged. During those months Juro had unquestionably been in California. And had unquestionably been in contact with the suspected intermediary, a Mr. Yawata.

⛩

"Yawata." Doug looked up from the morning *Times*. "Mr. Yawata. Wasn't that the name of one of the guys Juro hung out with?"

"He was associated with Toshiba in some way, yes."

"Your brother may have himself in a spot of trouble."

"Why do you say that?"

She put down "Opinion" and reached for the business section he had been reading. "Oh, my God." Even the baby became dormant in her body, as though it too suspended function. It was all over the first page: "The Kuril Island group, made up of Kunashiri, Etorofu, Shikotan, and Habomai, seem once again lost to Japan." The newspaper fell from her hand.

"I don't understand. It all went like clockwork. I shepherded it through myself. And now it's blown sky-high. What could have happened? What could have gone wrong? I've failed my father in this too. I can't imagine his anger when he learns of this, I can't imagine what form it will take. I've got to get a plane to Tokyo tonight."

"What are you saying? You're going to have that kid any minute."

"Juro's right in the middle, and I doubt that he knows it. Doug, don't you see, if Yawata's implicated, Juro could be too. I've got to go. You don't realize how serious this is."

"Miko, you can go after you've had the baby. It's just a matter of a few weeks."

"You don't know my father. No one crosses him. Not even Juro. I've got to get him out of Tokyo. After all, it's my fault he's there."

"You're overreacting, Miko. It's part of the pregnancy thing."

"You're wrong, Doug. I wish you weren't, but you are. I'm sorry, darling, I'm leaving tonight."

"You're really going?" Doug said as it sank in. "What will your father do when he sees you're pregnant?"

"He has two samurai swords in his office. He'll take the larger one, the *katana*, and behead me."

"Seriously?"

"I've no idea how he will react, absolutely none."

It had been her experience that every deal has a history and a context. This one had begun with a love affair and proceeded through a mistake and a tragedy to a secret marriage. She felt it was moving into the final stage. Soon the full text would be there, plain to see. And the text as far as Juro was concerned? He did not reply to letters, her only communication was with his computer. She left phone messages on his machine, but he never got back to her. A word now and again from Oba-sama told her that he seemed to be doing all right.

But in spite of availing himself of her advice in handling his investments, he refused more than this impersonal contact and kept her strictly out of his life. This continued sulking plagued her, but if he was in trouble she had to be there.

She was paging through her electronic phone book devoted exclusively to her father's unlisted and scrambled numbers, each worked out to fit into an overall code.

Miko reset her mind, Japanese time as opposed to Los Angeles time. She must track him down, she must have his permission to come home.

Where should she try? The trading house in the Marunouchi district? The floor of the Tokyo exchange? Trading ended there before the business day began here. She might catch him at the Nikkeiren, the Federated Employers Association, or at the Keizai Doyukai, the Committee of Economic Development. He could be closeted with any of the top executives of his six nucleus companies. If politics is motion, as former Prime Minister Tanaka once said, her father was a typhoon.

Of course he might be out of the country altogether, fine-tuning a deal on another continent, or golfing in Hong Kong, or relaxing in Hawaii.

She reached him at Mother's Place in Tokyo, and obtained his permission to return.

⛩

Akio ordered the *ofuro* heated and stepped into it, determined to relax. But the tightness seemed to be in the circuitry of his brain. No pleasant warmth could reach or soothe the despair that spewed out like a squid's ink, covering him. Juro was his heir. Juro must oversee his vast empire someday, and someday pray for him.

Juro, the child he and Sumie had thought so perfect, the boy who had grown up in a glow of health. This child carried a fatal seed that grew as he grew, undetected, like ARC before it becomes full-blown AIDS.

Akio spoke mantras to Noboru the Oka fighter, invoking his spirit. "I am utterly bowed down." Once this admission was made, it was easier to continue. "My son, your grandson, has dishonored us. Help me find the path that will reinstate the Sanogawa before our country and our Emperor."

After some moments the *kami* put into his mind the correct course to follow. He knew with certainty what he must do, and with the path of honor once again open to him and to Juro, he could continue to represent his family with pride. Mentally he bowed to the Oka fighter and drew his breath deeply.

Akio allowed himself to be dried and massaged with an emollient compounded of herbs, vitamin E, and the pulp of the aloe vera. He then retired and slept six hours. Waking refreshed, he rang for Kenji, who dressed him. He pointed to a white kimono that was reserved for rare ceremonies. He himself tied the *hachimaki*, the victory band, across his forehead. He sent for the Sanogawa swords, and he sent for his son.

Juro didn't like being summoned. Besides, there was the usual tinge of apprehension where his father was concerned. He was well aware that his carefree ways were anathema to the entire older genera-tion that had worn themselves out accomplishing the economic mira-cle. And now that Japan was the richest country in the world, they did not know how to loosen the traces they had tied themselves into, but, like old hobbled buffalo, continued to plod in the same grooves.

The few times his father unbent and made a conscientious effort to be buddies were strained and uncomfortable on both sides. Try as he would, Akio Sanogawa was not a jolly good fellow. Juro wished he felt the same sense of freedom Miko did with their father. But he didn't, and he hoped their recent evening out was not about to be repeated. It was impossible to forget who he was, and the grip he had over your life. One false step and—well, that was the point, you didn't really know. You knew the man's reputation for ruthlessness, but it was more what you felt about him. You could not even guess his *honne*, his real intent. But Juro sensed a raw power in his father that frightened him.

He reluctantly put his date for the evening on hold and braved Tokyo traffic for the pleasure of driving his Ferrari Testarossa sports car. How that baby handled with its space-age navigational system. An extra key locked off four of its eight cylinders so parking-lot atten-dants couldn't drag-race it. It had a fax, and the stereo was voice-activated. Fragrances were pumped through the air conditioner, and its windows adjusted their tint to the sun's glare. Finally, it unlocked only at the touch of his fingerprints. The exotic Ferrari was his special love; he understood Prince Charles had one. He planned to take it

into the country over the weekend and let it out. But for the moment
he inched through traffic, enjoying the envious stares of males and the
obvious admiration of girls in other vehicles. He had left his dinner
date tentative. It was possible he could still make it.

On reaching the house he spoke briefly to his mother. It was
almost like glancing into a mirror, they resembled each other so closely.
He was always pleased when she looked particularly lovely and, as
now, had taken extra pains with herself. He saw that she was getting
ready to go to one of her fund-raising auctions, and wondered that
a woman as attractive as his mother could interest herself in such
nonsense.

He continued down the corridor to his father's study. The shoji
screen was slid back by a servant who was expecting him. The room
was traditional, austere, without Western accouterments of any kind.

When he saw his father in a white kimono, with a *hachimaki*
around his head, Juro knew it was bad. He looked at the stern set of
his father's face; it held the hardness of carved stone.

Juro bowed, trying for a casual demeanor. "Good evening, Father." It came out much too high-pitched.

Akio did not respond. He did not even look at him. Juro resisted
the impulse to fidget. He would outwait him, he was determined to.

At last Akio's eyes shifted to take him in. "So you have come."

"Naturally, Father."

"It is natural for you to obey me, is that right, since you are my
son?"

"*Hai.*"

"I will bear that in mind. I want you to bring me the pair of
fighting swords, the *katana* and the *wakizashi*. Remove them and bring
them here."

Juro did as he was told. He recognized them as the ancient Sanogawa swords that had been returned to the family. They were usually
kept in his father's office; he wondered why they had been brought
here. What mummery was this, he wondered, returning with the props
to his father.

"Sit opposite me, placing the *katana* and the *wakizashi* between
us."

Juro assumed the *seiza* position, which had become almost foreign
to him.

"You may remove your jacket," Akio said.

Juro did so, folding it neatly and placing it beside him.

"We will share a cup of sake," his father said, "and then you will commit seppuku."

"What?"

Akio poured the sake and handed it to him.

"If this is humor, Father, isn't it a bit bizarre?"

"It is neither bizarre nor humorous. It is the way of your ancestors with whom you will shortly rest."

"Father, I'm trying to understand what this is about. Why are you dressed like that?"

"Because I will assist you. I will not allow you to suffer. On that you have my word."

"What are we talking about? Father, if you're trying to scare me, you've succeeded. Okay? Can we call it quits? Can we stop this? Can I put the swords back?"

"Do not touch the swords. Not yet."

"Not yet?"

"Not until I understand what the reason was for your betrayal of yourself and me and the country."

"I didn't betray anyone," Juro said, for in a rush he knew what was behind this. He too had seen the papers and Yawata's name. But as far as he knew there was no way to connect him with this debacle. Nevertheless the tight feeling in his chest increased as he said, "I don't know what you're talking about."

Silence closed around them for a full minute. "I am going to ask you a question. Before you answer, I want you to know that I will get to the bottom of this. So don't lie to me. I know about your swollen bank account. Explain how you came by such a sum."

"It was nothing. I played the market. I was lucky."

"I have checked the transaction tapes. The money is considerably more than your profit."

"It wasn't what you think. I needed cash. I couldn't ask for more allowance. My portfolio was totally tied up. I'd borrowed from Miko. I needed cash."

"If you wanted money, you only had to ask."

"I couldn't ask." Juro was backed into a corner, and it all spewed out. "I needed it for coke. You know, cocaine." He began to take pleasure in sticking it to the old man. "I put a fortune up my nose in California. Sometimes I freebased. Ask Miko. At first she tried to cover for me. But finally she gave up on me, put me in a sanitarium. Oh, I'm clean now. But I don't mind telling you, it was rough."

"You are telling me that you were, possibly are, a cocaine addict?" This was worse even than he had thought. The Americans attack in a cruel way. He should not have entrusted his children to them. It was a blunder for which he must bear a share of the blame.

"Father, I want you to believe me, I didn't know where this would lead. I'd no idea. When I read about the propeller deal the other day, I was surprised. Then I saw this name, Yawata. He was a friend of mine, a free-lancer with some kind of in at Toshiba. Well, I'd run out of moon rock, used up my allowance, sold off stock, borrowed, I didn't know what else to do. I had to have the stuff. It's not only that you want the high—you feel so damned rotten, physically you're sick. And Yawata said he had a contact who would pay to be put in touch with the top man on the silent propeller blade. It was so hush-hush that he hadn't been able to find out himself, so he came to me. All he wanted was a name. It didn't seem a big deal."

Akio nodded. "I have often wondered, in studying history, what rationale traitors prepared for their own consumption. The most perfidious act can apparently be couched in such a way as to make it seem almost a logical step. Certainly nothing momentous."

"I hope you believe that I'm sorry. I am. I know getting back the Northern Territories is important."

"Men shed their blood for those islands."

"If I'd had any idea, I never would have done it. You've got to believe that."

"I believe it."

"Well, I'm relieved to hear it. Can we put these away," he pointed to the weapons lying between them, "and go have a drink somewhere?"

"We are drinking the ceremonial sake I have poured."

Juro stiffened. "You're not serious? I've explained to you—"

"It is not a question of explanations, it is a question of facts. The fact is you are a traitor who sold out his country for gain and lost his Emperor territories that are historically Japanese."

"You'll get the damned islands back. You'll figure out another way."

"Perhaps. But even if that is so, it does not affect what you have done. Your conduct has covered me and the family in shame. That *haji* can only be expunged by your honorable death."

"Well, you're not going to have my honorable death, so you can forget it."

"Let us drink." Akio was imperturbable.

Juro struck the cup to the floor. "This sucks, you know it? This whole interview sucks. Go ahead, disinherit me, do whatever it is you have to do, I'm leaving." Juro in one motion got up and in the next reached the sliding door, which he pulled roughly aside. Yakuza stood there, three of them, arms folded.

Juro turned in a panic. "You can't behave like some medieval Shogun. You're a businessman, a man of the world. Those yakuza belong out in the garden, protecting the house. They've no place here, threatening me. That's insane. It's insane, Father. For God's sake admit that it's insane!"

"The sword is the only path of honor left you."

"I think you mean it." Juro began to cry. "Oh, God, you do, you do mean it." He stood in the middle of the room and screamed, "Help! Help!"

"Juro, things are not as bad as you think. Sit down again on the *zabuton*. I want you to calm down."

"How can I calm down when you want to kill me?"

"I do not want to kill you. I want you to kill yourself."

"Oh, well, pardon me," Juro fell back on the cushion, "that makes all the difference."

Akio, ignoring the sarcasm, said, "The first step is to remove your belt so there is no impediment."

"Of course. Remove the belt. Why didn't I think of that?"

"Remove it!" Akio commanded.

Juro did, unbuckling and passing it through the loops.

"Next the trousers are unzipped and rolled down under the belly."

Juro automatically followed this instruction with zombielike movements.

"The point of entry is just below the navel. The short sword of your samurai forefathers is lifted reverently in both hands. And you should prepare your mind, setting it above the concerns of this floating world. No cares can touch you now, you are part of the infinite. Your soul is with the *kami*. Take your handkerchief and wind it around the upper portion of the blade, it is an indication to you, you must give a mighty thrust. Only when you feel the cloth can you stop. At that moment your death is assured and you will slice the blade to the right and with your remaining strength to the left. With those thrusts you have regained honor, and I will strike cleanly so it will finish without prolonged agony." Akio bowed and held the *wakizashi* out to Juro.

Juro took it in both hands, looked down at it, and said, "You can't force me to do it, there'd be no honor."

"That is correct."

"Well, then, I've beaten you because I don't give a shit about honor. And since there's no way you can make me, you've gotten all dressed up in your white kimono for nothing." He began to laugh.

Akio regarded his son dispassionately. "I have not yet laid the alternative before you. It is this. You will undergo rehabilitation for your addiction. I know a place on the outskirts of town that treats both addicts and alcoholics."

"But I've gone through treatment. I'm cured."

"As a solicitous parent, I do not believe you are. And to ensure that you will not backslide, you will not be released. Of course every day you will be offered release. Every day you will be brought the sword. That is your release."

"Father . . ." Juro at this point was calm. "Don't do this to me. I have learned my lesson. I will be valuable to you from now on. I will do whatever you say, undertake anything you want. I'll sign a document of reflection, an official apology. You can print it in all the papers. Just don't do this."

Akio sheathed the *wakizashi* and, rising, returned both swords to their stand. Juro again slid open the shoji. At a sign from Akio the yakuza let him pass. Juro ran down the corridor calling for his mother.

Sumie had not yet left for her meeting. "Juro," she said in some consternation, "I thought I heard you. Is something wrong?"

"Mother . . ." He took both her hands, chafing them excitedly. "Mother, don't let me be sent away. I'm perfectly fine now, I'm not sick, I'm not addicted."

Sumie looked for an explanation to Akio, who had followed Juro in.

"My dear wife, I'm afraid our son has brought us sorrow."

"Sorrow? What? Will no one tell me what is going on?"

"He wants to shut me away, Mother."

"I'm afraid much of it is my fault," Akio put in. "I sent our son to America and he became infected with the virus of their streets, he is a cocaine addict."

"Oh, Akio. I didn't want him to go. I said so at the time."

"I should have listened to you."

"And now look what has happened."

"Mother, I've been in treatment. I'm okay now. I'm clean. Ask Miko."

"Miko? Was she responsible?"

"Mother, he never intends to let me out. He told me so, never."

Sumie patted the hand that clung to hers. "He'll let you out, of course he will, dear, when you're cured."

When Juro saw that all his protests were no good, he smiled at his mother. "You're right, of course." And without another glance at his father, he followed the three yakuza out.

Sumie looked to her husband for a further explanation. Juro was the only subject on which they communicated.

"To discover your only son is an addict . . ." she began.

Over the gulf of twenty years Akio reached out to her. "Is the meeting tonight something you could miss? Perhaps you could stay in and we could talk, Sumie."

Once she would have exulted at this moment. Now it was with indifference that she replied, "How unfortunate that this meeting is extremely important."

Akio bowed his head.

There were times when Miko regretted the Japanese manner of greeting after an absence. It was never with the hugs and kisses she had grown accustomed to in the States. Gifts took the place of affectionate touching. She followed the advice she had given Juro a year ago and shopped last-minute at the duty-free counters in Narita Airport.

She phoned her stepmother, Sumie, from a public booth. Sumie began crying and told her Juro was in treatment for drug addiction. "That's what they did to my son in America."

There was a pause before Miko asked, "Can I visit him?"

"No. They don't allow visitors, not yet."

"I see." Miko hung up. The worst had happened, then. She dialed her father at the number he had given her, but a secretary told her he was in conference, and made an appointment for the following morning.

She checked into the New Otani, kicked off her shoes, propped herself up on the bed with cushions at her back, and called her grandmother.

"Miko!" Oba-sama always recognized her voice no matter how long it had been. Her name came over the wires as an embrace.

"Grandmother, it's so good to hear you. Are you well? Are you fine? Let me pick you up at seven this evening. We're going to have dinner. It will be a wild celebration."

Immediately she hung up she redialed, phoning the Key Club. The maitre d' informed her they were not taking more reservations for this evening. She gave her father's name and a reservation was found.

A reunion with her grandmother was an event Miko looked forward to. She was Momoko's girl and always had been.

Oba-sama fed her broth when she convalesced from scarlet fever, read to her, and told her of her grandfather, the fearless Oka fighter. It was Momoko who noticed how quick she was at schoolwork and demanded an education for her.

She thought of these things as she got into her elegant maternity dress, a crepe material whose lines helped her overblown figure. Looking into the mirror, she fluffed her hair. Many people thought that a pregnant woman was at her most beautiful. Her face, she decided, reminded one of classic beauties in ancient block prints. As for the rest . . . She tried to imagine what Oba-sama would say, she'd given her absolutely no indication. Humming, she touched her breasts with perfume and was ready.

Miko left the cab waiting and went herself to the door of the house. The old place always produced a twinge. It was a bit ramshackle; God knows, Father could afford mansions. But this was the family home, the home of his childhood. It sat on a prime piece of Tokyo real estate, but nothing had been done to modernize or remodel. It was meant to be Western in style, but its austere lines and the curve of the green tiled roof were definitely Japanese. And there was no doubt about the combed gravel and gardens of its approach. But a Victorian veranda had been imposed on it.

Oba-sama opened the door. She wore a *homongi* that swept the floor, with motifs of plum blossoms and fans around the hem and sleeves. "You look beautiful, Grandmother," Miko said, bowing her glossy head.

Momoko caught her breath audibly at sight of her pregnant grand-daughter. "Miko, you have much to tell me."

"Yes, yes I have." Miko pressed the travel gift into her hand.

Momoko bowed in appreciation and Miko escorted her to the taxi. She found herself chattering away as though they had not been apart. How easy it was to talk to her grandmother. "Father always said the streets of Tokyo must be negotiated only in the deep trance of a Zen master."

Momoko laughed behind her hand, concurring with the idea, waiting until Miko was ready to confide in her. When they entered the club dining room with its chandeliers and crystals, its lush gilt and discreetly placed tables festooned with flowers and candles, their progress was noted by the other diners who watched the delicate, aristocratic women. Momoko's kimono rustled provocatively with each small, turned-in step.

When they were seated Miko said, "Let me order you a cocktail."

"I'll have a Bloody Mary," Momoko replied.

Miko hid her amazement by lowering her eyes. Her grandmother was full of surprises.

Momoko studied the menu raptly and ordered a New York cut with pickled eggplant on the side.

"Grandmother, this is fun. Why did we never do this? We must make it a custom."

Momoko agreed.

"It's a boy, Grandmother."

Momoko smiled. "They say if you dangle a cord before your belly and it moves perpendicularly . . ."

"No, Grandmother. It really is. This is the modern world. They can tell such things now, they have tests."

Momoko clapped her hands together in wonder and delight. "And you are carrying a son?"

"I am, yes. And what you are too sweet and dear to ask me is, am I married. I am. His name is Doug."

"Doug?"

"It's an American name, Grandmother. Scottish, actually. But he's Japanese."

The cocktail arrived. Miko smiled. "I'm not joining you on account of the baby." Her look became searching. "Grandmother, I don't know if you ve ever been in love. . . ."

Momoko nodded. "Oh, yes."

"But do you still remember?"

Miko didn't perceive the quickly suppressed expression that flitted across her face. "You'd adore Doug, Grandmother, because his own skin is no sort of boundary for him. Integrated circuits are his toys. The idea is to make them smaller and smaller and get more and more information on them."

Miko paused while the steaks were served, and Momoko waited for her to go on.

"Of course he hasn't had a Japanese upbringing. He's clumsy, like an American. And all the time he's figuring out how to control the path of electrons moving on these unimaginably thin scratches. He has extended his work to the edge of existing technology . . . and then taken a running jump. Another way to look at it is . . . Father takes a military stance, with a full war chest, an international organization, and legions of disciplined technicians he advances in kind of a Roman phalanx. Doug, on the other hand, just sits and thinks. Part of the work he does at the kitchen table. He's not disciplined or organized and he's certainly not militaristic. He gets ideas and then tries them out."

"And there is a market for this?" Momoko asked, trying to get her bearings.

"Oh, yes, the new supercomputers are crammed with microchips. If they save even a nanosecond of time it is significant. Who are his potential customers? Livermore Labs, Los Alamos, GM, universities, the Department of Defense, aerospace industries. That's what comes to mind to begin with."

"Then this improved microchip is vital in moving the supercomputer industry forward?"

"To use Father's favorite expression, 'They are the rice of the technical world.' "

Waiters hovered, clearing, pouring coffee. Momoko chose an eclaire from the passing cart of French pastries, but once on her plate she only cut around it with her fork. Managing a knife and fork took a good deal of concentration. "Try to be happy in your love, Miko." Then, casting back in her mind, she added, "You should make an effort to run after happiness."

Miko leaned across the table toward her. "Grandmother, I came back because of Juro. Do you know where he is?"

"He's in an institution just outside Tokyo."

"Grandmother, I'm worried about him. He's mixed up in one of Father's schemes. I'm afraid he's in over his head."

"You must ask for permission to see him."

Miko nodded. "How do you think Father will react to . . . my condition?"

"He will react strongly."

"Strongly good or strongly bad?"

Momoko hesitated, toying with the Bavarian cloisonné cups in which the demitasse was served. "Since he can no longer count on Juro, he needs this son of yours."

Miko waited in a large, boxlike room in which there were a half-dozen computer workstations laid out in a rectangle. She supposed that eventually someone would usher her into her father's office. At first she had been pleased at this early appointment, knowing he had postponed matters of urgency and put off cabinet ministers and visiting dignitaries to greet her. But as she waited she became convinced her father would castigate her over her pregnancy, be vituperous on hearing of her marriage, guess her panic over Juro, somehow penetrate her husband's secrets, and in general view her defection as a samurai of old. This was odd since she had never feared her father; as a small child she had the privilege of walking up to him and claiming his lap. Now, however, she could hardly repress the feeling that the office staff were retainers instructed to seize her for her crime.

And what was that crime? It was twofold. She was bringing him a grandchild and a valuable invention which could easily make him yet another fortune.

At last she succeeded in catching the eye of a young woman as she looked up from her machine. Miko bowed quickly and of course received a much lower bow. Once this acknowledgment had taken place, the "office flower" was obligated to leave her work and escort Miko into the innermost sanctum where Akio sat in his rather modest corner of the building. To his left were the Sanogawa swords that she recalled so vividly, mounted on an ebony display rack. They were the only personalized touch in the otherwise spartan room, which had an unused look; there was not a single sheet of paper or even an ashtray on the desk's surface. The almost shabby office was meant to convey that Akio Sanogawa was simply a servant of his companies. Most noticeable was the absence of bookcases. Books were not current enough for his purposes. Filed magnetic tapes held the information he required. The only indication of tenancy of even a transitory nature was a battery of phones with a scrambling device and a miniaturized dictating machine.

Thick, dark tea was served in ancient bowls. The young woman who officiated must have been trained on the bowing machine, so exact were her movements.

Setting down his tea bowl, Akio said, "I see you carry a child. Is a father permitted to ask if you are married?"

Miko bent her head before this curbed anger. "Forgive me, Father, for marrying without your consent."

"We Japanese have as many words for loyalty as the Eskimo has for snow. . . ."

She translated as they fell from his lips, *on, ko, chu, giri, gimu*—duty, obligation, fealty, loyalty, trustworthiness.

They were silent a long time before she spoke in her defense. "You have never lived outside Japan, Father, your visits abroad are lightning strikes. You don't know the alienation, the loneliness of not belonging. In my husband, Doug Watanabe, I saw my situation duplicated. His features were the features of my own race and I felt at home with him. If I did not have such a strong human feeling for him, I would not have acted as I have. I hoped that a grandson would make peace between us."

Akio's brows drew together. "Yes, it is a strong factor speaking to reconciliation. You have heard of our failure in connection with the Northern Territories?"

"I have searched my heart and my mind. I don't believe I was remiss. Someone sold out, but I've no idea who."

He regarded her with a long, level look. "I don't hold you responsible."

During the pause that followed, Miko summoned her forces for the attack. "When I got in yesterday the first thing I did was to phone the house. I was told about Juro. I'm very distressed. I want to see him as soon as possible."

"For the present, no one can see him. Perhaps in a week or two . . ."

"I would like to see him before then. I wouldn't stay long, or upset him in any way."

"The doctors advise against it for the time being."

"I see. Where is he staying?"

"I'll leave the address and phone number with my secretary and you can inquire after him."

For the moment she saw that she would have to be content with that. It was possible that everything was as it appeared. Her father had done no more than she herself had in placing him under treatment. But she had a strong presentiment that all was not well.

Akio swiveled in his chair to face the banks of windows that looked out at the Marunouchi financial district, the Ginza, and Tokyo Tower in the distance. He seemed to speak at random, but she knew this was not so. "Did you know," he asked, "that the word *market* also means 'sacred place'?"

"No, I didn't know that."

"Trade is still sacred. But do you think one of samurai descent owns trading houses and conglomerates around the globe to get rich?"

He paused to scrutinize her. "The answer is . . . of course. But not for me or even the family. It is *gimu* to the country. In your generation, Miko, it will come together. In spite of the setback we have received, it will come together. Americans like to think the war began with Pearl Harbor. But the day that will live in infamy is the day Commodore Matthew Perry and his black ships sailed into Uraga Harbor.

"In the eighteenth century we Japanese looked at the world and saw that we were outside it, a unique people existing on a chain of small volcanic islands. We did not share our language or our history with other peoples, we were free to choose the best of each. We went to England for our navy. France provided us the organization for our army. Germany was the model for our universities and our constitution. From England we took our civil laws, our courts, and our trains. In manufacture and commerce we patterned ourselves on the Americans. What a mix it proved to be! Confucian philosophy and German idealism met in Japan. That's the background of your modern intellectual, plus you can throw in a bit of Social Darwinism, a dash of Utilitarianism and a pinch of Rousseau. Graft this onto the traditional sword-wielding, haiku-writing samurai, and you had the prewar Japanese. He recognized that he was privileged, that he alone had not passively accepted the accretions of his culture, but taken the best the world offered—in short that he was ideally qualified to run it.

"He chose the way of the sword. Even in 1939 it was not the modern way. He was doomed to fail. He did, on a gigantic scale, in the Pacific."

Akio turned and pierced her with a terrible look. "He did not fail because his motives were wrong. They were not wrong. As a matter of fact, his preparation to this point was correct. Only the implementation was wrong. War in the conventional sense was wrong. Even then it was outmoded, passé. One could no longer win by such crude methods.

"The ultimate weapon could not be used. The spot where it fell is today a shrine, Peace Park. The whole world beats a path to Hiroshima every August sixth. At eight-fifteen in the morning everything in the city stops—buses stop, streetcars, motorcycles, automobiles, all traffic—and people pray with bowed heads as a thousand doves are released to the clanging of a temple bell.

"Not only Japanese pray—foreign visitors, *gaijin* pray as well. The granite tomb dedicated to the hundred and forty thousand dead is heaped with chrysanthemums, the flower of mourning."

Akio's words were of peace, but his tone seemed harsh, almost brutal. "In the report you just faxed me, you recommend that I look at the product of a novice electronics firm specializing in a new memory chip, with an eye to forming a partnership." Before she could respond he had rung for his secretary, who came in with a folio of papers Miko recognized. She had sent it from the States, after deciding it would be best to prime her father before this meeting. But now her heart began to thud against her chest. She tried for calm, measured breaths.

Akio reached out his hand for the report, and nothing was heard in the room but the turning of pages. Finally he spoke, but without looking up. "Doug Watanabe is, of course, your husband, and this is his company."

"Yes."

"This seems to be concerned with a chip etched by ion-beam lithography on a neodymium gallate substrate. Tell me"—he was still perusing the paper—"was I wrong to educate my daughter to take a place in my operations? Only you can answer, Miko."

"You were not wrong, Father," she said with what resolution she could summon.

"Really?" He spoke urbanely but with an edge of contempt.

All color left her face.

"You have presented me with a very interesting piece of work that does not seem to be complete."

When she and Doug discussed this eventuality, it had not seemed so drastic. "Doug is astute. The key is in his hands. He requires a signed fifty-fifty partnership, an agreement to develop, before relinquishing the final piece."

"I see. And how can I be sure there *is* a final piece?"

Her mouth had gone dry, she wet her lips with her tongue. "Father, he is a dedicated scientist. By withholding one element of the process he hopes to protect his interest, that's all."

Akio let out his anger. "You make a Kabuki production of giving me this worthless paper. It is pure duplicity on your part. Your pretended motives of loyalty to me are a lie."

She bowed her head. *"Shikataga arimasen,* it can't be helped."

Silence stood between them. At last he said, "I do not know what rules you play by. You were my *shosha*-man and at the same time secretly married to the man whose invention you want me to invest in."

Miko bowed her head against his wrath.

Akio paced up and down. He seemed to be wrestling with himself. Finally he came to a stop in front of her. "Miko, the past is done. We will forget it. You will stay here. Have your child here. He will be my heir. There have been few fortunes in history that match mine."

"Father," Miko said in a low voice, "I'm married."

"Doug Watanabe won't be the loser by the arrangement. I'll do as you suggest, buy into the company, let him run it. In return he'll give you a divorce and relinquish all claim to the child."

"Please don't go on, Father."

"I want you to think about it."

"No."

"Then phone your husband with my offer."

Miko hesitated.

"It's the sensible way out of this dilemma."

"There is no dilemma, Father."

"You have married without my knowledge or consent. How could you give yourself to the son of dirt farmers?"

Miko met his glance. "You would not see a grandson of poor farmers if you met him. You would see a brilliant, well-educated man who dreams many of your dreams."

"My dreams will swallow up America, supplant her. I do not think he dreams that."

"No, he doesn't. He believes that technology holds the key to a good life for people everywhere."

"There has always been a dominant culture. We have shed our blood for that privilege, it is ours. You do not see this because you are no longer Japanese. To have married without my consent or even my knowledge means you do not know *ko*."

"Please, Father, find a punishment for me so that I can be forgiven."

"I don't know if it is possible, Miko. You wear ribbons of shame."

Miko stood abruptly, but she looked as if she might fall. "What about my child? Does he wear ribbons of shame too?"

"The child is another matter. My proposition stands. In all fairness you must lay it before your husband, provided of course you are not afraid to do so."

Miko turned and fumbled for the door.

⛩

Momoko was preparing for the festival of Tanabata, which was only a week off. To her evening prayers she added another for the Cowherd and the Weaver, two stars known to the rest of the world as Altair and Vega. Their commemoration fell on the seventh day of the seventh month.

In ages past, two lovers had been discovered in an illicit affair and thrown into the sky. Their banishment did not end there. They were always to be parted by the Milky Way, except for one day of the year, the seventh of July, when, if the weather is fine, the two stars approach close enough to see each other. The *kami* named Tanabata the day of love's possibilities.

When she and Takeo went through a *giri*-divorce so many years ago, she had whispered to him not to be sad, that they would make this legend of love their own, that no matter in what direction fate took them, they would meet each year at the temple to celebrate Tanabata and feast their eyes on each other. And now again this was the only day left them.

The custom was to brush auspicious poems on brightly colored strips of paper and hang them on bamboo cuttings in the garden. Momoko was absorbed in composing garlands of poems, but a note of anxiety for Takeo's health crept into them. He had been seen in public, but, according to reports, still relied on a cane. She had even heard that when the doctors operated they found a more serious underlying condition. She had to wait for Tanabata to discover for herself how he was.

She was interrupted in her preparations by her granddaughter coming through the garden to her suite of rooms.

Even at at distance she sensed something was wrong and hurried to meet her.

"Oh, Grandmother . . ."

"He wasn't pleased about the grandson?"

"Oh, he was pleased all right, so pleased he wants him raised here. He wants me to divorce Doug and stay here with the baby."

"But that's mad."

"He offered a bribe. A big one. The child will be his heir. And Doug will be bought off by having his company financed."

Momoko sighed. "Your father believes that money will satisfy any appetite."

"He as much as dared me to call Doug. Grandmother, I'm afraid. That's terrible, isn't it? But suppose Father is right, and Doug agrees?"

"He would never agree to a thing like that."

"You don't know how hard he's worked for an opportunity like this, and how much he wants it. . . . Fuck, fuck, fuck," she said in English and continued in Japanese. "What should I do? Grandmother, tell me what to do."

Momoko looked into her garden. It was a source of strength, and she would need strength for Miko. Miko was her special responsibility. Special because it was she who had spoken up for a Western education. And she felt now she had been wrong. Miko reminded her of a bonsai tree, held by wires, twisted, taught to grow in a certain pattern. Once taken from its small container, transplanted, its wires cut, the tree can never be forced back, neither is it able to survive in a field. It no longer fits anywhere.

Returning her gaze to her granddaughter, she said, "It cannot be as bad as you think."

"But it is, it's worse. I wear ribbons of shame."

"What nonsense. Is this the Meiji era? No modern person speaks like that."

"Father does."

"Your father is not a modern man. He is a warlord. Oh, I know he is one of a small cadre of men who will bring about the next century. His *ura* was forged before his birth. I carried him in the last, most horrible days of the war. It scarred him. Even as a child he was not like others. His rages were terrible. Your great-grandmother thought there was an *oni* in him. He was seven years old when he underwent purification by a priest. But he was marked, he fights a war he cannot win. His abilities allow him to move the world forward, but it is never enough. He is a man who does not rest, a man of strife and conflict, driven by ancient values. He is, as I told you, not a modern man. He is a man divided against himself, who works to bring about a world that will destroy him."

"All right, Shinto devils and microchips fight for his soul. Why does he take it out on me?"

Her grandmother could not answer this. "Did you find out where Juro is?" she asked.

"Yes, I have the address and the phone number. But I won't be satisfied until I see him. I won't leave the country until I'm convinced everything is all right. After all, I've had a taste of what my father is capable of."

Momoko said, "I will attempt to learn the reputation of the institution and speak with his doctors."

"Yes, that would be helpful." But the immediacy of confronting her husband overwhelmed her. "Grandmother, what will I do about Doug? Should I call him? I suppose I might as well and find out where I stand."

"Perhaps," Momoko said slowly, "you should go on a pilgrimage."

This old-fashioned advice jarred her into the realization that Oba-sama was of another time, a time when protocol and correct actions solved problems. A time when a simple woodcutter, if he was of samurai blood, could win battles. She had been wrong to make a confidante of her. "Oh, Grandmother, what good would that be?"

"I don't mean to a temple. At least not a Buddhist temple. I mean the new kind, of steel and Lexan, the kind they are building in half a dozen places. I used to visit Kumamoto when it was known for watermelons. Now it is known for its laboratories. They are equipped with the latest robotic technology, all sorts of arms, pincers, and lasers working on flat television screens. Tsukuba is another 'brain city,' just fifty miles or so from Tokyo."

"Grandmother, what are you suggesting? That Doug and I develop the chip without Father?"

"I only suggest you make a pilgrimage."

This brought Miko up sharply. Oba-sama may have come from the time of the abacus, but she stood here with her now. Miko hugged her. "That's a crazy idea, Grandmother. We could never raise the capital."

Time wafted past them. "Perhaps *I* could," Momoko suggested.

Miko looked at her astonished. "Grandmother, you don't realize the sums involved."

"I'm sure that is true. However, let me speak in the ear of my friend."

Miko recalled that her grandmother knew how to order a Bloody Mary. What else did this woman of another time know? "It wouldn't hurt to make a pilgrimage," she conceded.

"And there *are* temples along the way. You might seek prayers for the life within you, for Juro, who I'm sure feels desperate. And for your father, who is so angry. We all need prayers."

Miko agreed. "We all need prayers."

⛩

It was against reason, Miko knew, to put credence in Momoko's vague plan. It called for a large injection of faith. The friend whose ear she would speak into, who could it be? Another little old Japanese lady like herself, who perhaps had savings she kept in a silk purse?

What a charming picture it made, a modern Japanese block print. Two old-world, elderly ladies as major stockholders attending business meetings in their finest kimonos. For all that she toted up what she herself could shake free in the way of assets. If she sold off everything, it represented a sizable sum. And Doug would contribute whatever he could in the way of contacts. Perhaps if they worked up a good presentation they could get additional financing. It wouldn't be on the scale they had envisioned; they wouldn't be equipped to distribute. But Doug might be able to keep control in his own hands. If they could make it, it would be without the aggressive political overtones her father brought to everything. With him it was a crusade. He wanted to shut the West, particularly America, out of the twenty-first century. Each deal he closed was a prescription for the eclipse of American technology. If they were embedding a thirty-two-megabit chip, Akio would bring out a sixty-four-megabit chip.

Grandmother knew him. She knew he was waging war and that his secret weapon was *o-kane.* Money. Finances. Through these means he meant to bring total power into his hands, and through him, to Japan. That he had been thwarted temporarily meant nothing. He would make an assault in another direction.

She had been blind not to understand how deadly the game was, and how high the stakes. If she had been successful in getting her father to fund Doug's process, she would have placed the two of them on a collision course. Doug was American, American to the core. Eventually, when he understood whose side he had come down on, he would pull out, and he would blame her as she blamed herself. She saw clearly that it was an act of war to stand with her father.

The other realization that came to her was that she must trust her husband. Together she and Doug must fight Akio. With this resolution it was easier to place the call.

When Doug's voice came over the coaxial cable she was unprepared for what the sound of him did to her. In that second he was conjured up, his American build, his sensitive Japanese face, the earnest look of him when he was working.

"Miko. Is that you?"

"Doug, how are you? I miss you."

"Yeah, me too. How's Juro?"

"I'm not sure. He's in rehab. I'm trying to get in to see him."

"And what about you?"

"I'm fine."

"And how are things going? Have you broached it to your father yet?"

"Doug, it didn't go well. That's the reason I didn't call right away."

"Shit."

"I know."

There was silence on the line.

"Doug?"

"So, that's that. The funding's out the window."

"Not necessarily. He wants me to put a proposition to you."

"What is it?"

She laughed a bit wildly. "He'll give you everything you want, let you write your own ticket. But this deal doesn't include me or the baby. You're to divorce me and give up your rights in him."

". . . . You've got to be kidding."

"No. He means it. In fact he challenged me to deliver the message to you." She paused. "So I have."

The line seemed dead.

"Doug?"

"Yeah."

"So what do you say?"

". . . . Had any good sushi lately?"

Miko rented a car and set out for the "brain city" of Tsukuba, northeast of Tokyo. She must see these new operations, and judge which of the high-tech facilities might be interested in joint manufacture in the United States.

She looked forward to the drive. It was a chance to renew her impressions. She soon left behind the triple-sided, hollow-cored, black-glass edifices, cosmopolitan, sleek, and sophisticated, the glamorous part of the patchwork that was Tokyo, splattered as it was with five and a half million vending machines, capsule hotels, Karaoke bars, no-panty coffee bars, and offices consecrated by priests. It was the most people-congested city in the world. Smart women shopped the boutiques of the Shinjuku, men practiced golf strokes on crowded station platforms, uniformed schoolchildren rode the subway to *juku* schools, and every cabbie could discuss the global situation, while parabolic antennas beamed uninterrupted streams of information to similar antennas on other continents.

Miko was glad to turn off the beaten path; the countryside was the true heart of Japan. She could proceed without hurry, stopping on the way to buy blessings for the future. She recognized in the marked dichotomy that even this short drive revealed something of the division of her own soul. It was more than the obtruding of an ancient past into a modern ethos. She thought perhaps it resulted from the American Occupation, which nursed her country into the twentieth century. Wasn't there a basic conflict in a military government attempting to foster democratic ideals?

This same dichotomy resided in Doug's micro-world. Motors refined to the size of a speck of dust would light up cities and light up minds. And yet she parked and entered the torii gates of a wayside shrine.

She didn't seem able to let go of the quarrel with her father. She knew how passionately singleminded he had been over the Northern Territories, and how bitter the loss of them must be. But she had felt at the interview that he did not blame her. And she did not blame herself; there was no way to foresee what had happened. It occurred to her that if things had fallen out differently, if he had funded the venture with Doug, it would have placed her child within his reach. She knew how important a boy was to the family, and she saw it as a blessing that he would escape his grandfather's influence.

She wondered why it had taken her so long to realize this. Her father was looking into the rising sun, and what happens when you stare at the sun? Darkness spreads over your vision. It spread over his, blotting out everything warm and human.

Communing with the life inside her, she asked, "What do I want for you? You will not be born owing *on* to family, country, and Emperor. Your *on* will be more than that. You will owe the Earth and mankind." This child must be part of the new world of new ideas. Nothing less was acceptable, nothing less would do.

Back in the car she drove slowly, passing closely packed mom-and-pop shops that opened onto narrow streets, enjoying their tumbled bins and baskets overflowing with cucumbers, stringbeans, radish bunches, and tubers, blending with yardage from adjoining shops. Cotton swatches bright with willows and birds competed with brocaded jackets laid out in crates and cardboard boxes.

The jumbled effect was enhanced by the linear Japanese script running down the sides of barrels and walls, while posters advertising a sumo match read from left to right, Western fashion. Familiar names, Nissan and Mitsubishi, were spelled out in English letters . . . a hodge-podge of culture and language. Paper lanterns swung overhead; beside them unshaded light bulbs looked down at racks of comic books and newspapers. Sounds of country-and-western from an unattended radio mingled with a television show and the shouts of boys playing baseball on a corner lot. Even for a pickup game they were outfitted in minia-ture uniforms. What a central place children held in Japanese families.

The window was rolled down and her arm rested on the frame. She took in the smell of fresh garden vegetables from which the dirt had not yet been shaken. "Yamato," she whispered, the old name for Japan. The essence of it was here in the houses with their rows of shoes inside the doorways, and their haphazard gardens, for no house was without its patch of garden. The country beyond was low, rolling hills into which forests of pine were settled.

". . . . Had any good sushi lately?" What did that mean? What was she supposed to think? Would he throw his lot in with her father after all? When it came down to it, she was not at all sure what Doug would do. That was why this trip was important. If it was successful she could place an alternative before him. If only things worked out.

A cricket sang from a bamboo cage, its cheeping sound continuing in her mind as she passed fields of rice that glinted in the late-afternoon sun. Wheat was the staff of life for Europeans, but in Japan it was rice. Rice was sacred. Prayers were said to it. She wondered if her child would understand this. If not, he would not understand his heritage.

Miko hardly noticed when she left the lanes of small homes with red peppers drying on their roofs, and shops with produce heaped on Coca-Cola cases. Scenes of women cleaning shrimp, sweeping floors, and hanging clothes from bamboo poles were replaced by the stream-lined architecture of a high-tech city, a Far Eastern Silicon Valley. Streets were broad again, filled with cars, bicycles, and motorbikes. People passed with Walkmen in their ears. She found a little fish house with a view of the bay of Kasumigaura, and sat down to a dinner that, even though she ate alone, she found she could not eat out of order. For too many years of her life she had begun with two sips of soup before proceeding to the rice, of which two bites were taken, from then on to be alternated with the main dishes—in this case, one of sashimi served with diced radishes and seaweed, the other *satoimo*, the grayish white potatoes that went so well with octopus. She finished

her soup and took a bite of melon. Buying a paper, she munched a
small confection and read about the new panda at the Tokyo zoo. She
checked into a hotel, but had difficulty sleeping. Would it be possible
on their own, or would tomorrow prove it was utterly beyond their
reach? . . .

In the morning, plum rain was falling in a gentle patter. She
made a series of phone calls. The Sanogawa name opened the right
doors. She stopped in at the local police office to pick up a loan
umbrella of lacquered paper, and stopped a moment more at the sight
of Mount Tsukuba looming above the city, draped in clouds.

She had appointments at both universities, then at a government
"think center," and finally at a private research institute. She looked
over physical plants, talking with chemists and engineers. Visitors were
requested to remove their shoes, and she put on rubber slippers to
prevent static electricity, the enemy of microelectronics.

At the institute she looked through glass walls into "clean rooms"
manned by robots. A speck of dust one-thousandth of the width of a
human hair could ruin the entire process of etching and photolithogra-
phy, doping, bonding, and sealing.

Originally robots followed magnetic tape or wires buried in the
floor. But these she watched had blueprints of the factory built into
their memory and were equipped with sonar senses for navigation.
She gazed with fascination at a wall-climbing robot that looked like a
cumbersome insect. Other robots were engaged in the delicate task of
assembling microchip components. More accurate and sophisticated
than anything she had seen in the States, this would be a must for
Doug's operation. Her guide explained that these models worked eighteen hours a day, and their MTBF or "mean time between failure" was
reckoned at two years. Miko made a quick calculation: that amounted
to ten thousand hours with no down time.

"Mechanotronics," her guide, an enthusiastic techno-warrior said,
"the fusion of machines and electronics, is the highest form of systems
engineering."

It produced an eerie feeling to see the cooperation between robots
as they fed each other drills and tweezers.

Satisfaction showed in the young scientist's voice. "They build
videocassettes, recorders, calculators, TVs, and VCRs. On the other
hand they are extremely versatile; they also perform such tasks as polishing trumpets or painting toilet bowls."

Although she had seen this before, now that she carried the future in her womb, she reacted differently. "What will become of people?" Miko's laugh was somewhat tremulous.

"People will improve their golf handicaps. It just takes one person at a command center to operate several factories like this on different continents."

Technology without borders. Miko suspected that the Western mind, with its Frankenstein hangup, would not take as kindly to a robotic world as her white-coated guide. The Japanese were more at home with the concept. After all, Shinto believed in the divinity of stones—why not robots?

Again she pondered the dichotomy of her country, with one foot in the sixteenth century and the other in the twenty-first. Not only the temples but these high-rises incubated the future and needed the mandate of heaven.

⛩

Momoko put the two dozen balls of peanuts rolled in syrup into a woven basket. Each was wrapped in cellophane and tied with a ribbon, to be presented to the priests this night of Tanabata.

She'd bought a kimono for the occasion. She wanted to appear fresh for this meeting with Takeo, which even Akio was powerless to forbid. She could not be young, but she would attempt the illusion of youth. Before dressing she held a sea sponge dampened in herbs against her face to press out wrinkles, then smoothed in a delicate, scented cream. She had told Akio no more than the truth, she had never felt guilty over her relationship with Takeo. Though her love had been outside the *ie*, she had given the family her physical strength, and the commitment of loyalty. There was no complaint they could lodge against her, she had never stinted in her devotion to them.

To see Takeo and be with him made her happy and Takeo happy, and it kept Noboru alive because they both loved him. What could be wrong in that? Now that it had been cut off, there was still Tanabata to keep sadness from overwhelming her.

The tokens of her feelings fluttered serenely in her garden. Speaking in different cadences and metaphor, the paper strips reassured her, for they were brighter than her thoughts, which surfaced with worry.

Had his health really deteriorated, or could such rumors be discounted? In the short time she would have with him she decided to ask that he make available to Miko the contacts she would need to set up her own operation. This would be nothing for him, she told herself, the man who returned from an Oka mission, the man who retrieved the Sano-gawa swords from Santa Monica, California, the man who, in her prayers, improved in health each day.

She arranged her hair with care and put a dab of rice powder on her nose and traced her brows and lashes with a wax pencil. Now it was time to fasten herself inside her new kimono. Then, taking her gift of sweets she stole into the garden, glancing heavenward for a sight of the lovers. There they were, the Cowherd and the Weaver, together for these few precious hours. With her eyes fixed on them she offered a thought-prayer asking that, in spite of being apart, the love between them continue clear and cloudless as this night. Making sure she was not observed, Momoko opened the gate and let herself into the street.

Immediately she was caught up in a holiday crowd, a young crowd of boys and girls. Was she the only grandmother who loved in this way that included wet love? Besides passion there had been the easy companionship of a friend. They were many things to each other, and all of it must be funneled into the short space of Tanabata.

Each year she watched the merrymakers grow fewer. Not too many people in Tokyo had gardens to decorate. In the old days young girls asked the Weaver to guide their fingers and make them skilled in needlework. But girls no longer wove cloth, nor did young men herd cows. Sumie told her that today many young women asked the Weaver to make them more proficient at the computer. But one thing did not change: there had always been lovers. And so she joined the throngs gathered before the shrine. Great banners many stories high waved above their heads, opulent in myriad shades and textures. The faces around her were animated and laughing, reflecting their sympathy with lovers. Perhaps because it was a land of arranged marriages, this senti-ment was especially strong.

Momoko left her sandals at the door of the shrine and entered with her gifts, which she placed on an altar already piled high with fruits, pinwheels, and rice cakes. Almost at once she was conscious of him at her side.

He emerged from the shadows, leaning on a cane, to place his gift beside hers. They looked at each other, their eyes smiled, the Milky Way between them disappeared.

But how frail he was. A quick constriction and coldness spread inside her. Even when he knelt in full candlelight the shadows remained in his cheeks and below his eyes. Illness was chiseled into his face. She saw the pain he attempted to conceal and guessed that even this meeting was an effort. In that moment she knew she would not place Miko's problems before him, or speak to him of Juro. He must get better, his health must improve before he could be burdened.

She tried to take joy in kneeling quietly beside him, but she had not foreseen that such a limited and restricted meeting would make her more lonely for him. She missed him more now, when his sleeve touched hers.

They walked out onto the steps together. How heavily he leaned on the cane.

"We can't talk here," he said, "but I've something to discuss with you, Momoko. Will you meet me Wednesday?"

She struggled to match his calm tone. "Of course."

Takeo bowed formally and walked away, attempting to minimize his limp.

She looked after him until he disappeared in the crowd. On this seventh day of the seventh month, in spite of all . . . rain had fallen.

Miko returned with contacts to be followed up and a sense of how a new company might be costed out. She was both hopeful and fearful.

At the Tokyo hotel she inquired about phone messages from the States. There were none. There was, however, a message that her father was trying to reach her. Had he reconsidered? She found herself wavering in her resolve to proceed independently. But only for a moment. After what she had seen she was almost sure she and Doug could pull it off.

She knew she owed her father, who had adopted her, an *on* she would now never pay. So she would pay some part of it by making peace. He was her father and Oba-sama was her family. She didn't want to be cut off from them. The *ie* was important to her in a way that Doug could not understand, that no one who was not Japanese to his fingernails could understand. She wanted this meeting to close this chapter in her life pleasantly.

She went up to her room and placed a call to the sanitarium, asking to speak to Juro. She was told he was not taking calls as yet. That was what they'd said last week, and they had promised that by now . . . "I'd like to speak to the doctor." The doctor wasn't in. She left her number.

The sense of panic that had brought her here was now full-blown. She was certain Juro had been incarcerated for his part in the sellout. What was the next step? How far would her father go?

Akio's secretary phoned to say he would receive her at home in an hour. She took a cab, and found to her surprise the outer gate guarded by yakuza who instructed her to go through to Akio's study. She was annoyed at this, and thought she detected someone in the garden as well.

This was the world as it had become. Reluctantly she conceded that protection was necessary for someone as prominent as her father. It still wasn't America, she consoled herself, there were no muggings, no skinheads or drive-by shootings. There were fewer robberies in a year than in two days in America. Walk-about police, with their white gloves and impeccable manners, approached one with bows. Doors here were generally left unlocked. There was no graffiti and no one bothered to count their change. This could be attributed, she thought, to the homogeneous population. No one was outside the system. To some extent you resembled everyone else, followed the same customs, said the same prayers.

In America the races seethed and vied with each other, and there were areas law enforcement would not venture into. Compared to this, yakuza were *manga* comic-book characters, proclaiming themselves by their dress and their swagger. They could not be taken seriously. Nevertheless, Miko was not pleased at their presence in the garden she had grown up in.

A servant escorted her through the house as though she were not expected to remember the layout of its rooms or the twists of its corridors.

She entered his study. Akio was playing go across a low polished table. He had no partner, he played against himself.

Quietly she took a seat and watched. She recognized that go was a ritual of great significance for her father. In his hand was a black stone; he laid it so that in conjunction with its fellows it threatened the bastion of whites. Akio was placing difficulties for himself for the pleasure of surmounting them. He planned both strategies, black and white.

Seeing him challenge himself had a strange effect on her. She sensed that what she observed was only a small part of what was taking place. Which stone was she? Which was the child? In an abrupt movement Akio brought reinforcements to black's position, throwing the game into *seki*.

Looking up, Akio nodded to a servant who waited just outside the partition. The servant disappeared, and a moment later Kenji brought Masaru in.

Akio announced to his cousin in a formal manner that his black had won. Masaru looked a long time at the go board. The foolish smile was no longer on his face. He bowed solemnly in Akio's direction.

Akio in turn bowed to him, his head slightly lower than Masaru's. Miko sensed she was witnessing an act of contrition. There were not many men to whom Akio would defer in this manner. How strange that it was to Masaru, his idiot cousin.

Miko always felt uncomfortable around Uncle Masaru. His fine features were untroubled by any thought, his clear eyes looked where there was no object and seemed to take pleasure in open spaces. Most eerie of all was the grin that passed with great frequency over his face. She wondered if it was related in any way to the emotion of happiness. She wondered what Kenji made of it. What did he think of the strong resemblance between them? Of course he said nothing. He never said anything. She thought he overdid the role of servant. Without glancing in her direction Kenji led her uncle out. Actually, she reminded herself, they were both her uncles.

Her father's attention, which had been given solely to Masaru, turned to her. "Miko, it is good of you to come. Sit and share tea with me."

"Thank you, Father." She bowed as a daughter and seated herself in traditional fashion.

Tea was served graciously by a servant she did not recognize, and Akio discussed for a moment or two the effect the early rains had had upon the crop. Miko struggled to free herself from the emotions this house set up in her. It took her back to the time when she ran about

in her bright child's yukata, talked to the *koi*, held *o-cha* parties for
her dolls under the willow tree, and pestered her grandmother for the
glazed chestnuts in her pocket.

Miko caught herself up sharply. She renewed her resolve to place
her single stone and leave.

"I have regretted," her father said, "that at our reunion you left
in anger. It was not my intention. You'll be interested to know that
in your absence a further, more detailed analysis was done on the
company of Doug Watanabe, and I am convinced he is a reputable
scientist with whom it might very well be advantageous to align
myself."

Resolution faltered. This was the solution Doug had dreamed of.
It was what her husband wanted.

Even as such thoughts crossed her mind, Akio moved on. "Of
course, my doubts of you remain, Miko. And they are grave doubts. I
don't know where your allegiance lies. Is it with your family to whom
you were born, who raised and educated you? Or is it to your American
husband?"

"Father, there is no conflict."

"It is to your father you owe *on*. And I must be able to count on
you. Especially as I do not have a son."

"I am deeply sorry about Juro, Father."

He regarded her in a lowering manner. "I perceive that you have
not rethought your position regarding the child. I see that after all you
are a woman who puts human feelings ahead of obligation. If you have
not modified your decision, it is my duty as your father to correct it
gently but with firmness."

"I don't follow you, Father. What decision?"

"I cannot permit you to return to America. Not until after your
son is born."

She seemed to miss a beat out of her life.

"At that time," Akio continued, "you may choose whether or not
to stay. But the child will remain here."

"My child? That's preposterous. There's no way I'll consent to
that."

"I do not require your consent."

Reality seemed to slip away, to have eluded her. "What then?
Am I your prisoner? Is that what you're telling me?"

"Only temporarily, until the birth."

"I don't believe what I'm hearing. Right now, this minute, I will not be permitted to walk out the front door?"

"You will occupy your old room. The time will pass pleasantly if you allow it to."

"You can't do this. My husband will come for me."

"That would be most unwise of him."

Miko heard the threat. "What if he does come?"

"I rely on you to see he does not."

"I won't submit to this. It's barbaric."

"No. It is Japanese. A father has the duty to guide a wayward daughter. The *ie* will take in the descendant of dirt farmers, adopt him, raise him to highest status. You should say prayers of thanks."

Miko tried to collect her thoughts. "Father, you live in the modern world, you run great multinational concerns, make decisions on the latest in high-tech circuitry, the most advanced DRAM systems. You can't seriously want to keep me prisoner and take my child. You can't run your personal life like a feudal warlord."

Akio dismissed this argument. "It is typical of your generation to react in this way." He walked to the door.

"Father," she called after him, "don't do this. It's ridiculous, it's archaic. Let me go. We can be friends, even father and daughter."

Nothing. No response.

"It won't work," she called down the hall after him.

"Shit," Miko said under her breath. Akio was no longer in the hall. She decided on a test. She had to know how closely she was watched. She slid back a door, and the garden flooded in, bringing a scent of jasmine.

She stayed still a long time. The yakuza moved first. She had misconstrued their role; she had supposed them to be her father's bodyguards when in fact they were her jailers.

He said he had given her back her old room, and she proceeded along the corridor until she reached it. Sliding open the door, she entered her childhood. What she remembered from those early years was her grandmother's lap. It was a safe place, a refuge, protecting and comforting. Once again she was as helpless as she had been as a child. Only now there was no refuge, no comfort and no escape.

Her father didn't care about her. That was the first thing to realize. He wanted her child, to rear and indoctrinate. He wanted to hobble him with what he owed his grandfather, the family and its holdings, the nation of Japan and its Emperor. She had no doubt that, fulminating in her father's mind, there were already plans whereby his grandson would reclaim the Northern Territories. He would be privy to plans for planting the rising sun on every continent. He would be weaned on tales of the samurai and the kamikaze, encouraged to be Susanoo-no-Mikoto, the screaming wind god. He would be raised as an instrument of revenge, his life dedicated to a bygone war.

She had been an idiot to walk into this. Still, how could she imagine that her desire to heal the breach with her father could lead to a situation where she would be a virtual prisoner? How could she have imagined he would go this far? The civilized world, she concluded, was no match for fanaticism.

She could not look to Doug for help, her father had made that plain. She was very much afraid for Doug, who knew nothing of *bushido* ways, which would cut him down before he had a chance to find out.

What kind of letter could she write him? In her mind she started to compose it, but it was hard to get beyond "Dear Doug." Dear Doug, what? I am a hostage in my father's house and your son has been taken away from you?

God almighty, she must do everything she could to prevent such thoughts crossing his mind. What reason could she give for staying on in Tokyo? . . . It is too close to my time to travel. . . . Fuck, that doesn't sound like me.

She put off writing.

A day wore away, and another. She walked in the garden, music and books were accessible. If one did not look closely it might even seem she was an honored guest, but a depression descended, warping her will. Her limbs had become heavy, her thoughts too; she had trouble connecting them. It did not seem it would be much use to do so. The anger and outrage she initially felt at her father were gone. Those emotions were too strong to sustain, they required effort, and lassitude had taken over.

The week continued to advance slowly, and a servant came unobtrusively with an invitation to a tea-luncheon in her grandmother's suite.

She was received in Momoko's private sitting room facing the sunny side of the garden. "The servants told me you have moved in. I am glad. Why should you stay in a hotel when you have a home?"

Hardly stopping to greet her grandmother, much less listen to what she was saying, Miko walked to the open door and slid it closed.

Momoko watched with surprise.

Miko spoke urgently, not holding back *ura*. "Grandmother, do you love me best? Do you love me better than anyone?"

"You were my child," Momoko said softly, waiting to be enlightened.

"But there was another child," Miko persisted. "My father. My father was your child."

"Yes."

"Grandmother, if we were drowning and you could save one of us, which would you save?"

Momoko considered this. "Akio could save himself."

"Then you would save me? Oh, Grandmother, you must save me. I don't know if you can, I don't even know what to ask you to do. But something."

Momoko listened without comment while Miko described the scene with her father. When she finished, Momoko did not immediately reply, but sat looking into the garden, communing with herself. At last she said, "It is sad for Akio. He controls the course that nations take, he dictates policy in Washington, D.C., in Taiwan and Korea, but he cannot control his children."

"Grandmother, tell me, what should I do?"

Momoko was still locked into her own thought. "He should never have let it come to this." And she bowed her head.

Miko was sorry she had confided in her, it only brought grief and could do no good. Momoko too was impotent to move against Akio.

As she reached this conclusion, her grandmother spoke. "I have seen the friend I mentioned to you. My friend has been ill, and for that reason I did not discuss the plans you have to start your own company. . . ."

"All that's beside the point now. The important thing is to get away from here."

"I don't know what to tell you to do." Momoko spoke disconsolately. "My friend cannot be approached right now. . . ."

Momoko's tone caught Miko's attention. She looked at her grandmother with new eyes. Youth was gone, but old age had not yet descended. Her carriage held the grace that only training in the traditional manner could achieve. Every line of her pliant body bespoke the breeding of a thousand years. Miko finally understood that the friend she relied on was not an aging Japanese lady as she had supposed, but a lover. Someone in the highest circles, someone able to stand against Akio Sanogawa, perhaps even bring him down. She bowed her sleek head, accepting the tea bowl from her grandmother's hand.

"Your brother also gives me cause for anxiety," Momoko said.

"Juro? Yes. Like me, he's kept incommunicado. Now I'm sure of it." A tear squeezed along her lashes. "I'll tell you something funny. I thought Father had some feeling for me. I was proud to be his *shosha-man*. That seems to be my favorite delusion, that people love me, my father, Doug. He hasn't called, Grandmother. He hasn't called me!"

Momoko looked at her with concern. "There may be a reason why he does not telephone, then you have upset yourself over nothing. Never mind, pregnant ladies are often not themselves," she said. "However, you must try to be more cheerful, for I have thought of someone I can approach, someone who has your good at heart."

Miko looked at her dubiously. "Who?"

"Your mother."

"My mother?" Miko couldn't speak for a moment. "My mother's alive? You know who she is?"

"Yes."

She spoke to her grandmother as she never had before, accusingly. "You've always known."

"Her name is Azuma. She is the proprietress of a restaurant in the Shinjuku district."

"A mama-san?" Miko said in disbelief.

There was a strained silence.

"A mama-san?" Miko repeated.

"On special occasions, when you entered school or brought home prizes, I sent word to her. She may be able to help us now."

"How? Someone like that?"

"Precisely because she is what she is, just to keep her business open it is necessary for her to deal with yakuza."

"But my father seems to own them."

"Only some. There are families, so I understand. A different family will take assignments from a different quarter."

"What kind of a person she must be," Miko said with distaste.

"We cannot judge her. Let me at least talk to her." Actually, Azuma had not occurred to her as a solution before; she had suddenly found the name on her tongue.

She had no idea if indeed Azuma had contacts in the underworld of crime and crime bosses. She thought it likely, but she didn't know. She had no way, either, to assess the woman's feeling for Miko. How real was her interest in a grown daughter? Did she care anything for the girl?

It was a gamble, but perhaps Noboru's *kami* guided her. Perhaps it was he who put the woman's name in her mouth. She prayed that night a long time before the *kamidana* and the young man in his flight uniform who never grew old.

In the morning Momoko made a discreet telephone call. The result was that two very different women peered at each other over the rims of their tea bowls.

Azuma was in a tailored slack suit with a good deal of jewelry. Momoko, as usual, dressed in kimono; the apartment was furnished austerely in a modern style she did not find comfortable.

Azuma had reservations as well. She had never spoken to a woman of this class. Their men, of course, she put to bed most nights of her life, but of a traditional woman such as Momoko she had no experience. She glanced furtively at her face. In spite of her years it was a lovely face, soft and gentle, deceptively so. These were the traits such a woman cultivated. Humble and withdrawn, utterly submissive with their husbands, they were hell on wheels with poor little daughters-in-law, many of whom escaped to her employment.

Before such a woman, a refined and cultivated woman of the old school, Azuma's insecurities surfaced. This woman represented the unattainable—position, family, birth. It took generations of breeding to produce such a one. Azuma dealt in pretty girls hired for beautiful faces. But how cheap and vacuous they were when set against a true aristocrat.

Momoko accepted tea graciously, murmuring, as etiquette required, praise of the fine porcelain.

Azuma felt helplessly inadequate, knowing she was judged by classic rules of comportment, standards she was barely aware of. She picked up the new ways, studied Western styles, and learned men's tastes in all things, from women to liquor. But the heritage of old Japan, with its complicated manners of harmonious behavior, was beyond her.

Momoko glanced at the Cubist painting on the wall, screaming in primary colors. Even the coffee table they sat at was a harsh, irregular glass shape. Still, she sensed Azuma's uncertainty and confusion, and felt something akin to compassion. When it was proper to do so, she spoke. "I have often wondered about you, Azuma. Did you, over the years, receive my small notes on your daughter's school progress?"

"It was most kind. I know I am unworthy to be the mother of such a well-bred, successful young woman as your honorable granddaughter."

Momoko's reply was self-deprecating. "I brought her up as well as I was able. Of course I do not understand the Japan of today. It is very different than the society I grew up in. I don't think I prepared Miko as well as I might."

"She has grown up to be a credit to you."

Momoko inclined her head.

Azuma waited. She was afraid to venture a further comment, not knowing where this was going or why the woman was here.

Momoko decided it was time to confide in her. "On her most recent trip to America, Miko married secretly." The words dropped from her lips as from a metronome.

Azuma's face did not betray that she knew this, and Momoko continued, "She is now pregnant with a son."

Azuma looked up sharply. "A son? But that is joyful news."

"Yes, in this modern age they have tests that tell such things." She pursed her lips. "It should be joyful, except that my son keeps her shut in the house. She is a prisoner until the child is born. Do you understand? My son intends to take the child away from her."

Azuma's hand trembled on the tea bowl. After a time she asked, "Why have you come to me?"

"You are her mother."

"Did you tell her that?" Azuma asked.

"I told her."

The small bowl clattered on the glass surface. "Was she upset? I mean, at who I am?"

The pause on Momoko's part was only fractional. "She was surprised."

"I see. Of course she was upset." Then, rallying somewhat, Azuma asked, "But why did you tell her, after all these years?"

"To give her hope."

The silence between the women became protracted. It took courage for Azuma to ask, "Why are you here, Oku-sama?"

Momoko looked at her steadily. "She must be gotten out of the house and out of the country. She needs a passport and a plan."

"Why come to me?" Azuma asked in a panic. "You can't possi-

bly think that I could go to the yakuza? It is impossible for me or
anyone."

"I do not ask anyone, I ask you."

"I wouldn't know how to begin, how to go about it."

"You are a resourceful woman."

"Akio-sama is my patron."

"And Miko is your daughter. And the child she carries is your
grandson. My son's interest is this child. Once it is born he will take
charge of it. I don't think Miko will be allowed to have much to do
with her son." Momoko paused a moment to let this sink in. "Actually," she continued, "you are very fortunate, Azuma, that in this life
you are given the opportunity to make restitution. It is rare indeed to
win the respect and gratitude of a child whom at one time you abandoned. You are indeed a woman who has been singularly blessed."

"But . . ."

Momoko held up her hand. "Surely you know the Confucian
saying: 'When the heart desires, the way opens. . . .' Well, it is late
and I must go." At the door she inclined her head almost imperceptibly. "I do not think we will meet again."

Azuma made a low obeisance that started a run in her sheer panty
hose. Bows and Western clothing were incompatible.

She hoped she had not left the grandmother with the impression
that she would try to help. She would never cross Akio.

She should have been firmer with the lady. Momoko was used to
being obeyed, and assumed too much. But she was not her servant.
She had been a lot of things, beginning with a little vixen of a street
prostitute, but never anyone's servant.

So once again Akio intended to take a child from its mother. She
knew that hurt, she knew the void it left.

Azuma pondered the problem. There were yakuza in her place
every night. The *oyabun* of the prefecture syndicate had his own table,
surrounded by *shateir*, young brothers, and one or two counselors.
Once, in an expansive mood, the *oyabun* had told her the structure of
their organization was no longer feudal; the eight major syndicates,
with a total membership of ninety thousand *wakashu*, were run along
the lines of any modern corporation. Although, he admitted with rel-
ish, the name *yakuza* came from the card game *hana-fuda*, a kind of
blackjack whose object was to get as close to nineteen as possible
without going over. So a hand with an eight or *ya*, plus a nine or *ku*,

and a three or *sa*, was worthless. *Ya-Ku-Sa—Yakuza*, the worthless ones! The *oyabun* roared with laughter.

Azuma considered. . . .

This woman of quality, who shared Miko with her, expected too much. Azuma knew, she didn't have to be told, that she in no way measured up, that it was only by a strange fluke of circumstance that she had borne Akio's daughter and Momoko's granddaughter. It was, she recognized, the finest thing that had come out of her life. It stood quite alone, the single outstanding, remarkable event, with no bearing on anything else that had ever happened to her. . . . A passport under a false name would be no problem to arrange. But to smuggle Miko out of Akio's house was another matter. Could she ever find the courage? It would be stupid to try, and she was not a stupid woman. On the other hand . . .

It was Wednesday. Momoko hastened to the small house with the attractive garden that now stood empty of all but the old servant.

Takeo was already there, walking in the garden, renewing his memory of it. At sight of him, fear again twisted in her. But she placed a smile on her face and, joining him, they walked together as though they had not been apart. They did not touch, they did not speak, they simply walked.

When he finally spoke, Takeo's voice was husky. "It is not good without you, Momoko."

"I know. It is hard for me too."

"As hard?"

"You know the answer, Takeo-san."

"Yes, well . . . it seems so natural to be here with you. I almost forget that it is forbidden." He sat on the bench and pulled her down gently beside him. "In a way this Wednesday is wasted time, as I do not speak to you of love but of business. Momoko, you remember over the years I would say, 'Buy such-and-such stock with whatever is left from your household money'?"

"Of course. I have a finance minister as my adviser. It is no wonder my holdings have increased unbelievably. Because of it I am a wealthy woman."

"This is the time to sell," he said without preface.

"Sell? But the Nikkei keeps going up."

"Momoko, this is in confidence. I speak from special knowledge and no one is to hear a word of it. It would be most serious if it were to get out. Do you understand?"

She nodded.

"The government is about to raise interest rates. The market will fall. Actually, I have stated it too mildly, the market will crash."

"Really? Like America in 1929?"

"Almost certainly. I want you to take everything you have out."

"May I tell Akio? He will be ruined."

"Tell no one, Momoko. Besides, why would you want to tell him? Look what he has done to us."

"He is my son. But you are right, the demon is still in him. He has done ruthless things and now it is quite out of hand. I shouldn't tell you this. I hadn't meant to, but he is angry with Miko. And it goes beyond that, he has lost Juro to drugs."

"I am sorry. I did not know this."

"Akio does not accept or submit. His way is to fight, even when it is a question of fate. Miko will soon have a child, a boy, as they can tell now. Akio wants to make him his heir. He is keeping Miko in the *ie* and won't permit her to leave. The *ie* that was Noboru's, and that I have struggled to keep together all these years, he is tearing apart." She began to cry into her hands. "I shouldn't have told you. You are ill. I shouldn't have said anything. There is nothing to be done. There is no way even you can stop him."

Takeo remained silent. Finally he said, "It distresses me to see you so unhappy."

"I feel there is much I am at fault in. Even your accident was my fault. If I had handled Akio differently . . . Takeo-san, be honest with me. Is your condition serious, is it grave? Why are you not better? What do the doctors say?"

Takeo took her hand in his. "At this time in my life am I to start listening to doctors?"

Momoko put her face against his chest. She cried quietly and his hand soothed her.

Takeo said, "If I could see how to help you, I would. But Akio has a great advantage over me. I love you. He, on the other hand, loves his image of you, and he will break every bone in your body to make you fit the mold."

Momoko's head sunk lower, and she held him tighter. But she was not able to hold him tight enough. At times they whispered together, at times they laughed. Momoko told him he must take calcium so that his bones would knit more strongly. Mostly they were quiet.

"Next year at Tanabata," she said softly, allowing herself this hope. He pressed her to him. "At Tanabata."

They left the little house with its quaint garden separately.

The wrenching interruption of her secret life with Takeo made Momoko face age and loneliness. She slipped from the *ofuro* into the folds of a large, fluffy towel held by her personal servant, put on the loose robe that had been laid out for her, and took her breakfast by the open door that looked into the garden. Surprisingly, she found the prospect of her future not too unpleasant. No one had the right to expect anything of her anymore. There should no longer be either chores or obligations. She had entered the free zone she had left behind as a child. Once again she was able to wear red.

She was free to dream, to remember, to wander the garden, to arrange flowers for her room, to pay visits to the nearby temples. Two things intruded on this gentle existence. Takeo, for whom her heart broke, but for whom she could do nothing. And Miko.

She could not close her eyes against the sun and rest. The survival of the *ie* depended on her. Choosing a single flower that lay on the heaven line of the arrangement on her dressing table, she brought it to her granddaughter.

Miko thanked her absently; she was not really interested in the shape of the curved stem or the delicate coloring of the petals. Instead of putting it in water she laid it carelessly on the table.

Momoko was forced to initiate the conversation. "I have spoken with your mother."

For the first time Miko showed some interest. "And she'll help?"

"I am confident that she will."

"But how? Did she say? Does she have a plan?"

"We must be patient. We must wait."

The momentary spark of interest drained out of her. "I suppose so. Yes, of course we must." She interlaced her fingers in her lap. "What was she like, Grandmother? Did you hate her?"

Trying to assess the woman across the gulf of their lives was difficult. Momoko pictured again Azuma's modern room, repressing her initial reaction as she did so. Their meeting had produced an almost

physical flinching, more from the life the woman led than from her
person.

It had begun with Shigeru, her brother-in-law, picking up a street
girl of fourteen or fifteen. She knew of this from Ryoko, who made
out money orders to cover gifts and finally an apartment, weeping with
jealousy as she paid the bills for her husband's escapade. She remembered laughing with Yoriko at the unseemly way Ryoko behaved.

She didn't believe she had ever known how Akio and Azuma
met. If she did she had forgotten. They must have been children, the
street girl and the son of samurai. She had not known there was a
child. Not until Miko stood, a tiny thing of four, with great fearful eyes,
in the entry of this very house. Akio simply said, "This is my daughter."

From the beginning Miko had been hers. She remembered feeling
a strange twinge of sympathy for the mother who had never known
her. But there must have been something that separated her from the
thousands of girls prostituting themselves on the street, something that
had gained her a patron. Even then Azuma must have possessed a
certain strength and resiliency, for Akio had never deserted her. He
set her up in business and adopted her daughter.

Why? The key was the woman herself, the tough fiber at her core.
It was to that quality Momoko appealed. She counted on the character
Azuma had demonstrated all her life to save Miko. After all, how
many Japanese women were as independent as Azuma?

As far as her feelings for Miko went, Momoko had detected an
eagerness when they spoke of her. Under the brittle façade she sensed
the mother.

And if she was wrong?

She answered her granddaughter. "I found her attractive."

"Apparently that's how she makes her living, being attractive. I
can't bear the thought of her. You've seen them, the mama-sans laughing with their customers, drinking with them. Those women are a
joke. And to think she's . . . When I was little I was sure my mother
was a princess, that I had gotten lost in the forest and she couldn't
find me. When I was older I thought she might be the daughter of
some powerful house. She'd fallen in love and had me in secret and I
was spirited away to be raised by this family. Mostly I guess I thought
she was dead. Grandmother, I don't want a person like that for my
mother. It's horrible."

"Have you considered that she risks a great deal if she helps you?"

"That makes it worse, to owe an *on* to such a person. I don't want to be placed under obligation to her, I hate her."

"You only hate the fact that she is your mother. But don't you think you are lucky that she is?"

"I don't know." She lapsed into silence.

"Put your flower in water and you will feel better."

A day went by, and another. Momoko did as Takeo recommended, and divested herself of all the stocks and bonds she possessed. But she struggled with herself over Akio. The question of the *ie* plagued her. Her entire life she had lived and worked for it. Could she really let it be financially ruined? Against this was her promise to Takeo. If only she could see him again, she was certain she could make him understand her duty to the Sanogawa, to Noboru's people.

She made her decision and, although it weighed heavily on her, sent a note to her son. Akio replied, agreeing to join her in her rooms as she requested. She looked forward to the interview with dread. It was terrible to violate Takeo's confidence. He had made it quite clear she was to tell no one. He impressed on her that it would be a serious matter if a hint of raised interest rates leaked out, that the government itself would be involved. But what else could she do? She could not stand by and see the family destroyed.

Akio came to her in her apartment and she poured tea for him. He sipped appreciatively, taking in her lovely corner of the garden. It occurred to him that he had not seen it often of late. It had been a long time since he had been invited to take tea. "I am glad of an opportunity to say good-bye, Mother. I am leaving for Okinawa on business. The trip should take only three or four days."

"Akio," Momoko said, brushing aside courtesy, "I have seen Takeo, but it was for a final time. He had information for me. I want you to know what he said."

Akio replied gruffly. "I'm not interested in what he said. And you had no business meeting him. I thought that was understood."

"It is, yes. But he works closely with the Minister of Finance, he knows that the government is about to raise interest rates. . . ."

"What? He told you this?" Akio's anger was replaced by an alert, almost predatory look.

"He told me to divest myself of all my holdings. The market will crash."

"He said this?"

"I made a pledge to him, I told him I would tell no one."

"He made you promise this?"

"He did."

Akio surveyed his mother with satisfaction. "You have done well, Mother. Your loyalty is here, to me and the family. Believe me, I will not forget this."

"Then let Miko leave." She was amazed to hear the bold words.

Akio smiled. "It is for Miko's sake, Mother." He took an envelope from his pocket. "Look, it is all settled. This is from Miko's husband, Doug Watanabe."

He put the envelope in her hand. The stamps were American.

Akio's smile broadened. "It has all worked out. Doug, as Miko calls him, jumped like a frog at my offer, as I knew he would. I am financing his entire operation, at the same time allowing him to run the company and retain ownership of the patent, subject of course to licensing agreements. The young man's achievement will command recognition from the scientific community. Wealth and recognition, who can ask for more?"

Momoko had not opened the envelope, she didn't even want to hold it. She gave it back to Akio. "And the price of this great good fortune is to give his son into your care?"

"I have softened my position, Mother. Miko can continue as my *shosha*-man, and she may do as she wishes in the matter of a divorce. As for the child, yes, he will be raised here, taking his place in the *ie*. He will be educated and trained as a Sanogawa."

"To fight."

"Of course to fight. Isn't that what life is about? Father's death taught me that."

"Is that what his death taught you?" Momoko lowered her head. When she looked up Akio had left.

⛩

Miko, as her time drew near, was more and more apprehensive. "We've waited too long," she fretted. "The baby's dropped." She also expressed her fear that Azuma would do nothing. She had stopped mentioning her husband. In the circumstances Momoko felt it was just as well.

She kept up a front for the girl's sake, but she had received no word or indication of any kind from Azuma. Perhaps after all she had misjudged the woman. The thought spurred her to action. She went into town and rented a Woody Allen movie to show on the VCR. She must keep Miko from brooding. It was essential that they laugh together at the American film.

In the meantime she had promised Sumie that she would take dinner with her and Ryoko. She couldn't think why she had accepted the invitation, other than that with Akio gone it was a house of women guarded by yakuza. She bathed, changed to a fresh kimono, and went to her daughter-in-law's quarters on the far side of the courtyard.

Sumie seemed to have shrugged off the unpleasantness of Juro's rehabilitation. Like a mother bird, once the fledgling is out of the nest she has done with it, thought Momoko. How differently she herself was constituted; she held to everything that was or ever had been a part of her. In that, Akio resembled her.

Sumie had made the room festive with candles and cut flowers, and she and Ryoko were in kimono in her honor.

"Is this some holiday," Momoko laughed, "that I have not remembered?"

"No, we are lonesome for you, that's all. You stay too much in your rooms."

"And how lovely you've made everything."

Sumie was delighted at this praise.

"Wait until you taste the dinner," Ryoko put in. "Fresh shrimp washed in salt, with peppers and fried tofu cakes and her special _nimono_."

Chattering, they seated themselves. Momoko thought how pretty Sumie still was, and Ryoko had managed to salvage her life with successful children who fortunately kept away. So the _ie_ continued, and she must see to it and not falter.

For dessert they were served sweet melon and sorbet.

Sumie urged her to taste the thinly shaved ices she had flavored so delicately, and afterward poured sake freely. Ryoko slid a folded copy of the _Shimbun_ across to her. "Did you see this? She's the one Shigeru was so infatuated with years ago. Do you remember? All the money he wasted on that little _onapet_. But things work out. Her place burned down last night, right to the ground. She owned a bar and restaurant, you know the kind. She was the mama-san. Anyway, the article says that she had been thinking of moving to Nagoya. And now she will. She intends to take the money from the insurance and open up a new place where the pace of city life is less hectic. I'd say it's a case of the dog trying to get away from its tail."

Momoko no longer heard. She looked at the picture in the paper; only one charred wall stood, the rest was rubble. That couldn't be Azuma's place. There had been a mistake. It belonged to someone else entirely. And the photograph reprinted in the paper? She tried to deny that too, but it was Azuma who looked out at her. Azuma had been taught a lesson, Azuma had been scared off. She was no longer a factor in their lives.

"Oku-sama, are you all right? You're not ill, are you? Did the account of this creature's misfortune upset you? You are too sensitive, she is just a mama-san. That kind always land on their feet."

Momoko murmured something about feeling giddy, and rushed down the hallway. Sure enough, Miko was commencing labor. Beside her on the tatami was the crumpled evening paper opened to the photograph of Azuma and the smoldering ruin of the restaurant.

Miko caught her hand, she was frightened. "I'm two weeks early, Grandmother."

Momoko sat with her and gradually the cramping subsided. "It is not unusual, especially with a first child. The next time the pains come they will be the real thing."

"It is not my child, Grandmother. He already belongs to Father."

"Hush," Momoko said, "hush."

But she could not hush her own anxieties. There was no help for Miko anywhere. Takeo no longer had the strength even for his own life, and now Azuma had been dealt with. But even this was not the nadir. The nadir was Doug Watanabe. She hadn't the heart to tell Miko that Akio had bought him.

Momoko continued to hold and stroke the girl's hand. Miko seemed incoherent; she was going on about something Momoko knew nothing of—America. Suddenly Momoko's woman's heart skipped a beat. She understood. Miko was saying she had aborted a child.

". . . a woman's right to choose, that's what they call it. I believe in that, I do, Grandmother. Only I chose the wrong way, wrong for me. I did not pay *ko*. And now *this* child will be taken away from me."

It was hard for Momoko to come to terms with such a thing. She felt old. Actually, she told herself, she *was* old, but she had never felt that she was, until now. Age had not been a factor in her thinking. Now it was. I'm not good for anything anymore, she thought, except to hold my granddaughter's hand.

The pains started in earnest. Momoko sent for a doctor, who transferred Miko to the hospital. The retinue of yakuza followed. The night was spent waiting and dozing. Toward morning the doctor approached and, bowing, announced the birth of a male child.

Miko had been returned to her room. She still slept. Momoko approached the bedside and peered down at the swaddled infant. He also slept, but even in sleep he had the proud features of the Sanogawa. She sent word of the birth to Okinawa, then struggled briefly with herself. The father had a right to know. Perhaps, in spite of all, he would come from across the sea and rescue both Miko and his child. One must have faith. Miko had forbidden her to contact Doug, but Miko must be overridden. It was clear to her that the husband was the logical one to act, not an old grandmother. He would put aside self-interest and act, and she would dress herself in red.

Momoko arranged for a message to be faxed to Doug Watanabe in California.

The next day there was still no word from Akio. However, the yakuza remained on guard at the hospital room door. They had taken it on themselves to do this, as repeated messages had not reached their employer. It was assumed he had cut short his trip and was headed home, but even this was uncertain, since no flight plan had been filed. Momoko thought privately that he might be on one of his human-feeling binges.

Whatever it was, it postponed the coming confrontation. Momoko shook her head as though to shake off the burden imposed on her. Why? Her complaint was visceral and agonized. Why had the *kami* chosen such an inadequate person as herself to stand against Akio? She was not capable of outwitting him. Even as a child he had been too much for her. It was always an unequal struggle, she fought not only him but the *oni* in him. And she must again.

The other quarter from which an absence of communication ensued was Doug Watanabe. Her fax might as well have fallen into the sea or been dissipated in the air. There was no response from him, no phone call, no wire. What, she wondered, had America done to Japanese males? What kind of men were they? If the birth of a son did not move them, nothing would.

As for Miko, the child seemed to give her courage. There was someone else now besides herself to set free. Momoko did not remind her that yakuza guarded the door.

The sound of the baby's contented nursing was calming. Momoko looked a long while into his face. A little samurai, a child pure as a cherry blossom.

She went downstairs, her mind circling the problem of how to evade the yakuza and get Miko and the baby on a U.S.-bound plane. The fact that there was no news of Akio gave them a chance. Tomorrow the mother would be stronger and the child a day older. Tomorrow she would buy a ticket, perhaps devise a bogus telegram that would send the yakuza on an errand, and—

She heard raised voices and looked up. In the entry a tall young man was arguing loudly with the servants, using a hybrid Japanese with a large admixture of English. It could, she decided on the spot, only be Doug Watanabe.

He was waving a sheet of paper in the air angrily and demanding to see her. The servants retreated at her approach, but Doug came directly toward her. He somehow looked American.

"Mrs. Sanogawa?"

Momoko inclined her head slightly.

"Did you send me this?" He shoved the fax under her nose.

"What is it?" she asked.

"It's a fax I received twelve hours and twenty minutes ago from Momoko Sanogawa. It says: *I fear for Miko. I fear for your son.*" He looked at her accusingly. "Now, you *are* Momoko Sanogawa and you *did* send this. So I'd like you to explain it. The baby's born? No, don't bother to explain anything. I'd like to see my wife, please."

Momoko did not reply. Obviously the young man was not in a state to listen to anything she might say.

One minute he balled the fax in his hand, the next he was straightening it out. "You can't just send someone a message like this, you know. I mean, I don't even have a flight bag with me. I took a plane the way you take a bus, the first one headed for Tokyo. And I had eleven hours to try to figure out what you meant by this. So now I'd like to know, where's my wife?"

Momoko just looked at him.

"If she's in this house I'm going to find her, I want you to know that."

Momoko listened courteously, but she did not participate in the conversation. Doug Watanabe seemed unable to withstand silence. He preferred to continue the one-sided dialogue. But he took another tack. "Look, Mrs. Sanogawa, I'm tired, I've come a long way, I'm sure you can appreciate that. Now I'd like to see my wife. You must know where she is. Is she here?"

He stopped to allow her to reply, but was faced with more incomprehensible Japanese silence. As a child he had encountered it sometimes from his parents, and it always frustrated him. But there was more than silence in her manner, there was coldness, and he realized that in spite of sending for him, it was quite possible she would not allow him to see her. With sudden intuition he realized something more, that she was protecting Miko. My God, he thought, she knows.

For the first time he really looked at her, the placid face, the demure carriage, the faded beauty like an old print. Then it came over him: her son had shown her his letter acceding to the proposal. Had he shown it to Miko as well? "Look," he began to stutter in both languages, desperate to make her understand. "I had to accept, I'd no choice. No, that's not right, I *wanted*, you understand, *wanted* the deal he was offering. It's beautiful, you can work all your life and never get handed a beautiful deal like that.

"Maybe if you understand the history, what led up to this . . . You don't know what I tried, copper wire, ceramics, the gallate compounds. I don't even want to think about the last five years. I mean, every once in a while I thought I had it. I'd turn in at three, four in the morning, thinking I had it. . . . But it always crashed. I kept running out of money, NSF money, personal loans, small grants.

"Then six weeks ago I got lucky. It worked, and in the morning it still worked. You don't know, you can't imagine what that means. All my life I'd heard about the hard life in Hiroshima-ken, where my family came from. Dirt farming, that's what Grandfather called it. My father didn't get out from under, either, he was a gardener. He sharpened his own tools. It was too expensive to take a lawn mower in for repair, he did it himself so I could go on to grad school. That's what drove me, I had to make it, pull it off, succeed."

For the first time Momoko spoke. What he was saying finally made sense to her. She nodded. "You owed your family *ko*."

"I owed myself. And by then there was Miko and a baby coming."

At the mention of Miko she once more drew the silence around her.

"I know what you think," Doug said, defending against charges she hadn't made. "But it wasn't just a question of vindication. My semiconductor has important applications. Your son could block its production simply by keeping it off the market. Or he could reverse-engineer it. You know what I'm saying, steal it.

"We kept back a small piece, Miko and I, but it would be no trick for his engineers to reconstitute it, and I'd simply be left out. Then what? It would mean starting at the beginning with another idea, going through the whole thing again. I couldn't do that."

Momoko's eyes had not left his face.

"You can't judge me, no one can who hasn't been there. I love Miko, and I want our kid. I don't even care at this point whether you believe me or not. And as far as losing the kid, that's a lot of BS. I know you don't know that expression . . . garbage, it's garbage. Things would settle down, work out. He wants his grandson raised under his roof. Okay, that's reasonable, the kid has a double heritage. Sure he's American, there's no way he'll keep from knowing what that means. And he'll be proud of his old man too, because I farm something more than dirt. I harvest ideas." He came to an abrupt stop, he could think of nothing else to say.

Momoko had only one question to ask him. "Why are you here?"

"Why am I here? You're asking me that when you sent me a message like this? I'm here, damn it, because I want my wife and I want my kid. And if that means going up against Akio Sanogawa, that's what I'll do, because I fear for them too. Without even knowing what it's all about, you got me worried sick. Will you please tell me where Miko is?"

Momoko had made up her mind. No matter how tempted he was to play Akio's game, the fact was he stood before her. "She's in the hospital. I'll take you to her. But I think you should not be hopeful. You renounced your child. I doubt that Miko can forgive that. I don't know that she should. She is the one to decide. However, I can tell you that your son was born yesterday at four-fifteen A.M. A fine, healthy boy. Congratulations." And Momoko extended her hand in the only handshake she had ever participated in. Taking it, Doug bowed to her, the only bow he had ever attempted.

The hospital was a short taxi ride. Momoko spoke to the yakuza at the door and they were passed in.

Miko looked up from the bed. Doug was larger than she remembered, and he moved like an American, looking ludicrously Western and out of place.

"Hi, Miko." The salutation was restrained and awkward. "Let me take a look at the kid. Say, he's a big one, isn't he?"

"And beautiful."

"Yeah? Let me look again." He continued in the old bantering way, but it was forced. Although Momoko stood unobtrusively in a corner of the room, he was conscious of her presence and knew what it meant. He would tell Miko or she would. "Miko, there's something I have to get off my chest. It's probably no news to you that my character isn't the greatest. So it won't surprise you to know that I've accepted your father's proposition. It's a damn good one, you know. The chance of a lifetime really."

She regarded him coolly. "If that's the proposition he told me of, and that I mentioned to you on the phone, it means giving up the baby."

"Miko, I know the way he put it, black and white. But it would only be like that in the beginning. You'd work on him a bit and he'd soften the rules."

Miko smiled her upside-down frown. He began to feel things were not going his way.

"Juro was right," she said. "He told me, 'If you're not a microchip you don't count.' "

"Come on, you don't believe that."

Miko was still smiling. "I'm glad you came, Doug. I'm glad you saw your son. There is a place for you here, but not in my life."

It took a moment to regain his balance. "And that's it?"

"Not quite. I assume that Oba-sama not only sent for you, but that she filled you in as to what's going on. Doug, I don't want my father's influence for our son. I want to get away. But he left yakuza as guards."

"I noticed."

"I'm going to ask you something, Doug. Will you help me get away with the baby?" She reached out and touched his hand. "Before you say anything, let me put it to you, there's no way back for us. And if my father thinks for a moment you had anything to do with helping us, it's the end of your career." She dropped her hand and studied his face. "So, what do you say?"

Without hesitation he replied, "I say we take a cab to the American Embassy."

Miko lifted herself against the pillows. "Doug, I see what you're driving at. It's brilliant. All we have to do is prove the child is American."

"That's right. We'll need a copy of our marriage license, my passport, and the baby's birth certificate. Then the Emperor himself couldn't keep him in Japan. The kid's an *American*."

She stared at him and shook her head. "And you're willing to take a chance like that?" The strange smile on her lips changed. "I'm glad," she said lightly, "that the father of my child is not a total bastard."

He made an eager gesture toward her, but she drew back.

"No, Doug. You're this wonderful but mercurial, undependable person that I've just realized I can't live with."

He started to protest, but she went on. "You know yourself, you can be this absolute bastard and then, like just now . . . make the grand gesture. That's what I love about you. Yes, I admit it, love. But I can't depend on these rare moments, no matter how marvelous. I want the everyday, ordinary kind of dependability, and that's not you, Doug. But I do thank you." She turned to her grandmother. "Grandmother, you haven't said a word. What are you thinking?"

Momoko bowed across the generations. "I am thinking that I am only an elderly Japanese housewife, I do not understand."

Takeo stood at the far end of the private airstrip, leaning with a great deal of pressure on his cane. He was deep in conversation with Kenji, whose resolution appeared to be wavering. Takeo addressed himself to those light eyes, allaying the fear and uncertainty he read there. "Think of your life in that household where you were never acknowledged. Who was your friend all those years? When the time comes you will know what to do."

Within a few minutes Akio arrived. Takeo hailed him. "Sanogawa-san, I think I am in luck. Your pilot tells me he is flying you back to Tokyo. I too am trying to arrange a flight. My plane's engine developed a bad cough and it looks as though there will be a considerable delay. Since there's no commercial plane scheduled until tomorrow, I wondered if I could impose on you to give me a lift."

This unexpected meeting and the surprising request pleased Akio. The thought of turning the tables and doing a favor for the unapproachable Takeo Kuroda filled him with a sense of satisfaction. Ever since the tea with his mother, he realized he had Takeo finally just where he wanted him. Not only had he sold off his stock on the tip from Momoko, but he had gone beyond that, dropping a word to his broker saying he had it on good authority that a crash was imminent. The man had been shocked and disbelieving. Akio, as though it were dragged from him, mentioned that interest rates were to rise. This, coupled with the name Kuroda and a stern caution that it was to go no further, was all it took. The scandal would rock the foundations of the LDP. Perhaps the government itself would fall. Certainly Takeo would be disgraced and forced to resign from the various committees he headed. Between them the world would no longer tilt. "I am delighted," he bowed ceremoniously, "to be allowed this opportunity to be of service."

"Good, then it's arranged. I was left property in Okinawa Prefecture that required my attention."

"Yes, I remember. I myself was here cementing diplomatic ties with the Americans, but I was informed that my daughter has given birth to a son. I am a grandfather."

"Congratulations," said Takeo courteously. "It is indeed an auspicious day."

"Yes, and although I am heading home, I did not allow the good news to interrupt business. On the advice of my honorable mother, who makes a study of these things, I liquidated my Nikkei holdings."

Momentarily Takeo's guard was down; his step faltered and he almost fell.

"Do you need an arm?" Akio asked.

"No," the other replied stiffly, "I'm all right."

"I heard you'd been in an accident recently. I'm distressed to see you still suffer from it."

"It's nothing." Takeo was in command again.

"I hope the prognosis is a good one."

"I tell you it's nothing."

They had been walking toward the plane, a sleek Cessna Citation III. Takeo paused to admire it. Akio said modestly, "It is more than I need. But my company insists on it. That DC-10 crash two years ago led to drastic new certification rules, and Cessna added numerous safety features."

Takeo smiled thinly and mentioned that his own plane would fit inside the Citation's cabin. "But then, the government is not renowned for pampering its civil servants."

Kenji helped Takeo mount the stairs. A damp wind was blowing from the east, with a promise of weather.

Takeo looked around the cabin at the carefully matched wood paneling and the deep leather seating for six that allowed for forward or club arrangement. "You have it nicely fitted out."

"I would prefer a less ostentatious interior," Akio said, waving him to a seat as Kenji began the checkout procedure. "Safety, durability, reliability—not luxury. The important thing is transportation."

Takeo inhaled politely at Akio's audacious pose. He happened to know that the sticker price for this transportation was 3.8 million U.S.

"This particular model," Akio went on, "commands a cruise speed of point-eight-three Mach, and a true airspeed of nearly four hundred eighty knots."

"Ah, yes, one of the highest in a private plane. I read about that. It's due to the tapered supercritical wing, which gives quite a bit more stability. Aerodynamic design has made great strides since the old Mitsubishi G4M.2e."

"The ones that carried the Oka bombs?" Akio smiled and inclined his head deferentially. "Odd, just the other day I was thinking of your distinguished war service. And the fact that you were my father's friend before you were my mother's husband."

Clearance had been received from the tower, and the Cessna was starting to taxi toward the runway when Kenji applied the parking brake with a jerk and, rising anxiously, saluted his employer. "I beg pardon, the tower informs me that I forgot to sign the flight plan. I'll only be a minute." The blue eyes sought Takeo's as he left, but Takeo ignored him.

"Shouldn't he have turned off the engines?" Takeo inquired.

"It's not necessary. He'll be right back."

"But with your very proper interest in safety, Sanogawa-san . . ."

And Takeo unbuckled his belt and crossed to the pilot's seat.

"It's not necessary," Akio repeated.

Takeo slipped into the pilot's seat and checked out the console. "Beautiful," he murmured. "Uncluttered, logical. Just as it should be. The switches are grouped by function with a 'normal!' position instead of an 'on-off.' You can see at a glance where things are. I've always believed switches and gauges belong on the panel, not overhead."

Akio brushed this off. "I try to be up to date."

"A Stormscope to supplement your radar . . . marvelous."

"Yes, sferics is the latest thunderstorm-detection technology."

"I see you use this small control wheel for taxiing and ramp maneuvering. Ingenious. And I like the additional authority of rudder pedals that allow you to steer with your feet for takeoff. But I do think we should turn the engines off."

"He *is* taking his damn time." Akio peered out the window.

Takeo gunned the jets. . . . He's turned the switch in the wrong direction, was Akio's first thought. And before he understood what was happening, they made a right turn and started down the runway.

"What are you doing?" Akio cried. He was still under the impression that Takeo had made a mistake.

Acceleration. Momentum. The plane was now thundering along the tarmac.

"You'll get us both killed!" Akio shouted, and then stopped as he realized this was Takeo's intention.

They were airborne, skyward at 1,210 feet per minute and climbing steeply with 176 knots to command. Akio half fell into the seat beside Takeo.

"This airplane likes to fly high," Takeo said with admiration. "I'll put her on automatic pilot for a moment while I take a look at your map projection screen. There's a spot in the ocean not too far off Okinawa"—this was offered in a tone of reminiscence—"where I almost died forty-five years ago. I wonder if I can find that spot."

Akio leaned back against the seat beside him. He was copilot on a one-way sortie. For it came over him that this was a Divine Wind mission. He closed his eyes, remembering the paper planes he used to fly, watching them intently as they hurtled to their end. This picture gave way to an Oka bomb, the one in the *National Geographic*.

A voice boomed suddenly from the radio, demanding that they return to the airfield. Takeo cut it off.

"When you were in my office last"—he spoke conversationally, he seemed to be completely at ease—"you mentioned go. I recalled that when you were my son, in my house, you particularly liked it when I got out the go board and allowed you to play with the stones. You liked the sound they made when they were brought into play."

Silence lengthened between them. There was no reverberation in the cabin. "I remember," Takeo went on, "the last time we had the board between us and I was showing you the moves . . . you were called away. We never finished. Would you care to play that game out now?"

"Why not?" Akio said, matching his nonchalance. "It may take you a while to find the particular patch of ocean you are looking for."

"It is only fair to let you know that I have given a good deal of thought to the many stones I can bring into play. Stone one . . . Masaru."

"What?" For the first time Akio's voice shook.

"Your grandmother Yoriko knew why the drowning occurred. Kenji learned of it from her."

"Kenji?"

"Yes, Kenji, the outsider. The cousin and brother that was never recognized, who was shunted aside, made to live with the servants. Kenji is the second stone I place against you."

Akio's fist knotted at his side.

Imperturbably, Takeo continued. "Stone number three, Shigeru. Stone number four, your wife, Sumie. My information again, courtesy of Kenji."

A strangled sound rose in Akio that he tried to repress.

"Stone number five, your son, Juro. Number six, Miko and your plan to separate her from her child. Number seven . . . and this is the most grievous, because it was against your mother, against Momoko that you moved, for she is the seventh stone."

The hum of the jet was the only sound. At last Akio asked the question. "Are you prepared to die to revenge yourself on me?"

"It was not a difficult decision. As you observed, I am in failing health. The prognosis in fact allows little hope. And since you informed me that a drop in the Nikkei is being bruited about, scandal must inevitably break around my head . . . making it even easier."

The sea sparkled below them. When clouds drifted into their path they pierced them.

"It was on a day like this," Takeo said, "that we flew from Mabalacat in the Philippines. We approached Okinawa, of course, from the opposite direction, so it is difficult to get my bearings now. It's odd, everything about those times comes back to me. Noboru, for instance . . . your father. He was crazy about American films. In fact he liked everything American. The war never really made sense to him. He didn't actively participate in it until the end. And then his stand in becoming a Special Attacker was to look past the war. Something you've never been able to do, Akio. To look past it and give us the courage and pride we needed for a surrender that would not defeat us. . . ."

"I always thought," Akio baited him, "that being an Oka pilot who returned required an explanation."

Takeo didn't answer him directly but continued. "I remember everything about that morning. The engine cutting out, being nursed back, sputtering again, stalling. I remember how the wind buffeted us. We went in straight down, rivets began popping out, the craft snapped over. The pilot was going through engine-out procedures when we hit the water."

"That should have been my father's mission. He should have lived and you should have died." The accusation burst from him without relieving him.

Takeo looked at his passenger. It was a long look with a tinge of sorrow. "Do you think this is the first time I have faced that fact? I have lived with it. But what happened as a result of my conduct was an accident. Your conduct is to manipulate and plan. For this reason yours is more heinous. But because Momoko loved you, loves you yet, I think, and because you were my son, I say to you, any life can be redeemed by a good death."

"I don't intend," Akio said slowly, "to plead for my life, if that's what you want. Besides being undignified, it would be futile. But if you carry this out, you will be thwarting our country's highest interest, standing in the way of the conclusion of the Pacific War."

"I was under the impression that it was concluded almost fifty years ago."

"Not necessarily. It has its soldiers, those of us who have not surrendered. Listen to me, Kuroda. We are blocked, at least temporarily, in respect to the Northern Territories. But I have devised a way to turn things around, to cast our net even farther. The Hawaiian chain, the original object of the war, will fall to us."

"You're dreaming," Takeo said.

"What if I told you that the initial steps toward acquiring the Hawaiian Islands have already taken place, that I have just met with prominent officials in the U.S. State Department?"

"Are you serious?"

"It's been done before. When their sun was rising, didn't they make the Louisiana Purchase? Now we are the rising sun."

"You actually believe America would sell us Hawaii?"

"In exchange for wiping out the massive U.S. debt, yes."

That gave him pause. "I don't know," Takeo said, "if this is genius or madness."

"And I tell you this initial meeting was positive. My contacts were more than receptive, they were eager. I can make it happen. We can own Hawaii."

"Perhaps . . . perhaps . . ."

Suddenly Takeo began to laugh. It was a laugh that didn't stop, that went on and on. "I must tell you something very funny. Perhaps, as you suggest, it is my duty to my Emperor and my country. But, if your father were here, he would tell you . . . we were never taught how to land a plane."

⛩

Slatted bamboo screens were lowered across the windows so that the sunlight reaching the room was banded. Momoko, watching a mote floating in a far corner, wondered if there was a prescribed way of grieving. She felt death in her womb where once there had been life.

Her womb ached at first and then seemed to shrivel up. Her emotions shriveled with them. Thought receded too, there was a kind of cessation. She had carried out the routine of her morning, bathing, dressing, accepting tea. It was the same world it had been. But like an onion or an iris bulb, her personal world had been peeled away, it no longer existed. She was the moon in a day sky, no longer belonging. Thoughts drifted, mind drifted.

A servant informed her in a hushed voice that Kenji was here. She nodded, she had forgotten she had sent for him. He entered, keeping his eyes from her. She tried to read his face.

"Sit down, Kenji, and tell me what happened."

He sat *seiza* fashion on the *zabuton*. She waited for him to begin. He started to cough. No, strangle. "Will I go to prison?" he asked. "Will they send me to prison?"

"I don't think so, but you must tell me what happened."

"Kuroda-san assured me, he said it was best for you. I swear to you, he said that, that's why I did it."

"Did you know they would both die?"

"Yes."

"But the plan was his?"

"Yes. He even piloted the Citation. The only thing I did was to prepare it for takeoff, then last minute say the tower wanted me to sign the flight plan, and leave."

"And that's what you did?"

Kenji nodded.

"What was Takeo-san's mood when he spoke to you? Was he agitated?"

"He? Never. He acted as though what he was asking me to do was my duty. He said I owed it to you."

"And you did not think it strange that a mother would want a son's death?"

"I didn't think of Akio that way, as your son. He was self-sufficient. He never needed you or me, or his wife. Only Masaru."

"And what about me? I am not so self-sufficient. Are you sure I didn't love him?"

"What kind of son was he? He spied on you, found out about your Wednesdays. He had Kuroda-san run down in the street. He committed Juro, and Miko wasn't allowed to leave the house. It goes back to the beginning, to the way the company and the fortune came into his hands in the first place. He had an *oni* in him."

"Yes, he had. That's what it means to have a vision. Akio had a vision. He saw the rising sun spread over the next century. He positioned Yamato for new conquests. He had *makoto*. And I, not you, killed him. I, not you, killed Takeo-san."

Kenji tried to protest, but Momoko went on, "If I had not seen him last Wednesday they would both be alive. As it is, the North Wind has stopped blowing, there is no longer snow and ice. But neither are there rivulets and tributaries, there is a drying up. The ground parches. There is drought. Susanoo-no-Mikoto has his place."

"Then I am a murderer." Kenji got to his feet.

She was lost in thought and forgot to answer him. He left without having gained a reprieve.

A subtraction, she thought, that's what death is.

Momoko turned to Akio's personal papers, which she had asked to be cleared from his study. Perhaps among the notes and memos there was a word in Akio's own hand that would reveal him. Perhaps she could still know her son.

She glanced at an appointment book. There was nothing there. She sifted through the pile, coming across an old *National Geographic* with a corner turned down at a mildewed photograph of an Oka bomb. It seemed to her that for the second time Noboru plunged to his death. She discovered there is no time factor in death. It no longer was important that Noboru had gone first, all those years ago. They were equally dead, equally separated from her.

She studied the Oka bomb with care. It depended from the belly of the mother ship, a Mitsubishi G4M.2e. It had started, then, when Noboru crawled into that space to die. That act of heroism, that death on the deck of an American cruiser, was the beginning. It set the Sanogawa apart. The seeds of Japan's recovery were sown in the Divine Wind that tossed the Oka fighters a final time. Akio was heir to a heavy burden. Takeo had said as much.

These thoughts did not proceed in orderly progression, but tumbled through a mind whose numbness held her immobile for hours at a time. Pictures formed too with sudden clarity. After the accident, when Masaru came home from the hospital, Akio sat him down with the go board between them. When she saw that he moved both the white and the black stones, she began to shiver and was unable to stop.

Momoko shook the recollection out of her head, and once more began sorting papers in the same mechanical manner, with the hope that in one of them there would be an explanation. But there did not seem to be this final clarifying word.

She came across a few clippings, an early grade-school award for proficiency in brushing *kanji*. And a newspaper posting of Akio's name among those who had passed the Todai examination.

What a terrible day. Akio had gone stiff all over at the sight of his name; she thought he was going to have a seizure.

She undid a legal document. It concerned Masaru, providing a small fortune for his care, stipulating he was not to be hospitalized. She herself had witnessed it. Yes, here was her signature.

Among the papers was a folded newspaper photograph. It had been taken of Takeo's new wife on the day of his marriage. She had kept the same photograph, but coming on it unexpectedly recalled the shock of the event. Takeo had tried to prepare her, but even though she believed him when he said he had no feeling for the new wife other than respect, it was hard to stare into that pleasant face and know she shared Takeo with this woman. Even more difficult were the births in the Kuroda household, two sons and a daughter. She could never get over the feeling that they should have been the children of her body, the children she gave him.

It struck her as odd that Akio had kept this clipping. She realized it must have been garnered at a later date, for he had been too young at the time. Then she saw that it was part of a report; she had simply opened to that page because of the bulkiness of the enclosure. She began to read through it. Incredible. Akio had a complete report prepared on Takeo; even their Wednesdays were noted here. At first she was described in the document as the woman Kuroda was seeing. Later there was a name, her name.

She folded it away along with the other hurts and joys. None of it mattered now, it was done.

She continued sifting pages, notes on the Northern Territories, business agendas, his son's name written on a blank sheet of paper and underlined several times. Whatever it was he intended for Juro could not be committed to paper. Had Takeo been right to do what he did? Was it the only way?

Had it not happened and they both lived, Takeo in all likelihood would have died a protracted death . . . and Akio would continue laying about on all sides, uprooting whatever was in his path. The North Wind had been stopped.

She got up and went downstairs. She kept her eyes fixed on the floor of the long corridor. Each board was known through the years of her life, how the pattern shaded from light to dark, where the imperfections lay. She knew it as well as her own skin. She approached the *kamidana* to look into Noboru's eyes. He gazed back at her with the grave determination that had held to the end.

"Noboru-san, your friend Takeo and your son, Akio, have left me for you. I am alone and I need your prayers. I am uneasy about Miko. She has been given a son, and a fortune. But she is sending her husband away. It is known that fish die if put into clear water. They need salt, sediment, even grit. Miko needs that too. I am uneasy, Noboru, because of the fish."

卄

The family gathered for the first official day of mourning. Sumie made a charming widow gowned by Chanel. Juro was already high, but not on drugs or liquor. It wasn't even beating the odds or his share of the fortune that was uppermost in his mind; it was his father's death he was tripping on. "I'm free. I don't mean the sanitarium, that Kafka-like hell. I mean free of him. We can stop fighting the war. Or are there more samurai out there with their *katana* and *wakizashi?*" He put an arm around Miko's shoulder. "Do you want to hear a story of a short and long sword, do you, huh?"

Ryoko came up to them. "The market crash didn't wipe him out. Akio was too clever for that. He liquidated everything."

Ignoring her, Juro asked Miko, "How is Grandmother taking his death?"

"Which death?" That was the question that hung over her. Oba-sama had withdrawn in her grief, no one was allowed to comfort her. She had not left her room since the news reached her. For some reason she held herself responsible. The servants reported that she had grown old.

Doug had been invited to attend this day of the dead; afterward he was leaving with specifications needed to mass-produce his microchip in California. He had been looking for an opportunity to talk with Miko alone, and when she took the baby out on the veranda, he followed her. "So, Miko, you've got six of the largest conglomerates in the world to run until our son is of age. Any particular plans for them?"

"Oh, yes. At first I felt totally overwhelmed. Our multinationals wield more power than most governments. They have more capital in many instances, and they aren't burdened by all the anachronistic accouterments of government, no military or fundamentalists, no aya-tollahs, no nineteenth-century nationalism. I'd say these global con-glomerates are the new force in the world. Remember, Doug, borderless economies? No tariffs, no protectionism. I'll bring my pigs to market and let the market dictate."

He stood somewhat stiffly beside her. "Are you sure you won't need help with all this?"

"I'm not sure of anything except that I'm going to be a player."

"Well," he said with a deprecating laugh, "I'll be off. I have a plane to catch. But if you want me, I'm in the book."

"Don't go just yet, I want you to say good-bye to Grandmother."

A small ripple passed through the company like an electric charge. The tiny old lady had entered the room, and with a smooth face bowed in greeting to her guests. Miko rushed up to her. "Grandmother, I knew you would come down. I am so sorry, Grandmother, so very sorry."

Momoko regarded her and the child with the same withdrawn expression. "Miko," she said, "I have a small gift for Doug Watanabe's journey. I forgot to bring it. Would you mind . . . ?"

"Not at all. Where is it?"

"In my room, in the old carved chest."

"Yes, of course, I'll get it." She shifted the baby to her other arm—the servants were not allowed to touch him—and left the room.

Momoko took the opportunity to speak to Doug. "You and Miko made a very fine son."

"Yes, he's all right, isn't he?"

"Miko is a woman who is not meant to be alone. And she is, after all, your wife."

"But I let her down."

"Fish die in clear water," was her reply.

"I'm afraid I don't understand."

"It is true that you have let her down. But because you did so once, it is not necessary to do so again." Momoko inclined her head and murmured once more, "You made a very fine son." Doug watched as she passed among her other guests, receiving condolences, graciously accepting the polite formulas, and hope stirred in him.

Miko burst into the living room, proudly displaying her child wrapped in a beautiful red silk bunting. "Look, everybody, at our little prince! I couldn't resist, Grandmother. I saw this gorgeous bunting hidden away under your gift in the paulownia chest. I didn't think you'd mind. After all, who else around here could fit into it?"

Momoko, like one mesmerized, staring at the child, saw another. She couldn't tell which child it was who grabbed her finger so strongly. She thought perhaps it was an *oni*. She wanted to pull away, but he looked so fine in his red silk bunting.